Also by H G

The Blood Series:
Hunted Bloodlines
Blood Trials
Blood Secrets Hidden
Coming soon Blood Secrets Revealed

African series:
Edge of Dawn

New Release:
Rules of Fate – scifi fantasy

For more information on upcoming books please visit us on Facebook:
https://www.facebook.com/vampiresandbloodlines

You can also visit her website on:
http://hashmigorauthor.wixsite.com/thebloodseries/books

Or on Instagram: @hashmigorauthor
Please leave a review if you enjoy the books.
Thank you.

Hunted Blood Lines

H.Gor.

Chapter 1

The rain was coming down in sheets reducing visibility to only a few feet as they walked to the car. Her mother was holding her hand securely as she tried to see where she was going. They had been shopping for a dress for her sixth birthday and had stopped for dinner at one of the small restaurants her mother loved. The taste of chocolate was still on her lips. Their footsteps echoed eerily along the empty street, her mother looking around for their car when something slammed into her, sending her flying to the ground several feet away with a sharp cry of pain. Her hand had been jerked away suddenly from her grip causing Eva to fall to the wet ground.

Looking up through her streaming hair she saw her mother a few feet away trying to stand up when someone appeared next to her, crouching over her. She thought she heard a low growl and something else flashed past her. She felt the air move from its passage, throwing her wet hair into her eyes, momentarily blinding her. By the time she had pushed her hair out of the way two strangers were leading someone away forcibly. A third stranger, a different one from the one before was kneeling next to her stunned mother, talking to her. Another blink and the stranger was kneeling next to her, staring at her with bright eyes, flecks of green in their depths. He lifted one of her curls away from her face gently, still staring intently at her face.

'Are you alright?' Eva nodded slowly, eyes wide as they took in his lean face, his jaw working as though he was angry, but his soft voice soothed her. He smiled kindly. 'Your mother is okay, help is coming; you are safe now.'

He lifted her gently to her feet and led her to her mother who was moaning slightly with pain. In the distance sirens were wailing. The tall stranger smiled again at her and brushed her cheek gently with his finger. 'Bye.'

Before she could say anything he vanished. The rain kept falling as the sirens got louder and the road became bright with flashing lights.

+++

She woke up with a start, her face and hands clammy from the cold sweat. Her breathing was ragged as though she had been running for miles. Her open eyes stared sightlessly at the darkened room, still seeing fragments of her dream, remembering the face that had haunted her for the past twenty years. Sometimes he appeared next to her mother, and sometimes he would already be there waiting for them. But it always ended with the wistful smile and the gentle caress on her cheek before he disappeared again.

She had begun to think she had imagined it all, especially when she had asked her mother about that night. Her mother had laughed gently and told her small daughter that it was the policemen she had seen. But Eva knew they hadn't worn uniforms and she hadn't seen him or the others again. She shook her head to clear it and tried to comb back her long brown hair with shaky fingers as she fumbled for the light switch.

'Forget him,' she mumbled to herself as the light shone painfully into her half-closed eyes. 'He's just a figment of your childish imagination. Half of what you remember doesn't make any sense!'

The clock face glowed up at her. It was seven o'clock in the morning, about time she woke up anyway. Swinging her legs off the bed she stood up and walked yawning into her en suite bathroom. Another busy day waited for her.

It's getting quite busy today, Nicholas thought as he walked up the wide stairs at the front of the courthouse. The rain was falling gently, sparkling like diamonds on his dark hair and coat. He smiled to himself as he passed several people huddled under umbrellas or running past him, trying to escape becoming wet. He kept up his measured pace, entering the courthouse leisurely and turned down one of the interminable corridors towards the courtroom at the far end. He could already hear the babble of voices clearly through the thick oak panelling and stone walls of the court. Speculation was rife on what the verdict would be for this case.

The spectators are waiting for the show to start, he thought as he entered the room. Sure enough the benches were packed with onlookers. Several people had decided to stand at the back rather than miss this trial. The trial of the year as it was beginning to be known in the media.

He walked past the babbling crowd, ignoring their speculations about him as he headed for the prosecutor's table. His steady gaze swept the defendant's table and stopped when they lighted on the bulky man sitting there. Jack Sharpe looked extremely calm for a man who was on trial for several murders in and around the state of Pennsylvania as he spoke to his attorneys. The number of murders was a monstrosity in itself but their nature made the bile rise in the public's throat. Seven of the women had been raped and left to bleed to death after their faces were cut several times. The other five had been mutilated beyond recognition before being burned.

As his eyes met the killer's, a low growl started building deep in Nicholas' chest. He stifled it with difficulty and sat down, staring at the paperwork in front of him, trying to calm himself. It didn't take him long to control his rage; he had had a lot of practice over the years.

'All rise!' The loud order emanated through the courtroom. The noise subsided as the judge entered and sat down, followed by the rest of the room. The trial had finally begun in earnest.

Chapter 2

'What are you listening to?' Eva asked throwing her bag onto a chair and removing her denim jacket.

The weather had deteriorated again sending heavy showers to obscure the scarce sunlight managing to get through the clouds. Summer had consisted of barely a day or two of sunshine this year, and the temperatures had remained low, deliberately thwarting any attempts the teenage girls made at tanning. The city of Erie had gotten the worst of the weather, remaining under a constant cover of cloud, even on the driest days. Despite the grey skies, the city still looked beautifully picturesque. Eva had managed to visit several museums and galleries and had also found time to walk around the Erie zoo. Although the weather wasn't what she was used to, she found the city more to her taste than Los Angeles. Plus the fact that she had landed a job at the Erie criminal lab as the youngest medical examiner was in itself a major plus point.

The blonde haired man she was looking at turned round with a grin, replacing the scalpel he was holding on the tray by his side. 'What? Don't you like the Monkees?'

'The Monkees?!' she laughed incredulously, heading for the CD player, 'Are you kidding? In this day and age?'

'Well, they are classic,' he replied with a shrug, turning back to the body in front of him.

'Yeah exactly my point! They are ancient!' She rolled her eyes and replaced the CD with the current trendsetter band, raised the volume a few notches and joined Matt at the table. 'So what have we here?' she asked, slipping on a pair of gloves.

'Sixteen year old female, found outside a nightclub last night in an alley.' He pointed at the paperwork stacked nearby. 'The police sent it all through this morning.'

'Goody!' Eva looked at the young girl's face. Even after working three years as a crime lab medical examiner she hadn't got used to the faces of the strangers that passed through her hands. She always felt a bitter sorrow at their loss and almost felt as though she knew them. Even while she worked she would sometimes chat to them as though they could hear her. All the girl's makeup had been washed away before the autopsy started, leaving her looking pale and very young.

'What do they think caused her death?' Eva was still looking at her face.

Matt sighed. 'The guys in blue thought it was a drug overdose; they found some speed in her purse.'

Eva shook her head sadly and touched the girl's face with her gloved hand. 'Poor girl, you hadn't even lived yet. I take it they want a full examination even though they have no doubt already closed the case?'

'Of course.'

'Alright.' She turned away to pick up a scalpel. 'Let's get to work.'

Two hours later she put the scalpel down and looked at their handiwork. No trace of drugs had been found in the blood samples, and no bruises could be seen. Except for a sprained ankle the body appeared very healthy. Matt had gone for coffee, announcing that the caffeine would help them figure out the cause of death. Something niggled at the back of her mind but she couldn't put her finger on it. Gently she moved the girl's head slightly, looking for any clues. Not seeing anything unusual she was about to re-position the head when she noticed a small wound halfway down her neck, most of it concealed by the girl's hair. She pushed aside the swathe of dark hair to expose it and her eyes narrowed as two small puncture wounds were revealed.

Two small symmetrical holes, she frowned thoughtfully. The girl didn't have any piercings. Maybe she had removed this one and the holes had healed? Taking a thin wire from the table they usually used for gunshot wounds, she slipped it into one of the holes expecting it to be shallow, only skin deep. To her surprise it went deeper than she had thought and it didn't seem to be connected to the one next to it.

'What did you find?'

She jumped at Matt's voice so close to her shoulder. 'Puncture wounds,' she replied recovering her composure. She showed him the marks.

'Hmmm…what do you think? Piercing gone bad?'

'I don't know, the wounds are too deep and they don't connect to each other,' she explained pulling out the wire.

'Probably a botched piercing job,' he shrugged nonchalantly. 'It happens,' he continued, moving away. 'My cousin had this piercing at the back of his neck, hurt like hell. Turns out it had hit one of the spinal bones, and you could hear it rubbing when he moved his head,' he shuddered at the memory. 'Anyway, he got it out pretty quick. Nearly sued the tattoo artist who had done it.'

'Your point being?' Eva asked raising a slim eyebrow at her partner.

'The point is people do stupid things all the time! More often in the case of my family.' He rolled his eyes expressively as she chuckled. 'Maybe this kid fancied a piercing because everyone was getting one, it got infected or something and she had it removed.'

'But why put it here, almost in her hair where no one can see it?' Eva argued, unwilling to admit defeat.

'I don't know; kids are weird. Maybe she was going to get her hair cut really short, or she didn't want her parents to know, or she just wanted a special person to find it, and I don't mean you.' He looked knowingly at Eva's uncertain face. 'If you know what I mean.'

'Surprisingly I do know what you mean and its gross! Plus it's weird coz I rarely run on your wavelength!'

'You should try it more often, it's an experience!'

'Yeah, I bet it is,' she agreed with a sarcastic smile.

As Matt tagged one of the girl's toes for identification, Eva couldn't stop thinking about the twin holes. Maybe Matt was right; she had to chill out more and besides kids *were* crazy nowadays, right?

+++

'We need the medical examiner to testify!' Sean said rubbing the back of his neck tiredly. The strain was showing on his handsome face.

Nicholas twirled his pen thoughtfully. The trial wasn't going too well. It had already been two weeks since that first day and he was realising how good the opposition were. The attorneys Jack had employed were the best in the game, probably paid handsomely by his mafia connections.

They had rolled out several arguments designed to nullify their opponent's attacks. The only thing they couldn't explain was the nature of the injuries and why they matched the tools found at the defendant's house. Plus who better to take them through the victims' last minutes than a medically trained witness? Nicholas agreed with Sean, the district attorney's office still had a card up their sleeves and it was time to play it.

+++

'You've been summoned!' Matt handed her the letter a few days later.

'Summoned where?' She glanced at the letter and blanched visibly.

'Only the biggest trial this year! Way to go!' Matt grinned across the table at her.

She swallowed convulsively, trying to speak past the large lump in her throat. The bodies she had examined for this trial had been gruesome. She could still see each mutilated face clearly and the memory of the smell still turned her stomach. She had been glad when they had finally finished and handed their findings to the D.A's office.

Now they wanted her to state her findings in court? What? Couldn't they read? Just great!

According to the letter she was still clutching in her hand one of the lawyers was going to prep her for her debut. She shuddered and pushed the letter away; there was no way she was going anywhere near that courtroom. No way no how!

Chapter 3

Two days later and Eva found herself walking down the old-fashioned, slightly musty corridor of the courthouse reluctantly.

'Don't worry you'll be fine,' Sean smiled at her reassuringly as they walked down the long, polished corridor to the courtroom.

She nodded, but she wasn't so sure. Crowds unsettled her. She had only been summoned once before for a small trial and she had hated every minute of it. Shifting uncomfortably in her suit and thinking of her favourite jeans, she followed Sean as they entered the court. She almost bolted back out when she saw the amount of humanity packed into the room. Steadying her breathing she walked past the audience and sat down a few rows behind the prosecutor's table. Sean left her, and went to sit beside a dark-haired man a few rows in front of her. She couldn't see the man's face but he appeared to be the one in charge of the case. She managed to calm herself as the court filled up and the judge entered.

'The prosecution calls Miss Eva Tanner to the stand.'

Here we go, she thought as she stood stiffly and walked to the front of the court.

+++

Nicholas' eyes narrowed dangerously as the short defending attorney tore into his witness mercilessly. They made it appear as though she hadn't really examined the bodies properly. He could see she was trying to hold her own but was steadily losing ground. His eyes lingered on the stubborn set of her jaw as yet another question was fired at her. It looked as though she was controlling her temper with difficulty. He would have been amused to see the slim brown-haired girl lose her temper at any other time, but he wanted her to control it here, almost tried to will her to do so. Besides, she looked too gentle to have much of a temper.

His eyes flicked over her slightly disarrayed dark hair framing the sweet oval face. Her wide eyes, which at this distance appeared dark blue or violet he couldn't quite decide, staring at the lawyer, reminded him of a deer caught in the headlights, the small delicate nose and the wide mouth that was constantly betraying her nervousness as her tongue flicked out again to lick her dry lips. For some reason she appeared familiar but he couldn't place her. He frowned as she answered the last question and the lawyer sat down, clearly satisfied with what he had achieved. Nicholas glanced at Jack Sharpe's smiling face and looked away quickly. He wouldn't be able to stop himself if he looked at the man again.

+++

'Well we couldn't have done more! He massacred our M.E on the stand!' Sean mumbled as he gathered the papers.

'Yes, *we* couldn't have done more.' Nicholas' deep voice seemed to echo with an underlying meaning.

Sean glanced at his profile from the corner of his eye. He hadn't known Nicholas long. He had arrived a few months ago and had become one of the lawyers in the D.A's office. Reputed to win more cases than he lost, Nicholas had practiced widely in the northern counties and Canada. Rumour was he was extremely rich and had owned his own practice before having a change of heart and wanting to help the less fortunate. Despite his incredibly stunning good looks, he emanated an air of indefinable danger that seemed to keep most people away from him. In fact he had never seen Nicholas outside of work.

As the thoughts flashed through Sean's mind, he suddenly became aware of Nicholas stopping in his tracks. Turning round he saw him staring at the crowd with narrowed eyes, his nostrils flaring slightly.

'Hey, what's up?'

'Nothing, I just remembered something.' Nicholas smiled with difficulty and willed his feet to move. But he could still smell that scent deep in his lungs. His nose was still questing the air but try as he might he couldn't place the source of that delicious aroma. The crush of bodies leaving the courtroom didn't help matters. He swallowed painfully and followed Sean back to the office, trying to erase the feelings aroused by that mouth-watering scent and failing miserably.

+++

'So, ready for another crack at the courtroom?'

Eva shook her head vigorously, 'I am never going into a courtroom again, ever!' Matt laughed. It was a week later and they were doing another autopsy.

'Let's not talk about it okay?' Eva cut through more tissue, slicing it cleanly. 'Besides I have enough problems dealing with your terrible taste in music!'

'The Bee Gees are not bad taste!'

'Yeah, whatever grandpa!' she teased glancing at his blonde classic good looks sceptically. Who knew they concealed such an old-fashioned taste?

A few hours later she placed the scalpel back on the tray and sighed.

'Another mystery,' Matt pulled off his gloves and lobbed them at the trashcan. 'Better get her tagged.'

'Wait, let me check something.' Eva lifted the girl's hair, to find the two puncture wounds she had half-expected to see. 'This is weird.'

'Yeah, another bad piercing, what are the chances?' Matt quipped.

'I really don't think that's what they are Matt.'

'What are you thinking?' His expression sobered slightly.

'Murders,' she replied grimly, 'I think we should let the police know.'

'Good luck with that.' He tagged the girl as Eva wondered how she would go about convincing the police detectives that she had a legitimate case. They weren't known for their patience with scientists. She sighed as she watched Matt, she would have to find a way.

+++

'Nick could you go down to the M.E's office to check out this case?'

'What is it?' Nicholas looked up as the file was dropped on his desk.

'One of the M.Es thinks she has spotted some trend; bodies from different cases or something. Thinks they are murders,' the man rolled his eyes and walked away.

Murders? Nicholas picked up the file and looked through the reports, his eyes widening slightly in surprise, before rising to his feet. They may not be murders but he had to see them to be sure.

Chapter 4

'Hey, there's someone here to see you!' Matt called out.

Eva left her desk and walked towards the door separating the lab from the front reception desk. As she came out of the lab, her breath caught in her throat as she saw the figure waiting at the counter for her. Well over six feet tall, the man's face was chiselled to perfection showing off high cheekbones, a firm chin that spoke of a stubborn streak, and smooth pale skin stretched flawlessly over his facial bones. His hair was jet black, swept back carelessly, slightly longer at the back so it fell in waves till it just touched the collar of his coat. But most arresting of all were his eyes. Pale silver with flecks of green in their depths, his pupils were as dark as polished obsidian. A dark fringe of long lashes swept his cheeks as he blinked and completed her undoing. One perfect eyebrow rose in query as he saw her staring at him.

She gulped and willed herself forward, trying not to think about how amazingly good-looking he was. Her eyes left his face in an effort to regain some composure, but they encountered his broad shoulders, filling out his designer suit jacket perfectly, down to narrow hips and long muscular legs enhanced by the superb cut of his grey trousers, ending in soft expensive-looking leather shoes. Not an ounce of surplus fat was discernible on his immaculate frame. A sigh almost escaped her, he would be any designer's dream...who was she kidding? He would be any woman's dream!

'Hello, I am Nicholas Rayne. From the D.A's office,' his deep voice seemed to resonate deep in her soul, as he introduced himself politely.

She could barely stop her hand shaking as it was encased in his gloved one.

'I...I'm Eva...Eva Tanner,' she replied stumbling through the phrase, her voice almost a strangled whisper.

His smile was devastating, his white teeth flashing briefly at her. She blinked and shook her head slightly before moving away from him.

'You are here about the bodies?' she asked, trying to speak in a normal voice rather than the croak that seemed to have taken up permanent residence in her throat.

'Yes.'

'This way.' She led him towards the lab, praying she wouldn't trip over something.

For a second he didn't move, couldn't move as her scent hit his senses, sending them reeling into disorder. He had to stay in control; he couldn't let go. He had to go through with this, if only to make sure the bodies were simply normal murders. He watched as the girl walked ahead of him. He remembered her from the courtroom, her large eyes staring at the lawyer, her set jaw, how he had thought she couldn't have much of a temper. Having seen her face more closely he realised that her eyes were indeed a unique shade of violet, almost mimicking the flower. They lent her ordinary features an air of mystery. He had never imagined the scent he was craving for could come from someone like her. Holding his breath, he followed her with difficulty into the sterile looking room.

'Here they are.' She pulled out the refrigerated drawers used to store the bodies. 'They both have the puncture wounds at their necks. The police put it down to drug overdose, but we didn't find any drugs in their systems.' She stopped to glance at his stony expression and quailed. He may be gorgeous but the way he was looking now, she had the sudden urge to run away, very fast.

He stepped closer and she instinctively shrank away from him. He didn't appear to notice her reaction as he lifted the girls' hair to see the marks. She thought she saw his jaw clench once and then he let the hair fall into place and turned to her.

'It's not much to go on. In any case we can't do anything until the police investigate further.' He looked closely at her stunned face and moved away quickly. 'We will deal with this once we have more evidence.'

'Right.' The sarcasm in her voice didn't escape him and he looked at her curiously as she put a strand of hair behind her ear and led him to the door. 'Thank you for coming all this way,' she hesitated, 'umm...I just wanted to say sorry.'

'Sorry?' He had been on his way out, but he whirled round to face her.

'For not testifying properly for your case,' she explained quickly, her wide eyes searching his. A distant memory stirred but was quickly stifled as he moved slightly closer to her.

'You did your best. Jack Sharpe will pay eventually.' He spoke in a low reassuring voice, his eyes shining with repressed emotion.

'Y...you have more evidence against him?' Eva whispered.

'Yes, its confidential.' He cleared his throat and stepped back hurriedly. 'I have to go.'

Before she could say anything else he had walked out of the room. *That was strange*, she thought as she turned towards her desk, she had felt as though he had been trying to make her understand more than what he had said on the surface. Plus there was still that niggling thought at the back of her mind she couldn't quite latch onto.

Chapter 5

'Hmmm, maybe it's a coincidence.' Chris looked at Eva's reports, missing the sceptical expression on her face. Why did everyone she spoke to about the case want to find a reason to dismiss it? She watched as he flicked through the pages. He was one of the police detectives in the homicide department, who had been assigned to one of the cases relating to the girls in Eva's lab.

'Well I could open their files again, and we'll keep an eye out for any leads.' He shut the folder with a snap and handed it back to her. 'Busy today?'

'Same old, same old,' she shrugged picking up the folder. 'Interesting case came in yesterday, a guy was killed with an icicle.'

'An icicle?' he looked at her uncertainly.

'Yeah, from a freezer. Forensics was having a hard time figuring out what the murder weapon was. No weapon, no finger prints, the perfect crime,' she smiled, 'People can be very creative.'

'Yeah and destructive,' he mused. His dark eyes looked thoughtfully at her. 'Are you enjoying being here?'

She nodded, it had been weird to come back after so many years away, especially since so little had changed. 'It's home.'

He stood up and came round his desk to perch on the edge. 'So do you want to go out tonight?'

'Can't, I have a lot of paperwork to catch up on,' she said, pushing her hands deep into her pockets, 'Can I take a rain check?'

'Sure,' he smiled, but his eyes showed a hint of impatience. Ever since Eva had started working at the lab Chris had felt an attraction between them. They had gone out together within the first week of her starting at the police department, and had gone out several times since then. But he always seemed to sense that she wasn't all there. It seemed like she was holding back and he was almost certain he felt more for her than she did for him.

'Okay, I'd better go...back to the dungeons.' Eva almost ran out of the office. Chris was a nice guy, and she knew he wanted some sort of commitment from her to move their relationship forward. But she wasn't ready for that. What was wrong with him anyway, she argued with herself. He was tall, dark and handsome, was a natural athlete playing basketball and rugby in the summer, and he was above all a genuinely nice guy. He ticked all the right boxes for becoming the perfect boyfriend, so what was the matter with her stupid heart? She had tried to hide the reason from herself, but it was obvious. Her breathing didn't change when he came close, nor did her heart speed up its rhythm. She could have kicked herself for wanting something that was a complete fantasy. Some people had to settle for second best; maybe she should too and make the best of it. She grimaced; yes... she would go out more with Chris Masterson and forget the fantasy.

She followed through on her plan a few nights later. Chris had been invited to a charity dinner and dance and he had asked her to go with him.

'It's a bit fancy, but we won't have to stay long. The chief really wants us all to go,' he had said rolling his eyes.

Dressy occasions weren't her forte either, but her mother had insisted on packing an evening dress for her. So here she was, dressed in the midnight blue gown that skimmed over her slight figure, clinging to her upper body before flowing elegantly to the floor. The outfit was held on by thin straps at her shoulders and had small sequins sewn all over it, so that it sparkled whenever she moved. It was simple elegance at its best. She had sighed in resignation when her mother had bought it, now she was glad she had.

Chris's reaction when he had come to pick her up had caused her to redden slightly in embarrassment. He had whistled under his breath and then kissed her quickly on the lips.

'You look great! I had no idea...maybe we should do this sort of thing more often!'

'No way! This will be the first and last time,' she had replied firmly, walking uncertainly in her heels towards his Toyota.

Having nearly keeled over half a dozen times on that short two-second walk, she now held onto his arm tightly. She was sure she was hurting him but he didn't show it, as they entered the huge hall. Chris knew several people and she hid a grimace as she was towed towards yet another group of strangers. She tried to hold polite conversation, but her attention was divided between them and the constant fear of falling flat on her face.

'Are you alright?' he asked at one point as she fumbled to regain her balance.

'Yup, never better,' she had lied through her teeth, trying to smile, certain that it resembled a snarl from a rabid dog. He had nodded and promptly continued to drag her across the floor.

'Ah Chris, I want you to meet someone. The police Chief's voice floated towards them. Chris turned round suddenly, almost catapulting Eva into the antique table nearby.

'Chris Masterson I'd like you to meet Nicholas Rayne, one of the finest lawyers at the DA's office.'

Eva had been busy trying to keep both feet on the ground, but hearing the introductions her head snapped up. Her eyes clashed with molten silver and held. Nicholas was dressed in a black tuxedo and crisp white shirt that fit him like a glove. His perfect appearance seemed to throw the other men into shadow.

His intense gaze left hers to skim down the length of her before returning to her face. She thought she saw something change in them but they shifted to Chris as he held out his hand.

'Mr. Masterson, I hear the chief is very proud of your work. Were you one of the officers on the Sharpe case?'

The men talked amiably, discussing cases they had dealt with and their opinions about them. Eva sighed, *thank god she didn't have to contribute to the conversation.* She could watch Nicholas to her heart's content without having to deal with that burning gaze on her skin. She blushed again as she remembered how he had looked at her. Almost as soon as she thought about it, those eyes were focussing on her once again, almost as though he had read her thoughts.

'I'm sorry, this is my date Miss Eva Tanner, a medical examiner at the police crime lab,' Chris introduced her to Nicholas having noticed Nicholas' stare.

'We have met before Miss Tanner. How do you do?' The softly spoken words seemed to caress her as she smiled politely at him.

'Fine, thank you.'

'May I compliment you and be so daring as to say you look absolutely ravishing tonight?' Nicholas smiled back at her, his eyes twinkling with amusement.

She couldn't help feeling his speech was more suited to a past era, as she swallowed nervously and tried to keep her smile pasted on her face. As to saying anything, it was impossible. Her heart had decided to stop beating and it seemed as though a flock of butterflies had taken up residence in her stomach. Her brain seemed to be frozen and try as she might she could not think straight.

'Thank you,' she managed to gasp, after what she thought was an eternity.

His eyes shone with suppressed laughter, before turning back to Chris to continue their conversation. She excused herself and teeter tottered to the powder room, eager to escape that stunning gaze. She touched her face. It was very warm and she could imagine how red it must be. She always did blush excessively, no wonder he had been laughing at her.

Glancing at one of the mirrors, she noted the tell tale blush on her cheeks and for some reason her eyes looked overly bright, which made them appear huge. She tried to breathe normally and slowly her heartbeat resumed its normal rhythm and the blush receded slightly. This was ridiculous, all this over a few polite words and some glances. It wasn't as though the man had even touched her.

But the mere thought of Nicholas' touch was enough to cause the blush to reassert itself and her heart to almost give up trying to be normal. She sighed and resumed her calming exercise. She must not think about Nicholas Rayne, or else she may not survive the night. She had enough trouble with her balance without adding a faulty heart and a tendency to turn red at the drop of a hat to the list.

Chapter 6

A few minutes later found Eva standing near a window, watching the dancing couples.

'Ah, there you are! Do you want to dance?' Chris stood next to her, a bright smile on his face. She gulped and shook her head firmly.

'I really don't think that's a good idea.' *That's what she needed, a dance, a dance to completely lose all sense of balance in these ridiculous sandals!*

He smiled down at her, 'I...' Before he could continue he was called away by an acquaintance. 'I'll be right back.'

'Do you dislike dancing?' the smooth voice set her pulse rate rocketing. She turned round slowly, carefully, to see Nicholas lounging against the wall.

Damn the man, she thought, he looked completely at ease.

'I don't dislike it, it's just not for me,' she replied using his phrase, trying to keep her voice steady as the silver gaze held hers captive.

'I see,' he glanced at the dancers, 'It's all about practice you know.'

'Of course, like everything else,' she conceded politely.

His lips quirked slightly in response to her polite answer, 'Exactly.' He seemed to be lost in thought for a few seconds, his eyes absently fixed on a distant spot, not registering the admiring glances thrown in his direction by the women present. 'Would you like to sit down?' he asked abruptly,

'Excuse me?'

'Would you like a seat?' he repeated slowly, his teeth flashing momentarily in a quick smile that had her mind spinning.

'I'm fine,' she replied stiffly. She would have liked nothing more than to sit down but that meant walking and she didn't think she could manage a single step.

'You look a little uncomfortable,' he continued as though she hadn't spoken, 'High heels seem to have that effect.'

'It's more than an effect with me, it's a catastrophe,' she admitted shifting slightly. She was holding onto the windowsill behind her tightly. Her frankness caused one corner of his lips to lift some more.

'Let's find you a seat,' he said as he pushed himself away from the wall. One dark eyebrow lifted slightly when she didn't move towards him. She looked helplessly at him and swallowed. What could she say? Sighing she shook her head.

'I can't move, I barely made it here from the powder room without falling. In fact,' she shifted again so he could see her hands grasping the sill tightly, 'the only reason I'm still upright is because of the windowsill.'

A low chuckle met her explanation and she looked up into his amused face and nearly let go of her support, shocked at the way laughter transformed his face. Unfortunately it enhanced his charm a hundredfold, which was almost a death sentence for her erratic heart.

'Careful!' he reached out to help her as she started losing her balance, but she leant back and grasped her lifeline more securely.

'Come along,' he said, moving closer to her and offering her his arm, 'You can't stay here forever.'

She glanced at his teasing face and sighed. 'You wanna bet? Alright, but not far.'

'Not far,' he agreed as he led her carefully towards a couch.

Having reached it without collapsing she sat down gingerly on the edge and watched in fascination as he manoeuvred his lithe body gracefully next to her, keeping a respectable distance between them.

'Why did you wear those shoes if you can't walk in them?' he asked idly once they were comfortable.

She shrugged, 'They go with the dress.'

He chuckled and looked away.

'What?' she looked at him confused.

'Nothing, you just sounded a lot like one of my sisters.'

'Your sister?' she looked at him blankly.

'I do have one you know,' he teased.

She shook her head to clear it, 'Of course, I'm sorry I didn't mean it that way. It's just I don't know much about you.'

He smiled at her contrite face. 'Don't be sorry. I have a few siblings, older and younger than myself. My parents died a long time ago.' A shadow crossed his face momentarily and then it was gone and Eva wondered if she had imagined it. He was smiling again at her in that devastating way. 'And you?'

'I'm an only child,' she replied her tone low, trying to keep her voice steady with difficulty.

'I see,' he nodded thoughtfully.

'You do?'

'Yes, you seem to enjoy being alone.' His eyes gazed into her wide ones, 'Don't you?'

She swallowed and nodded slowly, mesmerised. 'I guess so, but how did you figure that out?'

'It wasn't difficult. You just seemed happy on your own earlier on.'

She sighed. 'It was nice to get away from all the people Chris was introducing me to; to find some space. I don't really like crowds,' she confided wondering why she was telling him her most innermost thoughts so readily, she barely knew him.

'Bit difficult to avoid them in a city like this,' he mused, clearly teasing her again.

'I suppose,' she shrugged, 'So have you lived here long?' She was desperate to move onto any topic other than herself.

'No, we moved here a short while ago.'

'Oh,' she hesitated slightly, 'Where were you before that?'

He smiled absently as his eyes wandered around the room and for a moment she thought he wouldn't answer her. 'Many places.'

'Oh.' She looked down at her hands.

'Don't worry I'll help you get to the car park without falling.' The teasing voice was back and she looked up to see the serious expression on his face, whose effect was completely destroyed by the way his shoulders were shaking with silent laughter.

'Thank you but I wasn't thinking about that.'

'What were you thinking about?' he enquired softly, and she felt her breath catch.

'About...your family.'

He kept silent watching her from under his dark lashes.

'Could you tell me more about them?' She raised her eyes to his shyly.

He looked as though he was about to deny her request and then seemed to think better of it. 'I have two sisters and three brothers. Alena is very fashion conscious, you reminded me of her when you mentioned the shoes matching your dress.' He smiled as he thought of his sister and continued, 'My other sister is quite studious and couldn't care less about fashion. My brothers are just typical guys.'

'You really seem to love them,' Eva said slowly, noticing the tenderness in his eyes.

He shrugged, 'They are family.'

'Do you all live together?' She couldn't hide her curiosity about him.

'Sometimes, but we all lead our separate lives. We all own our own houses.'

'You all own houses?'

'Yes,' he looked at her questioningly.

'Wow! Do you live in the city?'

'My apartment is in the city but the family home is in the countryside.'

She was about to speculate on why he had two places to live in when he forestalled her with, 'It's more convenient for work with the traffic and all, plus I like my own space. Kind of like you.'

She nodded slowly, it did make sense but it still felt odd. She was about to ask him more about his family but Chris chose that moment to return to her.

Chapter 7

'Hey!' he bent down to plant a kiss on her cheek, 'I've been looking everywhere for you.'

'I'll leave you now.' Nicholas stood up fluidly, smiled at Chris and strode across the room. As soon as he was several metres away, he let out his breath and walked out into the gardens to inhale the fresh air. He couldn't keep doing this. He had thought he could ignore her scent but it was getting harder. He would have left her a lot sooner, but that would have been rude. He silently cursed his impeccable manners. As he turned to go back into the hall his ears caught the general babble of conversation and from amongst the chatter he managed to instinctively tune into the one conversation he didn't want to hear.

'So what was Nicholas Rayne saying to you?' Chris asked.

A smile touched Nicholas' lips, the handsome detective was a bit jealous.

'Nothing we were talking about his family,' Eva shrugged trying to steady her breathing.

'Weird.'

'Weird? Why?' she looked closely at Chris's face.

He lifted his eyebrows and laughed. 'You know…'

'No, I don't.' She waited for him to explain her brow furrowed.

'Well, did he tell you about his brothers and sisters?'

'Yes.'

'Don't you think it's weird?'

'What Chris? I don't understand.' She looked exasperated at his vague remarks.

'Okay, okay, look you don't know the full story. They aren't actually related, well not all of them. They are foster kids or adopted kids or something.'

'And?' Nicholas could almost imagine Chris's face turning red, and he chuckled, Eva was a hard nut to crack.

'Well, they all live together in this day and age…*weird*!.' His face looked immensely satisfied at spilling all his knowledge.

'So? They are a group of people living together, what's the big deal? Plus Nicholas said they don't live together all the time.'

'Yeah, guess that's what rich folk do,' he mumbled under his breath.

'Rich people?'

'Yeah didn't you know? Nicholas Rayne and his *family* own several businesses in the northern states and Canada. They are absolutely loaded!'

'So why does he work?' Eva looked confused.

'I dunno,' he spread his hands, 'I wouldn't if I was that rich. Guess he's bored.' He looked up and nodded at the small stage.

Eva turned to follow his eyes and found herself watching Nicholas as he adjusted the microphone and proceeded to give a short speech.

'Why is he…?' she looked at Chris and he smiled knowingly.

'He's the main benefactor of this charity.'

Her mouth dropped open and she listened mutely to his polite speech thanking everyone for coming and supporting the charity. She couldn't remember what the charity was and then her brain clicked into gear. It supported victims of rape and domestic abuse.

Chris leaned close to her ear to whisper, 'He's such a freak!'

'What?!' she whirled round on the settee to face him, she couldn't understand what he had against the other man.

'The guy's a freak, he's got a lot of money and good looks but he can't land a date? He's just odd, he gives me the creeps.'

Eva couldn't believe her ears. Could it just be a product of jealousy? It sure sounded like sour grapes to her. 'He's not a freak and I wish you wouldn't talk like that about him anymore,' she replied coldly.

Chris's eyes narrowed for a second and then he laughed aloud. 'You're defending Rayne? Trust me, you're not the only girl running after him.'

'I'm not running after him!' she snapped irritated at how accurate he was.

'Wow just a few minutes with him and you've forgotten me.'

'That's enough,' she stood up gingerly and glared at him, 'I'll see you at work Chris when you've had time to cool off.'

'Oh come on I was kidding!' Chris's voice followed her as she tried to leave gracefully but she barely managed to stumble towards the large doors at the other end of the room. As she walked through them the toe of her sandal caught on the hem of her dress and she toppled forward. She watched in shock as the concrete stair came closer to her face. Bracing herself for the impact she closed her eyes tightly and prayed it wouldn't be bad.

Suddenly she felt herself being grabbed by the waist and hauled into contact with a hard surface. She looked up half expecting to see Chris. Instead sparkling silver eyes assailed her own and she squealed in protest and tried to pull away.

'Calm down,' the smooth voice soothed her, 'you'll only get hurt.'

She stilled and let her senses exalt in his closeness. His arms were wrapped protectively around her, holding her securely. In fact she was sure her feet weren't touching the ground. Her cheek was pressed firmly against his broad chest. As she breathed in deeply trying to regain a normal heartbeat, the most fantastic smell wafted around her. It stirred her childhood memories. She breathed in again deeply and almost sighed in pleasure. It was definitely coming from him. The scent was of spices, rain on the earth and something else she couldn't place.

'Better?' Nicholas asked, his amused voice seeming to come from far above her.

'Y…y…yes,' she stammered, still trying to breath in as much of his scent as she could.

He released her slowly, almost reluctantly her foolish heart whispered. *He's just making sure I don't fall down again*, she told herself as she stood before him.

'You really should be more careful,' he said calmly, trying not to breath.

'Thank you for stopping my fall.'

'My pleasure.' He quirked an eyebrow at her, 'Leaving so soon?'

'Early morning,' she lied, trying to keep her balance.

'Of course. Are you driving?'

Although the question appeared on the surface to be mere courtesy, she had a weird feeling he knew she wasn't and had come with Chris. 'No, I'll catch a cab.'

'I'll call you one then, it's not safe to roam the streets at night.'

Before she could protest he had snapped open his cell phone and ordered her a cab.

'I could have done that, you didn't have to—'

'But I wanted to and I always do what I want Miss Tanner,' he said softly, his eyes alight with amusement.

She shook her head and kept silent, mentally cursing the heavy handedness of the rich especially rich good-looking men.

He seemed to sense her mood and she thought she heard a low chuckle. Glancing at his face she couldn't detect any humour, in fact it looked deadly serious as he said, 'Did you enjoy the party?'

'Very much,' she replied, a bit sarcastically, 'I was surprised when I found out that you are the main benefactor.'

He looked away quickly. 'My family helps many charities. I would prefer to be anonymous, but sometimes it helps to raise money if I am here.'

'Of course it's for a good cause,' she agreed, regretting the way she had almost accused him of keeping it a secret from her a moment ago.

He smiled down at her. 'So, Mr. Masterson has been telling you a bit about me?'

'How do you know it wasn't someone else?' she asked a bit defensively, her face already reddening slightly.

'Who else could it be? You have only spoken to him and myself the whole night.'

She couldn't believe he had been paying attention to who she spoke to during the evening.

'Okay,' she sighed resignedly, 'It was Chris.'

He nodded, a bit amused at her attempt to shield Chris from him. Maybe they were a serious couple, not just colleagues. He felt slightly uncomfortable at the thought, which surprised him. He never felt close to any woman, and would happily hand them over to their escorts once they had flirted with him. But this one was different his mind whispered insidiously, she was so small and yet had a stubborn independent streak which endeared her to him. And those unusual eyes, their colour seemed to have been stolen from nature's own treasure chest. Her humour exactly matched his own and she didn't appear afraid of him. Most other women, although attracted to him, were still too afraid on a primal level to really speak their minds. His sharp ears caught the sound of a vehicle and he turned to see the cab turning into the driveway.

'Your ride my lady,' he said smoothly, almost biting his tongue when he saw her looking curiously at him. *Old habits die hard*, he thought, silently cursing his mistake as he offered her his arm again and took her safely down the steps.

'Thank you,' she said as she got into the cab.

'No problem, I promised I would take you to the car park safe and sound,' he pointed out, 'Promise delivered.' He smiled and stood back as the cab drove away, not giving Eva a chance to reply.

She settled back into her seat and sighed. He really was an interesting man. Too interesting by far for her peace of mind, she warned herself. She couldn't let herself think about him or else she would become one of the women, as Chris put it, who were constantly chasing after him.

Chapter 8

Nicholas watched the cab as it turned the corner and disappeared into the night. He hadn't been kidding about the dangers of walking about at night, especially in this town. He glanced at his cell phone as he turned and walked back into the building. The dancing was back in full swing and he had to push through the crowd to find the person he was looking for. Ah, there he was. He moved silently and stood next to the Mayor and cleared his throat. The short balding man turned slightly and his eyes widened as they took in Nicholas' tall figure. He smiled and turned around completely to give Nicholas his full attention.

'Mr. Rayne, congratulations on throwing such a successful benefit!'

Nicholas smiled back in reply. 'Thank you Mr. Mayor, but unfortunately I am required elsewhere. Please accept my apologies.'

The mayor shook his head, waving away Nicholas' words. 'Don't worry yourself, I'm sure we will have plenty to talk about another time.'

Having excused himself Nicholas turned on his heel to find the chairman of the charity. She was standing a few feet away, but as soon as he caught her eye she moved towards him.

'I'm leaving now, looks like this was a great success, congratulations!'

'Thank you sir, for everything,' she replied with a warm smile. Her eyes travelled surreptitiously over his figure when she thought he wasn't looking.

Nicholas sighed silently, humans were so gullible; if the appearance was right they accepted it without question. He nodded to her and walked back to the car park where his car had been brought around. Sliding into the leather seat he dialled a number on his cell. After a few rings someone answered.

'I'll be late tonight, I have some unfinished business to sort out.'

He listened to the answer and smiled. 'I'll be there soon, don't wait up!' With that he switched off his phone and drove through the gates, heading several miles to a part of the city known to house the wealthy citizens of society.

+++

Jack Sharpe stood at the floor to ceiling windows of his apartment looking out at the city lights reflected on the lake. He sipped at his brandy as he thought about the court case. He could still see Rayne's hate-filled eyes in his mind and he smiled involuntarily. His lawyers had effectively killed the evidence leaving the prosecution floundering. He shook his head slowly; he knew the young lawyer wouldn't rest until he had found some more evidence against him. It wouldn't be too difficult to cause him to disappear just like the girls. His smile widened.

The sound of the doorbell echoed in the empty apartment causing him to glance at the clock, who could it be at this time? He moved towards the door the drink still in his hand. Opening it he stared at the visitor for a second before saying, 'Good evening, what a surprise!'

'May I come in? I have something to discuss with you,' came the quiet answer.

'Of course, of course!' Jack smiled knowingly as he turned back into the apartment, maybe he wouldn't have to worry about the young lawyer after all. The door shut with a decisive click behind him.

Chapter 9

'Hey guys!' Matt sat down at the table and pushed a chair towards Eva. 'Have a seat, you guys remember Eva.'

They were in the police department cafeteria, and Matt had finally convinced her to have the lunch they served. 'It's not healthy, but you'll love it.'

Love it was putting it strongly she thought as she looked at the array of chips, burgers and several unrecognisable dishes. She had finally asked for a salad much to Matt's disgust and had followed him to a group of people sitting several metres away.

'Yeah, hi, haven't seen you in ages,' a dark haired girl smiled as Eva sat down with her lunch tray.

Sarah, she thought delving into her memory. How could she explain why she had avoided coming into the cafeteria? After her experiences in high school she preferred to eat alone, away from all the popular kids who felt the need to taunt her. Instead she smiled in answer and looked around the table at the others, trying to remember their names. The red haired girl in the funky spectacles was Neave, next to her was Eric, the tall handsome chilled out looking guy, who was trying to take a book away from a shorter auburn haired guy with a serious face, Michael. Thankfully none of them resembled her tormentors from school.

'Here come the twosome,' Neave murmured as a couple approached the table.

'Hey Eric what's up?' the tall guy slapped Eric on the back in greeting.

'Trying to get Brainiac here to give up reading.'

'That's not going to happen,' Michael retorted grabbing the book back and smacking at Eric's hand.

'Yeah, Brainiac needs books like we need oxygen,' the pretty girl said with a smile as she sat down. 'So who's the new girl?'

'*New girl?*' Matt sighed, 'She's been here for a few months! Eva this is Tony and his current girl Meredith, our long lost sweethearts.'

'Current girl?! She's the love of my life!' Tony cut in theatrically, as he sat down next to Meredith.

'I'd better be if you know what's good for you,' Meredith replied, pushing him away.

'Hi,' Eva mumbled shyly.

'Hey.' Tony looked at her carefully for a full minute before Meredith shoved him hard. 'Get a grip Tony!'

He turned to her with a big smile, not at all abashed at being told off and put an arm around her. 'You know I love you!'

'Yeah for the next five minutes,' Eric retorted sotto voce.

'So how is the new ME doing?' Sarah asked trying to distract Eva.

'Great! I love it!'

'I'm sure you do otherwise you wouldn't be here! So have they been keeping you busy?'

'Overload,' Matt replied with a full mouth.

'Ugh! Didn't your mum tell you to eat with your mouth shut?' Neave grumbled.

'No!' he replied loudly still chewing.

'Any good cases?' Sarah ignored the bickering pair.

'Well—there is this one case. It s a bid odd.

'Tell me.'

Eva hesitated; Matt was still busy arguing with Neave. 'Two girls were sent to us from two different cases. Both have these small holes right here,' she pointed at a spot on the side of her own neck.

'Piercings?'

'Funny everyone keeps saying the same thing!' Eva complained in exasperation.

'Sorry,' Sarah smiled in apology.

Eva shook her head, 'No, I'm sorry it's just frustrating. They are quite deep, plus—,' she shook her head looking at the table top, 'I must be crazy.'

'Not at all, mysteries are what we live for!'

'Okay, the police are calling it drug overdose, but I haven't found high enough concentrations of drugs in their blood samples to cause death. In fact one of the girls didn't have any drugs at all.' She sat back feeling exhausted.

'So…are the detectives looking into it?'

'No, they tried to open the cases but they don't have enough evidence and they don't think the parents will want to delve any further.'

'That's understandable.' Sarah cupped her chin in her hand and stared into space. 'People lead bizarre lives,' she mused, 'Have you told anyone else about this?'

'Just Matt and the detectives.'

'Chris Masterson?' Eva looked into Sarah's green eyes questioningly.

'The word is he really likes you,' Sarah explained with a slight shrug.

'Yeah, well…' Eva looked down again, 'We have been out a couple of times.'

'So he couldn't help out?'

'No, he tried.' Eva smiled and looked across the table. 'By the way, what do Tony and Meredith do? I haven't seen them around before,' she said changing the subject.

'They are crime scene investigators like the rest of us. Tony is a whiz with cars, you know tyre tracks, interiors, engines and models? Meredith works with Michael, mainly researching anything and everything relating to the cases. Sometimes Tony helps out Neave with the forensic side of things, but he's such a clown she usually gets rid of him quickly. So he tends to hangout mainly with Eric and I at the crime scenes.'

'Hence the name Geek squad, ME,' Eric drawled popping a crisp into his mouth.

'Geek squad?' Eva asked timidly.

'Yeah, you know, the learned ones at high school,' Neave replied rolling her dark blue eyes skyward.

'Hey! I'm no geek, I'm cool,' Tony retorted heatedly, striking a haughty pose.

'Yeah whatever you say,' Michael said winking at Eva.

'You're not a geek Tony, umm…what's the braking power of a Lamborghini Diablo again?' Eric asked mischievously.

'It's…,' Tony glanced around the table at the knowing glances and shut his mouth quickly.

'Yeah, you're not a geek!' Michael said laughing at Tony's expression.

'Anyway, that's what we call ourselves, we are the best of the best,' Matt inserted smoothly.

'Hell yeah,' Eric said enthusiastically.

'It's not just the cases we work here, we are asked to consult in other states too,' Meredith inserted proudly.

'Murder capitals,' Tony grinned, watching Eva shudder involuntarily.

'Cut it out Tony!' Meredith said, looking at Eva sympathetically, 'Sorry about that, we tend to blow our own trumpet a lot nowadays.'

'Hey ME thought you dealt with death all the time?' Tony said, lifting an eyebrow,

'Doesn't mean I have to like it,' Eva retorted sharply.

'Whoa, the new girl has fire!' Eric said with a low whistle.

'You guys have no idea!' Matt agreed proudly.

'Good, you'll fit right in,' Sarah said, smiling warmly.

Eva returned her smile and listened as the rest of the team continued throwing insults back and forth good- naturedly.

Chapter 10

The next day, Eva walked into the lab almost groaning out loud as she caught the strains of music floating through the open door.

'Good morning Matt,' she called out over the jazz notes coming from the stereo.

'Hey,' Matt called back, lowering the volume of the music, 'Did you hear?'

'Hear what?' Eva shrugged out of her jacket and put on her white lab coat.

'About that guy you were testifying against...what was his name again? Oh yeah John Shark?'

'Jack Sharpe,' she corrected him absently, 'What about him?'

'It was on the news this morning, he was found dead at his home.'

'Dead?' Eva looked at him in disbelief. 'How?'

Matt shrugged, picking up a pair of forceps and turning back to the body on the table. 'They aren't sure. Sarah was on the case; she said they tried to dust for fingerprints...nothing. If you ask me good riddance.'

'Yeah,' Eva replied slowly her brow furrowed.

Matt turned slightly. 'Hey, I kinda need your help here.'

'Right, of course,' Eva shook her head to clear it and moved towards Matt, but her mind was still on what he had said. Suddenly an unbelievably handsome face popped into focus. She could still hear Nicholas' voice as he told her Jack Sharpe would pay eventually. That remark sounded awfully like a threat now. *But it couldn't have been meant as a threat, he was just saying that. Law enforcement people said things like that all the time didn't they?* She closed her eyes to block out the image of his intense face as he had leaned towards her, his eyes glinting. She had to concentrate on what she was doing. She opened her eyes to see Matt staring at her.

'You okay?'

'Yeah, absolutely, just a headache, it will pass.'

She sighed with relief when he nodded slowly and set about doing the autopsy.

A few hours later, Eva sat down at her desk tiredly. The girl had died from a stab wound. *Nothing unusual in that,* she thought as she started documenting her findings.

'Eva, I need you to drop off these files at the DA's office,' Matt said, placing a pile of files on her desk with an apologetic smile, 'I would take them but Sarah needs me to help her with a body they've found on the south side.'

'Of course,' Eva nodded and watched him leave.

+++

Why did I agree to do this? she asked herself half an hour later, as she walked up the flight of steps into the building housing the District Attorneys' vast suite of offices. All she could think about was accidentally meeting the devastatingly handsome Nicholas Rayne again. As though it wasn't bad enough he haunted her dreams, now even her waking hours were being spent obsessing about the man.

She stepped into the empty elevator and took herself to task. *Stop thinking about him, he's not interested in you. He was just being polite at the benefit. What would he possibly find attractive about you?*

She turned round to face the mirror at the back of the empty elevator and continued arguing with herself out loud as she was carried upwards. 'You are short, plain, your hair is limp... you look like a lab rat...!'

'Do lab rats look as good as this nowadays?'

Eva spun around, her face turning a bright red. Nicholas stood behind her, arms folded casually, leaning against the wall of the elevator. She hadn't heard the elevator doors opening but she had been so focussed on talking herself out of her obsession, she had probably missed it. And now here she was face to face with the object of that obsession…tongue-tied.

'Uh,' she swallowed quickly, 'What?'

'Lab rats, I don't think they are supposed to look like you.' His eyes shone with humour.

'Oh.' She could have kicked herself. Why couldn't she say something sensible and witty?

'Back to sensible shoes,' he said eyeing her trainers, 'Did you enjoy the benefit?'

'Yes, it was…' she hesitated, 'Fun.'

He laughed softly, 'I'm sure it was.'

'Did you raise a lot of money,' she asked trying to sound normal.

'Yes, it made a big difference.' His eyes locked onto hers and she felt goose bumps on her arms. He looked more handsome than ever in his dark suit, his hair casually swept back from his forehead. 'What brings you here?'

'Umm…files, I'm the messenger,' she replied shifting the pile she was holding in her arms.

'Let's hope it's good news, messenger,' he teased.

'Is it ever in our job?' she asked looking away. Suddenly she remembered what Matt had told her earlier. 'Did you hear about Jack Sharpe?'

'Yes,' he replied slowly, almost carefully, 'I want to say it's a pity but…' His face was taut as he let the words trail away.

'But he was found to be innocent,' she pointed out, wondering why she was fighting a killer's corner.

Nicholas' eyes flashed suddenly, 'Money has a way of manipulating the law, he was guilty as hell!'

She looked away from the fury in his voice. Almost immediately his face resumed its usual polite expression and his eyes looked apologetic. 'I'm sorry, it's just…the thought of criminals walking free; just because they have the means to buy lawyers and judges…it just doesn't sit well with me.'

Eva nodded, 'I know, but I guess some always slip through, right?'

He looked closely at her for a second and nodded slowly, 'Right, some do.'

The elevator doors chose that moment to open.

'This is my floor,' Eva said stepping away from him.

The doors slid shut behind her, but not before she heard him say with a chuckle, 'See you later…lab rat.'

She let out the breath she had been holding and started walking unsteadily towards the offices, trying to steady her erratic heartbeat. The conversation was still running through her mind. What had he meant by some do? It had sounded relatively normal but the way in which he had phrased it plus the look he had given her seemed to say so much more. If only she could understand what he meant. Most of his statements seemed to hold a cryptic message intentionally designed to confuse her. She put him firmly out of her mind as she walked through the door of the nearest office; she had work to do.

Chapter 11

The music was thumping against the club's walls, loud enough to be heard several blocks away. It was the newest club in the city and this was the opening night. The queue of eager youngsters waiting to enter it stretched for two blocks. The bouncers at the massive double doors were having a hard time trying to dissuade the crowd from pushing through the barriers they had erected. Even though they hadn't entered the club yet, most of the queue was swaying to the pounding notes causing the air around them to vibrate. The entire atmosphere was one of anticipation.

Inside the lucky ones were mesmerised by the bright décor, the lighting effects strategically created to enhance the party mood and the alcohol flowing freely. Crystal chandeliers hung from the ceiling glistening in the half-light while most of the walls were created to mimic the inside of a glacier. The floor was encrusted with sparkling stones and hidden floor lighting gave off a bluish glow. Professional dancers mingled with the crowd, setting the rhythm, while the best DJ in the state played the most up to date music adding his own special twist. Bouncers moved steadily amongst the youngsters looking for trouble, as the small army of bar tenders, the best in the business, juggled bottles and glasses as they poured out the myriad of special drinks, created specifically for the opening. The entire night was proving to be very lucrative for the club owners and very memorable for the patrons.

Jason and his crew had managed to get past the bouncers after waiting in the queue for over two hours. Adrenaline was rushing through their veins as they looked around them with wide eyes. Most of them were freshmen at college.

'I really need a drink!' one of them shouted.

The others nodded in agreement.

Jason smiled, 'Right go on then, I'll get us a spot.'

'Come on guys!' Danny shouted and headed towards the nearest bar, leaving Jason to shoulder his way into the crowd of dancing teenagers. Having been designated as the driver for the night he wasn't planning on drinking alcohol. He watched as several crews danced to impress, shaking his head slightly at their mistakes.

Danny, followed by the rest of their crew, found him a few minutes later.

'Right here!' Jason said loudly, jumping up and down on the spot.

'Cool, let's do this,' Danny shouted back. The rest of the crew formed a circle and started moving out into the surrounding dancers, forcing them to move and clear a space for them. Several of the teenagers stopped dancing and formed a circle around them as the crew started dancing in sync.

'Shorty's crew is here,' Danny shouted at Jason as he moved around him.

Jason's eyes lit with anticipation as they found the crew in question wearing black caps. 'They ain't got nothing on us bro!' he replied with a laugh and flipped upside down to start spinning on the floor, as the crowd cheered him on.

As he danced several girls moved closer, drawn by the fluid moves and his handsome face. His mates weren't far behind in the looks department and together with their ability to dance, they looked almost as good as the professionals. For a few minutes they held the small circle of dancers in thrall as they executed their practised moves with determined precision. They were all trying to attract the attention of scouting choreographers and dance directors, hoping to seal a contract to dance in some of the upcoming music videos.

Finishing with a complicated double somersault, Jason smiled up at the crowd of girls clapping enthusiastically. The entire crew vaulted upright and started mingling, watching the competition, and looking for any potential contacts they could use. ICE was the place to be tonight and they planned to make the most of it. Within half an hour Jason had the numbers of several girls written on napkins in his pocket and he was enjoying the latest song when he saw an unbelievably gorgeous girl staring straight at him. He felt the breath catch in his throat as she winked at him almost lazily. Without conscious thought his feet started moving towards her. She had the fairest skin he had ever seen, making her eyes appear large and almost pitch black. Her long black hair fell to her shoulders like a dark curtain and the dress she wore fired his imagination.

She had to be a model at the very least, he thought.

While the other girls were very pretty, they seemed to pale next to this gorgeous creature who looked like the proverbial ice queen. Having reached her, he stood still not sure what to say or do. But she lifted her hand to his neck cupping it gently and started to sway her body in time with the music. He followed suite, mimicking her moves to perfection. He didn't know how long they danced; it could have been mere minutes or hours.

She finally whispered throatily in his ear, 'Let's go.'

He didn't hesitate. She led him by the hand to one of the fire exits and pushed open the heavy door effortlessly it seemed. They slipped through and Jason found himself in an alley. The only illumination came from the flickering light coming through the open door. Once it was shut, the darkness claimed it again.

Turning to the girl by his side he breathed in deeply. She smelt divine. Without conscious thought he leant closer and found her lips. Kissing her deeply he almost fainted, as he tasted the sweetness of her mouth. The smell and taste of her made his heart beat faster. His pulse throbbed in his temples and his breathing was becoming laboured. He broke off the kiss at last, gasping for air. But before he could kiss her again she started kissing his cheek, trailing her lips down his jaw, nipping gently with her teeth as she moved back up to his ear lobe. He wanted to kiss her again, but her lips were on the move. This time they moved down his neck slowly, her mouth slightly open so she could taste his skin. Near the hairline she paused and sucked at his skin luxuriously, making his mind turn to mush with delight. Just as he thought he would crumble with anticipation he felt a slight prick at his neck.

He winced, 'Hey, gently girl.'

'Don't worry, this won't hurt,' she whispered into his ear.

He stared into her deep eyes and felt a cold shiver run down his spine, but before he could say anything else she covered his mouth with hers. Her tongue tangled with his in a complicated dance, and he gave up thinking as lethargic warmth spread throughout his body. He concentrated on her taste and smell and murmured in protest as her lips left his and went back to his neck. This time he barely registered the slight pain as she kissed him, her tongue licking his skin. He waited, anticipating another kiss, his eyes closed.

He couldn't decide how long he had been waiting, when suddenly he started seeing stars in front of his eyes. He blinked hard and tried to focus on a poster on the wall but it remained hazy. He felt his legs weaken and she must have felt it too because she pushed him against the wall, her mouth still locked to his neck. He started feeling dizzy and he tried to say something to the girl, but her fingers came up to silence him.

A few minutes later he slumped to the ground, pale and still as Marina wiped her mouth delicately with a tissue.

'Finished already?'

She swung round to see a tall figure lounging against the opposite wall, watching her with glittering eyes.

She smiled slowly, 'He didn't have as much as I thought he did.'

The tall stranger stepped closer, moving with a predator's grace and looked at the boy on the ground. 'Damn Marina! You didn't give him a chance!' he laughed softly, 'You almost gave him a heart-attack before you sucked him dry!'

She shrugged delicately, 'I was thirsty!'

He nodded, 'Shall we have dessert?'
She smiled back, 'I smelt some lovely girls in there.'
His dark eyes followed hers as they rested on the door leading into the nightclub. Wrenching it open effortlessly they slipped inside.
'After you,' he invited her, letting her move in front of him.

Chapter 12

Eva glanced at the clock and held back a sigh. She had stayed back to wait on a body being brought in by some police detectives. They had been delayed and when they had finally arrived it had appeared that the paperwork wasn't in order. They had left her to sort it out, and it had taken her an hour to organise the file and store the body for the next morning. It was almost midnight and she was just about ready to collapse with exhaustion.

Before switching off the lights, she took a quick look at the body again. It was a young man and she gazed at his peaceful face. He was only a teenager, probably a freshman in college. Gently she turned his head and peered at his neck, half-heartedly. Two small holes with several indentations around them barely showed up in the dim light.

What are the chances? she thought, quickly photographing the wound before pushing him back into the cooler. The kid had been dead less than three hours. It was almost one o'clock in the morning, by the time she had stored him safely and started switching off the lights and locking the doors securely behind her. A light drizzle started as she stepped onto the sidewalk. Pulling her coat closer around her she walked briskly to her car. *Why didn't I find a parking space closer to the entrance of the building*, she asked herself in annoyance as she almost tripped into a large puddle.

'Puddle? Yeah right! That's more like a lake!' she grumbled under her breath, shaking her jean-clad leg free of the water soaking through the material.

Still grumbling incoherently to herself she continued walking. Suddenly a sound stopped her in her tracks. Turning her head slightly she tried to place where it had come from when she sensed a presence next to her.

Automatically she tensed, clenching her fists, ready to fight. A second later she swung round, hoping to catch the person off guard. But the stranger was still next to her, so close she could almost smell his rancid odour, watching her movements with almost a disinterested patience, as though waiting for her to realise an obvious fact.

'Who are you?' she gasped, her eyes taking in his unruly hair, and dirty clothes.

'Someone who would like to know you better,' he replied his voice grating with menace as he moved closer.

She thought she heard him sniff the air appreciatively, like a connoisseur at a wine tasting, his face still in deep shadow. 'Well, I'm in a bit of a hurry…' she said, moving away from him as quickly as she could. She turned slightly to see another stranger blocking her way.

'Why in such a rush?'

The softly spoken query sent shivers down her spine. Some instinct made her wary of both men, but it wasn't just fear, it went deeper than that. Her brain seemed to be reacting as though a wild animal was hunting her.

They closed around her cutting off any escape route, coming closer and closer. She knew they would attack her in a few seconds, she had to make the first move and gain the element of surprise. Without a thought she lashed out at the nearest man. Her fist made sharp contact with his jaw, feeling as though she had smashed it into a concrete wall and she cried out sharply, but he didn't even flinch. Her fist on the other hand seemed to have shattered into pieces and she cradled it to her body, trying desperately not to scream out loud with the pain.

'You shouldn't have done that,' one of them chuckled with amusement.

'No harm done,' the other quipped and grabbed her shoulder, none too gently.

'Enough games, its time…'

'Let her go.' The quietly voiced command emanated from the darkness behind her, sending chills down Eva's spine, even though the pain made it difficult to register the presence of someone else in this nightmare.

'I don't think you want to be involved in this,' one of her attackers said, the threat clear in his voice.

'Are you certain about that?' A tall figure in a long dark coat moved away from the shadows, moving fluidly towards the group.

Eva raised her eyes to see his face but it was too dark to make out the features clearly. The voice however, that seductive, husky drawl…she shut her eyes as the pain rushed through her hand again.

'Leave her, she is outside your territory,' that lovely voice said in a commanding tone, penetrating the fog building in her head.

'And who the hell are you to give us orders?' it was almost a growl.

In reply a savage snarl shattered the silence and before she knew what had happened the hand grabbing her shoulder was no longer there, having been wrenched viciously away from her. There had been a sudden rush of air and she found herself kneeling on the wet ground from the force of its passage. Looking up she thought she saw vague shapes in the darkness, darting around each other, crouching, ducking and then vanishing to return from a different direction.

The snarls and growls intensified, and she had the vague notion she was watching wild animals fighting except that they looked human. Her mind was playing tricks on her again, she reasoned, or maybe she was asleep and all this was just a nightmare. She didn't know how long the fighting lasted, but before she knew it, it was over and Nicholas was again at her side helping her up; a strong arm around her shoulders. There was no sign of the others.

'Are you okay?' he asked her, guiding her towards a low slung black car a few feet away.

'Y…yes,' she stammered, wincing as her hand moved slightly.

Catching her gasp of pain he moved slower and didn't say a word until they reached the car. 'Get in, I'll take you to the hospital,' he said as he opened the door for her.

'I'll manage,' she gasped, 'You should go.'

He stood stock still, not moving until she sighed and got into the expensive looking car. She had a feeling he would have physically lifted her into it if she didn't obey. The door slammed shut and he slipped in behind the wheel. The engine was so quiet she barely registered it until they started moving. She stared out of the window, wondering what to say.

What can you say to someone who has possibly saved your life? 'Thank you!' she blurted out suddenly.

'You're welcome,' came the automatic reply.

She waited a few moments, expecting more. 'Is that all?' she asked finally in exasperation.

'Excuse me?' he was looking at her with raised eyebrows.

'Is that all you're going to say?'

He smiled gently, 'What do you want me to say?'

'Anything besides making this appear completely normal; it isn't normal. You just saved my life for God's sake and all you can say is *you're welcome*?!' Clearly the shock was getting to her and lending plenty of fire to her tongue, but despite knowing that she just couldn't seem to stop babbling.

'You said thank you,' he pointed out calmly, turning the steering wheel to negotiate a junction, 'You're welcome seemed appropriate.' His lips twitched slightly at the corners.

She glared at him and then slumped into the leather seat, resigned by his infallible argument. He remained silent, listening to her breathing, trying to determine by that how deep in shock she was. It calmed him to hear the regular breaths. If it weren't for that he would be speeding to the hospital to drop her off and then rushing back to hunt down those filthy mongrels.

He stifled the snarl rising in his throat at the thought of the attackers touching Eva. His mind had refused to consider anything when he had seen her in pain, her shoulder held by one of the men. His temper had almost boiled over then, and when his authority had been challenged his control had finally shattered and he had attacked with single-minded fury. Still, it hadn't been enough to kill them, which was what they deserved; he had been distracted by the gasps of pain coming from Eva. That had given his opponents the chance they needed and they had fled into the night, nursing their wounds.

'A lawyer by day, saviour of the weak by night?' Eva quipped, trying to forget the pain in her hand. Her voice drew his thoughts away from the attackers and any revenge he had been planning.

'What?' He stared at her, his gaze intense, his jaw clenched.

'I said...oh never mind I was kidding!'

'Oh...' he looked straight ahead again, not breathing.

She decided the one-sided conversation had gone on long enough. He may be gorgeous but she was damned if she was going to make an effort again, besides she was the one injured. She looked at his figure surreptitiously to make sure he hadn't been hurt. She hadn't even thought about that, but now her heart beat faster as she worried about any wounds he might have.

'How's the hand?' he asked quietly breaking the silence suddenly, catching her off guard as he turned his head to look at her.

She blushed, he had caught her looking at him, she was sure of it. 'It's pretty much broken,' she replied through gritted teeth, looking at it ruefully.

'You packed quite a punch!' He appeared quite amused and to some extent awed.

'Clearly not hard enough!' she muttered, thinking back to how it had made no difference to the man she had aimed at.

'I'm sure it would have sent anyone else to the ground,' he assured her with a small smile, seeming to read her thoughts.

'Anyone else?' she queried uncertainly, trying to block out the pain unsuccessfully.

'I meant...anyone less accustomed to living on the streets,' he amended hastily.

She nodded slowly still not able to fully understand his explanation. She sighed, the pain and the tiredness must be overriding her ability to reason; she wasn't usually this obtuse. She was about to ask him more about the men when he pulled up to the hospital entrance.

Before she knew what was happening he had helped her out of the car and into the waiting room, where he swiftly apprised the nurse in charge of her condition. Within seconds of revealing who he was, she was being led away gently down the crowded hallway, so that when she glanced back, she couldn't see him anymore.

Chapter 13

He's gone and you have to find a cab. Eva had been discharged an hour later, her hand firmly encased in a cast. Thank god she had broken her left hand. Apparently she had broken seven bones, pulled several ligaments and sprained her wrist to boot. The doctor treating her had raised several questions as to how she had managed to do so much damage and had looked extremely sceptical when she had told him.

'You must have punched more than just a face, unless it was made from steel,' he had said, waiting for a more reasonable explanation from her.

When she had remained resolutely silent he had sighed in resignation, given her a shot for the pain and advised her not to use the hand for several weeks if not months. She had been about to argue but his stern face had dissuaded her and she had walked out of the examination room meekly.

The doctor's right, that guy's face must have been made out of concrete, unless I did actually hit the wall and missed him completely, she mused glumly as she walked past the waiting area.

In mid-stride, she came to a jarring halt. A tall figure in a long dark coat was standing near the doors, raking his hand through his hair as he talked on his phone. Her heart thudded noisily, playing out a quick tattoo. *This is silly it can't be him,* she reasoned with herself half-heartedly. She was only a few feet away when he turned round swiftly, his greenish silver eyes clashed with hers and held. The cell phone was thrust into his pocket as he strode purposefully towards her, his eyes taking in the cast.

'Better?' he asked gently.

She nodded mutely, unable to find the words to answer him, still not able to believe he was standing in front of her. She felt her heart soar, felt so secure with him there, like she had finally come home. She blinked a few times to gain some perspective but the joy bubbling deep inside her refused to die down.

'You waited,' she almost whispered the words, afraid of shattering this beautiful mirage; just in case he wasn't really there.

'I waited,' he agreed, an uncertain smile playing on his lips.

'Why?' she asked, her wide eyes delving into his.

He took a deep breath and nearly groaned as her scent flooded his lungs. Controlling himself rigidly he exhaled smoothly with, 'How else were you going to get home?'

'Oh.' She looked away, trying to mask her disappointment at his reply, her heart plummeting sickeningly. She thought he had cared, but he was just being practical.

Seeing her face fall he sighed inwardly, unable to stop himself as the words spilled out. 'And I wanted to make sure you were safe and sound inside your house,' he murmured, almost hoping she wouldn't hear him.

But she seemed to have extremely sensitive ears for a human. She whipped her head round to look at him closely before a smile transformed her face. He was mesmerised, it looked as though the sun had burst forth from the clouds, as her lips widened and her teeth sparkled under the hospital lights. Her unusual eyes ordinarily a violet-blue now turned almost a brilliant violet and shone with happiness, and he found himself wanting to watch her for as long as he could.

A nurse walked past, reminding him of where they were. Clearing his throat, he moved towards the door, hearing her follow him. Once inside the car, they both appeared lost in thought.

He was still getting to grips with his reaction to her scent and now his sudden urge to keep looking at her.

'Who were they?' she asked suddenly.

Well, she didn't appear at all affected by him, she was still thinking about the attack. *As rational as ever,* he thought glancing quickly at her from the corner of his eye, *if only he could keep his thoughts away from her with as little difficulty.*

'Hmmm?' he reached out to turn on the stereo, flooding the car with soothing music. *What had she said? Oh yes, the attackers, maybe she would forget about it if he ignored her.*

'Who were they Mr. Rayne?'

He almost laughed out loud at her persistence. Bringing in the formal tone was aimed at making him remember their relationship. No, this girl was too stubborn to give up that easily.

'Call me Nick, Mr. Rayne is too formal after what happened tonight, don't you think?' he smiled at her, accelerating smoothly away from the traffic lights.

'Okay…Nick, you didn't answer my question.'

So much for trying to distract her, why wasn't she like the other women he knew, a small diversion from the main topic and they usually happily followed his lead. Not this girl, oh no, she had to be different. Why couldn't she just be glad she was alive? He could feel his patience waning and irritation taking its place. He swallowed and tried to hang onto his self-control.

'Just some tramps, I think,' he replied when he saw her staring at him fixedly, refusing to give an inch.

'What was that you said about territories?'

He glanced at her side-ways trying to hide his exasperation. She didn't miss a thing! That wasn't good; he would have to remember to be more careful in future. Future? What future? He wasn't going to see her again; shouldn't see her again.

'I always say too much,' he murmured under his breath frowning.

'What did you say?' the wide eyes were staring at him again.

'Nothing.'

He almost hit the steering wheel in exasperation, but caught himself at the last second. *How had she heard that? No human could hear his voice at such a low level. Maybe she wasn't human.* He quickly glanced at her from under his lashes, taking in the glow of her skin, its fragile texture, her features, and above all her scent. *No, she was human alright, just an exceptional one. Just my luck,* he thought, as he stared at the dark road ahead, *you had to pick the one human who not only has fantastic hearing but also the most stubborn streak you've ever encountered, not to mention the most mouth-watering scent on the entire planet you have ever come across. In short a challenge and a temptation all rolled into one.* He almost groaned out loud again, what was he going to do about her, or more to the point about this ridiculous obsession he was harbouring for her?

What was he supposed to do? Ignore the thirst? Suffer? He had stifled his desires for so long, they no longer mattered. But this was something else, something he almost had no control over. He glanced at her and clenched his jaw tight. Physically restraining himself from bending over her creamy neck. Something else was holding him back; the image of hurting her, holding her lifeless body in his arms, drained of warmth.

The thought was so painful that he nearly cried out. The pain numbed his primitive desire for blood, giving him some respite from his earlier agony. Maybe this was his punishment, sent directly from Heaven, a beautiful angel to torture him. But looking at her again from the corner of his eye he couldn't imagine her torturing anyone willingly. *Unlike me,* he thought. He could still remember Sylph's words when he had been a *neonate* all those years ago.

'Never break the Code, we live and die by it. No one can drink from the Bloodline, it's too dangerous.'

Her scent was saturating the air inside the car, driving him crazy to the point of no control; he needed fresh air. Lowering the window he almost gulped at the blast of air it generated. She was still staring at him like a curious child. Suddenly he knew why she had seemed so familiar when he had first met her. He glanced at her again, *yes, she seemed the right age and her hair was the same colour, just longer, the features*...he inhaled deeply...*the smell, more intense but still the same smell...it all fit, especially that amazing scent.*

'You still haven't answered me.' Her voice broke in on his thoughts again.

'What?' he asked in a disturbed tone, frowning at her.

'What territories were you talking about with those men? Do you know them?'

'No...' he cast around for a reasonable explanation, 'You must have misheard.' He accelerated some more, letting the wind cleanse the air, so that he could think clearly again without that disturbing fragrance clouding his mind.

'I didn't,' she retorted stubbornly, refusing to be placated, 'I know exactly what I heard...and saw.'

'Really? And what was that?'

'I heard snarling and growling and the three of you dancing around...'she stopped; it sounded ridiculous even to her own ears. His knowing smile didn't help her confidence.

'I think the shock could have caused you to hallucinate a little,' he replied soothingly, 'And you have been working all day.'

She sat back, her expression thoughtful as she chewed over his explanation, doubting herself.

He was waiting for another argument to erupt, but not hearing anything he relaxed slightly. Maybe she would forget and put the incident out of her mind. That was the safest path to take. *Safe*, he glanced at her again, wanting to stroke back the dishevelled hair as the strands fell onto her cheek. His eyes lowered to the white skin of her neck, peeping through the dark curtain of silky hair and felt his mouth moisten rapidly. Swallowing he looked back at the road, *this closeness could become a serious problem soon, and then she wouldn't be safe anymore.* His foot pressed down on the accelerator again, urging the sleek Mercedes forward at a speed well over the limit.

'Where do you live?'

'Rose Drive, on the other side of town.' She couldn't understand why the hands on the steering wheel tightened slightly, nor why he clenched his jaw, tension flowing freely from him. 'Is there something wrong with that?' she asked uncertainly.

'No, it's just...' he looked at her for a second before studying the road ahead and trying to relax, 'It's not a safe part of town.'

'Not a safe part? The real estate guy said it was the safest part!'

'So you haven't lived there long?'

'No, a few months. I used to live here years ago, but my mum and I moved to California.' Her voice became wistful as she thought about her mother.

'Why did you move back?' he asked, his voice betraying his interest more than he wanted it to.

'California didn't feel right,' she paused, wondering if she should go on, she hardly knew him and yet felt comfortable enough to tell him anything. Her reasons sounded hazy even to her. California had never felt like the place for her, it wasn't home.

'Right?' he prompted after a few seconds of silence.

'Yeah, I didn't feel like I belonged, plus I found a job here so...' she let her voice trail off.

'You certainly didn't come here for the weather,' he grinned at the windscreen as some raindrops hit it.

'I don't mind the weather, I love the rain.'

'All the time?' he teased.

'Okay, so I loved the warmth of California,' she sighed as she remembered the long sultry summers she had had with friends and family, the horse riding and the beaches.

'So you really miss it?' he had caught the slight melancholy tingeing her voice as she talked about her past.

'Just the weather…sometimes…and my mum,' she admitted, looking out of the window.

'I see.' He glanced in the rear view mirror and turned onto her street. 'Here we are.'

'Thank you again,' she repeated, as she was about to leave the car.

'Eva?'

'Yes?' she turned back to face him, her heart thudding a little faster at the sound of her name on his lips. Her eyes widened slightly as she saw how intensely he was looking at her.

He hesitated. 'Sleep well,' he finally said in a resigned voice.

She managed to smile at him and stepped out of the car, slamming the door shut. He watched her enter one of the buildings, clenching and unclenching his hands on the steering wheel. *What could he have said? Go away? Go back to California? You're in danger?* He grimaced as the minutes ticked by.

+++

This had been an unbelievable night. She still didn't quite understand what had happened but the cast on her hand proved that she hadn't been dreaming. She slept soundly for the remainder of the night, sitting up suddenly at five o'clock still shaking from the effects of her recurring dream. She glanced at the fluttering curtain…and frowned, she had no recollection of having opened that window.

Maybe she had forgotten about it, she had been so tired. Her mind flicked back to her dream. For some reason the unforgettable face from her childhood had morphed into Nicholas'. She sighed with frustration; her mind was playing tricks again. She wiped her hand across her eyes and lay back, trying to clear her mind and go back to sleep. After an hour of tossing and turning she finally gave up and went to stand at the open window.

Looking down at the dark street below, her eyes narrowed. Was that a black Mercedes parked at the curb? She squinted, trying to see it better. Didn't Nicholas drive a black Mercedes? She shook her head and sighed. *This is crazy, I have to stop obsessing about the man*, she thought, shutting the window decisively.

Chapter 14

'What the hell happened to you?' Matt asked as Eva walked into the lab the next morning.
She shrugged. 'I broke my hand.'
'Wow! What were you punching?' he asked, whistling under his breath.
'Apparently a concrete wall.'
He stared at her and then lifted his shoulders. 'Whatever you say. By the way that guy…Chris…has been calling here for the past hour. Can you give him a call so he can stop bothering me?'

Eva took the piece of paper he was holding out to her and glanced at the message. She sighed and went to call him. They hadn't spoken since the benefit.

'Chris Masterson.'
'Hi, it's Eva.'
'Hey!' his tone brightened instantly and she felt a warm glow at his obvious pleasure at hearing her voice. 'You got my message. I really am sorry for upsetting you at the benefit. I wasn't thinking straight. So, am I forgiven?'

She held back a sigh. He had been out of line, but maybe she had been too sensitive…especially where Nicholas was concerned. 'I guess.'
'Great! How about dinner tonight?'
'Sure, where?'
'How about the Italian on the High street, eight o'clock?'
'That's great. See you there.' She replaced the receiver and turned to see Matt eyeing her knowingly.
'Okay…what Matt?!'
'Chris Masterson…not bad…of course he's not as good looking as me,' he teased.
'Not many people are,' she smiled warmly at him, 'unfortunately from what I hear you are already taken.' She nodded towards his desk where he had placed a framed photo of his girl friend.

His gaze followed hers and his eyes softened, 'Yeah, she's my soul mate.'
'In everything including your lousy taste in music?' she asked laughing.
He made a face at her. 'So where is Chris taking you?'
'An Italian on the High street,' she replied, still laughing.
'Have fun, I hear it's really good.'
'Will do, now let's get back to work.'

+++

It was no use he couldn't concentrate on the work in front of him. He raked his fingers through his hair for the hundredth time that day. He glanced at the clock and straightened in his chair. *Five o'clock, she would still be at work, she would be safe there.* But he couldn't stop thinking that that was where she had been attacked last night. His eyes never left the clock, and when it struck five thirty he was up and out of his chair and through the office door, before anyone else had capped their pens.

Eva left the building at six o'clock and made her way to her car glancing around furtively for any strangers hiding in the shadows. Getting into the car she heaved a sigh of relief and drove out of the car park quickly. As she turned left, she thought she saw a black car and immediately took herself to task. She was obsessing again and that could not happen. Earlier she had asked Matt what he knew of the new attorney at the DA's office.

'Who? Nicholas Rayne?' She had nodded slowly, wishing she could stop being so interested in the man.

'Well, he's supposed to be this hot shot lawyer from up north. Apparently he's very rich, and this is just his way of giving back to society.' Matt had rolled his eyes. 'Why do you ask?'

'Oh nothing, just curious.'

She sighed now in exasperation, why had she asked Matt about Nick? She just couldn't get him out of her mind. She couldn't keep thinking about him, she had a date with Chris tonight. Pulling into a parking space outside her apartment she glanced in her rear view mirror just in time to see a black Mercedes turn down a side street.

Maybe those cars are very common in this area, she reasoned as she entered the building, but that didn't stop her heart pounding just a little faster.

Chapter 15

'What happened to you?' Eva raised her head as the now familiar question was asked yet again.

'I broke my hand,' she replied, trying to place the napkin unsuccessfully on her lap.

Chris's blue gaze rested thoughtfully on her face. 'And how did you manage that?'

She bit back a sigh. 'I punched a guy in the face last night.'

His eyebrows shot up in disbelief. 'Why?!'

'He and his friend were molesting me,' she admitted, trying to make it sound like a normal occurrence even though the mere thought of her attackers had her heart shrinking in fear.

'Molesting you?' Chris's voice was ominous. 'Where? When? Did you report it? Are you alright?'

She smiled reassuringly at his worried face. 'I'm okay. Really it was nothing. Nick took care of it.'

'Nick who?' his voice suspicious.

'You know, the new lawyer at the DA's office, Nicholas Rayne,' she clarified, feeling the heat suffuse her face. She hoped he hadn't noticed.

'Oh yeah, the rich kid.' Chris nodded in acknowledgement, but his expression remained serious. If anything he looked even more suspicious. 'What was he doing there?'

Eva shrugged. 'Dunno.'

'You have to be more careful Eva.'

'I didn't invite them to molest me you know.'

'All I'm saying is be careful. And not just with strangers.' His gaze shifted slightly.

'What do you mean?' Eva slanted him a curious look.

'I'm just saying...Nicholas Rayne may be rich and all, but he just gives me the goose bumps.'

Yeah me too, Eva wanted to say, but she was sure it was for a completely different reason. She cleared her throat softly, about to put Chris's concern to rest, when she saw him stiffen.

'Great,' he muttered under his breath.

She turned to see a couple being escorted by the maitre'd to a table a few feet away. She couldn't see the man's face but her heart started thudding a bit faster. She would know that figure anywhere. Her brain registered the fact that he was with a woman, and a shard of jealousy shot through her.

'The Raynes,' Chris growled.

'What?' Eva's eyes snapped back to his tense face.

'That's Nicholas Rayne and his sister...Leonara I think.'

'Oh.' Eva looked at them again, tearing her eyes away from Nicholas to focus on the woman next to him. Now that she knew they were related, she felt her breathing return to normal, and her brain started to notice the woman Nicholas was with; she looked absolutely stunning.

Her face was oval, with an aquiline nose, high cheekbones, and the same silver eyes possessed by her brother. If anything they were lighter in colour, almost tinged with blue. Her long tawny coloured hair flowed down her back like a mane ending at her slim waist. Dressed in black trousers, her legs seemed to go on forever. She moved fluidly next to Nicholas as he escorted her to the table. The smile she flashed at the maitre'd had the elderly man staggering slightly as he left them.

'What would you like to drink madam?'

She looked up at the waiter and smiled. 'Orange juice please.' He nodded and moved away.

She was about to say something to Chris when she noticed how quiet the restaurant had become. She turned to see most of the men at the surrounding tables staring at Leonara. *Men!* She thought, at least Chris was more of a gentleman.

As she turned back to him she sighed. He was staring at Leonara like a lovesick puppy. *Great!* She could have left the restaurant and he wouldn't have noticed. She wondered if the other women felt as deserted as she did. Glancing around again at the nearby tables, they all seemed to be staring too. She turned following their stares back to the Raynes' table.

Her eyes clashed with intense silver and she gasped. Nicholas was ignoring everyone including his sister and his gaze was fixed on her. She gulped and tried to smile. His lips twitched in reply. At that moment his sister touched his hand and he turned back to her.

Eva let out a sigh feeling her heart flutter. This was ridiculous; she was on a date. She glanced at Chris's rapt face and shook her head with a smile; at least she was supposed to be. 'Chris?'

'Huh? What?' Chris shook himself and looked at her questioningly.

'See something you like?' she teased.

As soon as she said the words the glazed look on his face vanished and he blinked uncertainly at her. 'What?'

'It's okay, you weren't the only one staring at her.'

'Staring at who?'

'Leonara Rayne.' Eva jerked her head slightly in the girl's direction.

'No way, she's beautiful but I wasn't staring! Come on Eva, we are on a date…together!'

In the silence following that statement she thought she heard a low chuckle from behind her. As she turned to see who was laughing, the restaurant seemed to come alive again. Conversations resumed, and cutlery clinked in the background. Her eyes focussed on the Raynes but they were deep in conversation. She looked at Chris again and sighed.

'She is very beautiful huh? '

'Yeah, but so are you,' he replied softly, leaning across the table to hold her uninjured hand gently.

'Yeah, thanks for making me feel better.' She sipped at her water and then looked up at him and smiled at his pained expression. 'Don't worry about it. How are your cases going?' she asked changing the topic swiftly.

It worked and he started talking about his current cases. Eva let her mind wander. That had been a bit odd. Everyone had stopped and stared at the Raynes, and then promptly resumed whatever they had been doing. In fact Chris didn't seem to remember it at all. But she had noticed the silence, the complete stillness. She had been the only one looking around in bewilderment. Except…Nicholas and Leonara, who she remembered had still been talking softly. Her brow furrowed as her brain continued to analyse what she had seen.

Chapter 16

Nicholas' eyes scanned the restaurant as he entered behind Leonara. She was dealing with the maitre'd so he was free to look for Eva. He had heard about her date with Chris when he had stood outside the forensics lab, listening to the conversations inside. Sometimes he was glad for the extra abilities he had.

He followed Leonara to a table and almost immediately her scent found him. Turning his head slightly he saw Eva sitting at a nearby table with Chris Masterson. He felt an inexplicable urge to rush over and pull her away from the muscular detective. Turning back to his own table he found Leonara smiling up at the elderly maitre'd who looked as though he had just stared at the sun.

'Better be careful Leo, you don't want to kill the man,' he teased, watching the man stagger towards the door.

'Oh, he seems fine,' she replied flippantly. 'Now, where is this girl?'

'Right there,' he moved his head slightly in Eva's direction.

'Well, she's no Madonna, but she does have a quiet beauty,' Leonara mused thoughtfully, letting her eyes travel leisurely over Eva's face.

Nicholas remained silent, he thought Eva had a unique ethereal beauty, but he knew Leonara would tease him mercilessly if he said so.

'Her date seems nice,' she continued as her eyes took in Chris's muscular physique and classic features,

Nicholas growled under his breath so that only she could hear him.

She laughed, a throaty laugh that had their neighbours looking at them in wonder. 'Do you want me to distract him a little?'

'You can't go over there,' he said quickly.

'Oh don't have to bro…' her face became intense.

'Stop,' he commanded quietly.

'Why did you bring me then?'

'For a legitimate reason to be here!' Nicholas rolled his eyes at her.

'Well it definitely wasn't for the food,' Leonara quipped, watching the patrons nearby eating a salad.

'Do you mind? Just be my date, okay?'

'Come on! I really want to show you what I've been working on!'

Nicholas sighed as she turned her pleading eyes on him. 'Fine, very quickly…' he warned her in a low voice, even though he knew no one would be able to understand their conversation, because of the speed of their speech.

'Excellent,' she nodded and the intense look came over her face again, just as Eva looked over her shoulder at them.

'She might notice!' Nicholas hissed at Leonara.

'She won't, she's a mortal,' Leonara smiled back at him nonchalantly.

Great! Maybe he should have asked Alena to dinner instead. At least she didn't have mad urges to show off her abilities in public. Actually that wasn't completely accurate, he grimaced as he remembered his other sister trying to show off and accidentally causing a flash flood during a severe draught in the town they had inhabited. The news reporters hadn't been able to stop commenting about how unusual it was for that time of year for weeks afterwards.

Leonara still had a smile in place and was telling him about how she had come up with her latest trick. Part of his brain registered her words but the other part wondered about Eva. Automatically he turned his head to look at her and inhaled sharply. She was staring straight at him, her violet eyes reminding him of the deepest oceans. Her faint scent drifted towards him, making his mouth water unbearably. Try as he might he couldn't tear his eyes away. She smiled slightly and he responded without thinking until Leonara touched his arm, effectively distracting him.

'What?' he almost snapped.

'Whoa,' she sniffed the air and her eyes darkened, 'Is that what I think it is?'

He looked away. 'Yes.'

'So, Eva is part of the hunted bloodline? And you knew all along?'

'Yes, and now you know why we have to protect her.'

'We?' she raised an eyebrow, 'I think we have enough on our plate already bro.'

'It's all connected,' he replied.

She looked questioningly at him. He was about to answer when he suddenly realised that that part of the restaurant was very quiet. He glanced up quickly and stilled. The women's eyes were fixed on him and the men's on Leonara.

'Uh, Leo?'

'What?' She turned slightly and then looked back at him with a sheepish smile.

He glared at her. 'Stop!'

'Looks like someone is already trying to,' Leonara shifted her gaze to Eva, who was talking to Chris.

Hearing Chris's answer, and seeing his almost lovesick expression Nicholas chuckled reluctantly. Almost immediately the silence evaporated and the patrons continued their conversations.

'What the...?' Nicholas' furious eyes met Leonara's again.

'Mass charming,' she replied softly, 'Don't worry they won't remember what happened.' Her gaze travelled slowly around the restaurant and she stiffened involuntarily.

'What now?'

'Your girl...Eva...she is the only one that looks puzzled, and listen...'

He focussed again on Eva's voice and almost paled as he heard her laughing at Chris's obsession with Leonara.

'Oh my god!' he breathed, 'Leo!'

'How was I to know she wouldn't be affected?' she asked, lifting her hands palms upwards.

He dropped his head onto his hand. No one at the nearby tables could hear him as he cursed, except for Leonara.

'Now, now, it's not that bad! She thinks it's just because of our looks.' Leonara was still focussed on Eva's conversation.

'That's just it! She is too stubborn! If she thinks there's something going on, she'll try to get to the bottom of it. She also seems to have amazing senses...for a human.'

'Hmmm...' Leonara looked thoughtful, 'This could be a problem.' She watched as Nicholas' eyes rested on Eva again before sliding away reluctantly. 'What's going on Nick? Do you like her?'

'What? No.' He hoped he sounded convincing. 'She's possibly the last of the bloodline. We are supposed to protect her, remember the promise?'

'Yes,' she almost hissed at him, 'Is this the girl attacked in our territory?'

'Yes,' his expression turned serious.

'I seem to remember saving a bloodline mother and child a few years ago,' her eyes widened suddenly, 'is she the little girl?'

'Yes,' he said softly, trying not to look at her, 'And I think she remembers us.'

'That's not possible!' Leonara looked shaken, 'How do you know that?'

'I heard her dreaming about that night...'

'Wait…you heard her dreaming? Were you close by?'

'Fairly close.' He looked away not wanting to admit that he had sat outside her apartment building, let alone that he had climbed up to her window and watched her turning restlessly as she dreamt.

'I still can't believe she remembers us, I affected their memories, I made us indistinct and she was so young…'

'Maybe, but you just saw what happened with the charming. Eva's not like a normal mortal,' he cut in tersely.

Leonara shook her head worry showing in her eyes, 'We have to let the others know.'

'We will, ' he glanced at Eva again noting the way her hair fell to her waist, 'But we can't leave now.' He glanced at his watch, 'The covens will be out.'

'You're right,' anger blazed in her eyes, 'Darius and his lot are causing no end of trouble.'

'Two bodies have been investigated by the police already,' Nicholas commented, watching Leonara's eyes widen.

'Oh no!'

He nodded slowly, 'And guess who has been examining them?'

Her eyes widened further, 'Eva?'

'Precisely!'

'Has she figured it out yet?' Leonara looked very worried now.

'I don't think so, but she did notice their wounds and asked me to investigate further.'

'So you managed to fob her off,' Leonara looked hopeful until Nicholas started shaking his head.

'No chance, that girl is like a bloodhound on a mission when she sniffs out a mystery.' He sighed in exasperation. *Why couldn't women leave things alone?*

Leonara smiled reluctantly and looked at the girl at the next table with admiration. 'I like her already.'

Nicholas raised his eyebrows. 'She's going to cause a lot of trouble.'

'Probably…but all good things are worth the trouble,' she replied sagely.

He looked sceptical but remained silent. No point in arguing with Leonara, she was as headstrong as she was beautiful. He tuned into Eva's voice and sighed inwardly as she laughed at Chris's joke…it was going to be a long night.

Chapter 17

'They're about to leave,' Leonara said softly, rousing Nicholas from his reverie.

He glanced quickly at the couple and felt an intense sense of relief. Finally the night was coming to an end. He couldn't remember the last time he had had to control himself so sternly. There were several times during the night that he had imagined killing or at the very least maiming Chris Masterson.

'What do you want to do?'

Nicholas smiled wryly imagining what he really wanted to do. 'I'll follow her home,' he replied instead.

'Alone?'

He looked at Leonara's anxious face and smiled. 'I've been on guard duty ever since the attack.'

'And she hasn't noticed?' His sceptical expression made her retort defensively, 'I know, but she's not a regular human, you said so yourself!'

'I think she has had other things on her mind,' he replied and his eyes focussed involuntarily on Chris.

'Well, he is cute,' Leonara admitted slowly, studying her brother intently. He looked like he could kill Chris given half a chance. 'But I don't think she's very interested in him.'

'Why do you say that?' he asked still looking at Chris from the corner of his eye as he escorted Eva to the door.

'Call it feminine intuition.'

Eva and Chris left the restaurant and Nicholas stood up. 'I'd better go, will you take care of this?' he asked nudging the bill with his finger.

'Sure bro…you owe me.'

'Right.' He strode out of the restaurant purposefully.

Keeping to the shadows he followed the couple to Eva's car. Once she was in it, he moved quickly to his own vehicle and got in. As he gunned the engine, Chris happened to pass right in front of the bonnet. It took all of Nicholas' self control not to run the man down. The effort again took him by surprise. What had Chris done? Nothing. He had only had dinner with Eva, and kissed her goodnight.

The thought of that embrace made him clench his teeth angrily, his fingers pressed against the steering wheel dangerously, and he had to remind himself that he loved his car and too much pressure would cause the wheel to crumble to dust. His mouth twisted into a wry smile at his reaction. *This was getting too serious. Maybe if he left town for a while…no, Eva would be in danger.* He shook his head to clear it and forced himself to relax.

From the corner of his eye he caught the flash of blue as Eva's car passed him. Pushing a CD into the player he settled into his seat and followed Eva home, preparing for another night in the car.

+++

'Where's Nick?'

Leonara raised her eyes to meet similar ones to her own, only they had specks of brown at the edges making them appear darker.

Seton Rayne the oldest of the family was seated on the couch next to her. Like Nicholas he was tall, broad shouldered with dark hair and flawless pale skin. He looked like he had stepped straight out of a romantic novel based in the nineteenth century. He was dressed stylishly in straight-legged pants and an open-necked shirt tucked neatly into the waistband.

'Uh, he's gone for a drive I think,' Leonara lied looking back down at the book in her lap.

'Leo?'

'He has!' she asserted, looking back at him with widely innocent eyes.

'Right. I know when you are lying Leo. Now what's going on?'

She sighed resignedly; Seton was always one step ahead of his siblings. 'Okay, he's protecting one of the hunted bloodline from the other covens.'

'Alone?' Seton raised his eyebrows a fraction in surprise.

She nodded and waited for him to speak. His brow was still furrowed in thought.

'The hunted bloodline; I didn't know any of them were in this area.'

'Apparently she moved back a few months ago, and Nicholas wanted to make sure she wasn't attacked again.'

'Again?' Seton's eyes narrowed dangerously. 'Leo, tell me what's been happening. And no more lies.'

Leonara related everything Nicholas had told her that night at dinner. She looked worried when she finished her tale.

'Are you implying that this girl is immune to your talents?'

'She seems to be; charming didn't work on her and Nick says she still has memories of us from twenty years ago.'

'Hmmm...and you say she was attacked. Did Nicholas save her?'

'Yes.'

'How did he explain that to her?'

Leonara shrugged. 'With difficulty?'

'I think we may have to sort out this problem.' Seton glanced up as a petite redhead with light blue flecks floating in her silver eyes, and a tall muscular sun-bleached blonde man with twinkling green eyes, the silver barely visible, walked in.

'And how are you two?'

'Just great!' Alena replied in her musical voice, almost dancing towards a chair. Kane followed her more sedately.

'Do you know where the others are?'

'Not really, Ashe and Eden are still in Canada. They should be back soon. No idea where Nick is,' Kane answered nodding a hello towards Leonara.

'They'd better be back soon, school is back on tomorrow.'

'Oh, they'll be back,' Alena smiled secretively.

'Now Alena, don't send out a freak storm,' Leonara teased her sister.

'Not at all,' Alena's eyes widened innocently, 'I wouldn't dream of it.'

'Yeah right,' Kane scoffed moving away swiftly as Alena threw a punch at his shoulder.

'Now, now,' a soft voice intervened from the doorway. Eleanor walked in and sat down next to Seton, kissing his cheek lightly, before turning her expressive eyes onto the playful couple. 'What's going on?'

'We are trying to bring the boys home,' Leonara informed her lazily from the couch.

'Really?'

'Alena wants to flood them out!' Seton supplied, his eyes glinting mischievously at his younger siblings.

'A bit messy,' Eleanor replied with a laugh. 'They should be back soon, they promised me.'

'In that case I'm sure they will keep it,' Seton reassured her, placing his arm about her shoulders and holding her close.

Leonara rolled her eyes at his certainty and went back to her book. Alena and Kane were still mock fighting when the roar of engines made them stop.

'Guess who?' Alena quipped as two forms rushed into the room pushing and shoving each other.

'I win!' crowed the blonde haired boy.

'Ha! In your dreams!' retorted the other, as they came to a standstill in front of Seton.

'Good trip?'

'The best!' Eden replied laughing, 'Totally beat the competition.'

'I believe I did the beating!' Ashe shot back as he pushed a hand through his messy blonde hair, launching another argument.

'Alright, that's enough,' Seton's commanding voice sliced across the fight causing the boys to look at him questioningly.

'We have problems to deal with,' Seton explained. He waited until they were seated and then resumed. 'Nick has found a girl from the bloodline and is protecting her from the other covens.' The others looked amazed, as he paused to let the statement sink in.

'Is she good-looking or just smells heavenly?' Ashe asked after a second, licking his lips expressively.

'Not the point Ashe!' Leonara said, glaring at him, 'She's the one we rescued years ago, she's moved back and has been attacked since!'

'Darius!' Alena growled under her breath.

'Not necessarily,' Seton replied.

'Then who? Come on Seton! He's the only one causing problems in this area at the moment,' Leonara argued glancing at the other faces. From the slight nods they appeared to agree with her.

Seton sighed. 'Innocent until proven guilty.'

'The human way?' Alena giggled disbelievingly.

'Seems to work.'

'Not always!' Kane retorted, as he caressed Alena's hand absently.

'Anyway, whoever it is we will have to protect this girl,' Eleanor said softly.

'Oh and another thing, she is immune to some of our talents,' Seton cautioned.

'*What?!*' Every face in the room registered shock.

'How?'

'Is she definitely human?'

'How did you find out?'

The questions were fired mercilessly at Seton.

'I tried to charm her and it didn't work and neither did my memory manipulation,' Leonara explained, quickly coming to his rescue.

'Come on Leo! Maybe you're just slipping!' Eden said with a short laugh.

Leonara glared at him, 'Then how did I manage to charm an entire restaurant and wipe their memories tonight while Eva just sat there looking confused?'

Eden shrugged with an apologetic smile, but a deafening silence had fallen on the room after Leonara's comment.

'Is Nicholas with her now?' Ashe asked suddenly.

Leonara nodded. 'Yup, he's on protection detail tonight.'

'How long has he been doing that?' Eleanor asked looking worried.

'For a while,' Leonara smiled reassuringly at her.

Seton was still frowning. He knew his brother well, and he had never seen him take on the protection of a human in the past. He treated them with respect but would never have got caught up so completely in protecting one. Normally he would have come to Seton and let him deal with it.

He preferred to carry out his self-imposed role as, what he called laughingly, the angel of death. That was one of the reasons he had decided to become a lawyer. It made it easier for him to judge the ones that escaped the human law. Made it easier to sentence them as they should have been sentenced if not for their tricks in court. This sudden interest in a human girl was a new development and he wasn't sure he liked it.

'Uh, there's more,' Leonara's voice cut into his thoughts hesitantly.

'Oh no,' groaned Eden dramatically, a twinkle in his eye.

'She's a medical examiner for the police and she's had a few victims of our kin on her table recently.'

'So? Humans usually don't care about stuff they can't explain even if they do see some unusual stuff,' Ashe said with a sigh of pure boredom.

'Have you not heard a thing we have said? This girl is unusual in the extreme and she's curious to boot!' Leonara snapped irritably at her younger siblings.

'What are you saying Leo?' Alena asked carefully.

'She's investigating the bodies and trying to get the police involved. She's not going to let it go.'

'Great!' Kane raised an eyebrow, 'What do we do?'

'First we protect her and talk to Nick. This is getting a bit out of hand,' Seton replied firmly, his face betraying his discomfort.

The others nodded in agreement, Seton was right, they had to tackle the problem soon.

Chapter 18

'Good to see you Nick. Leo told us about the...er situation.'

Seton had been waiting for him at his city apartment when he had returned from his nightly vigil for a change of clothes.

'Yes...' his eyes were impenetrable.

'This protection detail you've taken on...it's a bit unusual.'

'Why?' Nicholas' eyebrows rose slightly, still refusing to give anything away.

'Well, in the past you have always let the family protect the humans...but not this time.'

Nicholas shrugged defensively, 'You were busy with the other covens.'

It was now Seton's turn to raise his eyebrows, 'Indeed.' He waited for Nicholas to respond and when he didn't he sighed in defeat. 'Okay Nick, I won't pry, but this girl is in a lot of danger and you cannot hope to protect her on your own!'

Nicholas smiled coldly, remembering how he had managed to see off the two attackers. 'I have so far.'

Seton shook his head, 'But you weren't dealing with many of them. In spite of what you think you are capable of, I think you've bitten off more than you can chew.'

Nicholas' eyes met Seton's, a wry smile twisting his lips as he admitted silent defeat. 'Maybe you're right, I could use the family.'

'Good,' Seton smiled with relief. He looked again at his younger brother and decided to voice his thoughts, knowing Nicholas may not appreciate them. 'Does she know about us?'

'No!' Nicholas' exclamation rang out, 'I wouldn't betray us Seton!'

'I know, but this is different, her life is at stake.' He paused before saying slowly, 'Maybe you should tell her...'

Nicholas shook his head vehemently, 'She would be in more danger!'

'How exactly is that possible at this point?' Seton asked smiling disarmingly.

Nicholas sighed and then returned his smile reluctantly. 'I'm not quite sure, but I do know it's not a good idea.'

'How can we protect her without her finding out?'

'We have done it before!'

'Yes, but those were normal humans so to speak and not from the bloodline. From what Leo has told us, this girl is unusually...adept and is a walking temptation for any vampire.'

Nicholas stood up, raking his hand through his hair. Should he tell Seton everything?

'Nick?'

'I know what you're saying. She is a temptation.' Even thinking about Eva was causing his mouth to flood with moisture, but there was another yearning he couldn't place. Even while talking to Seton, he was conscious of wanting to be near her, to see her. An uneasy feeling gripped him as he thought of the danger she was in, and she didn't even know it!

'Yes, she is. You won't be able to control yourself if you are near her for long.'

'I will have to,' Nicholas replied from between gritted teeth.

Seton looked at Nicholas' tense back as he walked towards the fireplace; his hands clenched tightly by his side. 'You aren't telling me everything,' he stated softly. He heard Nicholas breathe out heavily. 'Do you like this girl?'

Nicholas bent his head and rested his arms on the fireplace, staring down into the hearth with unseeing eyes and nodded slowly.

Seton breathed in sharply, he had suspected it but had hoped he was wrong. Both he and Eleanor had hoped Nicholas would find that someone special eventually, but they had never dreamt it would get this complicated. He was starting to understand how Nicholas was feeling. If their situations had been reversed he would have killed anyone who intended to harm Eleanor. Looking at Nicholas now he felt a surge of sympathy.

Rising fluidly to his feet he walked quickly towards him and clasped his shoulder. 'You more than like her.'

It was a statement of fact for there was now little doubt in Seton's mind. Nicholas turned his head to look at his brother. His eyes told Seton everything he needed to know and he nodded with a small smile.

'That's good enough for me. Now how do we solve this?'

Nicholas' face glowed with relief and he covered Seton's hand with his own. 'Thank you.'

Seton shook his head, 'Don't thank me yet. We have to let the others know.'

'I'd rather not...' he could just imagine what they would say.

'They are family Nick and we need their support."

He sighed, 'Fine.'

'First things first...we need to get her to a safe place. Preferably based in our territory.'

'We can't do that!'

Seton looked at him, his gaze conveying the urgency he felt, 'We must. Which is why I think you should tell her about us.'

'NO!'

His firm denial made Seton raise his eyebrows. 'Are you afraid?'

'Yes! I'm afraid of frightening her. I'm afraid she will run away, but most of all...' Nicholas' voice trailed away as he realised what he was saying.

'You're afraid she won't want you near her, will be afraid of you?' Seton continued slowly, understanding dawning on him.

Nicholas nodded slowly, looking out of the window.

Seton sighed. 'I can't say I know how you feel, but her safety is paramount.'

'Let's try this without her knowing,' Nicholas almost whispered the words.

'Alright,' Seton agreed and walked towards the door, 'but you will eventually have to tell her.'

Nicholas heard the door close behind him and relaxed slightly. He knew this entire situation was impossible, but he still couldn't bear to see fear in Eva's eyes when she looked at him. They would have to think of some way to keep her safe without her being any the wiser. He smiled wryly, how would they manage to do that without arousing her over active curiosity?

Chapter 19

'So what's the cause of death?'

Eva looked into Sarah's blue eyes and sighed with frustration, 'I haven't quite decided yet.'

It was later that day and Eva had finally managed to get around to the body she had stashed on the night she was attacked. She still couldn't think about it without shivering.

'Oh?' Sarah looked at the body of the teenager closely. 'No bruises?'

'Nope.' Eva shook her head, 'It looks like he wasn't touched at all. No broken bones and no defensive wounds on his hands,' she turned his palms upwards to show Sarah what she meant, 'To all intents and purposes it looks like he dropped down dead.'

'What about drugs?'

Eva's head was shaking in a negative before Sarah had finished the question. She reached for the file she had compiled and flicked through it quickly.

'The tox report is clean, he didn't even have aspirin in his system, although…'

'What?'

'It *was* difficult to get a blood sample, I had to get it from a vein deep in his heart.'

'Is that…unusual?'

'Well, usually the blood starts to clot once it stagnates in the blood vessels but I can manage to get a sample without too much difficulty from the veins. But in this case the blood in the veins was so low I couldn't get a suitable sample.' She paused and then said almost to herself, 'It's almost like it was drained out.'

'There wasn't a blood pool at the crime scene,' Sarah replied quickly.

'No, I didn't think there would have been,' Eva agreed, 'There aren't any wounds big enough to cause such a loss of blood.'

She flicked through the file absently, still thinking about the blood when her eyes alighted on a Polaroid photograph. Her eyes narrowed as she tried to remember when she had taken it. Flipping it over she glanced at the date and time printed neatly in her handwriting on the back. Turning it face up again she picked up a magnifier and studied it closely.

'What did you find?'

'Have a look,' Eva invited, pushing the photo and magnifier towards Sarah.

Taking them, Sarah studied the photo before turning stunned eyes on Eva. 'It's the twin holes you were telling me about.'

Eva nodded, 'Yes but look at the marks around them.'

Sarah turned her attention back to the Polaroid and frowned as she concentrated harder.

Eva was still trying to place the marks as she watched the CSI. Turning the boy's head again she stared at the holes, but the marks had disappeared. *Now what could cause marks like that?* she wondered.

'You know these marks remind me of a hicky.'

Eva looked up sceptically, 'A hicky?'

'Yeah, you know…a love bite.'

Eva's eyes narrowed slightly, "So…he …was bitten?'

'Well…' Sarah shrugged with a wicked smile, 'that's what it looks like…obviously not by the love bug.'

'Okay…let's say he was bitten, why the two holes?'

'Maybe he was bitten first and then stabbed.'

'With what? No weapon or object I know of causes holes like that. Trust me I've checked,' she gestured towards another table where an array of forks and picks were arranged.

Sarah shrugged again, 'Hey I'm just the CSI you're the expert. But maybe it's a cult thing, you know, like in the old movies…who was that guy? Oh yeah…Dracula.'

'What did you say?' Eva looked up quickly from the body.

'You're the expert…'

'No, no, what did you say after that?'

'Uh…a cult…Dracula?'

Eva's eyes widened, 'Just maybe…'

Sarah shook her head, 'Kids are definitely weird nowadays.' Her pager started buzzing and she sighed looking at it, 'I gotta go, see you later.'

'Sure,' Eva barely looked up from the body as Sarah left the lab.

Dracula? A cult? She logged into her computer and started typing. Within minutes she had all she needed to know about bite marks. Scanning the Polaroid into the system, she started comparing it to the examples on the screen, her eyes widening as the program confirmed that they were tooth marks. But it couldn't seem to place the deep holes. It kept trying to superimpose the typical marks expected from the canines, but kept hitting an error. Maybe Sarah wasn't quite as off base as she had thought.

She walked to her desk and started searching the Internet for cults currently on the rise, interested in the ones mentioning any form of biting. A short time later she sat back and rubbed her eyes. In the USA there were over a thousand cults and those were only the ones that believed in causing bodily harm of some sort. Very few believed in biting, but a few did try to emulate vampires. None seemed to be practicing in this area officially, but maybe some members had joined up and started a different group? She sighed and stared at the body again, trying to arrange her thoughts.

Her eyes flicked back to the screen and scrolled down. A website related to mythical creatures caught her attention and she clicked on it, more out of curiosity than scientific interest. There wasn't a lot of information on vampires but apparently from the myriad of supposed sightings that were listed, people had noticed that their general appearance was very similar to humans, except for their flawless skin, intense eyes, and in some cases their magnetic personality.

She kept reading, her left hand automatically rubbing her right wrist as it started itching again; she had always had a small freckle there. When she had noticed it increasing in size a few months ago she had had it checked by a doctor. He had examined it closely and finally pronounced it to be a benign freckle. She focussed on the screen again dismissing the slight itch from her mind.

The website described these creatures as having the usual taste for human blood, but it also catalogued a list of exceptional traits such as their speed, strength, and abilities bordering on the supernatural such as shape-shifting or controlling people's minds. She almost laughed out loud as she continued reading. Some of the information read like the requirements for super heroes in comic books. *Well, no wonder some cults want to pretend to be mythical creatures*, she thought, a sardonic smile lifting the corners of her mouth. *What's not to like about having powers and killing people?*

Shaking her head she navigated away from the site, searching again for cults in the nearby areas. Although she felt the whole scenario of someone biting another person bizarre, she still couldn't understand why the boy had died. Correction, why three people had died so far from just two holes in their necks. The fact that the blood in the blood vessels wasn't what was normally expected added to the mystery. It was almost as if the bodies had been drained of their life-giving fluid. She shuddered involuntarily, and quickly directed her thoughts towards a different case as she pushed the body back into the cooler.

Chapter 20

Why could she not get him out of her mind? The man was embedded too deeply in her consciousness, so that every time she had an idle moment, her thoughts returned to him of their own volition. Even now she was trying desperately to bring Chris into the forefront but Nicholas' face simply smiled at her and refused to budge.

'Eva? Are you still there?'

She shook her head to clear it. 'Yes of course. Sorry I…I was just thinking.'

'Well, what do you say?'

'Uh…' *what had he said?* She tried to remember and then it clicked. 'Dinner tomorrow? Yeah, sounds good.'

'Great! I'll pick you up around seven?'

She tried to inject some enthusiasm into her voice, but it still came out somewhat resigned as she agreed to his plans.

As she put the phone down, she glanced out of the window and frowned. It was Sunday, her day off and she had decided to go for a walk on the beach nearby, but the sky was threatening. She sighed, how she missed the warmth of California.

+++

Dinner?! Again?! Nicholas' jaw clamped down as Eva's voice floated through the open window. He thought back to the last date he had had to sit through and winced. Leonara's charming foibles aside, it had been unbearable to watch Chris enjoying Eva's attention. All he had wanted to do was step in and stake a claim to her. Monopolise her attention so that she couldn't look at anyone else, couldn't listen to anyone else.

As his thoughts became more and more possessive, he suddenly drew himself up sharply, startled at the intensity with which he wanted to be with her. He had never had such feelings for anyone before. Even as he tried to reason them away, his mind refused to obey.

He decided to examine the situation differently. Chris was a good person, and Nicholas knew he wouldn't hurt her, then why this intense protectiveness towards her? Having hit an unanswerable question he concentrated again on the sounds coming from her apartment window. She was moving around the apartment now, he thought, hearing her gentle steps on the carpet. The sudden burst of music made him smile. Her taste in music was certainly diverse.

He sighed and leant back in his seat, listening to the song's lyrics. Inevitably his mind raced back to what she had said to Chris. *Dinner,* he cringed, *how could he avoid it? He could get one of the others to do it for him,* but he shoved the idea away quickly. He wasn't ready to hand over Eva's protection just yet. His mind whispered as to the reason for his reluctance, but he ignored it and concentrated on the dilemma. He couldn't ask the family to protect her yet, but they could be helpful in other ways. He smiled as he thought about it; *this would solve the problem with minimal fuss.*

+++

'I need a favour.'

Kane's eyebrows rose as he listened to Nicholas' plan.

'So what do you think?' Nicholas asked him slowly.

Kane's deep green eyes stared at him for a full minute, not blinking, before he finally smiled slowly. 'You won't like what I'm thinking.'

'Try me,' Nicholas invited.

'Okay, you asked for it. I think you are crazy in love with this girl and you need to tell her…and soon by the sound of it.'

Nicholas looked away from the knowing eyes of his friend. 'You're right…I don't like it.'

'Told you,' Kane shrugged and then smiled, 'but I'll do what you want.'

Nicholas whipped round to look at him, a smile of thanks lighting his face. 'Remember, nothing major.'

Kane nodded and left the room, leaving Nicholas to his thoughts. He had rushed to the family home as soon as he had seen Eva safely to the lab. He glanced at his watch and groaned he had to be at work in fifteen minutes. Rising swiftly to his feet, he rushed out of the living room, up the stairs and into his bedroom with lightning speed. Within a few short minutes he was back in the car, driving to work.

+++

Eva had just left work and was heading towards the car park, her fingers tapping out a beat at her side as a song ran through her head. It had been a busy day with back-to-back autopsies. The cases were picking up and everyone was run off their feet. She sighed tiredly as she got into her blue sedan. Just as she was about to rev the engine, her mobile phone started ringing.

'Hello?'

'Hey Eva, its Chris. Listen I seem to be having problems with my car tonight. Can we take a rain check?'

Her heart lightened considerably as she heard his words and she smiled involuntarily. Realising she wasn't supposed to be happy, she quickly straightened her face and tried to sound unhappy. 'Oh…well…guess it can't be helped. What's wrong with it?'

'The oil's leaking and I don't want to take a chance.'

Good one Kane, Nicholas thought, grinning as he listened in on the conversation from the other side of the car park.

'Oh…'

'Yeah, it's really weird, it's never had a problem before!'

'I'd get used to it if I were you,' Nicholas said softly, chuckling to himself. He listened as Eva reassured Chris. *Was she smiling?* He concentrated closely on her tone of voice and smiled. Yup, she was definitely not upset with the situation. Could it be she was actually glad not to be going out with Chris? He almost whooped with joy, but managed to stop himself at the last minute. He watched as Eva, having finished the conversation, revved the engine and drove out of the car park and followed her to the apartment, barely able to contain the happiness surging inside him.

Chapter 21

Half a mile away, two dark figures walked towards a group of dilapidated buildings on the outskirts of the city. The area looked severely neglected and several homeless people stood around fire barrels, warming their hands, trying to ward off the cold. As the couple approached they shrunk quickly into the shadows. Neither the man nor the woman seemed to notice them as they almost floated past, and entered one of the buildings.

Loud music was playing in the deeper recesses and they moved swiftly towards it. They paused at the doorway leading into a large room where several people were lounging in old chairs and settees or dancing to the loud music. Most were dressed in mismatched clothing and there was a faint rancid smell about them. Despite this their features were abnormally perfect with pale icy white skin, lustrous hair and every single one of them had dark, almost black, impenetrable eyes. Their beauty would have caused the fashion world to worship them, but their depthless, almost soulless eyes seemed designed to strike fear into the most courageous heart.

As soon as the couple entered the others stilled and looked up expectantly. A wave of the man's hand effectively killed the music. He let his gaze travel around the room cataloguing who was present. There were the usual crowd and some new faces.

When he didn't say anything for a few minutes one of the women seated on a nearby settee yawned and said, 'Why have you called us Darius?'

His eyes whipped to her face and narrowed dangerously, no one questioned him, least of all a relatively newcomer. *Savannah*, he thought as his eyes rested on her heart-shaped faced, deceptively innocent. She had flirted with him recently, and now seemed to think she had the right to question his authority, she would have to be taught a lesson, and he would enjoy doing so. She flinched slightly at the anger evident in his eyes and shifted her gaze to the woman next to him. She was smiling slightly at Savannah but her eyes were just as deadly as Darius'. Savannah stiffened her spine and glared back at Marina. It was common knowledge that Darius and Marina had been mates for years, but that didn't stop either from flirting with other vampires.

'We have things to discuss,' Darius' voice cut through the expectant silence.

'But it's time to hunt!' one of the others almost whined. The words could barely be heard but Darius' sharp ears caught them and an almost rabid snarl ripped through the air, silencing any more pending complaints.

Marina walked towards a chair and sat down gracefully crossing her legs and waited for Darius to continue. He in turn moved into the middle of the room and stared around him almost viciously, daring anyone to interrupt him.

'Any more questions?' A deep silence met his question and he nodded, satisfied, 'Right, I have some information about the girl.'

His words made the others shift with anticipation. The girl was uppermost in all their minds. Her blood was prized above all others and not one of them could think of her without saliva almost dripping from their mouths. Darius' eyes glittered as he took in their renewed interest.

'I have found a way to get at her.'

A startled laugh was quickly stifled as his eyes shifted towards the culprit.

'But...' his gaze shifted again and focussed on the man standing near the back, 'The elite one is looking after her.'

'We will delay him, and get her before he can come to the rescue' Darius clarified.

'But what if the other Elites are there? She is under their protection!' a small childlike voice piped up.

'She is in *our* territory, she is *ours*!' Darius growled in reply, his eyes daring anyone to contradict him.

'Why do we need a diversion?' another stronger voice asked, 'We can handle the elite male, and then just get her from her home.'

'Because...' Marina's smooth voice cut through the general babble of protests against and encouragements for this plan, 'We cannot enter her home without being invited in...you know that, and gaining her trust will take precious time.'

Darius clenched his fists at his sides, he was losing his patience rapidly and the others could sense it.

'So what is the diversion?' a male voice asked finally.

'Ah Tobias, always getting to the point,' Darius said, smiling at the burly man standing a few feet away, 'Not what but who.'

'But that is suicide!' a female almost wailed, fear rampant on her face.

She was standing a metre or so away from Darius. Before she could react, he had moved behind her to sink his teeth firmly into her neck. His patience had finally evaporated. Biting down hard he wrenched most of her throat away, almost separating her head from her body cleanly. There was a horrific cracking and splintering sound as though a structure of concrete and hard wood had been cut in half, as he pulled away, leaving her in a heap on the floor.

'Any more questions?' he asked the rest, his eyes glinting with menace.

No one made a sound.

'Good,' he approved, walking back to the middle of the room. He didn't have anything against the girl whose existence he had just ended, but he couldn't vouch for his temper. Now that it had run its course he felt more in control. *A pity*, he thought, *the girl would have been an asset in the coming days*. 'Any one of us can come to our end, is it not better to do so while trying to get the girl's blood? Besides,' he licked his lips, 'we can easily keep the elite male busy.'

The others nodded slowly, but none of them truly believed him for a second. Darius was ruthless, and he constantly flaunted the vampire laws, but the rest of them were in awe of the Elites. They had powers the rest of them didn't. But anything was better than meeting an end at Darius' hands.

He was pacing now, looking closely at each face. 'Luke... and Anna,' he said smoothly.

The two of them walked forward. Luke was built like a tank, while Anna was very petite and looked extremely fragile next to Luke's massive frame.

'You will be the diversion, make your preparations.'

They nodded and almost flew out of the room, their feet seeming to float above the floor, leaving Darius to look coldly at the others, gauging their expressions, which ranged from shock to relief.

Marina rose from her seat and moved to his side, reaching out to slip her arm through his. 'I can understand Luke, but Anna?' she queried gently, wary of rousing his anger.

Darius smiled down at her, his white teeth flashing, 'You underestimate her, she is very fast. Besides,' he leaned forward to kiss her lingeringly on the lips, 'the only other exceptional vampire I could think of was you.'

'Yes, but against the Elites ...! ' she tried to continue, ignoring the thinly veiled threat.

'All we need is a few minutes!' Darius growled suddenly, effectively ending the conversation. He turned to face the others, his eyes glittering again in the half-light. 'Time to hunt!

Chapter 22

Nicholas braked gently at the traffic lights and watched in exasperation as Eva's blue sedan drove through.

Blast, he thought, *why hadn't he accelerated?* He waited impatiently for the lights to change. It was evening and he was escorting Eva home. It had been weeks since the attack but he wasn't about to relax. He knew how tempting she was to his kind, and he knew to what lengths they would go to get what they wanted. He thought back to last night when the family had had a meeting.

'Darius' coven is growing stronger by the day,' Ashe had remarked as he sat down.

'Are you sensing them Ashe?' Seton asked.

'Yes,' the blonde head nodded an affirmative, 'Especially when I go towards their lair.'

'What were you doing in that part of town?' Eleanor asked, worry showing in her eyes.

'Oh, we were racing,' Ashe shrugged nonchalantly, drawing a disapproving look from Eleanor and a roll of the eyes from Leonara.

'Yeah and you lost,' Eden piped up shoving his brother.

'Yeah well...!'

'Enough!' Seton put an end to their bickering, 'Let's not get into such petty things, Darius is our problem at the moment.'

Alena shook her head, 'Where is he getting his recruits?'

'Who knows?'

'Is he making them?' Leonara wondered aloud. The rest of the family stilled, their expressions worried.

'I don't think so,' Ashe volunteered finally, his brow creased in thought, 'their movements aren't frantic and they don't smell part human like *neonates*. These are seasoned ones.'

'I don't know if that's better or worse!' Kane grumbled with a sigh.

'Well at least they haven't attacked Eva again,' Eleanor said comfortingly.

'Yet,' Nicholas added, his voice sour, 'You can bet they are waiting for a chance.'

'Maybe they are too scared of us,' Alena said hopefully.

Nicholas shook his head, 'No, Darius doesn't care about the laws, he is planning something.'

'Bring it on!' Eden said firmly.

'Yeah we can handle it,' Ashe added, smiling with anticipation.

'Morons!' Leonara hissed at them. 'Don't you see? There are more of them!'

'We can take them,' Eden said, smiling at her charmingly.

'I would love to see you try baby brother,' she replied acidly, smiling sweetly back at him.

'Oh...oh...sounds like a challenge bro,' Ashe quipped slapping his brother on the back.

Leonara shrugged, 'You couldn't take me on, let alone Darius' lot.'

'Let's take this outside,' Eden invited, starting to stand up.

'Later, we are still discussing Darius,' Nicholas broke in, pushing his brother back into the chair.

'Nick I think you should take at least one of us with you when you look after Eva,' Seton said calmly, looking at his younger brother worriedly.

'That may draw too much attention,' Nicholas argued.

'And what if you are attacked?' Seton asked his eyes piercing Nicholas'.

'I can handle it,' he asserted firmly.

'Nick, Seton's right I wish you would take Ashe with you,' Eleanor said pleadingly.

Nicholas walked towards her and bent down to kiss her cheek. 'I'll be fine. You worry too much!'

She smiled up at him and sighed, 'And you never listen!'

'Just like these two,' Leonara said, moving fluidly towards the door as she led Ashe and Eden outside.

The rest of the family followed in resignation, they wouldn't have any peace until Eden and Leonara had had their competition. The garden consisted of beautifully manicured lawns with old oaks standing tall against the sky. The flowerbeds were weed-free thanks to Eleanor's loving care. Eden crouched down, bracing himself, planting his feet firmly in the grass. Leonara yawned and stretched luxuriously before moving to stand a few feet away facing him, her eyes lighting with amusement as they watched him. When Eden didn't move she lifted her hand, palm upwards and gestured him to come forward, tauntingly.

With a growl he launched himself forward, speeding towards her so that it seemed he was flying. Leonara stood stock still until it seemed he would crash into her, and then she quickly sidestepped him, the wind caused by his passage causing her hair to fly around her face. He turned almost immediately, another growl emanating from his throat as he leapt into the air, arms outstretched to grab her. But she was too quick as she ducked and turned sideways at the same time, leaving him to flail at the air as he landed several feet away.

'Tired yet brother?' she asked glancing nonchalantly at her nails.

'I'm just getting started sis,' he replied with a snarl.

'Ten on Leonara,' Nicholas said to Ashe.

'I'll take that bet,' Ashe agreed.

'I'm in,' Alena said with a smile, 'ten on Eden.'

'I'll come in on that,' Kane replied, throwing an arm around Alena.

'I can't believe you're betting against your family,' Eleanor said, shaking her head with mock horror.

'Put me down for Leonara,' Seton added, smiling at his wife's disapproving face.

Eden was circling Leonara slowly now, his eyes determined not to miss any of her moves. He launched himself at her again, but she smiled as soon as he moved causing him to shake his head, to clear the indecision fogging his mind. Before he knew it, he had sped past her and his head felt fuzzy as though he had forgotten something important.

He glanced over his shoulder and growled. 'Not fair!'

Suddenly he disappeared and reappeared just behind her. 'You're not the only one with talents sis,' he almost whispered.

She smiled in reply and then leapt straight into the air, twisting herself as she fell to the ground neatly avoiding Eden's outstretched arms. Landing on all fours she crouched low to the ground waiting. As he came forward, she lashed out with her feet, lifting them to catch at his, but he had already disappeared. She vaulted upright and blocked the punch headed her way.

Eden kept attacking from all directions, disappearing and reappearing at different positions all around her, but she avoided or blocked all his blows, until he increased his speed to such an extent that neither adversary was visible to the others. Suddenly they both stopped; Eden had a hold of Leonara's hands and he was smiling at her.

'Give up?'

'Never!' she hissed and twisted in his grip, almost doubling over backwards before tangling her legs with his, causing them both to sprawl on the ground. Having freed herself she leapt onto him, locking his arms swiftly with her own and holding him down as she stared intently into his face. Before long he had stopped struggling and a blank expression fell over his features.

'Wha...? Where are we?' he asked in a dazed voice a few seconds later.

Leonara smiled and flung herself away from him before standing up and flicking away the grass on her clothes. 'Checkmate.'

'Pay up!' Nicholas laughed at Ashe, slapping Leonara on the back as she came towards them.

'Aww, you cost me ten big ones Leo!' Ashe complained.

'Then next time bet on me not against me,' she advised him with a wink.

Eden was still shaking his head, slightly confused and still sitting on the ground.

'Maybe I should go tell him what happened,' Alena offered.

Ashe shook his head. 'Nah, let him be,' he looked at Leonara speculatively. 'How long does this last Leo?'

She shrugged, 'A few minutes I think.'

'Great!' Ashe started running at full speed towards the huge garage at the side of the house.

'Where are you going?' Eleanor asked suspiciously.

'To race, hey tell Eden we are racing when he comes around will you? I'm getting a head start!' he shouted back, chuckling as he revved his bright yellow Kawasaki Ninja motorbike and roared down the drive.

It had taken Eden several minutes to recover from Leonara's effect. Scowling when he heard where Ashe had gone, he had got onto his bright red Fireblade, and roared through the gates, disappearing from sight as he used his teleporting skills to catch up to his brother. Two defeats in one day would be unbearable.

Chapter 23

Nicholas smiled as the lights changed to green and he accelerated past them, eager to catch up to Eva. His thoughts returned to the discussion he had had with the family before the fight had broken out. Seton was right in a way maybe he should have one of the others with him. But he hadn't wanted Seton to know that he didn't fully trust the others around Eva.

Taking Leonara for dinner to the same restaurant as Eva had been difficult for him, but he had been pretty confident he could subdue her if the need arose; he wasn't so sure about his brothers, and now having watched Leonara fighting Eden he was beginning to think that he might have been overconfident about his abilities. He shuddered as the thought crossed his mind.

His foot pressed the accelerator, hitting a speed well in excess of the legal limit. Just as he was about to turn a corner, he felt a sharp jolt. Before he knew it, his car door was ripped off the hinges with a sickening squeal of protesting metal, and a huge hand caught hold of his shirt collar, dragging him onto the road. His body slammed into the edge of the open door, ripping apart the doorframe leaving the car to crash into a wall nearby at full speed.

Instinct kicked in and Nicholas hit back at his adversary. In the darkness he could just make out the huge shape of a man. There was no doubt in his mind what he was up against, and he unleashed his rage from the severe restrictions he usually placed on it. He pulled away savagely leaving the man with most of his shirt still clutched in his hairy fist.

With his torso now bare, he whirled around and leapt at the man. Catching hold of his massive shoulders he held on grimly as his victim thrashed from side to side. *Kind of like catching a whale,* Nicholas thought smiling slightly.

Almost effortlessly it seemed he was plucked from the man's back and thrown several feet away. He landed against a stone wall, sending cracks all the way through it. Luke smiled cruelly and flexed his arms; *this was going to be too easy.*

Nicholas got to his feet snarling in challenge as his eyes took in Luke's hulking body. Strength clearly wasn't going to help, but speed might. He crouched low, and then raced towards his target dodging swiftly, trying to confuse Luke. He was circling him now, looking for an opening. He finally saw it as Luke turned to his right, Nicholas doubled back swiftly on his left and leapt, his teeth bared. He knew if he missed this opportunity he would have a hard time disengaging, possibly risking death. As the thought flitted through his mind he felt his teeth sink into the man's neck, burying deep in his flesh.

Luke howled in agony and tried to claw at Nicholas' chest and face, but Nicholas held on with all his strength, bracing himself against his adversary so that the muscles in his arms stood out in sharp relief. He pulled sharply backwards, pulling part of the neck out with a sound similar to the squeal of metal as it is pulled apart. Before Luke could recover, Nicholas was crunching down again, biting deep and tearing at his flesh. Before long his adversary was reduced to dust on the ground with Nicholas crouching nearby, recovering from the fight, and trying to ignore the taste of ash in his mouth.

As he was about to rise to his feet, a small dark shape launched itself on him. For a second he thought it was a small animal, but the body his hands grappled with had a human form. He threw it off viciously and his eyes widened slightly as he took in the petite female hissing and spitting at him like a cat. He clamped down on his innate loathing of fighting with a female. This was no time for chivalry.

There was no doubt in his mind that this particular woman would kill him if she could, but why? His eyes narrowed momentarily as she started circling him. Although she was still hissing like a feral cat, he thought he could detect a trace of fear in her dark eyes, as they watched his movements. Could she be an unwilling adversary? And if so, why was she attacking him? Suddenly Eva's face flashed into his mind and his eyes widened as understanding dawned. *This was an ambush!*

He glanced at his wrecked car and almost groaned it wasn't going to be going anywhere for a long time. In fact it barely resembled the sleek machine he was used to. Just as he was contemplating the alternatives the female launched herself at him again. He ducked and rolled below her, biting her hand as it passed him. *A small reminder* he thought grimly, as he heard her yelp of pain, *for attacking an Elite*. Rising to his feet smoothly, he suddenly leapt several onto a nearby wall. His face took on a blank expression and a second later he had disappeared. Anna watched in astonishment as a large black bat flew high into the air, got its bearings and flew swiftly towards the girl's house.

Chapter 24

Eva glanced in her rear view mirror and sighed in relief as the black Mercedes stopped at the traffic lights. She was sure it had been following her for a few days and getting closer and closer each day. It un-nerved her to see the sleek machine so often mainly because it reminded her of Nicholas. She hadn't heard from or seen him for several weeks and she kept telling herself she was glad. After all, he was way out of her league. She sighed again if only Chris would consider her below his league then she wouldn't have to keep making excuses not to see him. But he just didn't seem to understand her.

She grimaced and turned a corner. As she did so she thought she saw someone waiting in the bushes, but in the gathering darkness she couldn't be sure. Shrugging she glanced again in the rear view mirror and relaxed. The black car was nowhere to be seen. She kept driving, trying to forget Nicholas' face as it taunted her enticingly from the recesses of her mind. Parking her car at the curb, she stepped out and walked to her front door. She was about to insert the key to unlock it, when a low voice resembling a growl spoke close to her ear.

'Hello again sweetheart!'

Whirling round quickly she nearly lost her balance in her attempt to move away from the large figure standing next to her. He laughed at her antics and leaned against the doorjamb, folding his arms.

'So jumpy,' he observed, his voice still amused.

Eva swallowed nervously, and tried to think what items she had in her handbag that she could use as a weapon. Her fingers tightened convulsively... of course the keys! She manipulated them in her hand, still watching the man warily. Having gripped one of them securely she lifted her chin slightly to meet his dark impenetrable gaze. What she saw there made her heart quail with fear but she gritted her teeth resolutely.

'What do you want?' she asked, glad her voice didn't shake, too much.

'Now is that any way to talk to a friend?' another rough male voice asked from behind her.

She jumped and turned slightly, starting to move backwards, away from the door and glanced at her blue Chevy parked a few metres away.

'Don't bother honey.' A female was standing at the bottom of the short flight of stairs looking intently at her nails. When she looked at Eva fleetingly her dark eyes were just as menacing as the men's.

'Wh ...what do you people want?' she asked again, her voice now shaking noticeably.

'You,' one of the men replied simply as he moved forward.

She gripped the keys harder and tried to breathe slowly. *Calm down*, she told herself, *just wait, wait ...* she watched as the man continued to move closer. *Now!* Without warning she whirled around and ran down the steps, straight towards the woman, who was still looking at her nails. Eva was almost on top of her as she lifted her hand, the key aimed for the woman's face. Her fist struck the pale skin followed by the rest of her body.

The key snapped against the woman's cheek, causing the broken piece to pierce Eva's palm, while the impact of the collision had her falling back onto the stone steps. Eva shook her head slightly, not able to believe what had happened. She looked up expecting the woman to be sprawled on the pavement at the very least, but she was exactly where she had been before, not a scratch on her beautiful face.

'Nice try,' she drawled, but her voice had changed subtly. She was no longer portraying the calm façade.

Her companions were laughing as they watched Eva try to raise herself from the ground.

'She's a fighter,' she heard one of them say admiringly.

'Yup, they are always more fun,' the other agreed, licking his lips with anticipation.

Eva finally managed to rise from the ground, her legs shaking with terror.

'No more tricks, honey,' the woman said with forced sweetness as she caught Eva's arm in a vicelike grip, 'Time to go.'

'Aww, we were just about to have some fun Marina!' one of the men said sulkily.

Marina's sudden snarl silenced him. Eva's eyes opened wide as she glimpsed her glistening teeth. She blinked and looked back at Marina's mouth, but it was firmly shut. She could have sworn she had seen razor sharp canines. She shook her head to clear it; she must be in shock…again.

'Have you forgotten…we grab the girl and leave!' she was saying to the men.

Her two heavyset companions glowered, but neither offered any further objections.

'Come my dear,' Marina crooned, as she forcibly pulled Eva along the street, the other two following close behind.

Chapter 25

They walked for a few hundred yards, Eva trying every so often to free herself but Marina barely noticed her feeble attempts as she almost floated gracefully along the side-walk.

Eva grimaced as the pressure on her arm increased. She glanced at Marina's beautiful, cold face and shivered involuntarily. She didn't know where they were going or why she was being dragged along. She hadn't even met these people before. Was this to do with her work? Maybe they were part of the cults she had researched earlier on.

Suddenly there was a loud crash on a side street. Marina glanced at her companions and motioned them towards the noise. Both men almost flew into the street to find the cause, leaving the two girls to continue along the street alone. Eva blinked a few times and refocused on a spot further along the street, *was that an animal?* A pale shape flew past another street lamp and she gasped. Marina turned her head to look at her and then away, not slowing down.

Eva suddenly felt another hand on her arm and she shivered again, believing it to be one of the men. Before she could move, Marina's hand had been removed and the woman had been thrown against one of the brick buildings at the far side of the street. A snarl ripped dangerously through the air and Marina was once again standing in front of Eva glaring at the tall man next to her.

'Stay away from her,' Nicholas growled, his eyes deadly.

Marina smiled mirthlessly, 'And you are?'

Nicholas' eyebrows rose a fraction, and his hand tightened its hold on Eva. 'Your worst nightmare.'

'Ah, the dramatic nature of the Elites,' Marina mocked, curtseying low to the ground.

'Not the only nature you are familiar with, I hope, commoner!' he replied smoothly.

Marina's smile slipped and her eyes grew cold. 'She is ours.'

'She is under my protection. You should read the treaty more often.'

Marina almost growled with frustration. Footsteps behind them heralded the presence of the others. Eva sucked in some air but her throat felt as though it was lined with sandpaper. She could barely breathe as she watched Marina's dark eyes duel with Nicholas' steady silver ones. Glancing at him now she shrank back with fear. He looked furious and his eyes glittered like a predator's, cold and deadly.

'Watch your manners commoner,' he said haughtily, 'Or else I will have to teach you and your friends a few much needed lessons.'

Eva didn't know how she knew but she was certain he was truly worried about this situation, and he was trying desperately to bluff his way out of it. Apparently it was working because Marina's eyes flickered away uncertainly from his steady gaze.

One of the others growled and Nicholas' head twitched slightly in his direction but he continued to watch Marina, knowing it was her orders the men would follow.

'We are leaving.' He caught hold of Eva's hand securely and almost dragged her past Marina, his long strides carrying him quickly over the ground so that Eva had to jog to keep up.

He maintained his speed for three blocks and then turned a corner sharply and stopped. Eva almost collapsed against the wall with relief and opened her mouth to speak, when he lifted a finger to his lips and motioned in the direction they had just come. She nodded in understanding and listened with him. It was then that she noticed that he wasn't wearing a shirt. His bare chest gleamed in the half-light thrown by a nearby streetlamp, emphasising the sculptured muscles just below his skin. She gulped and reluctantly looked away.

'Good, they aren't following.' He looked down at her and smiled, reverting to the Nicholas she had come to know. 'Time to get you to a safe place.'

Before she knew what he intended to do, he had lifted her in his arms effortlessly and started running down the street. She could feel the wind hitting her face. A few seconds later the wind speed increased considerably and she buried her face closer to his chest. *It must be very windy tonight,* she thought. She focussed on the sound of Nicholas' feet hitting the sidewalk and then frowned. There was no sound whatsoever except for the sound of the wind in her ears.

She opened her eyes a fraction and then wider, blinking a few times and then stared in disbelief at the fast moving surroundings around them. The buildings were practically flying past them, and the streetlamps were just flashes of light in the darkness. She tried to say something but the force of the wind stole what little breath she had left, leaving her gasping.

Nicholas must have heard her because he lifted her higher so that her face was pressed securely against him, his arms protecting her from the whiplash of the wind. She breathed in deeply and sighed silently as the warm spicy fragrance tingled her nose. *That's one hell of an aftershave,* she thought hazily. *Sell that in a bottle and most of the men in the world would be irresistible!*

Before she could think about it anymore, the wind died down and their speed decreased. Buildings stayed steady and she could make out the shape of streetlamps clearly again. She opened her eyes wider and lifted her head from its muscular support, looking around her in surprise. They were standing outside one of the largest hotels in the city centre. She glanced up at Nicholas' face confused.

He was smiling down at her. 'You will be staying here tonight.'

'What?' she asked shocked.

He bent to release her, and then straightened again. 'You can't go back home,' he replied reasonably.

'But...'

'There's no point in arguing, Eva,' he said before she could get the words out. Once he was sure she wasn't going to continue, he took her arm and steered her towards the brightly lit entrance.

'But you don't even have a shirt!' she whispered urgently as they walked across the huge lobby.

He smiled down at her as they reached the massive reception desk, ignoring the whispers as the patrons stared at them.

'Mr. Rayne?' the receptionist looked up, successfully masking her surprise, 'Your usual room?'

'Yes and a white shirt please,' Nicholas said in a low voice.

'Of course.'

One of the porters guided them to the elevator. Almost immediately the doors opened and they stepped in. The elevator ride ended on the twenty-second floor and they stepped out onto a deep red-carpeted hall with an ornate door facing them. An embellished letter R graced the front of the door in glittering gold. The porter inserted a card into a small slot in the door and waited for a small light to turn green, before swinging it open and standing aside to let his guests enter. Eva stepped into the room first at Nicholas' urging and gasped.

The entrance hall was done in white and gold. The floor made of white marble glistened with gold specks, while the wallpaper had a delicate swirling gold design running through it. As she moved further into the room, the hall opened onto a massive lounge, complete with white leather couches, framed paintings from artists even she had heard of, and a huge fifty-two inch plasma screen television taking up most of one wall.

At the far end the entire wall was made of glass and looked out onto the city lights and beyond them to the dark waters of Lake Erie. She spun around when the front door clicked shut. Nicholas stood just inside it, watching her carefully. She swallowed and tried to smile as her eyes took in his calm expression and then moved of their own volition to his still bare chest.

'This is amazing!' she finally blurted out.

He didn't respond, instead he moved slowly forward. He was still watching her as he sat down on the leather couch and gestured for her to do the same. 'We need to talk.'

She hesitated and then nearly fell into the nearest seat, which was so large she felt completely enveloped by its softness. Her eyes met his steady pale ones for a second. When he didn't say anything she drew in a deep breath to steady her voice.

'What a weird night!'

He nodded slowly. 'Yes it is. No doubt you have many questions.'

She looked at his face; he appeared almost resigned. 'Well, I do have a few.'

'Shoot,' he invited her as he leaned his head back against the cushions and closed his eyes.

Relieved that he was no longer watching her with that all-seeing gaze, enough of Eva's courage returned for her to say, 'Umm...who were those people?'

He smiled slightly. 'Not very nice people.'

She sighed in frustration; he wasn't going to answer as fully as she wanted him to. 'I gathered that much, I meant...' she hesitated as he opened his eyes, watching her as she struggled, 'You seemed to know them,' she finished lamely.

He closed his eyes again and didn't answer. Just when she thought he had fallen asleep his low voice cut through the silence. 'Yes, in a manner of speaking, I know of them.'

Eva frowned, *what did that mean?* She stood up abruptly. 'Well, if you're not going to tell me anything!'

She heard him sigh softly. 'I am trying Eva, but this is difficult to explain let alone understand!'

She shook her head and let her gaze wander aimlessly until it settled on a nearby painting, prompting her to say involuntarily, 'This place is just...beautiful.'

He nodded in agreement, his eyes still closed. 'Are these original?' she asked, her tone betraying her fascination.

When there was no answer, she turned slightly to see Nicholas standing just behind her looking at the painting. She hadn't heard him move and it took her by surprise.

'Yes,' he quirked an eyebrow at her, 'You know about art?'

She shook her head. 'Not exactly, but I have seen these in books.'

He smiled, 'I don't either, but my sisters insist on buying and displaying some of the masters.' He waved at another painting, 'I believe that's one of the lesser known Van Goghs and that is a Puccini, or so they tell me,' he shrugged, pointing across the room.

'That's impressive!' she gulped, her eyes wide.

He shrugged again and walked to the front door just as the bell rang. The porter stood outside with a white shirt. He thanked the man and shrugged into the shirt, buttoning it up swiftly as he walked past Eva to stand staring out of the window.

Eva remained near the painting, not sure what to say or do, but she couldn't stop herself from asking timidly, 'How did you manage to lose your shirt?'

He laughed in surprise. She never said what she expected her to. 'I ran into a bit of trouble before I found you.'

'Oh...'

'Eva...' he pushed his hand through his hair, he couldn't keep evading the questions he knew where coming. *Just take the bull by the horns and say...* 'I need to tell you something.'

She looked at him enquiringly.

He sighed and turned away from her. 'I'm not what you think I am.'

She looked at his stiff back in surprise, but remained silent.

'I didn't want to tell you, but…after tonight…' his shoulders sagged slightly.

She wanted to go to him and tell him everything was going to be okay but she couldn't, not truthfully.

'Wha…what do you mean?'

'I'm not like you.'

'I can see that!' she looked around the room, 'I could never afford this place!'

He shook his head impatiently and turned around to face her. 'That's not what I meant.' He met her eyes squarely. 'I'm not…a human.'

'What?! What are you talking about? Of course you are!' she replied with a laugh, her brain not registering his words.

He sighed again this was going to be almost impossible. And when she did understand she would run away from him screaming. And then what? How was he going to protect her then? But looking at her confused face he knew he would have to tell her.

'The people who attacked you, they are like me.'

She still looked confused. 'Like you? How is that possible?'

He moved towards her very slowly so as not to frighten her. 'I'm a vampire.'

There he had said it, he glanced at her expecting her to be horrified, but she looked calm now, maybe too calm.

'You mean you are *like* a vampire,' she said slowly, trying to wrap her mind around this new development. So he had a hobby.

'No, I am a vampire.'

'So you belong to a cult?'

Now it was his turn to look confused and then understanding dawned. Smiling he shook his head. 'No, I don't Eva. I'm not a human wannabe vampire. I am a vampire.'

She shook her head slowly. 'That's not possible.'

'I wish!' his smile disappeared and he stared past her at the painting.

'So those people are also…?' she swallowed, starting to realise that he wasn;t joking. He nodded absently and then shifted his gaze to her.

'And your family?'

'Yes.' He waited patiently for her to register his full meaning and start running.

She nodded slowly and sat down on one of the couches almost wearily. She looked thoughtful as he sat opposite her, still studying her expression, looking increasingly worried at her lack of fear. She finally focussed on him after what felt like hours.

'The bodies in the lab? That was one of you?'

'It was the vamps who attacked you tonight,' he explained softly. 'How did you…?'

'Figure it out?' she smiled, 'The internet of course! Those holes only resembled one type of weapon, canine teeth.' She paused remembering the glimpse she had caught of Marina's mouth and said slowly, 'very *large* canines.'

He nodded. 'And you thought it was due to a cult?'

She nodded in reply, 'There are so many out there!'

Suddenly his eyes fell on the telephone by his side and he lifted the receiver. 'Excuse me while I make this call,' he said as he started dialling rapidly, his fingers flying over the keys.

'It's me,' he said by way of a greeting when the call was answered. 'I'm at the Regency hotel with Eva.'

He listened for a second before saying, 'We were attacked.' He paused again before smiling into the receiver, 'She's fine, don't worry.'

Eva looked at him curiously, but he was still talking into the receiver.

'I'll need some help.'

A few more minutes of conversation later he replaced the receiver to look at Eva's puzzled face.

'I had to call the family,' he explained.

'Oh.' She didn't know whether to be relieved or worried.

'They'll be coming over shortly to protect you,' he continued, watching her face for her reaction.

'They know about me?'

'Of course!' he looked quizzical, 'we don't keep secrets from each other. Well,' he smiled, thinking back, 'Not for long anyway.'

'Are they okay with this?' she asked hesitantly.

He looked away and laughed softly. 'They don't have a choice now.'

She settled back on the couch and crossed her arms. 'When can I go to my apartment?'

That caused his eyes to narrow and the laughter died swiftly on his lips. 'Never if I can help it!'

'Why?' she looked stubborn and he sighed inwardly. *Why couldn't women just blindly accept what they were told for their own good?*

'Because of what happened tonight, because those people are dangerous, and because they are vampires! Do you need any more reasons?' he took a deep breath and watched her eyes widen slightly, and immediately felt guilty for being so harsh.

'Eva,' he controlled his voice into a softer tone, 'those people won't stop until...until...' he stopped, wondering if he should continue and risk scaring her even more.

'Until?'

'Until they kill you,' he almost whispered the words, hoping she wouldn't hear them. Of course that possibility didn't exist with this human.

'But why? I mean there are other humans out there right?'

He shook his head slowly. 'They still want you. Remember the night you were attacked outside the lab?'

'That was them?' she grimaced at her stupidity, of course, she knew she had seen those men before!

'Yes.'

'Well, I must have the worst luck in the world huh?' she quipped, but he was shaking his head again.

'It's more complicated than that,' he drew in a small breath and tried to ignore the smell that came with it. 'You are special, your blood draws us like bees to honey.'

Her eyes widened a fraction, and she whispered, 'Why?'

'It's the chemical mix in the blood, determined by your genes.' He shrugged, 'In short you are irresistible to my kind.'

Chapter 26

Eva couldn't believe what she was hearing but there was only one thought that was uppermost in her mind. *She was irresistible? Did that mean...?* She just had to ask. 'To you too?'

'Yes.' He closed his eyes as his mouth watered uncontrollably.

'So why did you save me?' She was trying desperately not to think about being irresistible to the gorgeous man sitting opposite her, even if he was a vampire.

His eyes opened at her question, glinting in the light like polished platinum. 'I can control myself. I'm not an animal like those filthy...' he stopped himself and cleared his throat painfully. 'My family has sworn to protect you.'

'Protect me? But why?'

He smiled slowly his eyes softening and she watched mesmerised. 'It's a long story, perhaps too long to finish tonight.'

'I want to know!' she insisted.

'You are part of the hunted bloodline. My family made a promise a very long time ago to protect any descendants from vampire attacks.'

'So if it wasn't for this promise, you would...' she couldn't say it aloud, but her face told him exactly what she was thinking.

He looked away from her. 'Possibly, but I would try very hard not to.'

She believed him without quite knowing why.

'But the other covens wouldn't.'

She frowned, puzzled again. 'Coven?' She had read that word before during her research on the Internet but didn't know what it meant.

'A group of vamps,' he clarified.

'Like your family?'

He nodded. 'In a manner of speaking, but the ties holding us together are stronger than what you would normally find.'

She looked thoughtfully out of the large window for a few minutes while Nicholas continued to study her face. When she looked back at him she was still puzzled and he could almost see the questions rushing through her active mind. He smiled to himself; she really was very unusual for a human, blood type aside. No screaming and no running...yet. He clenched his fists and then relaxed his hands, waiting for her to speak.

'If I am so irresistible,' she swallowed nervously, trying to gather enough courage to go on.

'Yes...?' he raised his eyebrows slightly, instinctively knowing what she was about to say next.

Eva licked her lips and forced the words out through her dry mouth. 'How can you stand to be so close to me?'

'I'm not breathing,' he replied matter-of-factly.

'Not breathing...?' her eyes dropped to his still chest automatically. 'How...?'

'I don't need to breathe Eva, I'm not technically alive you know.' His tone was bitter.

'But you were once?'

He nodded. 'A very long time ago.'

'When did you...I mean...' she hesitated, not sure how to say what she wanted to.

A shadow crossed his face as he answered softly, '1820.'

Her eyes widened in shock, but she managed a small shaky smile, 'You look very good for a...200 year old!'

'I try,' he replied, his eyes lighting with humour.

She stared at his face, the shadow had gone and he was back to the person she knew. 'It must be difficult not to...you know...'

'Yes, but the thought of hunting an innocent person...of hurting you...' he shook his head vehemently, 'Is unbearable.'

She was about to speak when the doorbell rang. Nicholas stood up fluidly and looked down at her. 'Don't worry, that must be my family. You're not scared?'

She shook her head, hoping her face didn't betray how scared she really was.

He stood still for a long second looking at her and then leaned forward to touch her cheek gently. 'Everything will be okay, trust me.'

He moved away leaving her frozen. She touched her cheek and shuddered as memories flooded through her mind. She closed her eyes and immediately saw the dark street, her mother smiling at her and then being pulled away, her terror, the pale shadow passing her so swiftly and then the tall stranger lifting her up and then finally the gentle touch on her cheek.

She gasped as Nicholas' face jumped into startling focus, his silver eyes with green flecks looking at her kindly in the half light of a streetlamp, and then the touch on her cheek before he disappeared, leaving her with the sudden courage she had needed as she had tended to her hysterical mother. Although she had known it in her bones it still took her by surprise to realise after so many years that her dreams had happened in reality, and now it seemed that she owed Nicholas her life at least three times, not to mention her mother's.

Her eyes flew open as she heard the door close and words being exchanged at high speed between what she perceived to be a very beautiful group of people standing just inside the hallway. She tried to understand what was being said and failed. *There was no way they were actually talking that fast right?* She closed her eyes for a second and opened them and nearly screamed. One of the women was sitting next to her, watching her silently. Nicholas stood near her now talking to a tall distinguished looking man quietly. Her eyes moved to settle on another couple by the door who were also silent.

Seeing her startled face Nicholas moved closer and smiled gently. 'This is Leonara, I believe you saw her at the restaurant a few weeks ago?' He nodded towards the gorgeous woman next to her.

Eva swallowed the lump in her throat and nodded.

'Nice to meet you,' Leonara smiled back, her pearly white teeth flashing, but she made no move to touch her, for which Eva was grateful.

'And this is my elder brother Seton,' Nicholas continued, indicating the man next to him.

'A pleasure,' Seton said with a slight bow. He followed her eyes as they rested on the couple by the door. 'That's Alena and Kane,' he explained.

Alena turned her head and waved at her, while Kane smiled and nodded.

'They are all here to keep you safe,' Nicholas told her gently.

She looked at him with a frown. 'But...tomorrow I have to work.'

He nodded. 'You will.'

'But my clothes, my things...' her voice trailed off.

'I wouldn't worry,' Leonara smiled kindly at her.

'Of course not!'

Eva gasped as Alena flashed to Nicholas' side a holdall in her hand. 'Sorry!' she smiled at Eva before glancing at Nicholas apologetically, 'I'll have to move slower.' She turned to Eva again, 'Here, I thought you'd need this.'

Taking the large bag, Eva slid open the zipper and glanced at the contents curiously. There was a pair of jeans, shirts, trousers and shoes. An inside pocket held all the make up she might need plus any other essentials.

She looked up at Alena with wide eyes. 'How did you know my size?'

'Oh, that was easy,' Alena shrugged eloquently, 'I hope you like it.'

'They are lovely! Thank you.'

Alena's smile widened, nearly dazzling Eva before she danced happily towards Kane. 'I'm glad someone appreciates my talents!'

Kane smiled and gathered her close, murmuring in her ear.

'Talents?' Eva asked looking at Nicholas.

He laughed softly and shook his head. 'Alena loves fashion. I'd bet those are the trendiest clothes she has managed to find, although I did warn her that you were a bit conservative.' He grinned as Eva started to shake her head. 'Don't say a word, she already despairs with the rest of us. But she already likes you a great deal because you accepted that bag without argument.'

'How long do I have to stay here?'

'As long as it takes for us to make sure you are safe,' Leonara said, before Nicholas could reply. 'Besides...' she looked knowingly at her brother, 'You are special.'

Eva smiled politely. 'Yes, Nicholas mentioned the bloodline.'

'That too,' Leonara agreed cryptically, causing Eva to raise her eyebrows slightly, but she didn't explain.

Seton sat down opposite her and smiled. 'Leo, Alena and Kane will stay with you, while the rest of us solve this problem. Tomorrow Leo will drive you to work and escort you back.'

'Consider us your personal bodyguards,' Leonara piped up helpfully.

Eva looked stunned. 'But I can't expect you to always be with me!'

'Why not?' Leonara asked.

'Well...I bet you have other important things to do besides babysitting me all day!'

'Not really, and I can do whatever I need to while you work.'

'But what about...?' she glanced towards the door.

'Alena and Kane?' Nicholas shook his head. 'They both agreed to do this.'

'That's right,' Kane drawled. He had moved to stand beside Nicholas so quickly that Eva hadn't noticed him.

'So it's settled,' Nicholas said, his tone final.

Seton stood gracefully and motioned to the others to follow him. As they walked away, Eva looked up at Nicholas imploringly.

'Why are you doing this for me?'

'I told you...,' he looked away. 'The promise...'

'Yes, but all this is too much. You don't even know me.'

'Do I not?' he was looking strangely at her now.

'It was you wasn't it? The one that saved my mother all those years ago?'

He sighed in resignation, there was no point denying it now, 'Yes.'

Eva could feel her heart beating double time and she swallowed. Suddenly Nicholas was seated beside her and he took her hand gently in his cold one.

'Do you trust me?' She nodded slowly unable to speak, and watched fascinated as his face lit up with a smile. 'They will look after you.'

'When will I see you again?'

'Soon,' he promised and gently touched her cheek again as he looked into her violet eyes. She held his gaze for a full minute before she felt a presence next to her. She looked round to see Alena smiling down at them.

'Come along, I'll show you the bedroom. Leo is ordering dinner.'

Chapter 27

Eva woke up the next morning to find herself lying on a huge bed staring up at a white ceiling. She pushed herself up and looked around. The room was larger than her entire apartment. A mahogany dressing table stood against the far wall, dominated by a circular mirror. Near the picture window stood a small table with two couches arranged around it. The built-in wardrobes were concealed behind more mirrors making the room look twice as big. A thick cream carpet covered the floor with swirling golden thread running through it to match the wallpaper. She lay back and stretched, closing her eyes against her expensive surroundings.

Her mind was blank, exhausted, and then the events of yesterday rushed back in full force. Her eyes opened wide and she sat up again. She must have dreamt everything. Of course she had, there was no way any of it could possibly have been true! And yet…she looked around the unfamiliar room again…here she was. Okay so maybe three odd people had attacked her and Nicholas had miraculously helped her again. He must have been joking about the vampire bit, after all vampires were mythical creatures, figments of some over-worked person's mind. She frowned, the way his family had talked and moved had been unnatural, not to mention the way in which she had been brought here.

Imagination and tiredness clearly created a very potent fantasy she thought. Her mother had always said she had too much imagination even as a child. But the dreams she had been having for all those years…she laughed out loud, the human mind believed whatever it wanted to. She was still chuckling to herself when there was a soft knock on the door. The laughter dried up quickly in her throat and she stared at the door unseeingly for several seconds, wondering what figment of her overactive imagination would walk through it, before she remembered to say 'Come in,' in a choked voice,

The door opened a fraction and Leonara's immaculate face peered around it.

'Are you awake?' she whispered.

'Yes,' Eva replied in a whisper, wondering why she was whispering too. She cleared her throat as the door opened wider and Leonara walked in with a breakfast tray balanced expertly in her hand.

'You really didn't have to…' Eva started to shake her head, but Leonara walked to the table and deposited the tray before turning round with a smile.

'No problem, I hope you like what I've ordered.'

In a few minutes Eva realised with dismay that the entire breakfast menu was sitting in her room. She glanced at her companion and wondered what to say.

'What's wrong?'

'Nothing, it's just that…umm…' Eva chewed her lips indecisively and decided to tell her the truth. 'I don't think I can afford this.'

Leonara stared at her and then burst out laughing. Her deep-throated laughter was so loud that Alena popped her head into the room, a mischievous look on her pretty face. 'What's up with Leo?'

Eva shrugged helplessly and sat down on the bed. 'I have no idea. All I said was that I couldn't afford the room service and this menu,' she explained miserably.

Leonara was still giggling uncontrollably and gesturing at Alena who chuckled and walked into the room to sit next to Eva.

'What exactly did Nick tell you before we turned up?'

'That I couldn't go home and I was to stay here,' Eva said still looking downcast.

'I see,' Alena glanced at Leonara, but she was still trying to stop laughing. 'Did he happen to mention that we own this hotel?'

Eva's jaw dropped and her eyes widened in surprise.

'Men!' Alena exclaimed in disgust, taking in Eva's shocked expression.

Eva managed to shut her mouth and look around the huge bedroom. 'You guys own this place?'

'Yup!' Leonara confirmed as she leaned against the wall weakly, a large grin on her face.

'He did talk about the paintings in the lounge,' Eva tried to defend Nicholas, but a snort from Leonara made her turn towards her.

'Nick couldn't tell a Picasso from a Puccini!' she said sceptically.

'Well, neither can I,' Eva admitted sheepishly, but Leonara smiled kindly at her.

'I don't expect you to, but Nick has been around for a very long time, and he is always surrounded by art.'

Eva digested this slowly and then glanced at the two girls shyly. 'So, I didn't dream all that stuff? You guys really are…uh…'

'Yup, we're vamps alright,' Alena said.

'In the flesh,' Leonara grinned, 'So to speak!'

Eva swallowed, trying to think of something to say.

'Hey, don't worry we're the good guys!' Alena reassured her when she saw Eva's worried expression.

'Yeah, I mean you smell amazing, but there's no way any of us would even think about…' Leonara trailed off with an expressive look.

'Hell, it's been years since one of us did that!' Alena continued.

'Oh good,' Eva replied weakly, trying not to show how scared she really was.

The others exchanged glances and then Leonara shrugged and waved at the breakfast tray. 'Your breakfast is getting cold.'

'Oh yeah.' Eva stood up hastily any excuse to put a bit of distance between them and her sounded like a good idea. She walked to the table, picked up a large pancake and bit into it hungrily. Before she knew it she had devoured not only the pancakes but a bowl of cereal, a couple of toast and a cup of tea. Just as she was sipping at her second cup of tea she lifted her eyes to look at her friends. Well she supposed they were her friends now. They had been chatting amicably and ignoring Eva while she ate. But now that her stomach was full her mind flicked back to them and she was horrified that she hadn't offered them any of the food.

'I'm so sorry!' she blurted out.

Alena raised her eyebrows in surprise. 'Why?'

Eva looked despairingly at the empty dishes. 'I didn't offer you any food!'

Leonara started giggling again and Alena smiled. 'No need, we don't eat anyway, so don't beat yourself up!'

'You don't eat?'

Alena shook her head, making her shoulder-length hair bounce.

'Never?'

'Nope!'

'But can you?'

She looked closely at Eva and nodded. 'We can but we can't really taste it and it doesn't satisfy us or give us energy, so it's a bit pointless.'

'I see.' That sounded reasonable. She glanced at her watch and paled. 'Oh my god! I have to get to work!'

'No problem, get ready and I'll drive you,' Leonara promised as she walked towards the door with Alena.

Within minutes Eva had showered and changed into the new clothes Alena had brought yesterday. Looking at herself in the mirror she had to admit they fit perfectly and she looked…well…polished. The material looked expensive and she knew the cut was created by a designer's hand. She couldn't bear to think about how much they must have cost, and she knew Alena wouldn't tell her, even if she asked. She stepped out of the room and into the huge lounge. Both Alena and Leonara were waiting for her. She smiled at them and then her gaze shifted to the person standing near the window in surprise. She remembered seeing the tall, muscular man yesterday, *what was his name? Oh yeah...Kane.*

He smiled at her and moved forward slowly until he was standing a few feet away. 'Hi, I'm Kane. We met briefly yesterday, but I'm sure you were too tired to remember!'

'I was tired but I do remember you,' Eva replied cautiously.

'He's a bit hard to forget huh?' Alena asked cheekily. 'Don't worry, he's one of us!'

This caused Leonara to giggle and Kane to grin warmly at Alena.

'Come on we have to go,' Leonara said rising quickly from the couch.

The ride to the police lab could only be described as terrifying. Leonara seemed to have no concept of speed limits and appeared to dodge other vehicles with inches to spare. Eva tried to make conversation to distract herself from the wild ride she had unwittingly agreed to.

'So Kane is your brother?'

'Nope.' Leonara swerved across two lanes to avoid hitting a car. 'But we treat him like one.'

'I don't understand.' Eva gripped the door handle tightly.

'Alena and Kane are a couple, so are Seton and Eleanor.'

'Oh. Do you have other brothers and sisters?' Eva was trying desperately to stay on her side of the car as they swerved again.

'Yeah, you didn't meet the two most annoying ones. Ashe and Eden.'

'So do they have girlfriends too?'

'There's no way a girl would even think of going out with those two crazy boys!' Leonara laughed aloud at the very thought as she manoeuvred expertly around a few more cars.

Eva expected sirens to start wailing at any second, but they arrived without incident at the lab. She got out on shaky legs and nearly collapsed when she tried to walk.

'I'll pick you up at five. Stay inside till I arrive,' Leonara cautioned. Somehow she had jumped out of the car and was standing next to her without Eva realising it.

Eva swallowed and nodded.

'You okay?'

She looked up to see Leonara's worried face. 'I'm fine, just recovering from the drive.'

'Why?'

'It was a bit faster than I'm used to,' Eva admitted.

'Yeah, I suppose so. It's good to have certain talents,' Leonara chuckled and nodded at the lab entrance, 'You're on time though.'

Eva looked at her watch and her eyes widened. She was actually early. The drive, which would have taken her half an hour, had only taken ten minutes. She shook her head in disbelief, thanked Leonara and walked into the building, feeling Leonara's eyes on her back the entire way.

Chapter 28

Nicholas looked expectantly at Seton as he paced the length of the room. They were in the huge living room in the family home. Despite several white couches placed around the room it still looked vast. Eleanor was curled up on a nearby chair, watching her husband calmly as he turned and walked towards her.

'Are you sure it was Darius' coven that attacked you?' he asked finally, coming to a stop in front of Nicholas.

Nicholas shrugged, 'Who else would it be?'

Seton smiled at his naïve reply. 'How many vamps do you know who are currently in this area?' Another shrug of the broad shoulders answered his question. 'Even if you're right, if we confront him, he will deny it,' Seton mused.

'We can't just let this go!' Nicholas said looking at Eleanor for support.

'Seton's right, we cannot fight without absolute proof.'

'But attacking an elite…!'

'If we find your attackers and they admit to being from Darius' coven…' Seton paused looking at his brother expressively.

Nicholas' eyes glinted with fury, 'I killed one of them, and you know as well as I do that the rest won't be found. They have either disappeared or Darius has destroyed them.'

'Perhaps.' Seton nodded.

'Nick is right, we won't find them.' Eleanor stirred in her chair. Her wide eyes focussed on Nicholas. 'We have to set a trap.'

'I know what you are going to say and the answer is *no*!' Nicholas almost growled.

'She will not come to harm, but it's the only way to drag Darius out of hiding.'

'He might send his entire coven instead. There is always the risk that she would be killed,' Nicholas argued, his eyes flashing.

'Yes, there's always a risk,' Eleanor agreed, 'but we either face it or run.'

Running sounded pretty good to him at the moment. He opened his mouth but his voice died as he looked around the room, the paintings, the expansive gardens and the woods beyond the French windows. They had never run from anything before. They had always lived courageously, without fear. They were the rulers and expected to be obeyed. Sacrifice was something they had learnt a long time ago, and had this decision come a few months earlier he wouldn't have hesitated. But Eva's fate was paramount and he wasn't about to endanger it.

'No,' he smiled sadly at Eleanor causing her to blink in surprise, '*We* will not run. I will take Eva and leave.'

Seton shook his head, 'The family stays together. Do you think she will be safer elsewhere? Do you remember what happened to the family we found in Russia?'

Nicholas' eyes glazed over with the memory of watching an entire human family wiped out by a small coven; in the end the Raynes had destroyed the coven but it had been too late.

'That was a smaller coven than Darius'!' Eleanor almost whispered the words. Her eyes were sorrowful as they gazed at Nicholas. She had been close to the children.

'Why don't we attack Darius?' Nicholas asked exasperated, but he already knew the answer.

'The treaty,' Seton replied grimly as he lowered himself into the nearest couch.

'I don't think we should rush this,' Eleanor began slowly, 'Sometimes decisions are made for us.'

'You think they will attack again?'

'I'm almost counting on it,' she replied with a small smile.

'How dare you return to me without the girl?'

Marina raised her eyes to Darius' furious ones and quickly looked away. 'An elite came to the rescue.'

'And?"

She looked back at him in shock. 'We couldn't stop him.'

'Why not? He was alone right?'

'Yes, but the treaty…'

'That is just as excuse. To hell with the blasted treaty!' Darius spat out.

'The Elites would have attacked if we had killed him,' Marina continued softly.

'And we would have won!' Darius snarled at her in reply.

'It wasn't our fault,' a male voice piped up.

'Oh, and how do you figure that?' Darius turned on the large vampire standing beside Marina.

'The diversion should have worked.'

'Indeed, and one did. Luke is dead and there is no sign of Anna.'

'We scoured the area,' another voice spoke up, 'She is nowhere to be found.'

'Did you get rid of Luke?'

'Yes, we buried him.'

'Good, now go and find Anna. If she isn't dead bring her to me. She has a lot to answer for.'

Five vampires flashed out of the room to do his bidding.

'She is very young,' Marina tried to defend Anna. 'It was probably a mistake.'

'Her first and last' Darius promised darkly.

Chapter 29

Eva stepped through the glass doors of the lab building to see Leonara waiting for her a few feet away. The whole day had passed in a blur for her. The morning had been filled with several autopsies. At lunch the geek squad were in full swing in the cafeteria.

'You're awfully quiet today.'

She had lifted her head to see Matt staring at her. The others were too busy arguing to notice her silence. 'Yeah, I'm not feeling too good.'

'You're working too hard! You should take some time off.'

'No!' she said quickly, not realising she had raised her voice until the entire table fell silent. 'I mean I don't need a break, I'll be fine.' Work was the only thing keeping her sane. If she got time to think about all that had happened she would go crazy, she just knew it.

'Okay, I hear you,' Matt smiled at her. 'You know you're one hell of a workaholic!'

She returned his smile with difficulty and tried to eat some of the food on her tray.

'I really think we should have a night out, you know a party of sorts!' Eric's voice floated towards her.

'Yeah, about time,' Tony agreed enthusiastically.

'And who are you bringing?' Neave asked him innocently.

'Well...' he glanced around the table speculatively.

'Don't bother!' Meredith said flipping her hair over her shoulder as his eyes settled on her.

'Oooh, looks like you're in the doghouse man,' Eric sympathised.

'She'll come around,' Tony promised with a wink, 'They always do!'

Sarah rolled her eyes expressively at Eva.

'What happened between Tony and Meredith? I thought they were quite close.'

'Who knows? I bet Tony was up to no good as usual! Knowing Tony he probably flirted with another girl.'

'Does he do that a lot?' Eva asked.

'Well, let's put it this way, I've known him for a few years now and he rarely goes steady.'

'Oh.' Eva looked at the handsome guy exchanging high fives with the others at the other end of the table.

They finally decided that the party would be held next weekend, at one of the nightclubs in the city.

'You will come won't you?' Sarah asked Eva as they left the cafeteria together.

'Uh...'

'You have to! Even Neave is going,' Sarah smiled at the redhead as she passed them.

'Whatever!' Neave replied throwing her hands up in surrender, 'Just keep Tony away from me!'

Meredith who was just behind them laughed softly, rolling her eyes, 'Bet he's got eyes for someone else!'

They all turned to see Tony escorting a tall policewoman towards the elevator.

'So are you going or not?' Sarah looked quizzically at Eva again.

'Ummm...'

Chapter 30

'So what did you say?' Leonara asked as she navigated away from the lab.

'I bluffed out of it, what could I say?' Eva slumped in her seat tiredly. For all intents and purposes she was under surveillance. She couldn't do anything without her bodyguards nowadays. Since the night of the attack, the Raynes had seen to her every need. Her belongings had miraculously appeared in her hotel suite a few days later courtesy of Eden.

She had finally met the rest of the family at the large mansion on the outskirts of the city. She had never been in the area before. It was lush with dark forests full of tangled undergrowth covering the ground and almost creeping up the tree trunks. Only the first few trees could be seen, the rest swallowed up in the darkness of the interior. The deep gloom she glimpsed in the forest's depths sent chills down her spine. She was seated beside Nicholas in a different black car she didn't recognise. Glancing at him now, her eyes travelled hungrily over his rugged profile.

'Are you cold?'

She jumped guiltily and concentrated on the road ahead, her heart thumping. Did he know how he affected her? Did he know she was looking at him just then? She shook her head in answer to his question when she felt him looking at her.

Nicholas sighed softly, breathing in the sweet scent floating around him. Strangely it wasn't causing his mouth to water excessively. He still craved it but it didn't have a firm hold on him anymore. He smiled to himself; maybe he was becoming immune. He flexed his fingers on the steering wheel, attuned to every movement Eva made. He had wanted to return to the hotel constantly for the past week to check on her, but between work and constantly patrolling the city looking out for Darius' coven he hadn't managed to be with her. Eleanor had also devised ways of keeping him away from the hotel; she wanted him to carry on with life as he had before Eva had come into it. She had noticed his obsession and feared for him as Seton had found out when she had confided in him a few days ago.

'He should stay away from her.'

'My love, how can he?'

'Oh no, you don't suppose?'

Seton nodded his head slowly, 'I'm afraid it's too late.'

'No! It is too dangerous! We must talk to him. *You* must talk to him!'

Seton put his arms around his wife's slim shoulders. 'Whatever we say it won't make any difference now.'

'You've already spoken to him?'

'Yes, and I fear he is too far gone,' Seton said trying to keep a straight face.

Eleanor looked up after a second to see him smiling into the distance. 'You always were a romantic!' she accused him, trying to pull away. 'But this is dangerous. You know that as well as I do! A vampire and a human? The Council will never agree!'

'You said the same thing when we got together,' he reminded her, 'and look where we are now.'

'That was different as you well know!' she replied struggling against his arms.

'So sweet when it goes your way,' he drawled, tightening his embrace, 'and such a fury when it doesn't!'

She stopped struggling and slanted him a wicked look. 'You're not an angel either you know.' He bent his head to kiss her before releasing his hold. 'Does she know?'

He shook his head with a sigh, 'I don't think so.'

'Well for better or worse, ' Eleanor smiled grimly, 'We will have to help him when the time comes.'

Nicholas turned his head sharply when he heard Eva's gasp. His eyes followed hers to see the family mansion sitting on the summit of a raised stretch of ground, overlooking the surrounding forests and fields.

'It's beautiful,' Eva whispered.

He nodded. 'It's been in the family for years.'

'That's where we are going?' She shifted so that she could see him properly.

He had barely nodded in reply before he guided the car onto a narrow track hidden from the main road by the undergrowth. It had been a bright cloudy day until they turned off the main road. The track ran between the huge trees, winding and twisting unexpectedly, the dense leafy canopy overhead enveloped them in an ethereal greenish world that grew darker as they travelled further into the forest. Nicholas had slowed down a little to negotiate the turns. Five minutes later they drove through an ancient wrought iron gate.

The driveway wasn't as dark and the light grew stronger as they advanced allowing Eva to see the grounds flanking the drive on either side through the gaps in the trees. There were formal gardens with overflowing flowerbeds, gravel paths winding haphazardly between them. Further on she spotted a huge Rockery with waterfalls glistening in the crevices, and as they neared the house the gardens levelled off into beautifully maintained lawns that stretched to the front steps of the house. A large stone fountain dominated the end of the driveway. At least five metres in diameter it glistened in the dull light, the water spewing forth from the gaping mouths of stone fish and vessels held by all manner of mythical creatures arranged in an ascending spiral which reached several feet into the air.

They drove around the fountain and stopped at the front steps. Before Eva could open the door, Nicholas had left the car and was holding it open for her with a small smile.

'Welcome to my home,' he said formally and put out his hand.

Chapter 31

She looked at it for a second before placing hers in it gingerly. Her fingers were immediately clasped gently in his as he helped her out. They walked to the front door hand in hand, neither willing to break the contact. Opening the door, he guided her in.

'Before you meet them, just remember you are safe here,' he whispered close to her ear, and his fingers tightened slightly on hers.

Her breathing sped up as she looked around her, trying to avoid looking at his intense eyes as they rested on her pink face. She suddenly realised what the house reminded her of. It's what she had imagined Mr. Rochester's house would have been like in Jane Eyre, one of her favourite books; only this had more light and was much grander. The hall was done in dark panelling, possibly walnut; the floors shone from the years of polish applied to them. In the centre stood a circular table with a vase full of hothouse flowers lending the room a more homey feeling, which put her a little more at ease. Nicholas led her past several rooms before halting in front of a pair of closed double doors. His hand on hers and the warm look he directed at her gave her some courage as he opened the doors and strode inside, pulling her with him.

She gasped when she saw the room. It was a huge living room, panelled like the hall but it felt more modern. The couches were cream in colour and the tables and cabinets a dark mahogany. Photographs of the family, paintings and statues stood on every surface. Along one entire wall built-in bookcases almost groaned under the weight of their load while a small alcove to the left of the door housed all manner of musical instruments, from a baby grand piano to a violin. A bookcase nearby seemed to be dedicated to only sheets of music. Large tinted windows on most of the walls flooded the room with light. A state of the art television and stereo system stood to the right of the door. Vases with cream and dark red roses were placed strategically around the room.

Suddenly Eva's gaze fell on the two people sitting nearby watching her. She recognised Seton who was smiling at her warmly and motioning her forward.

'I hope you are well, Eva,' he greeted her as Nicholas led her to a seat across from them.

'Yes thank you,' she replied quickly, aware of the piercing gaze of the woman seated next to him.

'This is Eleanor, Seton's wife and my sister-in-law,' Nicholas introduced the slim, blonde to Eva, exchanging a slightly nervous look with Seton.

'Nice to meet you,' Eleanor said, a small smile on her lips. She turned to the two men. 'I think you can leave us now.'

Nicholas looked slightly uncomfortable until she smiled at him reassuringly and winked as Seton led the way out. Once they had gone, she turned back to Eva with a smile. 'Now we can talk in peace without them hovering over us.'

Eva swallowed with difficulty. She was now accustomed to Alena, Leonara and even Kane, but there was something about the woman sitting opposite her that made her appear very distant. Maybe it was her elegant dress, or her perfect face. She had a regal air about her which the others didn't and when she smiled her pearly white teeth appeared sharper and more pronounced. Her eyes glittered slightly despite their pale colour, flecks of darkest ebony floating within their depths, reminding her of her attackers.

'Don't worry my dear, I will not harm you.'

She started in surprise. It was as though she had read her thoughts. 'I'm not worried,' she lied quickly.

Eleanor's laugh was like the tinkling of wind chimes. 'You don't lie very well. That's a good sign.' She peered closely at Eva's face and smiled approvingly. 'You have courage, but do you have enough I wonder? You know what we are and yet you are here.'

'I...I trust you,' Eva whispered softly, her heart hammering painfully in her chest.

'Trust is fragile, it can be broken. But love...' her eyes narrowed as she watched the blood tinge Eva's cheeks, 'Love is stronger.' She sighed in resignation and sat back slightly. 'Do you know why you are here?'

Eva let out the breath she had been holding, 'To meet you?'

'Of course, but also to learn more about our kind. Nick thought it would be a good idea for me to tell you.'

'Oh.'

'But where are my manners? Would you like some refreshments?' she indicated a pitcher of juice and a plate of biscuits on a table.

'No thank you,' Eva replied politely.

'Very well. First, do you have any pressing questions? Nick tells me you are very curious by nature.'

'Umm...' Eva's brow furrowed as she thought about it and then nodded. 'Yes...I heard Nicholas talk to the other vampires about Elites and territories when I was attacked. He didn't really explain...'

'Ah yes, a good place to start. Well, to answer your first question we are the Elites.' She paused for a second and then resumed, 'Vampires, you have to understand, are creatures of habit and custom. We love pomp and ceremony, and although old habits die hard we try to nurture them. Most of us were born in the old days and some of us still live that way now.' She paused watching Eva's eyes travel around the modern room before adding, 'Not this family of course but several do. There are three tiers in our world. The Elders Council are the rulers, the law-keepers and judges. Any vampire breaking our laws is punished by them. The Elites come next, the upper class of vampires who do the Council's bidding and are of an elevated status.

'The rest are commoners, your typical vampire nomad moving from place to place, surviving on what they can find.' She broke off to tip her head to the side as though she was listening intently.

Eva couldn't hear anything, no matter how much she strained. But Eleanor was looking at her curiously again. '"Does that answer some of your question?'

'Yes, but the territories...?'

'Every country in the world has been divided into segments according to how rich or popular certain areas are. The best areas are given to the Elites to control and no other vampire can hunt in these territories. The human inhabitants are unknowingly under their protection. The rest serve the commoners.' Noticing Eva's pale face she quickly moved on. 'The Elites may roam where they will, territorial boundaries are not for us.' She allowed herself a small smile and shook her head, 'You see we still believe in the social classes.'

'So...the ones that attacked me were...commoners?'

'Undoubtedly and they defied Nick for which they would have to pay a high price. But we cannot prove under whose orders they were acting, which is why we cannot attack them nor ask for justice from the Council court.'

'Nicholas said I had a different type of blood...'

Eleanor's eyes darkened and she licked her lips slowly, making Eva feel distinctly uneasy. She eyed the door judging the distance and heard that tinkling laugh again.

'You would never make it my dear! But thankfully I am harmless. You must forgive me the mere mention of your blood has the ability to make my darkest desires surface, but I can control them well.' She watched Eva relax slightly and smiled, 'Nicholas is right every vamp in the world is after your blood, hence the name of your bloodline. We call you the hunted.'

'Are there many like me?'

Eleanor shook her head 'Not nearly as many as there used to be. Being desired by one of us is not a good thing. We protect the bloodline but the others crave it.'

'But why?'

'You are part of our legends, there is a myth of sorts which says the blood of a pure heart is very powerful. So powerful that when drunk by a vampire whilst still warm will enable that vampire to be stronger, faster and altogether unbeatable.' She looked at Eva's stunned face and smiled kindly, 'Every commoner and elite wants to rule our world. None will say so but they all think it. They are all looking for the hunted ones. Of course only one coven has ever carried out the legend, and it has been said there is more to the myth but no one truly knows.

'So, the vamps kill the hunted ones indiscriminately hoping for glory, but none has attained it so far. The Council are duty-bound to protect any of the Hunted Bloodline to prevent being overthrown.' She paused for breath and to gauge her guest's reaction.

Eva nodded slowly her eyes glazed over with memories. 'When I was attacked as a child?'

Eleanor nodded, 'Yes, they were after your mother. You were too young to have a lot of blood, and the chemicals hadn't been fully produced yet.'

Eva swallowed, 'Are there other Elites here?'

'No, we are the only ones. Sometimes there can be more than one coven but it depends on the size of the territory. We don't like to be too close to our own kind, and it's not healthy for the local populace either,' she added wickedly, watching Eva's pupils dilate with fear. 'I'm sorry, our humour does run into the dark side occasionally.'

'Of course,' Eva smiled with difficulty, her fear of the woman opposite her still present. It was her eyes she decided, they were very different from the others'. She watched as Eleanor reclined against the cushions, her hair spread around her creating a halo effect.

'Can I ask you something?'

'Of course, that's why you are here!'

'Uh...your eyes...they are different from Nicholas'. In fact they are all different, the others had odd black eyes...' she trailed off uncertainly.

'You notice a lot,' she mused, 'Yes, the silver colour strangely depends on our diet. We drink mainly animal blood, clean blood so to speak and the colour shows our purity. The flecks you see are from our other life, remnants of the colour they used to be. The black eyes you saw in the others showed their dark nature and their dark deeds. The colour is of emptiness. You have heard it said that the eyes are the windows to the soul? Well, ours prove it.' She smiled again almost wistfully. 'Listen to me! You'd think I was a poet or a romantic!'

Eva smiled in reply, not wanting to do anything that could be construed as an insult. Despite her assurances, Eva couldn't feel completely at ease with Eleanor. Suddenly she heard a sigh.

'You still do not trust me, but you will,' she said almost to herself, and then a little louder so Eva could hear clearly, 'Let's move on to happier topics. Let's see,' she appeared to think for a minute and then smiled, 'Do you know of our talents?'

'Talents?'

'Yes, I should have told you this at first, it's the most interesting part and the least scary.' She kept her lips firmly together now when she smiled, 'The Elites are chosen according to their gifts. All of us either have a talent or have fallen in love with an existing Elite. Take myself for example, I am not vastly talented, but I can sense people's feelings to some extent and I seem to create loyalty easily. When a promise is made to me it has to be kept. It is a very intangible gift and very flawed but there it is.'

'So you can tell what I'm feeling?'

'Yes, but then again you are very easy to read. It varies with different people.'

'What other talents are there? I mean if you don't mind me asking.' She was feeling better now that some of her fear had been replaced by curiosity and the growing interest in what she was learning.

'Ask away dear, you need to know to stay safe. Let's start with Leo, she is a charmer.'

'A charmer?'

'She can make people do what she wants to some extent. I believe you witnessed it at the restaurant. It works on most people, even vamps but...not you.'

Eva's eyes widened as she remembered the sudden silence and the stares. 'That was Leonara?'

'Yes, she's getting very good at it, but you baffle her.'

'Yes...I was able to look around at everyone else when they were staring at her and Nicholas. Why was that?'

Eleanor shrugged eloquently, 'Who knows? But I can tell you it worried her a lot, especially the return of your memory about the night we helped you as a child,' she chuckled, 'It takes a lot to knock her confidence and you managed it!'

Eva looked contrite. 'I honestly didn't mean to!'

'Of course you didn't! Some people are able to withstand our talents. Don't worry, she got over it quickly enough and now seems to really like you.' She smiled when she saw Eva relax slightly. 'Now Alena is completely different. She is possibly the most powerful one here.'

'Really? What does she do?' Eva couldn't imagine the petite red-haired vampire capable of anything very powerful.

'Well, she controls the weather.'

'*What?* That's not possible!'

'Neither is this situation but here we are, a vampire and a human talking as though we were old friends,' she smiled warmly, 'You will see many things that are impossible. Yes, weather control. She is getting better at it but she too has a lot to learn.'

'What about...' Eva swallowed nervously, not sure she wanted to know the answer, 'What about Nicholas?'

'I'd rather he told you himself. In fact here they are now.'

Chapter 32

The door opened and Nicholas entered silently with Seton, followed by two teenage boys. Nicholas headed straight for Eva's side and sat down with a questioning look. She smiled with relief and almost automatically his lips widened in an answering smile. Eleanor watched the pair avidly as they stared at each other. A part of her was glad, but a slow dread was gripping her heart. Her thoughts were interrupted as Seton sat next to her and covered her hand with his. She looked up at him, her eyes silently conveying all she was feeling. He nodded, a slight smile on his lips and petted her hand reassuringly.

Nicholas glanced at Eleanor and at her nod, seemed to visibly relax. He looked back at Eva and indicated the two boys sitting near Seton.

'I have more of the family for you to meet if you're up to it. That is Eden.' The taller of the two smiled mischievously at her, 'And that is Ashe,' he continued. The blonde-haired boy yawned and waved lazily to her.

She smiled at them, they reminded her of normal teenage boys and she wasn't quite sure what to say. Her mind was still digesting all she had learnt so far.

'Did you have a nice chat?' Seton asked his wife.

'Yes, we learnt a lot about each other, didn't we my dear?'

'I hope it wasn't too much for you,' Seton said kindly, looking at Eva.

Eleanor said something in a low voice to him, which Eva couldn't hear and he laughed with a slight shake of his head.

'No, not at all,' she replied instead, her voice fairly steady.

Nicholas gave her an approving look, which made her blush slightly.

'I think we interrupted you,' Seton continued, ignoring her reaction.

'We were almost done talking about our talents when you arrived,' Eleanor said.

Before Seton could reply, Ashe quickly interrupted with, 'Did you tell her about mine?'

'Why would she when mine's the best?' Eden piped up, forestalling Eleanor.

Ashe was about to retort when Eva quickly said, 'What do you do?'

He smiled and cleared his throat. 'I can detect others like us!'

'Like I said, mine's better!' Eden said with a scornful laugh.

Ashe was seething with anger, but Eva stepped in again. 'What is your talent?' she asked Eden.

'I think showing you will be better.' And he vanished in front of her startled eyes.

She gasped and would have stood up if Nicholas hadn't stopped her with a hand on her shoulder. 'Where did he go?!'

'Over here!' Eden's laughter came from behind her and she started nervously. Before she could turn round to see him, he had returned to his place next to Ashe, a big grin on his face.

'What was that?' she asked shakily.

Nicholas was glaring at Eden, but he smiled and replied loftily, 'Teleportation! I can disappear and reappear wherever I choose!'

'Oh,' Eva blinked and tried to breathe normally.

The day was turning out to be quite extraordinary. She would never have believed any of it if she hadn't seen it for herself. As a scientist she still couldn't quite believe any of it but the evidence of her eyes and what she had been through the past few weeks couldn't be ignored.

'This is the entire family, don't worry, no more for you to meet,' said Nicholas with an understanding look.

Soon after Ashe and Eden left the room, bored and seeing no further opportunity to frighten her. A look from Seton caused Eleanor to rise as well and having thanked Eva for coming to meet her left with Seton, leaving her and Nicholas alone. As the door closed behind them, he heaved a sigh and settled back against the cushions.

Eva's puzzled look made him say, 'I'm glad that's over and done with!'

'Same here, and I'm glad you agree!' she replied with a shaky laugh.

'I have been on tenterhooks for a while now. I didn't know how you would take the family and more importantly how Eleanor would react.'

'Only Eleanor? Why?'

He looked at her steadily, seeming to take in every detail of her face before he replied. 'She's...sceptical about everyone and everything until she has...let's say...vetted them.'

'Is that why you left me alone with her?'

He nodded. 'She sees what others are feeling and gets an idea of who that person is. Having someone else present makes it more difficult for her to sense the true person inside,' he paused before continuing, 'and she is the best person to tell you about our kind.'

'Why?' she was starting to understand more about the strange interview she had had.

'Because she is older than the rest of us and she was part of the ruling Elders until she met Seton. She was very influential, but when she fell in love with him she had to give up her position.'

'Wow!' Eva looked impressed and she now understood the regal air Eleanor seemed to have about her, and then her face fell visibly.

'What's wrong?'

She shook her head. 'I don't think she likes me.'

Nicholas smiled. 'I'm sure she does. It takes us a long time to truly like anyone, and even longer to show it. Plus you are a human and she isn't in the habit of making friends with mortals.'

Eva smiled in relief and stifled a yawn.

'About time I got you back to the hotel. Your guards will not be happy, I have it from Leo that she will personally harm me if we are very late!'

They were driving back to the city when another thought occurred to Eva. She peeked sideways at Nicholas' face and was startled to see he was looking at her from the corner of his eyes. Both of them averted their eyes simultaneously and she could feel a ridiculous urge to giggle.

'You have another question don't you?'

The quietly voiced question made her jump. He was staring at the road ahead and she noticed they weren't travelling as fast as they had when travelling to the mansion.

'Yes,' she hesitated and then decided to just ask him. 'Eleanor was telling me about everyone's talents...but she said she'd rather you told me about yours...'

Nicholas' smile dazzled her and her heart started racing again. Suddenly he pulled into the side of the road and turned to her, his eyes shining.

'Do you really want to know?'

'Yes.'

'Are you not too tired?'

'No!'

'You won't be afraid?'

'Uh...I don't think so.'

'Well, if you can handle my being a vamp and meeting my family, this shouldn't be too hard for you,' he mused, a half smile playing on his lips.

She held her breath, waiting expectantly. He was still scrutinising her face intently, noticing the dark shadows under her eyes and the paleness of her skin, the slight dullness of her eyes betraying her fatigue.

He sat back and shook his head, 'I think you've been through enough for today, maybe another time.'

And with that he sent the car roaring back onto the road.

Eva blinked in confusion. 'But I'm not tired and I want to know!'

'And you will when the time comes. Plus I'd rather you saw it, it's difficult to explain in words.'

She slumped dejectedly in her seat having realised he wasn't going to change his mind. Darting a quick glance at her Nicholas couldn't help but be amused at her childlike posture.

Chapter 33

A week later and she was back at the Rayne mansion sitting again in the same room, flanked by Alena and Leonara. The entire family was present. Watching them she couldn't believe how much they behaved like a normal human family. Ashe and Eden were busy arguing, Leonara was torn between asking them to stop and holding a conversation with Alena. Kane and Nicholas were playing chess on the other side of the room.

All at once everyone stilled and the room became silent. It seemed as though they were all trying to listen to something. Suddenly a draught of air hit her as the door opened and shut and she looked round to see Eleanor and Seton seated nearby. She blinked in surprise, they hadn't been there a second ago, she was sure of it.

'What happened?' asked Nicholas. He had left the chess game and was now standing facing his brother.

Seton shrugged. 'It appears they have been eavesdropping. Our plan might just work.'

'We will need the entire family for this,' Nicholas warned. Seton nodded his consent.

Eleanor was looking at Eva with a sympathetic light in her eyes when she caught her eye and smiled slightly. Wedged between her two friends she felt more secure than she had when she was alone with the elegant vampire.

Nicholas was still speaking to Seton in that odd high-speed way she had started getting used to. A few minutes later he looked at Eva and jerked his head towards the door. She stood up on shaky legs and walked carefully across the room to his side. She could feel the Raynes watching her as she left the room with him. He led her to a smaller room a few doors down. As soon as she was seated he cleared his throat.

'What was all that about?' she asked, her eyes wide, clearly something was going on.

'Nothing, just the usual. We are tracking other vamps in the area.'

'The ones that are after me?'

He nodded slowly. 'Amongst others.'. He took a small breath and said quickly, 'I need to ask you a favour.' She looked surprised as he continued, 'Leo told me about the party...'

'Don't worry I'm not going,' she broke in, 'I already told her that.'

'I know, but I want you to go.'

'What? Isn't that dangerous?'

'A little, but it would help us out a lot. We have a few things to deal with and we can't leave you alone. If you are surrounded by people you are less likely to be in danger. Which is why I need you to stay close to a friend.'

Understanding dawned and she smiled shakily, 'Alright I'll go.' After all, she thought, she couldn't expect them to look after her all the time.

'Good,' he smiled gratefully but he didn't miss her look of unease as she turned away from him. Why was she not happy about the party? He wasn't particularly over the moon but he had very good reasons for his reluctance.

+++

'I am so glad you decided to come!' Sarah said hugging Eva.

They were standing outside a new nightclub on the east side. The guys had hired a room at the club and from a few people the whole thing had exploded into a massive affair. Most of the crime lab were now milling around them, eager to get in. Eva hadn't realised how many people would be present and looking at all the faces around her she wanted to turn and walk away very fast. Only by remembering Nicholas' face was she able to stop herself.

'Here are the others!'

She turned to see the rest of the Geek Squad strolling towards them.

'This place is heaving!' Eric exclaimed as several teenagers pushed past him.

'Told you it was hot!' Tony agreed, bobbing his head to the loud music.

'What's it called again?' someone asked.

'ICE!' someone else shouted out and before Eva knew it, she was being carried along by the crowd into the club. She held onto Sarah's arm as people shoved and pushed eager to get in. They managed to eventually move towards the reserved area they had hired.

'Hey, I thought it was a room?' Neave said looking around the fairly small cordoned off area which sported a balcony overlooking the packed dance floor below them.

'Well…' Tony shrugged nonchalantly as he gulped at his beer.

'But anyone can enter it!' Neave continued.

'I don't think they'll get past those guys without these armbands,' Eric replied soothingly nodding towards the two heavily muscled bouncers.

'I guess so,' Neave smiled and turned to Sarah and Eva. 'Want a drink?'

Chapter 34

It was an hour or so later and she was still in the cordoned off area. The girls had tried in vain to get her to dance but she had refused. She was fingering the small talisman Nicholas had insisted she wear before he had left her the night before at the hotel.

She looked up to see Tony standing next to her with a frown.

'Come on!! Look Sarah will come too! You have to dance! It is a night club!'

After five minutes of his pleading she finally relented reluctantly, and was almost dragged down the steps and into the crowd of dancers. Two songs later she had to admit she was having fun. The music was intoxicating and Tony was a really good dancer. As she danced she tried to forget everything, letting the music dictate her moves. When the song changed Eric stepped in. Looking around her she couldn't see anyone else she knew in the crowd.

Several songs later she looked up to be confronted by a sea of strangers. Most were ignoring her and others were looking at her in what she thought was an odd way, but when she looked again they had moved away or were looking elsewhere. She shook her head to clear it. *You are going paranoid!* she thought, *not everyone is out to get you! There are no vamps here.* She looked around her again, this time paying close attention to the several pairs of eyes near her. Not one of them had that dead black look about them. Closing her mind to the scary thoughts floating through it regarding vampires, she continued to dance.

Suddenly she started feeling very warm and dizzy. Opening her eyes she groaned, the entire club was rushing past her, careening wildly. The faces were now an indistinct blur and were taking on a grotesque appearance. Even the music was causing her to feel nauseous and the electric blue under floor lighting was giving her a headache, dazzling her so that she had to close her eyes again. The press of bodies was making it difficult to breathe and she felt like she was drowning slowly as people shoved and pushed against her, moving her inexorably to an unknown destination. A forceful shove from behind and she felt herself falling. Although she tried to stop herself all she could do was watch the blue lights come closer and closer. With a dull thud she hit the floor, landing on her knees, still staring at the floor as it continued to spin wildly.

Just as she was thinking about lying down and praying for the headache to pass, someone grabbed her arm and helped her up. She tried to thank them but she couldn't quite get the words out. She was expecting them to leave her, but the firm grip remained, moving her to the edge of the dance floor. Expecting to see one of the bouncers next to her, she turned her head and squinted her eyes against the bright flickering lights, to see a tall girl she had never seen before. As they moved she could hear the girl apologising to the dancers they brushed past. Once they were out of the crowd, she tried to pull away from the girl with a quick thank you, but the grip tightened and the girl shook her head.

'You are not well. Come on I will help you.'

And with that assurance she pulled Eva towards a side door. Pushing it open she helped her gently out of the club.

'But my friends...' gasped Eva, stumbling along next to her escort.

'They are all inside. Once I've made sure you're okay I'll let them know what's happened. Don't worry.'

Eva frowned as her mind cleared slightly, 'But you don't know them.'

'Oh, I'll manage. They were on the balcony right?'

Eva nodded a lethargy spreading through her body. She let herself be led along the dark alley they had entered.

'Where are we going?' she asked after a minute or two of walking in the dark.

The girl didn't answer at once instead she walked faster towards a white van parked at the end of the alley.

Here we are!'

'Where?' Eva almost whispered the words, the pounding in her head had gotten worse and now stars were floating in front of her eyes.

'The ambulance of course! They will help you!' the girl promised.

The side door slid open with a grating sound which caused her to squeeze her eyes shut, as the pounding increased. Just as she opened them again, a pair of hands caught hold of her arms and pulled her in. The girl gave her a slight push and then followed.

It took Eva a few seconds to adjust to the gloom inside the van. She found herself seated on a wooden bench nailed to the floor. She sensed other people around her besides the girl as the door slammed shut and an engine started.

'I just need painkillers! Where are we going?' she protested weakly as she felt the van begin to move under her.

'We have to go to the hospital, you are too sick!' came the immediate reply. It was a man's voice and she frowned again, did she know that voice? Of course not! She had never met these people before. She shook her head, trying to clear it, but the pain was too penetrating and she lay back exhausted, feeling herself slipping away into the darkness.

Chapter 35

Sarah looked around the dance floor and frowned. She couldn't spot the dark head she was looking for. She had left Eva with Tony while she went to the ladies. Sensing that she didn't like crowds she had made Tony promise he wouldn't let her out of his sight. She picked him out dancing a few feet away with a blonde. Making her way through the press of moving bodies, she tapped him on the shoulder. He turned around in surprise, but seeing her smiled.

'What's up?'

'Where's Eva?' she asked close to his ear.

He looked around at the nearby dancers and shrugged. 'No idea, I left her dancing with Eric.'

She frowned at him as he pointed out the tall man. 'There he is.'

Without bothering to thank him she moved in the direction he had indicated, expecting to see Eva next to Eric.

'Hey, where's Eva?' she almost shouted at him when she realised he was dancing with a complete stranger.

'What?' he asked leaning down slightly.

'Where's Eva?' she repeated louder still.

'No idea! She must be here somewhere. We got separated,' he explained casually, and turned back to his partner, leaving Sarah looking worried.

She decided to scour the dance floor for the girl. She couldn't be far. After an hour she had to admit defeat, Eva was not in the nightclub. Maybe she had wandered outside? Sarah hoped she hadn't but decided to check anyway.

She left by the front doors, having asked the two bouncers if they had seen anyone matching Eva's description. When they shook their heads in a negative, she walked along the street peering into the shadows. The music from the club was so loud she could still hear it clearly as she walked further into the darkness. The street looked deserted and very dark. Most of the street lamps weren't working and those that were shed a feeble yellow light that made the atmosphere even more eerie. She was passing a narrow alley when she heard a noise. Peeking in she could just about make out that there was someone there in the darkness.

'Eva?' she almost whispered her name and saw something raise its head.

'Eva? Is that you?' she repeated louder this time, moving into the alley.

The clouds chose that moment to part and a moonbeam shone through lighting the alley. Sarah gasped in horror. Several people were lying on the ground motionless. As her eyes adjusted to the half-darkness she saw some more people who had been crouching stand up.

'What's going on?' she asked suspiciously, moving slightly towards them.

They were too far for her to see their faces clearly. All she could see were the black cloaks they wore and as the moonlight brightened what she thought was red paint on their faces. The wind changed direction and she almost gagged. A thick rusted iron-like smell assailed her nose and she staggered back involuntarily.

Her foot fell into what looked like a puddle. Looking down she gasped again. Her trousers shone darkly with a sticky fluid and the smell caused her to gag again. Her mind reeled and she looked up again quickly at the strangers who were advancing slowly towards her.

She thought she could see them smiling and her heart nearly stopped as she realised that the red paint was in fact blood. Without another thought she whirled and ran out of the alley, headed straight for the club's entrance. She couldn't hear any footsteps behind her but she wasn't about to stop and make sure. She was panting uncontrollably as she saw the brightly lit entrance with the two bouncers chatting to each other.

I'm almost there, she thought and increased her speed, her lungs now painfully taking in the little air she could suck through her open mouth. For some reason she could still smell the blood, the thick clogging stench seemed to coat her tongue and throat so that every breath seemed tainted. She almost gagged again as she ran up the steps and nearly collided with the muscular man at the top. He caught hold of her and she sagged thankfully against him, staring fearfully in the direction she had just come from.

'Help!' she gasped, her words barely audible.

The man looked confused. 'Are you okay?'

'Blood...all those people...' she was shaking as she gripped his arms firmly.

'I think she's drunk,' the other bouncer volunteered uncertainly.

'No!' she exclaimed, sucking in more air, 'Call the police. People are dead!'

The other man looked uncertain until she turned on him with blazing eyes. 'I said call the police! I'm from the crime lab!'

Seeing her anger, he promptly ran into the club to follow her orders. The man still holding her lowered her to the ground gently and knelt beside her as she panted heavily, trying to breath normally. He didn't say a word and she was grateful to him. She kept glancing down the road, still expecting the cloaked strangers to emerge from the darkness, with the blood smeared smiles she knew she could never forget.

Finally they heard sirens and two squad cars screeched to a halt outside the club their blue lights flickering over Sarah's ashen face. Her breathing was back to normal but she was still shivering uncontrollably despite the thick jacket the bouncer had thrown over her shoulders. Even after the squad cars arrived she kept looking nervously down the street.

'Miss?' one of the policemen was kneeling next to her now, 'Miss are you alright?'

She nodded and identified herself as a crime scene investigator. In as few words as possible she told him what she had seen and a description of the cloaked strangers. She could see the disbelief on the man's face as she spoke, so she shifted her body and pointed at her right shoe. He looked down at it and recoiled when he realised it was covered in blood. His eyes moved up her trouser leg to see it was also spattered with blood.

'Is that yours?' he asked gingerly.

She shook her head impatiently. 'Go to the alley, second right down there,' she pointed, 'Please, they may still be alive!'

Hearing this he sent the rest of his men down the street. He looked at the bouncers. 'Did you see anything unusual tonight?'

They shook their heads and said some people had left the club but they had thought nothing of it. It was normal for drunk teenagers to be escorted out by their friends during the night. They hadn't heard any screams or any sounds of fighting and they couldn't remember anyone wearing a black cloak. A shout from the street made the policeman look up.

'We found them sir!' shouted one of his men.

Sarah made as if to get up but he restrained her gently. 'I think you should go home and rest. Do you have someone to help you?'

She nodded and gave her friends' names to the bouncer who quickly went to find them. The other one stayed with her while the policeman left to talk to his men. The squad cars were summoned to the alley and positioned so that their headlights could flood the area.

Sarah closed her eyes and leaned against the wall, trying to forget what she had seen. She was used to dead bodies but she had never encountered so many at once, had never seen the murderers in the act and had definitely never had to smell the overpowering stench of so much fresh blood. Just the memory of it was threatening her control on her gag reflex. Before she knew it Neave and Meredith were standing next to her with Tony, Eric and Matt.

'Are you okay Sarah?' Neave asked as she knelt next to her, looking shocked at the state her friend was in.

Sarah nodded and looked around her hoping to see Eva. 'Where's Eva?' she asked.

The others looked at each other with vacant expressions. Sarah could feel the tears behind her eyes as she imagined Eva in the alley. She told the others what she had seen and Eric, Matt and Tony all left to see what they could do to help, after promising her they would let her know everything as soon as they could. The girls called a cab and herded Sarah into it despite her protests.

'But Eva…'

'The guys will find her. Don't worry. She's probably in the club,' Neave reassured her.

'Yeah, but you need to chill! You look terrible!' Meredith said with a forced smile.

Sarah tried to smile and share her friends' optimism but she couldn't help fretting about Eva.

Chapter 36

Nicholas watched as Eva took a sip of her drink. He was hiding behind one of the marble pillars, watching out for Darius and his friends. The others were similarly employed, either inside the club or outside. Suddenly a blonde-haired girl passed close to his hiding place and he stiffened. She was definitely one of them. His eyes followed her as she walked onto the dance floor. Making sure Eva was still with her friends he followed, staying out of sight.

The blonde danced for a while and then walked up the staircase leading to the upper floors of the club. Nicholas turned to see Leonara watching Eva. Having signalled to her he followed the leggy blonde. She disappeared into the ladies as he walked up the stairs, so he waited outside looking inconspicuous as he mingled with the teenage crowd in the corridor. A few minutes later she emerged and headed for the back of the building. He was expecting her to seize a human or return to the dance floor but she turned into an office at the far end and closed the door.

Moving closer he stood nonchalantly with a drink in his hand, leaning against the railing overlooking the packed floors below. He was paying little attention to the dancers or the teenagers streaming past him. He was focussing on the conversation taking place inside the office. Even at this distance he could make out the words as though they were being exchanged right next to him.

'You're back!'

'Yes.'

'So have you enjoyed the club?'

'It's wonderful. So many humans! It makes me thirsty just thinking about it!'

'In good time my dear. My partners are happy for us to use it. But its reputation is important you understand.'

'Of course, Darius understands only too well.'

'Good, now tell me what has been happening since I was last here.'

The girl seemed to hesitate and then told him all the news. When she mentioned Eva's name Nicholas stiffened.

'Ah! One of the Hunted Bloodline! That is good news.'

The man sounded educated and his accent was uncannily familiar. What had he meant by the vamps could use the club? Nicholas looked around at the crowd of teenagers and his eyes widened in horror. The club was like honey to the youngsters. It was being used to lure them to the vamps. He shook his head, he didn't have time to worry about them; he had more important things on his mind tonight. He listened closely as the two people in the office continued to talk.

'I hope Darius knows what he's doing.'

'Don't worry he does,' the girl assured him.

'Well, feel free to pick whoever you choose.'

'Actually we are having a banquet tonight, it will kill two birds with one stone.'

Silence greeted her statement and then the door opened. Nicholas melted into a crowd of college kids coming up the stairs, still watching the girl closely as she looked around her quickly; making sure she wasn't being observed and then flashed to the window at the far end of the corridor and leapt out. He waited to see if anyone else was going to follow her but the office door remained firmly shut. He walked casually to the window and stared down.

It was two floors up and he couldn't see any sign of the girl not that he had expected to. Not wanting to lose her he glanced over his shoulder and then jumped out, leaving his drink sitting on the windowsill. He landed on his feet and began walking quickly along the street, following the girl's scent. He followed it for several streets, winding haphazardly into areas no respectable citizen would be seen in at this time of night. As he turned a corner he froze. Just ahead of him stood the girl, her blonde hair flying in the slight breeze. He was about to attack her when she turned round and his mouth fell open in surprise.

'What are you doing here?'

'I was following one of Darius' lot,' Eleanor replied looking equally shocked to see him. 'What about you?'

'A female vamp.'

She was about to say something else when he motioned her to be silent. Further down the street two people were walking towards them. They crouched low, ready to defend themselves if necessary when Leonara's voice made them stand up and flash forward, Nicholas reaching them sooner than Eleanor.

'Where's Eva, Leo?' he asked urgently.

'In the club,' she replied trying to hide her surprise at seeing them.

'What are you two doing here? You were supposed to look after her!' Nicholas almost growled, fear lending his voice a cutting note.

'We were, and then this vamp turned up and I followed him,' Leonara explained defensively.

'Yeah, and Eva went onto the dance floor and I lost her for a few minutes, but then I saw someone like her wearing her coat leave through the front door so I followed. After a while I realised it wasn't her so I turned back and bumped into Leo,' Alena said quickly.

Nicholas looked helplessly at Eleanor. 'We've been tricked.'

'We have to get back,' she replied.

Before she could finish the sentence Nicholas had flashed to the end of the street heading for the club. He slowed down to a human-paced run as he neared the club, the others following closely. As they came in sight of the front entrance they froze. There was a lot of activity, police cars with flashing blue lights crowded the street and policemen patrolled with flashlights. An alley to their left seemed to be attracting a lot of interest.

Chapter 37

The Raynes slunk back into the shadows as a police dog-handler started towards them. The dog would find them at once and flush them from their hiding place. Eleanor touched Nicholas' shoulder and he nodded. Although it was pitch black the others could see his face clearly as though it was noon. A strange concentration gripped his features and his eyes glowed as he muttered under his breath. The advancing police dog raised its ears and whined. And then wagged its tail before leading it's handler safely away from the concealed vampires.

'Why are the police here?' Alena wondered out loud, her voice so low no human would hear it.

'We will have to find out.' Eleanor motioned to them as she headed back the way they had come. They trooped behind her, Nicholas hanging back slightly, keeping a lookout for any more police dogs. When Eleanor was certain they were standing in an alley parallel to the one the police were interested in she motioned upwards.

Without waiting for the others, she started climbing the sheer wall of the nearest building with lightning speed. She was so fast that she had reached the roof of the four-storey building within seconds. The others followed closely and then crawled carefully along the roof till they were looking down at the narrow alley filled with police. They had smelt the blood long before they had climbed the building but even that had not prepared them for the carnage that met their eyes now.

Along the alley's entire length dead bodies lay haphazardly. Many looked as though they were sleeping but even from this distance Nicholas knew they were dead. And he had no doubts as to what had caused their deaths. Large pools of blood already congealing glistened in the pale moonlight and he could feel the others move restlessly next to him. He scanned the pale faces below him, dreading the second he recognised Eva's. Although several women lay below him, none of them had Eva's features and after a minute or two he relaxed and heaved a sigh of relief. The others too had been looking for her and were glad when they couldn't see her, but Eleanor was frowning.

'What is it?' Leonara asked her finally.

'Why such a massacre?' Eleanor mused. She glanced at the large number of police still swarming over the area. 'They had to know this would get a lot of attention.'

'You think its Darius?' Alena asked, her pale blue-ringed eyes wide with worry.

'Yes,' she replied with a simple certainty, 'But why?' She looked around at their worried faces and motioned them away from the edge. 'We have to get the others and find Eva.' She looked at Nicholas' grim face. 'Check the club again, the rest of us will search the surrounding areas.'

She didn't say it but Nicholas knew she was expecting to find Eva's body. He leapt from the building silently landing again in the alley parallel to the crime scene. He dusted off his clothes and circled around the police barricade, weaving in and out of several streets before reaching the club from the opposite direction. Just as he walked up the steps of the club a burly policeman blocked his way.

'Sorry sir, the club is closed.'

'Why? What happened?'

The policeman swept a flashlight on his face. 'Nothing to worry about sir,' he finally said with pursed lips. 'Why are you in this area?'

'I am meeting a friend,' Nicholas replied smoothly.

The policeman looked unconvinced and was about to say something else when another man approached them. 'Mr. Rayne?'

Nicholas shifted his eyes to take in Chris's puzzled face. 'Detective Masterson,' he greeted the man slowly.

'I'll deal with this,' Chris dismissed the policeman and he left reluctantly. Turning back to Nicholas with raised eyebrows he said, 'Funny to see you here at this time of night,' a suspicious gleam in his eyes.

'Not at all, I was supposed to meet a friend here.'

'Really? And that friend's name?'

'Why is that important?' Nicholas asked casually.

'It is an investigation, you know we have to ask these questions,' Chris replied with a seemingly harmless smile.

'Tom Jefferson,' Nicholas said with a shrug, 'You haven't seen a slim man with brown hair, about this tall have you?' he asked placing his hand a few inches lower than his own head.

'No.' Chris didn't look convinced.

Nicholas shrugged again. 'Maybe he didn't turn up.' He looked round as he heard the sound of sirens and a few vans drew up. He recognised Matt talking to one of the drivers and looked back at Chris's face. 'Out of curiosity, have you found a body?'

'Why do you ask?' Chris's look of suspicion increased ten-fold and didn't lessen when Nicholas smiled disarmingly.

'I know a medical examiner's van when I see one.'

Chris sighed in resignation. 'Yes, a few bodies.'

Looking closely at the man, Nicholas asked slowly, 'Anyone we know?'

Chris shook his head. 'I don't think you know them, but...' he hesitated, 'There are several from the crime lab.'

Nicholas' face paled visibly in the moonlight. 'One of our own?' Chris nodded. 'I worked closely with the crime lab, could I have a look at your list?'

Chris was about to shake his head, but when he saw the earnest look on Nicholas' face he sighed. 'Here, these are the ones that have been identified. There are more but they are all civilians.' He handed over the list and watched as Nicholas flipped through it. 'It's crazy how they were all out together for once and this happens...' he blurted out.

Nicholas was still flicking through the list his eyes scanning it avidly, searching for the one name he hoped he wouldn't see. 'Did you say that most were from the crime lab?' he asked, masking his look of relief as his eyes failed to see the name he had been dreading.

Chris nodded. 'Yes and several from the police department. Apparently they had organised a night out.' He glanced over his shoulder as several stretchers with body bags were loaded into the waiting vans. 'There's still a lot to do tonight.' He looked sympathetically at Nicholas. 'If I see anyone with your friend's description I'll let you know.'

'Thank you,' Nicholas said gratefully and watched as the detective walked down the steps.

Well he hadn't found Eva dead or alive and he was glad for it, but there was always the chance the others would. He couldn't have borne it if she had been one of the pitiful souls in that ghastly alley. He didn't envy the policemen as they went about their work. Even he, who knew what had caused the deaths and should have been immune to it, could not stem the sadness and horror that gripped him. He left the scene and walked quickly to his car parked a few streets away. Gunning the engine he drove to the mansion, his thoughts still revolving around what had happened.

Chapter 38

It was the disgusting stench that she noticed first. It reminded her of what a butcher's shop smelt like, but with rotting meat and blood instead of fresh corpses. Having dealt with dead bodies for several years she was used to such smells but it was the insistent humming that she couldn't place. She frowned as it became louder and her eyes flickered open.

She found herself lying on an old ragged couch, her head against the armrest. She closed her eyes again trying to remember. Oh yeah, the white van, even now she couldn't quite believe it was an ambulance, but she had been feeling so sick. She was still so confused. So this must be the hospital? But why was she on a couch? She opened her eyes again and tried to sit up.

A sharp pain shot through her head stopping her. She lay back and tried to move only her eyes, looking at her surroundings. What she saw made her gasp. The room had all the signs of a dilapidated building. The paint was peeling off the walls, the underlying bricks crumbling with age, the mortar that had once held them together having disappeared a long time ago. The floor was littered with old magazines and rubbish, while the rest of the furniture, like the couch she was on, was old, the fabric ripped to shreds and the stuffing pouring onto the floor.

She turned her head slightly to see what was making the humming noise she had heard. It seemed familiar and then it came back to her. It was the same sound the Raynes made when they were talking to each other in that high-speed way she couldn't understand. They must have brought her here. She turned ready to call out to Leonara and Alena when a white flash next to her made her scream involuntarily and sit up quickly ignoring the severe burst of pain filling her head. A beautiful woman was looking at her steadily. Eva looked into the empty black eyes and her heart quailed with fear, she was not an ally.

The way in which the woman stared at her, the grotesque smile and the sharp teeth gleaming in the dim light when she opened her bright red lips, licking them slowly made her shiver with horror. The woman laughed when she saw the terror on Eva's face and leaned closer to her, breathing in deeply. Eva's eyes widened in disgust as she saw saliva drip from the red mouth.

'You smell so good!' the woman whispered, her teeth a few inches from Eva's face. She turned her face away, holding her breath for the woman smelt of rotting flesh.

'Don't touch her.' A sharp voice cut through the growing fog enveloping Eva's mind. For a minute she had actually felt safe and warm. The woman next to her reeled back with a contemptuous laugh and turned to her companion.

'*You* are ordering me?' she spat out.

'These are Darius' orders,' came the reply and another woman flashed into view.

'Darius wants her for himself. He will not share her with us,' the first woman snarled, but she moved away from the couch reluctantly.

'He promised he would,' the second woman smiled, 'And we have o choice but to believe him Savannah.'

The woman called Savannah growled half-heartedly in protest. 'She smells too good Marina, I cannot stop myself.' And she shifted slightly closer to where Eva cowered against the couch.

'She is not to be harmed,' Marina said again crouching low and Eva realised she had seen her before outside her building, the night she had been attacked. She was the one Nicholas had called a commoner. 'You will have to go through me to get to her.'

Savannah's eyes blazed with a terrible anger and Eva shrank back further as she turned and glared straight at her. And then she swept through the door, her enraged snarls echoing around the room. Marina looked after her, a bitter smile on her face. She turned swiftly to Eva but kept a respectable distance from her.

'You are lucky Darius holds you in such high regard and has an important use for you. Savannah and all the others would think nothing of killing you.'

Eva gulped. 'Where am I?'

'In our lair, hidden away from those damnable Elites. They will not find you here.'

'What do you want from me?' she asked her voice pitifully small.

'I would have thought that was obvious,' Marina smiled cruelly, her eyes fixed on Eva's throat. 'You got away before, but not this time. Savannah is right, you smell...' she moved so quickly Eva flinched. She was now kneeling next to the couch, her face close to Eva's white neck. 'You smell delicious,' she breathed, her rancid breath flowing over Eva's face so that she had to hold her breath to stop from gagging.

That heavy drugging fog was coming over her again and she felt sleepy and oh so warm and comfortable; she could feel her eyes getting heavier and even the smell was starting to lose its potency.

Marina put out a finger to touch the vein throbbing just below the white skin when a spark flew at her and she was thrown back forcefully with a harsh cry. Eva flinched and her eyes flew open to see the vampire sprawled several feet away. As she watched Marina stood up and shook her head in disbelief.

'What the hell is going on?'

Eva looked equally shocked.

'What did you do?' Marina growled again and flashed back to Eva's side, careful not to touch her.

'N...nothing,' Eva whispered, her heart thudding. She gulped wondering how she had managed to throw off the woman in front of her.

'Darius will deal with you,' Marina promised darkly and flew out of the room. Eva barely had time to digest her words before the door slammed shut and the lock clicked into place.

Chapter 39

So she was being held captive, and from the looks of it they weren't taking any chances. She shuddered and looked down at herself with a frown. How long had she been here? She was still wearing the same jeans and T-shirt she had worn to the club. She looked around for her jacket. She must have left it at the club, great! She had no idea what day it was but the daylight filtering through the tattered curtains next to her and the time on her watch confirmed it was ten o'clock in the morning. She cursed herself for following the tall girl from the club into the van.

Why had she done it? She had known even then that the van wasn't an ambulance, but she had felt so powerless and had been so grateful for the girl's help. She remembered how the girl had held her arm securely, refusing to let go. Was she a vampire too? Then how had she managed to touch her when Marina couldn't? But Marina too had managed to touch her that night in front of her apartment building.

She could still feel the pounding headache at her temples, but it was nothing compared to the pain she had suffered at the nightclub. A sudden thought made her gasp ...*the headache, the helplessness...I was drugged! But by whom?* All her drinks had been brought to her by her friends. Could they be involved?

Don't be ridiculous! She chided herself, none of them knew about vampires! Then who?

Maybe it was the bartender, a small voice inside her head suggested.

But why would a bartender do that?

Maybe because he was paid to whispered the voice insidiously.

Perhaps...but the girl? Maybe she wasn't a vamp the voice continued, maybe she was human, or maybe she was immune to whatever had affected Marina. The thudding at her temples had decreased and she tried to sit up gingerly. All this speculation wasn't doing her any good; she had to find out where she was and most importantly how she could get out.

She walked quietly to the door and turned the handle gently, praying it wouldn't squeak and alert anyone on the other side. She didn't want those women anywhere near her again. The door remained shut and she sighed, well it was worth a try. She headed for the single window.

Maybe she could jump out or yell for help. Pushing the disintegrating curtains aside she sneezed as the dust flew around her in a huge cloud. She looked through the dirt-caked glass but couldn't make out anything except for the wall of the building next door. Not seeing a latch she gripped the bottom of the window and tried to lift it up. It didn't budge. Taking a deep breath she tried again putting all her strength into the effort.

It creaked slightly and then after a few more tries, grudgingly lifted by a few inches. It wasn't much but she was grateful for the slight breath of fresh air, even though it was tainted with the smell of open gutters and rubbish. Anything was better than the unbearable stench in the room she decided as she gulped at it greedily. The gap wasn't big enough for her to look through and see the street below. Looking through it though she could just make out the surrounding buildings, which looked old and abandoned.

Her hope for rescue from that quarter was slowly fading away especially now that she realised she was on the third floor. Even if she could open the window and escape it was too high for her to land safely and looking around the room there was nothing she could possibly use to climb down. Besides judging from the state of the neighbourhood, no one was around to help her even if she could attract some attention.

She sat back down on the couch and stared at the faded wallpaper, trying desperately not to cry over the predicament she was in. *Nicholas will find me*, she thought. Just thinking about him cheered her up. She didn't know how long she sat staring at the wall, her mind discarding endless possibilities and ideas of getting out of the room.

Finally she glanced at the window and was stunned to see what little she could make out of the other buildings fading as the sun set. She had been left alone for the whole day with no food or water and now she realised how thirsty and hungry she actually was.

As the last rays of dim sunlight faded and the room darkened, she rose to close the curtains, leaving the window open. She had seen a light switch by the door. A dull yellow glow fell over the room, making the shadows in the corners appear more sinister when she flicked the switch. Not sure what to expect next, she sat down again and waited. Unconsciously she started scratching her right wrist. It had been bothering her more and more recently. She glanced at the bluish freckle and frowned, was it larger than before? She sighed it was probably nothing besides she had more important things to worry about. She sighed as she looked around the room again. Surely someone would come for her sooner or later.

It turned out to be sooner for she had barely made herself comfortable when she heard the door being unlocked. She sat up hastily and clenched her hands together to stop them from shaking and giving away how scared she really was. The door opened and a tall dark-haired man entered flanked by Marina and another woman she hadn't seen before. They all looked related from their flawless pale skin to their dark inscrutable stares. Clearly the man was in charge and Eva assumed he was the one Marina had mentioned...Darius. He strode forward silently and stopped a few paces from her.

For a minute no one spoke. Eva lifted her chin defiantly and held his gaze, refusing to break eye contact even when he raised an imperious eyebrow at her. His eyes seemed to overshadow his classic equine nose, full sensuous mouth and firm chin which had a slight cleft in it. Eva could easily imagine him being the most popular boy in high school and college with girls fawning over him. Oddly his good looks only made him appear more sinister.

'You have courage' he said slowly. Even his voice was sensuous, but with a dangerous undertone. 'No human I have met can hold my stare for so long.' He smiled and Eva's eyes widened as she caught a glimpse of his razor sharp teeth, sparkling in the dim light. 'I'm Darius, you have already met Marina and this is Lea.'

The shorter of the two women smiled, but Eva didn't respond. The woman was more petite than Marina, with a narrow waist accentuated by the long dress she wore from a previous decade. The golden curls falling untidily over her shoulders gave her the appearance of a young child. At any other time Eva would have liked her but the way in which her large hungry eyes were fixed on her face made shivers run down Eva's spine. She quickly looked back at Darius and found him sitting on a nearby chair.

'Marina tells me you have special powers. That she tried to touch you and couldn't. Why?'

'I...I don't know,' Eva admitted truthfully.

'I see, let's test them shall we?' He motioned Lea forward lazily and she moved in a blur, her skirts rustling, until she stood close to Eva.

He nodded when she looked at him and then lifted her hand. She moved it closer and closer until it seemed she would touch Eva's shoulder when a white spark flew from Eva and hit the blonde vampire, hurling her several feet into the air. She fell to the floor with a crash, but was instantly on her feet, an angry snarl ripping through her throat past the usually pouting lips. She flew forward in a rage but Darius had risen and now stood between her and Eva.

'Enough!' he commanded and Lea shrank back obediently throwing Eva a dirty look.

'Hmmm, this makes things difficult,' he mused, returning to his seat. He glanced at Marina. 'I have never seen this happen before.'

'It looks like some sort of protection...a spell...a charm,' she said slowly.

'Yes, it is old magic, but how do we get past it?' He stared at Eva contemplatively for a few seconds before a small smile stretched his lips. 'You have family.'

Eva felt as though a cold hand had just enveloped her heart.

'She has a mother,' Marina clarified, and the cold hand squeezed tighter, making it difficult for Eva to breathe.

'Like mother like daughter,' Darius intoned and a wicked gleam entered his eye, 'Is Marina right?'

Eva shook her head quickly, 'No!'

Darius laughed delightedly, 'I don't believe you. Tell us where she is.'

'Never!' Eva spat out.

'We will find her with or without your help,' he promised, 'but we will not hurt her if you help us.'

'No!'

'Maybe if you understand what we want,' he said soothingly, 'You see we don't want to kill you. All we want is your blood. You already know you are different from other humans.' He was almost crooning to her now, 'Your blood is strong, it gives us strength. Do you understand now? We can't kill you, otherwise where will we get another supply?'

'Take it from me then!' she gasped, fighting the lethargy spreading through her limbs his words had somehow created, 'Leave my mother out of this!'

'I would, but we can't get near you,' he looked at the women who were still staring at her. 'They need to know you are useful otherwise I won't be able to stop them.'

Eva looked closely at him, a plan forming in her mind. For a split second her mind cleared. 'You are lying!'

His eyes widened in surprise, 'What?'

'You heard me. You just said you can't get near me! Even if they tried, they can't do anything.'

Darius smiled dangerously, 'Ah you're right! But what about your mother? The Elites haven't got to her yet; they haven't put a charm on her. She is still vulnerable.'

Her throat constricted as he continued mercilessly, 'We will find her and when we do we will drain her blood until there's nothing left!'

'You wouldn't!' she gasped in horror.

'Do you want to take that chance?' he purred.

She dropped her eyes to the floor, trying to steady her breathing. Finally she said hesitantly, 'If I give you my blood...what happens then?'

Darius sat back with a small sigh and the lethargy invading her lifted some more, 'We won't hurt you.'

'I would be free?'

He laughed and shook his head, 'Free from this room, but not from us. You would be mine.'

'What?' she frowned, confused.

'You would give me blood whenever I wanted it. You would be my human, I your protector.'

'Your human? You would own me?' She was starting to feel sick.

'Yes, we have several, like the girl who helped you in the nightclub.'

'She's a human?' she looked shocked.

He nodded slowly. 'We feed off our humans whenever we are a little thirsty and they get whatever they want in return, usually protection. We call them *vassals*.' He smiled as he saw the confusion on her face. 'You're right, we also kill, if we are very hungry or we just want something new.' His eyes rested hungrily for a second on her throat, 'Let's just say this deal is very sought after.'

'But what if she told others about you?'

'She wouldn't,' Darius replied with a finality that made her cringe.

She knew instinctively what would happen if she did. He was staring at her ashen face and smiled gently. 'You know you would like being mine,' he said softly, 'even the blood taking isn't painful, in fact it can be quite pleasurable...for both parties.'

Eva shuddered and felt the nausea rising in her throat. Suddenly Darius' eyes shifted to the window and he frowned. She couldn't understand what had caught his attention until she heard a dull flapping sound.

'What the hell is that?' he growled with irritation.

Marina flashed to the window and threw open the curtains violently, almost ripping them off their supports. Outside Eva could make out a large dark shape hovering. Almost immediately it disappeared into the night.

Marina returned to her post by the door with a shrug. 'Just a bat.'

Darius turned back to Eva. 'I will leave you now to think about all this. Let me know by tomorrow.' He licked his lips quickly still staring at her, 'I think I'm ready for a drink.' He stood up and walked to the door. As he was about to leave he turned back. 'Marina will bring you some food.' With that he left, the women following him.

As the lock clicked into place, Eva slumped back against the couch, tears already pouring down her cheeks. Darius had made it very clear. She would either have to agree to give him blood and become his slave for all intents and purposes, or else they would murder her mother. She gulped for some air. It was a no-brainer; she wouldn't let anything happen to her mother.

Chapter 40

'Eva!' She looked up but she couldn't see anyone.

'Eva! Help me!' Again she looked around her.

The street was crowded people were rushing past intent on getting to work. It was warm and the buildings looked terribly familiar. She was back in California she was sure of it. She looked around again the voice calling her name was also very familiar.

Then she saw her. It was her mother running towards her through the crowd with outstretched arms. The people were just pushing past her, not letting her get closer to Eva. She couldn't move either and then she realised with a shock that there was someone running after her mother and she tried desperately to move but she just couldn't, the crowd was just too thick around her. As she watched in horror dozens of black clad figures with pale skin, black eyes and sharp fangs appeared through the crowd. They completely ignored her and started circling her mother.

'Mum! Run!' she yelled, trying to fight the crowd.

'Eva!' for some reason her mother stopped running and instead turned to face one of the figures in black…Darius.

'Mum don't! He's a vampire!' Eva shrieked as she continued to fight to get closer.

But her mother was now smiling at Darius and he was kissing her hand. Suddenly she lost sight of them. She continued to move through the crowd with difficulty as they pressed closer, her heart pounding painfully. Finally after what seemed an age the crowd parted and she could make out a huddle of cloaks in the centre.

She ran forward and they moved apart so that she could see her mother in Darius' arms. He was holding her close and she thought he was kissing her until she turned her head to the side and Eva saw his mouth firmly at her throat.

'NO!' she screamed and flew towards him, ready to rip him away from her.

'Get away from her! Mum!'

Her mother was smiling at her dreamily now and then her eyes closed and Darius lifted his mouth away. Eva couldn't speak. His mouth was bright red with blood which dripped down his chin and fell onto the sidewalk. His black eyes stared at her mercilessly and then he smiled.

'It's all your fault!'

She tried to say something but the other vampires came at her and everything went dark. She could hear flapping around her like dozens of wings and she knew it was the sound of the black cloaks as they moved around her.

Suddenly she sat up a scream on her lips and looked around expecting to be on the street with the vampires surrounding her. But she was back in the dark, smelly room again. She groaned and put her head in her hands, trying desperately not to weep with the horror of the nightmare. But the flapping, she could still hear it.

She looked around her expecting to see Darius, but the room was empty. Even the dishes from her small meal still lay on the table undisturbed. She listened carefully, there was that flapping again; she wasn't imagining it. She stared around her, slowly trying to place the sound until her eyes focussed on the window. It was definitely coming from outside the window. Or was it just the curtains?

She stood up and pushed the tattered curtains away and nearly screamed as a large black shadow swooped at the small opening. She fell backwards tripping over her own feet in her haste. As she lay on the floor stunned, her eyes still staring at the window, she started as a black bat, larger than she could have imagined, settled on the window sill, peering at her with its beady eyes. She felt a trickle of horror skim its way down her spine. She had never been afraid of the creatures but the prospect of spending time with one in this room was unbearable.

As she watched it clawed its way under the gap and sat on the threshold, still staring at her. She wasn't sure what to do, so she shuffled backwards, having heard that they carried several diseases. As thought it had read her thoughts it flew into the room and she shrieked, ducking behind the couch. Raising her head so that she could peer over the edge of the couch she found it sitting quite calmly on one of the chairs. She blinked in surprise as a light mist surrounded it and a second later it dissipated leaving her staring in wonder at the man sitting in the chair.

'Did you miss me?' he asked quietly, his silver eyes shining.

She jumped up and ran towards him, the tears flowing freely. She didn't care if he was a figment of her imagination. Throwing herself at him she buried her face in his shoulder and cried in great racking sobs. Nicholas, although surprised at her reaction, was more than happy to wind his arms protectively around her. He stroked her hair absently as he looked around the room not having expected it to look so horrible, listening for any sounds coming from the rest of the building. Satisfied that no one was going to enter the room any time soon he relaxed and concentrated on soothing the sobbing girl in his arms. They stayed like that for several minutes while Eva's sobs continued, dying away gradually until he felt her body relax against his. He tightened his arms reassuringly. She lifted her head, her face wet with the tears, her eyes bright red.

He smiled at her when she lifted a hand and childishly rubbed her nose. 'Better?'

She nodded and tried to move away suddenly self-conscious. He let her go reluctantly, there was no need to hug her now. Although that was exactly what he wanted to do. When he had seen her looking out of the window earlier he had felt so happy he hadn't been able to contain himself. To see that she was safe was like breathing oxygen again after being deprived of it for so long. He had been terribly worried about her and had finally taken Ashe with him to find Darius' new lair. Eden had offered to teleport into Eva's room, but he had refused, saying it was far too dangerous for her if Darius found out. Besides they had to find out what Darius was planning first. He watched her closely now as she shifted her eyes away from his shyly and awkwardly stood up.

'I'm sorry,' she apologised meekly, trying not to blush.

'No problem,' he replied, wondering why they were being so polite all of a sudden. He watched her try to walk away and stumble. Before she could steady herself he was out of the chair and lifting her easily into his arms. She was about to protest but the safe feeling of being in his arms was too good to resist and she relaxed involuntarily closing her eyes. He walked to the couch and sat down, depositing her next to him gently. 'Are you okay?'

She nodded with a tired sigh; all this was really taking a toll on her. 'I'm dreaming right?'

'No, I'm real,' he smiled, 'just like you.'

'I don't believe it! You were a bat' she complained dazedly.

'Would it help if I pinched you?' he asked amused.

She nodded sleepily and he gently pinched her arm, careful not to harm her. She yelped and her eyes flew open and stared at him as though for the first time that night. Before he knew it she had flung her arms around his neck saying, 'I am so glad you're here! I was so scared!'

'Shh…' he whispered stroking her hair again, 'You're safe.'

She pulled back, tears threatening again, 'They are going to kill my mum!'

He frowned. 'No, they won't.'

'But he said…'

'Nothing will happen to her, I promise. Leo and Eden are already on their way to protect her.'

Eva's looked at him in surprise, 'But how did you...?'

'I was listening in when he threatened you earlier,' Nicholas replied through clenched teeth as he forced himself to stay calm. When he had heard Darius it had taken all his willpower not to transform and kill him. In fact he had been so close to losing control he had flown into the window.

'The bat earlier? That was you?' He nodded and she turned paler. 'You can turn into a bat.' The idea was still incredible to her, and her tired mind hadn't yet processed it.

'And other creatures,' he shrugged, 'I told you, you had to see it to believe it!'

She shook her head to clear it. 'That's your talent?'

'Yup,' he replied laconically and then caught her hands in his. 'Don't worry it's still me. Plus I can keep a better eye on you.' He paused to watch as his words sank in. 'But we don't have time, it's almost sunrise and they might check on you before going to sleep.'

'What?'

'I'll explain later,' he promised hastily, 'but right now I need you to have faith and be brave. Leave your mother to us, and whatever you do, don't give your blood to Darius. I'll return tonight.'

'You're not taking me with you?' she asked in a small, confused voice.

'Not tonight, but you are safe as long as you keep the charm I gave you.'

'But...'

'Shh,' he pressed a finger gently on her lips, 'Trust me.'

She was about to argue when there was a small sound in the corridor. Nicholas leapt to his feet and flashed to the window. 'See you tonight, remember what I said.'

Eva watched aghast as he vanished and the bat sat on the windowsill for a second looking at her before it clawed through the gap and flew away, its huge wings flapping strongly against the wind. She turned away from the window, just as the door opened and Marina walked into the room.

'Not asleep yet?' she asked, looking around the room quickly.

'No, I uh...had a nightmare,' Eva explained weakly.

The vampire smiled sweetly, 'I'd expect a lot more in the future, if I were you.' She laughed at Eva's white face and walked out locking the door securely behind her.

Chapter 41

Fey Tanner smiled at the blonde woman as she put her purchases through the till. She owned the small shop just outside the city centre in Los Angeles, catering to all homeopathic needs. The shelves were packed to the ceiling with buddhas, good luck charms, aromatherapy oils, pot pourri and candles of every colour imaginable. At the far end bookshelves containing books on witchcraft, myths and spells stood in chaotic order.

She watched the woman walk out and then locked the door. It was almost five o'clock, closing time. Checking to see everything was stocked for the next day she walked into the back room to get her coat and bag. She lived several blocks away in an old apartment building on the second floor.

She hadn't owned a car in years, believing it polluted the environment. In fact she only used modern amenities with the utmost reluctance. Eva had had to plead for months before she relented and bought a cell phone, and that was only so she could keep in touch with her daughter in Erie.

As she walked home several people turned to give her a second look. Being almost forty-four years old, her skin was still smooth and unblemished, her hair fell in a smooth dark curtain down her back, and her eyes, the same violet as Eva's, sparkled with laughter. No one could believe she had a twenty-five year old daughter. But it wasn't her stunning good looks that caused people to stare. It was her dress sense. She loved vintage and rarely bought any new clothes. She preferred to hit the charity and second hand shops instead.

At the moment she was wearing an old T-shirt with a faded logo on the front, a small lime green chiffon scarf tied at her throat, a short red leather jacket worn out at the elbows and a long flowery skirt which skimmed the ground, its hem dragging in the dirt. Her black combat boots peeked out of its folds showing off their scuffed toes. Her large yellow bag completed the outfit, bouncing with every step she took.

Reaching her apartment building she unlocked the door and slipped in, oblivious to the three pairs of eyes trained on her. Leonara and Eden were perched on one of the nearby roofs following Fey closely. Leonara had already established that Fey unlike Eva was prone to her powers. She had entered the small shop, bought a few things, tempered with Fey's memory and left. Within an hour she was back to be greeted by Fey's puzzled face when she enquired about Eva.

'Do I know you?' she asked, frowning slightly.

'We met a while ago,' Leonara replied, smiling with relief. She had quickly left, erasing Fey's memory again.

They had kept a close eye on her since early morning. Neither Leonara nor Eden was sure about how to get her to the mansion but they knew Nicholas would be very upset if they didn't. They were still deciding on a strategy when Leonara lifted her eyes in time to see a stranger walk across the street and enter the same building. They already knew what Fey's neighbours looked like and this woman was not one of them. She nudged Eden and he followed her gaze.

'Who's that?' he wondered.

'No idea, but you'll have to find out,' Leonara replied.

He knew what that meant. He smiled at her and disappeared. He had aimed for the second floor landing. It looked deserted but he could hear footsteps on the stairs below. Quickly he teleported into the huge air vent running above the floor and peered down as the woman they had seen reached the top of the stairs. She looked around carefully and then walked deliberately to Fey's door. Maybe she was just a friend Eden thought. He could tell she wasn't a vampire from her scent. He relaxed slightly but continued to watch her. The door opened and Fey's puzzled voice reached him.

'Yes?'

So not someone she knew, he frowned, then who was she?

'I was wondering if I could have a word?' Fey looked surprised and nodded, letting the stranger into the apartment. Eden groaned silently and teleported back to where Leonara waited impatiently. He told her what had happened and she cursed.

'Relax, maybe she's just selling something,' he tried to reassure her.

'Really? Did you see any brochures?'

He shook his head slowly, worried now. 'But she wasn't one of us.'

'You know that doesn't matter, Darius still uses human vassals to do his bidding.'

'Well, we have to get her out of there,' Eden replied. Taking her hand firmly, he teleported both of them back to the landing.

Standing outside Fey's door they listened intently to the voices inside.

'So you have to come with me.'

'How did this happen?' Fey sounded distressed.

The two vampires exchanged glances, looked like the vassal had done her job.

'I'm not sure, but you will come?'

'Of course!'

They could hear movement and then footsteps approaching the door. It opened and the woman glared at them icily. 'Yes?'

'Uh…' Eden looked confused but Leonara stepped forward slightly, careful not to cross the threshold.

'We're selling advertising space in a new magazine.'

The woman's eyes narrowed suspiciously, 'Which magazine?'

'The Vintage,' Leonara replied smoothly.

'We don't want any space,' the woman replied an odd look on her face, and started to close the door.

Fey was peering anxiously past the woman's shoulder. 'Aren't we going?'

'Yes, but these people are outside,' the woman explained.

Fey looked puzzled. 'So?'

At a loss for words the woman opened the door wider and started to walk out. Leonara stood in her way and when the woman looked at her she blinked in surprise. Leonara was smiling at her, her silver brown eyes intense. Suddenly the woman closed her eyes and would have fallen if Leonara hadn't caught her. She laid her on the floor and looked up to see Fey looking horrified.

'Oh my god! Is she okay?'

'She's fine,' Leonara said reassuringly, 'May we come in?'

'Why?'

'We need to speak to you about Eva. Whatever this woman told you it isn't true,' Leonara said nodding towards the unconscious woman at her feet.

'She said my daughter's in danger!' Fey replied, shaking with emotion.

'No, she is safe,' Leonara said firmly. She smiled sweetly and a confused look came over Fey's face. 'Can we come in?'

'Yes, come in' Fey replied automatically in a daze.

Leonara stepped over the sleeping woman and entered the small apartment, Eden following closely. It was cluttered with books and candles. The carpet was old and the walls needed a fresh coat of paint. But it was clean and very homely, the feeling accentuated by the scent of freshly baked cookies permeating through the air. Leonara smiled and Fey's eyes cleared.

'Who are you?' she asked in a dazed voice.

'I'm Leonara and this is Eden,' Leonara introduced them and then led the way to the couch. 'We are Eva's friends.'

'Like that other woman?' Fey asked slowly, shaking her head in an effort to clear it.

'Not quite, she was lying to you.'

'What? Why?'

'We'll explain later, but right now we need to get you out of here.'

'But...is Eva alright?'

'She's fine,' Leonara replied.

Eden had been wandering around the room while they talked. When he reached the kitchen door he stilled and his eyes narrowed as the familiar scent hit him. He turned quickly to alert Leonara but a powerful arm pulled him into the kitchen. Leonara looked up and frowned at the sudden sound of pans falling.

Where was Eden? She rose up, her senses on high alert, when suddenly something flashed out of the bedroom and tackled her to the ground. Fey screamed and stood up hurriedly, watching in horror as Leonara fought the large man. He looked massive, built like a wall. Fey reached for her bag, about to pull out the can of mace she always carried with her when she became aware of another person behind her. Before she could turn round something hit her head and she blacked out, crumpling to the floor.

Both Leonara and Eden were still fighting when they heard the front door open and close. Leonara had just managed to grab her assailant's hands and was about to use her powers when he threw her off and flashed to the nearest window. Before she could reach him he had leapt out. She looked around the room and cursed soundly, Fey had gone. Hearing the noises from the kitchen she flew to the door to see Eden staring at the window.

'Are you alright?' she asked.

'Got jumped!' he replied incredulously. 'Where's Fey?'

'They took her,' Leonara replied agitatedly.

'How the hell did they get in?'

'The vassal...she must have invited them in,' Leonara guessed.

'We have to get her before Darius does,' Eden said grimly as he grabbed her hand and teleported them to the street below. Leonara followed Fey's scent while Eden scoured the surrounding streets. They had to find her, who knew if Darius would keep his word?

+++

Eva was exhausted. The lack of food and sleep whilst worrying constantly about her mother was starting to take a toll on her body and mind. She hadn't done anything the whole day and by the time sunset had come round she had almost been glad to see Darius stroll through the door.

'Have you decided yet?' he drawled.

For some reason he looked several years younger. She would have placed him closer to twenty than thirty now. She glanced at the two women by the door. They too looked much younger than what she remembered, what was going on?

'I...uh...need more time,' she replied haltingly.

Darius' face remained calm but his eyes flashed with suppressed anger. 'More time?' he mused. 'Okay, I'll let your mother know that her life hangs in the balance while you decide what to do.' He was about to leave when Eva stood up and blocked his way.

'My mother is here?' She could barely speak.

'She will be in a few hours. I'm sure she will be pleased with your answer after I've drunk from her.' He tried to move past her but Eva stood her ground even though her knees were shaking.

'Y...You said you wouldn't hurt her.'

'Yes, but I didn't say I wouldn't use her as collateral,' he replied with a smile.

'I want to see her first,' Eva said slowly, her eyes clouding over, 'I want to make sure she is okay before I agree to your terms.'

'Done.' He leaned forward slightly and inhaled deeply. 'Don't make me wait too long,' he whispered close to her ear, careful not to touch her.

Eva leaned back nauseated by his closeness. He laughed softly before pulling away and exiting the room with the women, leaving Eva to sag slowly to her knees and weep uncontrollably.

Chapter 42

Leonara and Eden stood in the living room shamefaced. They hadn't managed to find Fey and had finally decided to teleport back to the mansion to let the others know.

'YOU WHAT?!' Nicholas almost shouted when he heard their story.

'I'm sorry Nick,' Leonara raised her eyes to her brother's furious ones. 'We tried but they had planned the whole thing.'

He flung away to stand at the large window, his desperation knowing no bounds. He had promised Eva her mother would be safe. Now that she was in Darius' hands he could no longer keep that promise. If anyone knew Darius, he did. He clenched his teeth his jaw working agitatedly.

Seton glanced at his brother's rigid back before clearing his throat. 'We don't have a choice, we have to get Eva and her mother out of there, Darius is not bound by any laws. If I know his thirst for power he will keep them both as vassals.'

'With them on his side he could overthrow the Council and the Elders,' Eleanor said slowly. She stood up and walked towards Nicholas. Placing a hand on his shoulder she said, 'We swore to protect them, let's not fail now.'

He nodded and turned to the others. 'Once we are sure Fey's in the building we can go in.' He looked at Eden. 'Can you manage two passengers?'

'Hell yeah,' he replied, some of his cockiness restored.

Nicholas smiled in answer, 'Let's go.'

+++

Chris was at the police station going through the evidence they had collected from ICE and its surroundings on that fateful night. The nightclub was open again and the usual crowd of teenagers were flocking to it as though nothing had happened. His eyes fell on a crumpled car number plate inside a sealed plastic bag. It might be from the murderers' car he thought. He sent it and the rest of the items to the forensic lab downstairs and waited impatiently for the results.

He had asked for the number plate to be traced first. Within half an hour they had tracked down the model, colour and the type of tyres it used. But what made Chris's eyes widen in shock was the owner's name. In fact he had to look away rub his eyes vigorously and then look again at the report. Yup, there was no mistaking it…Nicholas Rayne. It was there in black and white.

Chris sat back exhausted and confused. How could he have killed all those people? And if he had then why had he come back to the scene of the crime? Was he just over confident or was it a ploy to mislead the police? But if that were the case why leave the number plate where they would find it? He stared at the report, frowning.

Nicholas Rayne…the powerful assistant district attorney, younger brother of Seton Rayne, a millionaire with estates and property all over the world, who donated lavishly to several charities. The Raynes were never in the media, keeping themselves to themselves, but anyone who was anyone knew who they were. It was their money that kept hospitals and research facilities open, their money that was poured into restoring old buildings around the country. Seton was the face of the family. Passing mention of the others in the media usually meant they weren't recognised in public unless they appeared at an exclusive event.

Chris shook his head, he didn't particularly like Nicholas, especially since Eva seemed to have developed a crush on him at the charity ball, but he couldn't believe he would be involved in something like this. He pushed a hand through his dishevelled hair, but evidence was evidence. He picked up the phone and dialled.

'Find Nicholas Rayne and bring him in for questioning.'

He replaced it tiredly, wondering not for the first time where Eva was. They had tried to find her, leaving numerous messages on her answering machine and her cell phone, but no one had heard or seen her since the party at ICE. Some people were already whispering that she might be dead. He clenched his hands into fists, if Nicholas was responsible, he would pay dearly.

Chapter 43

Eva's ears pricked up when she heard voices in the corridor outside her room. She sat up on the couch and waited, barely breathing. A few seconds later and the door opened. A huge man was carrying someone in his arms. Her mouth fell open as she recognised her mother's limp body. She stifled the urge to cry out.

The man dropped his load unceremoniously onto the couch and disappeared through the door, leaving them alone. Eva leaned over her mother's pale face, searching for any sign of life, her heart beating painfully in her chest. She watched with relief when her mother's chest rose slightly as she took a breath. She turned Fey's head to the side, searching her neck for any telltale marks. No holes. She could have cried with joy. At least they hadn't fed on her. She glanced at the window, hoping to see a flapping shadow hovering, but there was nothing there.

Her heart dropped with disappointment; she wanted to leave this place with her mother. She shuddered as she remembered Darius' foul breath caressing her skin when he had leant closer to her. She would rather die than have him feed on her and become his vassal. As these thoughts ran through her mind, her mother stirred and opened her eyes.

'Whe...where am I?' she asked groggily, trying to sit up.

'Be careful mum, you're with me,' Eva said, her voice cracking with the relief she felt as she helped her to a sitting position carefully.

'Eva?' Fey squinted at her daughter and threw her arms around her, hugging her tightly.

'Good to see you too mum,' she said, her voice muffled against Fey's shoulder.

'What's going on? Where are we? How did I get here?'

Eva sat back and sighed. She had a lot of explaining to do. Fey was looking around the room in horror. 'What is this place?'

'It's an abandoned building in Erie. Mum I don't want you to freak out okay?'

'Okay,' her mother said slowly.

Eva took a deep breath. 'We have been kidnapped by vampires,' she said in a rush.

'Vampires?' Fey shook her head. 'Eva, are you on something? I thought we agreed when you were fourteen that you wouldn't touch drugs.'

'And I haven't. Just listen to me; I can prove it all. But you have to listen.'

Fey sat back, a doubtful look on her face, her eyes searching her daughter's. Not finding any obvious sign of drug use she folded her arms and stared at Eva.

Taking another deep breath, Eva told her everything that had happened so far, from discovering the twin puncture holes on the corpses to the present moment. The only part she left out were her feelings for Nicholas. She didn't think her mother could handle that at the moment. Fey's eyes had widened considerably during Eva's story and now she leaned forward, gazing deep into her daughter's eyes.

'Mum? What are you doing?'

'Checking for dilated pupils,' her mother replied. Satisfied she sat back. 'So you're not on drugs, well, as far as I can tell. But vampires? There must be another explanation!'

Eva sighed, her mother wouldn't believe her until she saw them with her own eyes. Hopefully she wouldn't have to wait too long.

'In any case we have to get out of this horrid place!' Fey continued.

'Don't worry the Raynes will come for us,' Eva replied confidently.

'Are you telling me they were the ones at the apartment?' her mother asked suddenly.

'Yes, Leonara and Eden,' Eva smiled at her mother's horrified look.

'But they were attacked by those people, and I was going to use my mace...' she looked around, 'Where's my bag?'

Eva shrugged. 'It's not important, trust me.'

Fey leant against the couch. 'Then something hit me. I don't remember anything else, until I saw you looking at me just now.'

'It was Darius' vampires that attacked them. Do you believe me now?'

'I can't,' Fey replied helplessly.

Eva shrugged. 'You will.'

As she said the words, a familiar flapping noise came from the window and Eva looked round to see the black bat aiming for the gap.

'Mum,' she said urgently turning back to her mother, 'don't scream. That bat is Nicholas Rayne.' As she spoke the bat landed on the windowsill and crawled in.

Fey had been about to protest but her eyes widened and she gulped, but Eva was smiling with relief. As they watched the light mist surrounded the animal and Nicholas stood at the window, looking at them with a small smile. Eva couldn't help but notice how handsome and debonair he looked in his black wool coat over a crisp white shirt open at the neck, and beautifully cut black trousers. His face shone and his black hair looked casually dishevelled as he bowed formally to Fey.

'I hope I didn't startle you ma'am?'

Fey gulped again and shook her head in a negative.

'I'm Nicholas, one of my brothers will be along in a minute to help us.' He looked at Eva and smiled, but made no move to come closer. Eva was grateful; she didn't think her mother could have borne it. Nicholas was listening intently and then nodded, there wasn't anyone in the corridor. He looked at Fey.

'We have to leave now it's not safe. I hope Eva has told you everything?' He looked quizzically at Eva who nodded in answer.

Fey cleared her throat. 'She did but I can't believe her, except...I saw a bat and now you're here...' she shook her head. 'I'm not feeling well. This has to be a dream.'

Nicholas smiled at her reassuringly. 'You will feel better when you're away from here.' He was about to continue but his attention was captured by Eden suddenly materialising next to Fey.

She screamed loudly and promptly fainted on the couch. Nicholas moved with lightning speed towards Eva, shooting an exasperated look at his brother. 'Eden will take you to the mansion. Don't be afraid.' As he spoke he led her firmly towards Eden who had already lifted Fey easily into his arms.

'Hold my arm tightly,' he instructed Eva. She grabbed it and took a deep breath.

'I will see you soon,' Nicholas promised, as the door crashed open and Darius and at least a dozen vampires flew into the room.

'GO!' Nicholas urged and Eden teleported them away, not giving Eva a chance to protest.

'NO!' Eva screamed as buildings, streets and people blurred into indistinct shapes around her.

Chapter 44

In less than a second she was standing in the Raynes mansion, still holding onto Eden, tears pouring down her face. She could just make out the shapes of the family through them. Alena rushed forward and helped her to one of the white couches, while Eden lay Fey down on another. Seton came forward and examined Fey gently. Satisfied he nodded and shifted his attention to Eva.

'Are you alright?'

She shook her head, not registering his question, still unable to talk. They had left him, *she* had left him alone to face Darius and his horde. She squeezed her eyes shut, trying to block out the look of hatred on Darius' face as he had entered the room and the hunger evident on the others' faces. *They wouldn't...couldn't kill him...right?* She opened her eyes to see the Raynes staring at her sympathetically.

'We left him,' she whispered.

'Yes,' Seton nodded. 'We had to, to save you.'

She looked at Eden with wide eyes. '*Go back for him!*' she almost sobbed the words.

'We don't need to,' Seton replied, as Eden looked down and shook his head silently.

'But you can't leave him there!' she wailed in anguish.

'Don't worry,' Alena soothed her, 'He'll be okay.'

'No he won't! You don't know them! They will kill him!' Eva hiccupped uncontrollably.

Eleanor glided forward and sat next to Eva, patting her hand. Eva flinched involuntarily and Eleanor smiled.

'Love blinds us, my dear. You forget that Nick is one of us, an immortal; he is strong. He is stronger and braver than you can ever imagine.' She looked at Fey still lying on the opposite couch. 'You should think about your mother now. This will be very difficult for her.'

'Oh my god! Mum!' She had almost forgotten about her. She jumped up and kneeled next to her.

'She is fine, just fainted,' Seton said softly. 'I can wake her but you will have to reassure her.'

She nodded and he touched Fey's clammy forehead with one finger for a second and then moved back as her eyes fluttered and then opened fully.

'Mum, are you okay?'

'Yes, I...I just had the weirdest dream. We were in this horrid dirty room, you were talking about...' her voice trailed off as she looked around at the Raynes standing silently around them.

'Who are they and where are we?' she whispered.

Eva followed her gaze and smiled, no wonder Fey was surprised, the Raynes looked like models as they stood around the room. 'These are the Raynes. I told you about them remember?'

'Raynes?' Fey's face paled further. 'But you said they were vampires...' her voice faded away and she grasped Eva's shoulder. 'This is another dream right?'

'No, it's real.' She gestured towards her friends. 'You remember Leo and Eden?'

Fey looked at them and nodded slowly. 'You were at my apartment and those horrible people were fighting you.'

Both Leonara and Eden nodded, thinking it best not to upset her further by speaking.

Fey shuddered uncontrollably at the memory as Eleanor walked towards her. 'Can I get you something to drink?'

Fey recoiled when she saw the elegant vampire looking at her, and shook her head, but Eleanor smiled and motioned to Eden. He disappeared and reappeared with a glass of brandy.

'This will make you feel better.'

Fey grasped the glass as Eden handed it to her, and sipped at the golden liquid, looking away from Eleanor's warm gaze. She stopped trembling as the fiery liquid burned down her throat. For the next few minutes no one said a word as she drained the glass and sat back against the couch, Eva next to her.

'Better now?' Eleanor finally asked.

Fey nodded and found her voice. 'Thank you.'

The regal vampire inclined her head and sat opposite her. 'I know it's a shock for you, but everything Eva told you is true. You will feel better able to cope with it in the morning.'

Fey sighed. 'It just doesn't make any sense.'

'I know. We'll talk in the morning.' Eleanor rose and asked Alena to show Fey to one of the guest bedrooms. 'I've made sure your room is next to Eva's.'

Eva kissed her mother's cheek and watched as she followed Alena's slim figure out of the room. She turned to Eleanor once the door closed, only one thought uppermost in her mind. 'What about Nick?'

Eleanor sighed, she knew Eva loved Nick but she had never guessed at how much. But she knew if their roles were reversed she would have been standing in front of Seton shielding him from harm.

'You worry too much about him. Now, how are you feeling?'

'I'm fine.'

'Would you like some brandy?'

'No, thank you.' Eva had a stubborn look on her face now.

'In that case you should get some sleep, it's very late.'

Eleanor stood up before Eva could say anything else, and almost floated out of the room, followed by everyone except Leonara who escorted her to her bedroom.

'Leo…'

'Shhh…go to sleep,' Leonara said with a smile, leaving her outside a closed door, before walking away.

Eva opened the door and walked in slowly. She barely registered the beautifully appointed room. She was still thinking about Nicholas. She couldn't understand how the family could be so calm when one of their own was in danger. She closed her eyes as she leaned against the door and pictured his face. The pale skin; raised chin; the firm but mobile mouth, his hair all dishevelled so that she wanted to rearrange it and those eyes. His silver green-flecked eyes that laughed one minute and flashed with fury the next.

She sighed happily lost in her memories and then she remembered with a sickening jolt where he was and tears pricked behind her eyes again. She knew he was immortal, but she still didn't know enough about it to feel confident, the way Eleanor and the others had. Maybe they were right, she was worrying about nothing.

But Darius was immortal too right? But Nick could move really fast, not to mention become a bat! She took a small breath, plus the Raynes would have helped him if they thought he was in danger right? She shuddered, would they know if he was in trouble? Would they help? After all they weren't actually related. Her fears returned tenfold and the tears flowed silently down her cheeks again.

Chapter 45

Nicholas crouched snarling as Darius rushed forward. He stopped a few steps away and his eyes glinted with fury. He had seen Eva and Fey disappear and knew exactly who was responsible. The rest of his coven came to a standstill behind him once they realised who was facing them. Some moved back slightly, but Nicholas didn't notice. All of his attention was focussed on Darius. Suddenly Darius stood up to his full height, giving up his fighting stance. Nicholas was caught off guard but he wasn't taking any chances.

'So…you found me,' Darius drawled.

'You're difficult to miss brother,' Nicholas retorted as he straightened. He sent a withering look towards the others. 'Friends of yours?'

Darius flicked his hand and the room emptied.

'After all these years…' Darius shook his head. 'I always wondered which coven you had joined.' He sat on the couch and stretched lazily. 'Now I know.'

Nicholas refused to sit; he stood in exactly the same spot, watching Darius cautiously. 'Now you know, what of it?' he asked matter-of-factly.

Darius shrugged. 'It amuses me.' He turned his head to look straight into Nicholas' eyes, his own dark ones in direct contrast to the paler ones staring back at him. 'To think you are the Elders' lackey.' He grinned as Nicholas' eyes glowed ferociously.

'You know that's not true,' Nicholas said through clenched teeth, controlling himself rigidly, so that the muscles stood out in his neck. 'You chose your way and I chose mine.'

'You're right, I chose power and you chose to be a servant!'

Nicholas shook his head slowly. 'We will never resolve this Darius, you and I are too different, we always have been.'

Darius chuckled. 'You have always followed the Law and I never have, and yet your precious Elites can't touch me.' He glanced at Nicholas' set face. 'You know I will get her sooner or later.'

Nicholas took an involuntary step forward. 'You will *not* touch her ever again brother if you know what's good for you,' he said evenly.

'But I almost did,' Darius replied. 'Oh, don't worry, your pathetic spell worked but I did manage to get to her past you, not to mention her mother.' He licked his lips. 'Did you know she was that beautiful? I should have made her mine as soon as I found her.'

Nicholas shook his head. 'And we would have destroyed you, if you had.'

'With their blood in my veins, the Elders couldn't stand in my way, let alone the Elites,' Darius sneered at him.

'Darius, there is still time, stop coveting power. I'm sure we can put in a good word with the Council on your behalf.'

Darius snorted in disgust. 'The Council. They preach but they can't follow their own rules. Look at Eleanor. Such a powerful Elder and she fell with temptation.' He smiled, 'No brother, the time has come for a different way that allows us to be powerful, to rule over humanity as it was intended from the first. Nicholas we are gods!'

'If that is your decision, I cannot say more,' Nicholas said with finality and walked to the window. He turned to the figure still sitting on the couch, 'If you persist brother, I will have no choice but to fight you, even though our blood was once the same.' With that he transformed and flew out into the night.

+++

Eva wasn't sure how long she stood against the door. She felt a draught and opened her eyes to gasp in shock. Nicholas was sitting on the king size bed watching her intently. She blinked a few times and shook her head to clear it, but he was still there, except that now his mouth was twitching as he stopped himself from smiling.

'Are you planning on standing there all night?' he asked seriously.

She let out the breath she had been holding and shook her head. 'You're here.'

He shrugged nonchalantly. 'So it would seem.'

She moved slowly forward, desperately trying not to throw herself at him. She was still living down the embarrassment from the last episode. In fact her face was already turning slightly red as she thought about it. If he noticed he didn't say a word.

She stood next to him, looking at his face. Her eyes were devouring his features hungrily, trying to imprint them on her brain so that she would never forget. He moved slightly.

'There's plenty of room if you want to sit down,' he invited.

'When did you get back?' she asked, lowering herself onto the bed next to him.

'Just now,' he smiled, 'I decided to sit while waiting for you to open your eyes.'

She turned redder and looked away. It was painful to see his perfect face and remember how she had left him alone. 'I'm sorry,' she whispered, her vision blurring as more tears threatened. 'I shouldn't have left you there.'

'What?!' he looked shocked.

She lifted a shaking hand to her eyes to wipe them. He watched her and then gently turned her face towards him and looked closely at her tear-stained cheeks. She wanted to jerk away, cover her face so he couldn't see its haggard appearance and the redness of her eyes from crying too much, but his hand was firm on her chin, holding her captive as his eyes assessed her features intently.

'You're crying? Over me? Why?'

She shrugged half-heartedly, 'I thought...Darius would...' she gulped convulsively not able to finish the sentence.

He smiled and handed her a glass of water from the bedside table. She drained it and handed it back, feeling a little better.

He watched her for a second and couldn't stop himself from finally touching her nose gently with the tip of his finger. 'Silly child, I was never in grave danger.'

She looked at him through the tears, blinking in confusion. 'Really?'

'Of course,' he smiled and glanced at the clock on the bedside table. 'Time for you to sleep now. We will talk later.' He stood up.

'C...could...could you...?' she blushed as he looked back at her.

Understanding the unspoken request he nodded. 'I'll stay. But don't worry, Darius can't enter the Mansion.'

Reassured she slipped between the covers. Almost as soon as her head touched the pillow, she fell into an exhausted dreamless sleep. Nicholas watched her and sighed with relief when her breathing became more regular. Darius' words were still echoing in his mind. He had to speak to Eleanor and Seton soon, they would know what to do to protect Eva and Fey. He settled himself into a nearby armchair and prepared to wait for Eva to wake.

Chapter 46

'You are upset?' Seton asked his wife as they entered their room.

Their master bedroom was on the other side of the Mansion, tastefully furnished with a king-sized bed, dressing table and seating area near the picture window looking out at the now dark grounds surrounding the house.

Eleanor walked past the bed and into the walk-in wardrobe. Seton followed her and together they opened an invisible door in the back wall leading into a huge windowless room. For all intents and purposes it resembled an ancient library. Books and scrolls were placed on all the shelves, crammed until no space could be seen between the tomes. There was a large wooden table in the centre with several open books on its surface. All around it piles of more books and scrolls stood in disarray. Eleanor paced to the far wall leaving Seton to sit at the table, watching her.

'She is in love with him,' Eleanor said slowly in a hushed voice.

Seton didn't answer, he was studying her face intently as she moved closer. Several emotions flitted across her smooth features, but they were all overshadowed by despair.

'We knew that,' he finally said gently.

'But not to this extent!' she contradicted. 'Human love is fleeting, we've seen it before over the ages.' She shook her head. 'This is different. It is too strong!' Her eyes became icy as she said the words.

'I know it's the law but...' Seton's voice trailed off as his eyes met hers. What he saw in them silenced him.

'This is how it started all those years ago,' she replied gesturing to a large leather bound book placed in a position of honour on a stand in a glass case near the wall.

He glanced at it and paled. The book was covered in worn leather and weighed like a ton of bricks. The writing in it was golden, written by an immaculate hand in an ancient language. It was their history, something every Elite was required to study.

'What do you propose?'

'We have to meet with the Elders, this has gone far enough. It's not safe for the Bloodline to remain here.'

'And Darius...'

Eleanor sighed. 'They will decide.'

'You know Nick will never agree to do that,' Seton said, avoiding her eyes.

'If the Elders command it, he will. After all, blood has been spilt before.'

Seton wasn't so sure.

+++

Eva woke up and stretched languidly. The sun was filtering through the curtains, bathing the beautiful room in a golden glow. As her eyes adjusted to the light, she glanced around her. Suddenly she sat up; all the events of the past two days came flooding back. She looked around frantically for Nicholas and then saw him seated in the armchair smiling at her. She smiled back and caught her reflection in the mirror opposite the bed.

The smile disappeared quickly. She looked like something out of a really bad zombie movie! Her eyes were still bright red from all the tears she had shed, her face was pale and tired-looking, and her hair...she closed her eyes in horror. Her hair was mussed and stood out in all directions. She took a deep breath and nearly gagged; *what was that smell?!* She lifted her hand slightly and her eyes flew open in shock. It was her; the smell from the room she had been held captive in had permeated into her clothes and skin, making her smell like a butcher. She jumped out of bed quickly, about to apologise but Nicholas was already standing next to her.

'Good morning.' He raised an eyebrow as she scooted away from him.

'Don't come near me, I stink!' she gasped.

He laughed softly. 'Fine, I'll leave you to get cleaned up. Alena has left some clothes in the closet.' He waved at the myriad of doors along one wall and let himself out silently.

Having had a shower and made use of the marble bathroom and its various lotions and perfumes she emerged to find some clothes. The closets, as she had expected, were crammed full of beautiful clothes she was too scared to touch. She managed to find a pair of designer jeans and a fairly simple looking white T-shirt made of the softest cotton. She walked out of the room a few minutes later after throwing her dirty clothes into a laundry basket she'd seen in the bathroom. She never wanted to see them ever again.

Walking along the carpeted corridor wondering where everyone was she heard laughter. She followed the sound, entering a dazzlingly white kitchen complete with stainless steel worktops and a breakfast bar. Nicholas was seated at the bar, while Alena busied herself at the stove. Kane was tinkering with the radio. As she entered Alena smiled at her and motioned to a seat.

'Sit!' she ordered and turned back to the stove.

Kane handed her a steaming cup of coffee with a wink. She smiled gratefully and sipped at the strong-flavoured drink. She could feel Nicholas' eyes on her but she was too shy to meet them.

'What are you cooking?' she finally asked Alena.

'My special pancakes and amazing omelette,' she replied, busily flipping a pancake whilst beating the eggs simultaneously. 'Hope you like it.'

'I'm sure I will. Thought you guys didn't eat?'

'Oh, sometimes we like to play at being the perfect American family,' Nicholas replied and nodded towards the patio doors opening onto the grounds and a grassy tennis court. Two figures were flashing around the court, so that Eva couldn't quite make out who they were.

'Who's that?' she wondered aloud.

'Ashe and Leo,' Kane yawned. 'They're playing tennis, our way.'

'Seriously?'

'Yeah they're pretty good,' Nicholas said as Alena placed a plate piled high with pancakes in front of Eva. A second plate appeared with a fluffy omelette filled with cheese and ham.

'Bon appetit!'

Eva's eyes widened. 'Are you guys eating too?' She couldn't imagine one person eating so much at one sitting.

'Yeah but ours is special,' Kane replied as he opened the refrigerator door and flung some steaks at Alena. She caught them deftly out of the air and put them on a frying pan.

Eva looked away as she served them on plates, still very rare, the blood still evident on them. She averted her eyes and ate her food as Kane took a mouthful of the bloody meat.

'Chow time!' Alena called out.

Before Eva could turn round, two blurs materialised at the breakfast bar and started eating. Leonara and Ashe smiled at her, but continued with their meal. Within seconds the four vampires had finished and there was no evidence of their meal. Leonara and Ashe excused themselves and left.

'Where are they going?' Eva asked still trying to finish her first pancake.

'Ashe is in high school and Leonara is working at the research centre downtown,' Kane replied. He winked at Alena, 'We'd better get a move on too, girl.'

She shrugged. 'Plenty of time.' Eva's confused expression made her explain. 'I'm a dance instructor and Kane is a swimming instructor at one of the high schools.'

Normal jobs? Did vampires do that? She looked across at Nicholas who was still watching her. Well, he was a lawyer she supposed. She readjusted her thinking. They weren't blood feasting monsters like Darius and his lot. She shuddered involuntarily. Just thinking about him was enough to bring back the fear she had felt. She smiled a farewell when Alena and Kane left a few minutes later, leaving her alone with Nicholas.

'Did you sleep well?' he asked conversationally.

'Yes, thanks.' She glanced at him shyly. 'Did you stay the whole night?'

'I promised didn't I?' he asked his eyes amused.

She nodded, she hadn't really expected him to, but she was very glad he had. 'Has mum woken up yet?'

He shook his head. 'She was very tired, so Leo made her sleep a bit longer. It gives us time to talk.'

She nodded in understanding. He obviously didn't want Fey to hear more than she had to.

'Finished?' he was looking at the empty plates and she nodded. 'We'll be more comfortable in the study.'

Chapter 47

He stood up and led the way to a smaller room across the corridor from the kitchen. He settled himself into an old leather couch, while she perched nervously next to him.

'Go ahead,' he invited, leaning back slightly so that he could watch her easily.

She looked at him surprised. 'What?'

'I know you have a load of questions,' he explained with a knowing smile.

She blushed; he was right, she did have a load of questions she was dying to ask. 'I don't know where to start.' She sifted through her mind as he watched her silently. Suddenly she raised her eyes to his and she knew immediately what she wanted to say.

'Can you be hurt? I really need to know.' It was for the sake of her sanity, if he was ever in danger like last night.

He shook his head. 'I'm immortal Eva, and I'm an Elite. I can't be hurt by just anyone. Only another vampire can harm me.'

'Like Darius?' she asked slowly, her throat closing up.

'Yes,' he looked thoughtfully at her, 'but he wouldn't.'

'Yeah right!' she retorted, sceptical of the certainty in his voice, she wasn't so sure. 'What makes you say that?'

'He wouldn't because...' he sighed uncomfortably, not entirely sure he should tell her. 'We are brothers.'

'WHAT?!'

'When we were still mortal, we were brothers. He was my younger brother.' He watched her eyes widen as his words sank in.

'But...he's so evil!' she whispered, 'and you...' Her eyes took in his perfect features, so different from Darius'. He scared her as soon as he walked into the room while Nicholas exuded comfort.

'He wasn't always like this. It's his lust for power that led to this.' His eyes dimmed as he remembered what had happened all those years ago.

He glanced at Eva's intense face and sighed inwardly. Why was he always compelled to tell her everything even if he really didn't want to? It was as though she could pull the truth out of him.

'We were part of an ancient family, rich and powerful. Our days were spent hunting, attending parties and being the most eligible bachelors of London's Ton. All the debutantes wanted to marry us, but we were too wild to settle down.' A slight smile flitted across his face as he remembered his youth, but it quickly disappeared as he continued.

'And then it all changed. I still remember the day Darius found our great grandfather's diary. He became obsessed with it. It talked of life after death, of being able to live forever, to be as handsome as we were then. Possessed by this need he frequented all the lowest places he could find, hoping to find and convince a vampire to turn him.

'I tried to stop him, God knows I did, but he wouldn't listen. It is said if you look hard enough for something you can even find God. He found what he was looking for.' Nicholas was staring intently out of the window. His clouded gaze seeing the crowded London streets, the dark alleys, and finally the sumptuous ballroom where his brother had found him.

'I remember the night it happened when he told me. He looked so much younger and full of life. He wanted me to share it with him; he called it a gift. But I shunned him; it was an evil I wanted no part of. That night as I slept he entered my room and turned me against my will.' His voice had changed subtly taking on the accent and feel of the English gentleman who had lived so long ago. He turned his head slowly to look at her and she couldn't help gasping at the anguish in his eyes.

'I left, I would not feed on humans as he wanted me to. The Elites found me, starving, on the brink of death and still too stubborn to feed. They had heard of our change. They took Darius and I to Italy, to teach us, to keep us safe and to keep humans safe from our voracious appetites. Once we could control ourselves we returned to London and led normal lives. We faked our deaths once it was convenient to do so, having made sure our family would still go on. We took on different identities and continued to learn about our kind in Italy under the Elders. When it was time they wanted to see our powers. I had shown the promise of transformation, a shape-shifter.

'But Darius couldn't perform any particular feats. They sent him forth as a commoner, for they had seen his dark nature and his craving for power. They placed me with Seton's coven. As you can imagine Darius' anger knew no bounds and he vowed to overthrow the Elders.'

He glanced at Eva who was leaning forward, absorbing his words like a sponge. She continued to stare at him curiously, not sure what to say or do. He was obviously still hurt by his brother's actions, even after two centuries.

He smiled casually, trying to lighten the moment. 'That's why he would never hurt me.' He had reverted back to his old self.

She sighed and sat back slightly. His explanation did make sense. 'And the others knew?'
'Of course!'

That explained a lot. 'So you can also put spells on people?'

'Yes, like the protection charm. Only the Elites can touch you as long as you have the charm I gave you.'

'I see.' She bit her lip as another question surfaced. She wasn't sure if Nicholas would answer it but she just had to ask. 'Darius...well he...he spoke of *vassals*.' Nicholas remained silent as she fumbled for words. 'Do you have them too? I mean...do the Elites have *vassals*?'

'No, that practice was invented by the Dark Ones. We kept *vassals* centuries ago, but technology has advanced so far that they are no longer necessary.' He sighed, 'That power demeans humanity. *Vassals* are not their own masters; their master controls their will. They are slaves.'

'But how does that happen? Are they under a spell?' Eva was trying desperately to understand what he was saying.

He looked deep into her eyes, wondering if he should tell her the truth. Once again the large violet eyes staring back at him seemed to drag the words out of him.

'When a vampire feeds on you, part of you joins him. He is more powerful than you, and so he controls you. When you are both equally strong it only makes you both stronger.'

'But how can a human be as strong as one of you?' she asked confused and a little freaked out. She was trying not to show it, but her hands were trembling at the mere thought of what she had been prepared to do to save her mother from Darius.

'Never a human, but if two vampires exchange blood they become tied for eternity, stronger together than apart.'

'Two vampires? You mean like...Seton and Eleanor?'

He nodded. 'It's our way of marrying, but it is so much more. We call it the *Cruor Acquiesco* - the blood agreement. No one can break it, and no one can come between them.'

He let himself imagine them sharing the agreement, being inseparable, so strong that even the Elders couldn't part them. It took an effort for him to come back to reality and focus on Eva again. They could never be together like that; he wouldn't let anyone turn her.

'That's amazing!' Eva breathed, her eyes wide. She had never imagined all this existed in the same world she had inhabited a few months ago.

Nicholas shrugged with an easy smile at her awed reaction. 'We have many rituals.' His eyes travelled over her clothes, taking in the T-shirt and then following the line of her arm to her hand resting over the other one, rubbing idly at a spot on her wrist. His eyes narrowed and he froze.

Eva frowned, why was he staring at her like that? She looked down at herself; wondering what he was looking at. The T-shirt moulded to her body perfectly and she blushed as she wondered if he was looking at her curves. But it wasn't her body he was staring at; he seemed to be looking intently at her right wrist. She stopped rubbing it when he suddenly reached out and caught her wrist gently, turning it towards him. She looked up in surprise to see him frowning.

'What's wrong?'

'How long have you had that?' he asked in a strained voice she had never heard before.

'Uh, since I was a kid, I guess. The doc said it was just an unusual freckle.' She shrugged nonchalantly, wondering why he was asking.

He touched the faint blue spot gently, and then pulled his hand back. 'Has it changed since you were a kid?' he asked, trying to sound mildly interested.

'I think it's a little bigger and maybe a bit darker.' She was looking more and more puzzled as he continued to stare at it. 'Why?'

He shook his head and smiled. 'Nothing just curious.'

But she wasn't fooled. He still looked shaken. She had never thought anything could make him look like that. He was always so self-assured and confident. He now looked as unhinged as she always seemed to feel when he told her more about the vampires. It was odd, the way he kept darting quick glances at her wrist when he thought she wasn't looking. He had changed the subject, and showed no inclination of returning to what was pre-occupying both their minds. She rubbed her wrist protectively, something wasn't right.

Chapter 48

She took a tentative step forward. It was so dark she couldn't see anything in front of her. She knew buildings surrounded her, but she didn't know how she knew that. Suddenly she caught the faint smell of iron, and knew instinctively it was the smell of blood. She tried to stop, but her feet carried her forward, deep into the darkest parts.

She could finally see a dim light further ahead, as though she was reaching the end of a long tunnel. She moved faster trying to ignore the smell, but it was all around her now making her gag. As the light grew brighter she could make out figures. Dark cloaked figures crouching on the ground. Her heartbeat increased rapidly as she took another step forward and heard a splash. She looked down to see a huge puddle. It drenched most of her leg and the smell intensified. She knew it was blood, not hers because there wasn't any pain, but it was from someone she knew. It was as if someone had whispered it in her ear. She opened her mouth to scream when one of the cloaked figures flew at her. Bony fingers clutched at her throat stifling the scream.

She woke up gasping, clawing at her neck desperately. Her eyes opened to see her room, the moonlight shining through the curtains. She stared wildly around ready to fend off her attacker, but the room was empty. She lay back, wiping the sweat off her face. Sarah had been having similar nightmares ever since she had witnessed the massacre in the alley. Not being able to sleep for the past two weeks, she looked constantly tired and the dark circles under her eyes had intensified each day.

She still hadn't heard from Eva and each day dreaded someone finding her body. The rest of the team was worried too but they had a lot on their minds. The lab had been extra busy since the ICE massacre. That's what the CSIs were calling it. To a man they had sworn to find the murderers. Crime was committed all the time, but when it was directed at one of their own it became intensely personal. Most of the other cases had been pushed aside as the police and the CSIs worked extra shifts to uncover the culprits responsible for that night.

+++

'She has the Mark!'

'Are you sure?' Eleanor sat next to Seton, staring at Nicholas in shock.

They were in the hidden library in the master bedroom. Eva had gone to check on her mother and Nicholas had sought out his brother, eager to speak to him.

'Yes!' he almost hissed and put his head in his hands. 'This is getting too complicated.'

It was bad enough that Eva was a mortal and one of the Hunted Bloodline, but this? Having the Mark was the worst thing that could have happened. He still couldn't believe it. He could hear Sylph, one of the Elders telling him about it. It was a severely debated topic amongst the Elders.

'Describe it,' Eleanor ordered.

'It's the Mark. It's blue, slightly raised, about two millimetres in diameter on her right wrist,' he almost groaned, this shouldn't be happening.

Eleanor sighed and looked at Seton's set face. 'I thought she looked familiar when I met her.' Perhaps too familiar! She had hoped to make the girl disappear but this new development had effectively destroyed her plans.

'You think she knows?' Seton asked slowly.

Nicholas shook his head. 'I don't think so, she thinks it's a normal freckle.'

Seton nodded and looked away, *what were they going to do?*

As though she had read his thoughts Eleanor's voice broke into his concentration. 'We have to tell them.'

'But...' Nicholas tried to protest but Seton was nodding.

'I agree,' he said looking apologetically at Nicholas, 'They will know what to do.'

'Like, kill her?' Nicholas asked sarcastically.

Seton shook his head. 'You know they will never do that now.'

'Do I?' Nicholas almost laughed out loud. 'I would have thought they'd be glad to.'

Seton's eyes pierced his brother's suddenly, 'You don't know the half of it. Did Sylph never mention it?'

Nicholas shook his head, puzzled. He thought he knew everything about their history, but Seton's question made him wonder just what was being kept such a secret, even from him. Seton noticed the confused look on Nicholas' face and glanced at Eleanor. He didn't know what to say.

Nicholas looked from one to the other. 'What is it? You have to tell me sooner or later.'

Eleanor nodded. 'You're right, but it may be better if Sylph told you. She is after all the historian.'

He sat back, his arms folded. 'It must be something big then if she has to tell me. But whatever it is, I won't let Eva be harmed.'

Eleanor looked deep into his eyes for a long second seeing the determination there and nodded. 'Understood.' She sighed. 'We have to go to the Reliquary. We leave tomorrow.'

+++

When she was told they were leaving Erie, Eva was stunned. 'But where are we going?'

'Italy,' Nicholas replied, looking away from her.

'Italy?!' She had always wanted to visit Europe but this didn't sound anything like a vacation. 'Can you tell me why' she asked tentatively.

Nicholas' face remained passive and he shrugged. 'We have business there and we can't leave you here alone.'

She nodded automatically, not believing a single word he had just said. Something had happened. Something big and she had an odd feeling that she was responsible; to be more specific the itchy freckle on her wrist was responsible. She had never given it much thought, but when Nicholas had questioned her about it, she had stared at it for ages, trying desperately to see what he had. But no matter how closely she looked, all she saw was a slightly raised blue spot, hardly anything at all. She had even asked her mother about it, but Fey had shrugged.

'It's always been on your wrist, even when you were a baby.' She paused, lost in thought before saying, 'But I do remember it became red at one point and we had to use a cream on it. Then it quietened down, became a little bigger and that was it.'

Eva sighed, none of that had explained Nicholas' reaction and now they were jetting off to Italy? Maybe she would learn more once they got there. Looking at his face now, she knew he wouldn't tell her anything else until then.

Preparations for the trip were already underway. Besides Nicholas and herself, Seton and Eleanor were also going. The rest of the Raynes were staying in Erie to look after Fey and continue living as mortals to stop suspicions arising. Eva had asked about Fey's safety, but Nicholas had squashed any worries she may have had by making sure one of the family was always with her. He also asked Eleanor to give her a protection charm, much stronger than the one Eva had.

Eva was relieved when all the safety arrangements for Fey were made. She didn't want to leave her mother anywhere Darius could find her. She had called the lab and asked for some time off. They had agreed immediately, knowing she had been at ICE during the massacre. In fact her superiors were just glad to know she was alive and well. When asked why she hadn't contacted them till now she had quickly lied and said she had been given strong painkillers for a migraine that had kept her sedated. Matt had talked to her briefly and mentioned the deaths.

'What?!' Eva paled, clutching the cell phone tightly, 'How many Matt?'

She could sense his unease as he replied, 'Fifteen.'

She had almost dropped the phone in horror. Fifteen of her colleagues had died and she hadn't known? Several questions popped into her mind. Did Nicholas know? Had he known all along? And if he had known why hadn't he said anything? Even now as she sat next to him in the plane, he appeared distant, almost closed off from her. His face was grim and his eyes were hard as he watched the in-flight movie on his personal monitor. She didn't know how, but she knew he wasn't really paying attention to it. It was as though his mind was elsewhere. In fact all the Raynes looked uncomfortable. Seton and Eleanor were seated across the aisle from them and were also staring at their screens, not moving. They all seemed obsessed with their innermost thoughts.

Chapter 49

They landed in Rome in the early morning. A luxury saloon was waiting for them. Seton got behind the wheel, Eleanor taking her place next to him, leaving Nicholas and Eva to settle into the backseat. She wasn't sure where they were going but as soon as they left the airport she didn't care; the sights and sounds of Italy delighted her. The old buildings looked so stately and magnificent. She could almost pretend she was in a bygone age and glancing at Nicholas, he looked like he was still part of that bygone age. He pointed out several interesting features she would have otherwise missed.

Seton drove as fast as he dared through the traffic. On the whole, she wished they could have spent more time in the city exploring with Nicholas by her side. But the Raynes were eager to reach their final destination. They were still very friendly and looked after her well, yet there was something different in their eyes and manner when they looked at her. But she just couldn't put her finger on it.

Suddenly she heard Seton say something. She leant forward, frowning. If she really concentrated she could just make out what he was saying.

'I think you should tell her. It will be less of a shock if she knows.'

Nicholas looked at the driver's seat, his face uncertain. 'It might scare her. Plus they might not approve.'

'Who wouldn't approve?' she asked, regretting her words immediately when Nicholas turned sharply towards her.

'What?!'

'I said, who would not approve?' she repeated, her eyes wide, her cheeks turning slightly red under his scrutiny. He looked shocked and when she looked at the front both Seton and Eleanor were very still, listening intently.

'You could understand us?' Nicholas asked slowly.

They had been speaking in the high-speed vampire way, which to humans was undetectable or at the very most a low hum. He shook his head thoughtfully, it was worse than he had thought. They all knew what was happening but none of them had expected her to progress so quickly. He had hoped all this was a coincidence, but he remembered how he had thought she was exceptional even when they first met.

'Yes, if I really concentrate,' Eva answered, looking baffled. 'Is that weird?'

'Yes,' he said flatly and then met Seton's eyes in the rear view mirror.

They seemed to exchange an odd look, and almost immediately the car slowed down and they pulled into a side street, coming to a stop. Simultaneously Seton and Eleanor exited, walking away and leaving Eva and Nicholas alone.

'What did I do?' Eva asked even more puzzled.

'Nothing, you're just very special,' Nicholas assured her with a warm, sad smile that made her heart turn over. He looked uncomfortable and she felt like a child who had done something wrong and its parent was trying very hard to hide the reason why. *Special? Was he kidding?* That was making her feel even worse in fact it was starting to scare her.

Some of what she was feeling must have shown on her face because he sighed and pushed his hand roughly through his hair, a sure sign of discomfort. 'Okay,' he took a deep breath, 'the others want me to tell you where we are going. I suppose they're right, but I need to tell you a lot more for you to understand and I'm not sure you're ready for it.'

He looked closely at her and she nodded. 'I'm ready. I mean it can't be worse than what I already know right?'

He smiled. 'You can decide after you've heard what I have to say.' He shifted so he was more comfortable and a faraway look came into his eyes as he remembered the past. 'Do you remember the Elders?'

She nodded, prepared for a long story.

'No, I'll have to start further back.' He paused. 'In the beginning, God created the angels. They were divided into three categories, the Triads. The first two were the angels of Heaven, they protected God and Heaven, rarely coming to Earth to deal with mortals. The third Triad were divided further into three groups. The Principalities, Archangels and the Angels. They were more involved with humans, but it was the Angels who were sent to guide mankind. They were the messengers between Heaven and Earth.

'To help humans, God granted the Angels special powers like telepathy, so that they could plant ideas into their minds unobtrusively. Some were more powerful, able to control the weather and the elements.' He looked at her trying to judge her reaction, but she was looking at him calmly. And not for the first time he thought how singular she was. Anyone else would have told him he was crazy, freaked out and probably tried to run away, but not her.

'They could not appear in front of mortals but some of the Angels weren't careful and humans caught glimpses of them. They believed them to be gods and so they started to worship them, and called them the Olympians and various other names.'

Eva's eyes widened, 'As in the Greek gods of Olympus?' She couldn't believe what she was hearing.

'Precisely,' he nodded, 'Some of the Angels started to believe that they were gods, put on Earth to control man. They still had their powers and they still helped people, but only for their own pleasure and only the selected few. Seeing their weakness, God became angry and punished them by cursing them to live on Earth, banished from Heaven until they repented. Once they realised what they had done, several of them repented and returned to the old ways, but many refused to do so.'

He sighed, his face grim. 'The two factions fought each other. Only an Angel can kill another Angel. Many died as a result. Since their powers were no longer part of Heaven, they remained in the world, free to find suitable hosts... mortals.'

He watched as Eva's expression changed slightly. She was beginning to understand where this was headed, but she remained silent and let him continue.

'The Angels who returned to the old ways are called the Enlightened Ones, the Elders. They are the original Angels that didn't die during the battles. They have a duty to find the mortals who now have the angelic powers, make them immortal, and teach them to help humans. Only when all the powers from the original Angels are found can there be any hope of Salvation.

'But even now, once they have been converted, there's still the age-old lure of the Darkness. The Elites are the most powerful after the Elders. All our powers found us when we were still mortal, and we all survive on animal blood. It's part of the original curse. The Dark Ones, who are against helping humans and want to still dominate them as gods, like Darius, are cursed to drink human blood and live in the dark.'

Eva looked away thinking. Darius' name still sent shivers down her spine, but it all made sense, except one thing. 'If the Elites and Elders are so powerful, why not defeat the Dark Ones?'

'Because we would lose the powers again,' he replied softly. 'We believe in negotiating, and hope we can bring them to the light eventually. We control them at the moment, but it is a tenuous balance. Not all the Dark Ones have powers. But they have been recruiting and turning normal mortals which is forbidden. We try to stop them, but we are often too late.' He smiled at her. 'Had enough yet?'

She shook her head and swallowed, trying not to show how scared she really was. 'Not yet.'

The gravity on his face told her he was deadly serious. This was not fiction, although a part of her wanted it to be just that.

'It's just a little unbelievable,' she whispered uncertainly.

'Like a story, but it's not. That's what's so scary isn't it?'

She nodded. 'I guess, but like all stories there's always a good guy right?' And she knew exactly who she would have picked for that role.

His lips twitched. 'And I guess you expect me to be the good guy?'

'You're perfect for the part,' she laughed shakily, wondering if he could read minds. 'But you still haven't told me where we are going exactly.'

'The Elders' headquarters in Vatican City.'

'The Vatican?' she looked at him surprised. Of all the places she had expected the Vatican hadn't even remotely made the list. 'You mean it's near the Vatican?'

'No, I mean in it. Actually it's under St. Peter's Square to be more precise.'

'No way!' Eva shook her head, 'That's crazy! Didn't they excavate the area before building the square?'

'Yes, but there is a huge Necropolis under the city and they are still discovering it. Besides it's easy to stay invisible if you know people in high places,' Nicholas shrugged, his eyes twinkling at the double entendre. 'We also use charms and spells to keep humans away from us, and you would be surprised how many well-known people are actually Elites living as normal mortals.'

'Wow,' she breathed.

His easy manner all of a sudden was seriously affecting her breathing and her heart rate had tripled. She hoped he hadn't noticed or hopefully thought it to be because of all he had told her. Thinking about it, she couldn't imagine anyone suspecting that the biggest lair of vampires was under the holiest place on Earth, visited by thousands of people every year. Although having heard Nicholas' story where else would ex-angels reside? She shook her head slowly, never in a million years would she have thought all this existed if she hadn't seen it for herself.

She looked up as the car doors slammed and the engine came to life. Seton and Eleanor were back and Nicholas was nodding at Eleanor as she raised an eyebrow in query. He turned his silvery gaze back to Eva, catching her unawares.

'Okay?' he asked, looking carefully at her, noting her slightly flushed cheeks and her slight breathlessness, trying to detect what she was really feeling.

She didn't appear scared, but he knew from past experience that she was very good at masking her feelings. He felt relieved, he had expected a much more explosive reaction, but again he had misjudged her. All he could see was a burning curiosity. He had expected her to act like any other human, and had forgotten that she wasn't like other humans. He frowned; that fact reminded him of the Mark, something he didn't want to think about, not yet at least, and he hoped she wouldn't ask him anything he couldn't answer.

She smiled in answer. She saw his frown and bit her lip. She wanted to ask him so many things, but she knew that she probably wouldn't get the answers. She was still puzzled about this whole trip and his reaction to the freckle. And why was she now able to follow their high-speed conversation? She scratched at her wrist absently. So many questions that needed answers but suddenly she wasn't sure she wanted to find out.

Chapter 50

'And therefore x is equal to sixty-four...'

Mr. Caldwell's droning voice reverberated through the silent class. Most of the students looked suicidally bored, barely managing to keep their eyes open, while the few who weren't comatose were exchanging notes or were busy on their cell phones.

Ashe yawned and looked out of the window that overlooked the football pitch. The cheerleaders were in full swing despite it being a frosty day in April. He spotted Eden warming up on the side-lines, ignoring the girls as they called out to him. Ashe turned his attention back to his classmates. As his eyes moved around the room, several of the girls smiled coyly at him. He barely acknowledged them. Ever since he had moved to Erie, the girls had been hoping for either of the Rayne brothers to ask them out. The two brothers were thought to be the best-looking students the school had ever seen. Their extra-curricular activities on the sports teams had also elevated their status. Teachers loved them too, because their grades were consistently high.

His eyes fell on the blonde sitting in the centre of the room. She was easily the most attractive girl in the school, coming from one of the richest families in the state. And true to form Taylor Vaughn was the most spoilt girl he had ever met. Her group of girls always surrounded her doing everything she wanted them to. Most of the guys in the school were also her groupies and were constantly asking her out. Until a few months ago she had been seeing the captain of the football team. But when she realised that he was no longer as popular as the Rayne boys, she had dumped him like a hot potato and single-mindedly pursued Ashe and Eden. Eden was a master at disappearing whenever he saw Taylor approaching, so it was usually Ashe who had to fend her off.

Today she was wearing a pink miniskirt, which in Ashe's opinion was something even a hooker would blush to wear. Teamed with a tight black T-shirt and six inch stiletto heels. Her face as usual was impeccable, the makeup flawless. She was a stunning girl, he had to admit that much, but nothing about her seemed genuine. It was a picture that was too perfect. He quickly looked away as she turned towards him. Mr. Caldwell was busily scribbling on the board again. Ashe sighed, school was becoming tedious; he wanted to be in Italy with the others. Racing exotic cars and sipping champagne with the gorgeous models he always seemed to find. Sometimes his powerful senses came to very good use.

Something fell on his desk and he frowned. It was a note and he didn't need to look round to see who it was from. The perfume on it practically screamed her name. He opened it lazily, taking his time. He knew she was fidgeting with impatience. Waiting would do her good.

Are you coming to my party this weekend?

He smiled to himself. The party Taylor hoped would be the best thing ever seen in Erie for the past decade. He wrote back, his handwriting neatly formed.

I haven't decided yet.

He folded the note again and flung it casually towards Taylor. He didn't turn to see her face but he knew she wasn't happy. The party would only be a success if all the popular kids turned up, and at the moment Eden and Ashe were on the top of that list. He had never considered high school parties to be a lot of fun. They were full of pretty girls and muscled jocks, all wanting to get wasted on the cheapest beer available. He would have to check with Eden anyway, he might want to hit it after they had been to the underground racing circuit.

He looked around the room again, his eyes coming to rest on a small dark-haired girl sitting as far away as possible from Taylor's group. She was nothing like the other girls. Dressed in tattered jeans, sneakers and a baggy T-shirt under a hooded black jacket, with her hair hanging straight down her back and no makeup on her face, she resembled a geek in every sense of the word.

Lainey was the brightest student in the class and Ashe knew that she had a kind heart. She constantly helped the jocks with their homework or tutored the prettier girls. But for all that she was still an outcast. Not fashionable enough to hang out with Taylor. As far as he knew she didn't have a lot of friends. He looked thoughtful; maybe they *would* hit Taylor's party after all. She had invited only selected students, so it was very exclusive, but she had no say about who those students came with, right?

+++

Lainey bent to pick up her books from the floor. Jerks! She thought as she blocked out the laughter. Five boys had pushed her aside and her books had fallen all over the corridor.

'Hey let me help you with that.'

She turned her head in surprise. A tall, blonde-haired boy was kneeling next to her picking up her history textbook. She knew he was in some of her classes, what was his name again? Oh yeah, Ashe. She hadn't paid him much attention. Having learnt from an early age that good-looking people preferred the likes of Taylor, she simply blocked them out of her conscious mind. But even she had been awed by his gorgeous face. She distinctly remembered that he had an equally gorgeous brother in the same school. He handed her the books and she smiled her thanks before standing up awkwardly.

She was about to walk away when he said, 'You're Lainey right?'

She stopped in her tracks, surprised that he knew her name. 'Yeah,' she frowned, 'Why?'

He shrugged, 'Just curious. I'm Ashe.'

'I know,' she replied and started walking towards the front doors of the school leading to the car park.

'So what are you doing after school?'

He was still there, walking next to her? What was this? Some kind of bet? She looked at him with a raised eyebrow. 'Why?'

He smiled, 'Just asking.'

'If you need help with your homework, just ask,' she said tiredly. *Why else would this gorgeous guy be talking to a nobody like me?* she thought, hefting her backpack further up her shoulder.

'Help?' He sounded amused.

'Yeah, is it maths?' she asked, remembering seeing him in Mr. Caldwell's class earlier.

'Uh…no, but thanks.' He walked next to her till they got to the car park. She was dying to know what the deal was.

'Okay what do you want?' she asked finally, coming to a sudden standstill and turning to face him.

Ashe looked taken aback. 'Nothing, I just thought we could hang out.'

'Hang out?' she asked incredulously. 'You and me?'

'Yeah, you know, grab some coffee or something.'

'Okay what's the bet?' she asked desperately, looking around for a group of jocks eagerly watching them. But she didn't see anyone.

'There's no bet Lainey, I'm just trying to be friendly.' He smiled disarmingly. Wow she was really wound up.

'Well, stop it. It's unnerving,' she snapped and marched to her small car.

As she drove out of the car park she barely glanced at him as he waved farewell. *Crazy! Didn't he know she wasn't popular? That she wasn't like Taylor?* She glanced down at her clothes and laughed out loud. He must be really dumb if he thought she was one of that group!

Chapter 51

Ashe found Eden lounging against the inconspicuous car they used for school. The Raynes tried to fit in wherever they could. Following that rule meant not throwing their wealth around and much to Ashe's disappointment, no flashy cars. Eden winked at him in greeting.

'So how was your day bro?'

'Alright,' Ashe sat in the passenger seat as Eden gunned the engine. They didn't notice most of the girls in the car park turn round to watch them drive away.

'Are you still up for the underground this weekend?' Eden asked, glancing at his brother.

'Uh...I meant to talk to you about that,' Ashe began slowly.

'What? Too scared to be beaten...again?' Eden teased.

Ashe clenched his hands. 'No.' He took a deep breath. 'What do you think about going to Taylor's party instead?' He shut his eyes knowing the answer he would get.

'You must be kidding! Blow off a race to hang out with that girl? Are you crazy? Man, what are you on?' Eden laughed incredulously. 'Don't tell me you've fallen for her?'

'Ugh!' Ashe made a face. 'No way! But I figured we could help someone out.'

'Really?' Eden looked at him long and hard, steering the car by instinct. 'And who are we talking about?'

'Lainey.'

'Lainey?' Eden frowned trying to place the name. And then his eyes widened in disbelief as a face popped into focus. 'The quiet brainy girl? How would we help her exactly?'

Ashe shrugged. 'If we go with her to the party, the kids will look at her differently. And,' he added wickedly, 'It would drive Taylor insane with rage! Wouldn't you love to see that?'

Eden shook his head slowly, staring at the windscreen. 'Does she want to be like them?'

Ashe thought about that for a second. 'I don't think so, if she did I'd lose respect for her.'

Eden agreed; he couldn't stand the in-crowd and their pretentious exclusivity. He had seen too much of the world to believe only in appearances.

'So we're not helping her,' he said slowly.

Ashe sighed in resignation, 'It seemed like a good idea at the time!'

'Let me guess, you were bored and were sitting in Caldwell's class right?'

'Yeah and Taylor was right there...' Ashe shook his head. 'She needs to be taught a lesson.'

'All in good time. So we're back on for the race?'

'I guess,' Ashe replied, looking out of the side window. Even though he wouldn't take Lainey to the party he decided to continue being friendly. After all there was no harm in that!

+++

Lainey bit her lip and glanced out of the corner of her eye. She could feel his eyes on her and she didn't like it. Or did she? She couldn't quite make up her mind. For the past few days Ashe had been very friendly, talking to her in the halls, saving her a seat in the classes that were too crowded, although she had declined politely. Even the jocks had stopped pestering her and she had a feeling he had something to do with that too. *But why?* That question stayed uppermost in her mind. *Why would he help her? What was in it for him? The most popular boy in school lowering himself to talk to her? It was unbelievable!*

She darted a look at the other side of the class. Taylor was glaring at her furiously. *If looks could kill...*Lainey thought.

Clearly she had noticed Ashe's behaviour and it infuriated her no end, that he would rather spend time with that mouse than with her. She was surrounded by her usual fawning friends and one or two of the boys were sending her notes, but she only wanted Ashe to look at her, like he was looking at that nobody. She seethed, *what did he see in her anyway?*

Lainey slumped further down in her seat, trying to become invisible. She was good at that; always had been. Only the teachers really noticed her and that was only because of her high grades. Otherwise they wouldn't either. The hairs on the back of her neck rose slightly, but she refused to look up. Ashe was still staring at her. Since he had helped her pick up her books a few days ago in the corridor, she had managed to find out that he wasn't the typical jock she had expected him to be.

His grades rivalled hers, even though he rarely paid any attention in class, and she wanted to laugh at herself for thinking he needed her help with his homework. He didn't stray anywhere near Taylor or her crowd, kept himself to himself and seemed on the surface at least to despise the attention he naturally attracted. *An enigma*, she thought, as she tried desperately to ignore him.

As soon as the bell rang she leapt out of her seat and literally ran for the door. She didn't know what was worse, Ashe's friendliness or Taylor's obvious hatred. But she wasn't going to stick around to find out. He unnerved her and she had heard what happened to people Taylor didn't like. It was the end of the school day and she hotfooted it back to her car, eager to leave.

She left the school building and stopped dead in her tracks, causing a few people to slam into her from behind. She barely noticed their muttered curses. Standing right next to her car was Ashe. Hadn't she left him in class two seconds ago? How had he got here so fast? She considered turning round and walking in the opposite direction, but Taylor's too loud laugh was coming from the hall behind her. She took a deep breath and walked slowly towards the car and the gorgeous boy next to it. Maybe if she moved quietly he wouldn't notice her. She frowned when he picked her out from the crowd and smiled. *Damn! So much for being invisible.* She sighed in resignation and having reached the car unlocked it quickly.

'Trying to avoid me?' he teased, leaning casually against the bodywork.

'Yes!' she snapped, dropping her books onto the backseat. She turned to see his amused face. 'Why don't you leave me alone?'

'Good question,' he frowned and then shrugged. 'No idea. I guess I like people who are different.'

'You mean geeks?' she asked caustically, causing him to raise an eyebrow.

'If that's what you think you are, you couldn't be more wrong,' he said gently, surprising her into silence. She had been about to reply rudely, but his tone of voice touched her.

She blushed and looked away. 'Just shows how much you know,' she countered lamely.

'I know a lot Lainey. For example,' he pretended to think. 'I know you're really clever, you don't get swayed by people's appearances and you are kind.' His eyes crinkled at the corners. 'And apparently you don't make friends easily.'

She humphed and was about to get into the car when he stopped her with a hand on her shoulder.

'I don't make friends because there's no one here worth being friends with,' she replied defensively, suddenly close to tears and not knowing why. He had touched a raw chord. She shrugged his hand off.

'You're wrong. Not everyone is a jerk,' he answered, a small smile lighting his face. 'Don't cut yourself off from people Lainey, it's very lonely.'

'I think I can handle it, but thanks for the advice Einstein,' she said sarcastically, getting into the car and slamming the door shut.

He watched as she left the car park. He had the oddest feeling. A small voice in his head was prompting him to follow her. But why? He looked towards the main school entrance and frowned. Taylor stood with her cronies glaring at him. He had no doubt that she had seen him talking to Lainey and that just increased his uneasiness. He had seen the cruelty etched on her features and he knew she would go to any lengths to get what she wanted.

A few minutes later and he was running behind Lainey's car, still not quite sure why. He had let Eden know he would get home late and had ignored the questions in his brother's eyes. Now he was running through the quiet streets of Erie's suburbs, trying to avoid humans.

He sensed rather than saw Lainey. Eventually they reached her house and he stood behind a large tree across the street and watched as she left the car in the driveway and jogged up the shallow steps to the front door. The house was large by Erie standards. Clearly her family wasn't poor and that surprised him. *Did she dress the way she did purely because she wanted to? This was one interesting human,* he thought. He sensed that she was alone in the house and sighed. He didn't know what he had been expecting to happen, but that small voice stayed with him, prompting him to stay just a little longer.

Chapter 52

Lainey opened the front door and walked into the empty house. She passed through the vestibule and headed up the long winding staircase to her bedroom. She entered and slammed the door shut. It was a mess as usual. Books littered the floor and half of the bed. Her desk looked like an explosion had occurred.

She dropped her backpack on the floor and fell onto the bed, closing her eyes. She hadn't been able to stop thinking about Ashe during the drive home. He still puzzled her and his words continuously rang in her mind. She squeezed her eyes tight shut, trying to force him out of her mind. He had almost made her cry! *No one has been able to do that since kindergarten*, she thought tiredly. She had never let anyone get close enough to do that. She even kept her family at arms' length.

Her workaholic father and her constantly criticising mother rarely had time for their daughter's problems. Her brother had left home to go to college a year ago, leaving her stranded. She had always looked up to him and spent all her time with him. Now that he was gone she tended to bury herself in her books rather than actual people. Maybe Ashe was right. He had seen right through her and she despised him for that.

On an impulse she stood up and walked out of her room and into her brother's room next door. It still smelt the same; his clothes and books were where he had left them. This room was in direct contrast to hers. Where she revelled in chaos, he preferred structured order and not for the first time she heard her mother's voice in her head.

'Why can't you be more like Steven? Look how tidy and well presented he is. You look like a frump!'

She shook her head to dislodge the memory and turned to leave when she heard a sound. She looked back, her hand on the doorknob. The sound had come from the en-suite bathroom. No one else was at home; no one ever was at this time of day. But it had sounded like a bottle bouncing off a hard surface. She turned towards the closed bathroom door and reached out to open it.

It's probably just a cat, she thought, stamping down firmly on the twinge of fear. The door swung open and she started in surprise. A petite girl stood in the middle of the floor holding a shampoo bottle. Her hair was dishevelled and her clothes were in rags, but through the dirt on her face, Lainey could tell she was beautiful. The stranger stared at her in horror and then sniffed. Lainey was about to move forward to comfort her when the girl's dark eyes stopped her dead. They didn't look friendly or remotely sad. They looked terrifying.

Lainey swung round to run through the bedroom door but the girl was already there. Her little pink tongue licked at her red lips. The movement caught Lainey's attention and she stood mesmerised. A cold dread was seeping into her limbs and she couldn't move. She blinked and the girl was right in front of her. A lethargy was spreading through her body and she felt sleepy.

Maybe all this is just a dream, she thought tiredly. She felt so heavy and tired all of a sudden.

'LAINEY!'

Was that what she thought it was? No way, she was definitely dreaming, he couldn't be here. She struggled to open her heavy lids and saw the girl leaning closer to her. Suddenly something threw the girl against the bedroom door, making Lainey fall to the carpeted floor in a daze. She opened her eyes wider to see the small girl slumped on the floor and then felt herself being lifted gently and deposited on her brother's bed. She watched confused as someone dragged the dark-haired girl out of the room, as she snarled like a wild animal. The door slammed shut so she couldn't hear anything else. She didn't know how long she lay on the bed, but when she opened her eyes again Ashe was looking down at her worriedly.

'Are you okay?' he asked, his eyes travelling the length of her body and making her blush. She nodded and sat up slowly. 'What are you doing here?'

'Uh...' he looked confused. 'I was in the area.'

'Oh,' she accepted it without question and he sighed inwardly with relief.

'Where's the girl?'

'What girl?' he asked innocently.

She stared at the closed door. 'The small dark-haired girl.'

'There's no girl Lainey, you fainted and I heard the crash of bottles in the bathroom. So I investigated and found you on the floor unconscious. I put you on the bed,' he explained easily.

'No,' she shook her head. 'There was a girl and her eyes were so...scary. I wanted to run, but she was there at the door so fast and then I felt sleepy and I heard you calling my name.'

He was nodding now. 'Yes, I called out to you when I was coming up the stairs.'

She looked at his innocent face and sighed. She could have sworn she had heard his voice from behind her. She glanced at the only window in the room, expecting it to be broken or at least open, but it was firmly shut, like it always was. She touched her temple uncertainly.

'Are you sure you're okay?' he asked again, watching her intently.

Where was Leo when you needed her? he thought with exasperation. He had taken the female vampire down the stairs, locked her in the kitchen cupboard and called Eden for help. As soon as Eden had arrived they had over-powered the girl and Eden had held her securely in his arms as he teleported them to the Mansion. Ashe had flashed back to the bedroom, dreading what he would find. He half expected Lainey to be dead; he wasn't sure he had arrived in time to save her.

She stood up shakily now and he immediately steadied her with an arm around her slim waist. He thought she was going to protest and was surprised when she let him help her to her own room. He made her sit on her bed and promised to return as soon as he could. Running down the stairs, he found a bottle of brandy in the kitchen, measured out a small dose in a glass and then loped up the stairs, making sure he moved at a normal human pace.

'Wha...?'

'Just drink it, you'll feel better,' he ordered.

She sipped at the dark liquid and gasped as it slid down her throat. 'Mum will kill me for drinking this,' she managed to say between sips.

'I think she'll understand,' he replied, relief flooding over him. She looked shaken but he hadn't seen any fang marks on her skin, even though the strange vampire had looked starved. Was she one of Darius' coven? Why was she here? This was Elite territory. He frowned deep in thought...and why Lainey? She wasn't part of the Hunted Bloodline. Was this a plot against the Elites? And how had he known something would happen today?

He had stayed behind the tree, feeling foolish until suddenly he had felt another vampire's presence. He had gone closer to the house expecting a vampire to pass along the street. But when the scent had come from inside the house and mingled with Lainey's he had leapt up the wall and opening the window had seen Lainey swaying from the lethargy vampires created in their victims before feeding.

The girl had been holding her and was bending towards Lainey's neck, her fangs glistening wickedly as they almost touched the fragile white skin. He hadn't thought, just acted by instinct and apparently called out her name. Launching himself at the vampire, he had thrown her back against the door with enough force to stun her, whilst he picked up Lainey from where she had fallen. When he had grappled with the girl she had fought back, but he sensed she was weakened from lack of blood and had quickly overpowered her. He wasn't sure what they would do with her, but he knew one thing for certain, he would not let her harm Lainey.

Now he sat next to Lainey and watched as she drank the rest of the brandy hesitantly, colour returning to her cheeks. He left the house a few minutes later, when she professed she was feeling better. Once outside, he stayed in the shadows, patrolling the area in case the rest of Darius' coven was nearby. Once her parents returned he felt she was safe enough and returned to the Mansion eager to find out more about their captive.

Chapter 53

The Raynes had been talking amongst themselves in a completely different language as they drove through the city. *Probably to stop me from understanding them*, Eva thought as she rested her head against Nicholas' shoulder. He automatically put his arm around her and shifted so that she was more comfortable. He saw Eleanor's look of disapproval, but ignored it. She may have been an Elder at one point but even she had relented to the call of love. How could she expect him to be strong against its power when she had caved in so completely?

They reached Vatican City at last and Eva leaned closer to the windows to take in the massive stone walls, several inches thick, surrounding the city. They passed through the gates where, after several security checks by the Swiss Guards, they were allowed to enter the most sacred Christian stronghold. The streets were teeming with tourists and devotees, all of them there to experience the Vatican, home of the only true monarch in Europe. She had heard a lot about it, but had never thought she would ever visit it.

They parked the car and she followed the others as they walked through the crowds, towards St. Paul's square, and headed for an ordinary looking building on the south side of the square. They entered it through a heavy wooden door leading into a musty corridor. Seton locking the door securely behind them. Eva expected them to continue walking but they stood still listening. She looked up at Nicholas' severe face puzzled.

'What are we waiting for?'

'Shh,' he cautioned and then she felt a draught.

A man was standing a few feet away, dressed in the blue, red, orange and yellow raiment of the Swiss Guards, the military force of the Vatican. He approached them and spoke to Eleanor and Seton in a low voice in rapid Italian. Eleanor answered him in what Eva considered a regal tone of voice and he stood back. Raising both hands, he faced the stone wall and muttered an incantation. The wall seemed to disappear in front of her stunned eyes and the Raynes entered the dark opening following the guard. She held back uncertainly but Nicholas grasped her hand and urged her forward, pulling her with him.

They entered a dark passageway and she heard a rumble behind her. Looking back she could make out the stone wall, intact once again. The passage was lit with flaming torches held in the wall sconces. Their flickering light lent the place an eerie feel that Eva didn't really care for. The deep shadows between the fire lit areas made her shudder and involuntarily think of Darius. It was only Nicholas' firm grasp on her hand that prevented her from baulking and running back the way they had come. The passage seemed to widen and then double back on itself before opening onto a landing. They descended several flights of stairs, following the guard deeper and deeper underground. Having followed the man for what seemed an eternity, they reached the bottom step, facing an ornate door.

Eva peered around Seton's shoulder to see it better. The door must have been constructed several centuries previously. It was made of a heavy wood she didn't recognise, with metal studs and reinforcements all over it. Carved intricately with religious symbols. The guard again lifted his hands and uttered a few words. The door swung open slowly and they walked through. Another dark passage led them deeper into the dark until she felt she couldn't walk any further. Just as she was about to say as much to Nicholas, the passage widened and they stood in front of another door.

This one was more ornate than the last and Eva gasped when she realised it was made out of pure gold, studded with jewels. It shone dully in the flickering light and opened at the guard's command. He vanished and Eleanor led them forward into a room of indescribable beauty. It was a long banquet hall, with ornate chairs placed along its entire length. A different symbol was carved on the back of each. They were all empty except for the ones standing on a dais at the far end of the room.

As she walked forward, Eva couldn't help but stare at the treasures the room held. The floor was inlaid marble. Ancient tapestries which hung on the stone walls; depicting battles and Greek gods; brushed shoulders with artistic masterpieces long lost from the outside world. The high vaulted ceiling had a gothic feel, further enhanced by the lack of windows. *No wonder,* she thought, *they were probably several hundred feet below the earth's surface.*

She shifted her attention to the dais. Several people were either sitting on the throne-like chairs or standing behind them, each as stunning as the Raynes. The ones sitting on the thrones seemed to emit a glow, which made her think of heavenly beings. She felt no fear, only a calm, lulling her senses gently.

Nicholas glanced at her, trying to gauge her reaction. She appeared unafraid and he was glad. He didn't feel as secure as he looked at the Elders. They obviously knew they were coming to meet them, he thought. He glanced at Eleanor; she must have sent a message beforehand. They reached the shallow steps leading up to the dais and stopped, no one was permitted to walk up those steps except the Elders and the Machai, spirits used to protect the Elders, who were standing behind the thrones.

'Welcome,' a voice boomed out, startling Eva who grasped Nicholas' hand more firmly.

All the Raynes bowed in answer and Eva followed suit. She glanced at the man who had spoken. He wore a small crown on his fair head, his golden curls falling about his shoulders. His handsome face shone with an inner light making him appear painfully gorgeous. All the people on the dais were dressed in flowing silks and satins from a bygone age, giving her the impression of being in a royal court.

'It is a pleasure to see you again, Eleanor,' one of the women sang out. Her platinum blonde hair fell to her waist and when she smiled the whole room seemed to light up.

'You too sister,' Eleanor replied courteously.

Eva stared at her as the two women exchanged nods. *Sister?*

The woman on the other side of the golden haired man nodded at Eleanor but Eva felt it was a cold greeting.

'You look well.'

'So do you Arri,' Eleanor replied, turning to her, her voice tinged with hauteur.

There was no sign of the warmth she had shown to the silver-haired woman. Arri's eyes narrowed. She was just as beautiful as the others with deep red hair arranged in a thick plait over one shoulder. Before Eva could look questioningly at Nicholas, the man cleared his throat, dispelling the tension.

'Seton, Nicholas.' He looked at Eva and frowned thoughtfully. 'And guest.'

'This is Eva your Grace,' Nicholas introduced her quickly.

'Eva,' he nodded at her, his silvery eyes seeming to pierce her soul and she gasped, bending her head low as though he had made her do his bidding without lifting a finger. He turned his attention to Eleanor.

'She is the One?'

Eleanor nodded and Eva could see his indecision. Abruptly he glanced behind him and one of the men leant forward obediently.

'Take them to their rooms. Fulfil their needs,' he commanded, and then looked at the group in front of him. 'Rest, we will speak later.'

Without another word they all bowed again and followed the man through a small door to the side of the dais. Eva looked back at the Elders and saw them talking to each other in hushed tones, their heads close together. The golden-haired man's eyes met hers just as the door closed behind her.

Chapter 54

What had he meant when he had said is she the One? The One for what, exactly?

They had been escorted to a suite of rooms, furnished as though for royalty. They all had separate rooms with a shared living room. As soon as they entered the suite, the guard disappeared at Eleanor's command. She had so many questions but the Raynes didn't look as though they would welcome them. She turned to Nicholas. Seeing her worried face he smiled and led her to one of the bedrooms.

'This is yours,' he explained. She barely looked around the luxurious furnishings.

'Great,' she said hastily, dismissing it completely, wanting to talk about what was bothering her. 'Nicholas, I really need to talk to you.'

'I know,' he sighed and for the first time she noticed the worry lines on his face. He looked tired and more on edge than she had ever seen him.

She had a sudden urge to smooth away those lines and her hand lifted involuntarily. But she checked herself as he lifted his eyes to meet hers. She didn't know how he felt about her and she wasn't so forward as to ask him. Her hand dropped to her side and she looked away quickly, avoiding his gaze.

'I have so many questions.'

'Which will be answered soon,' he promised cryptically, but she was shaking her head vigorously before he had finished speaking.

'I really need some answers now, otherwise I'll go mad!'

'We can't have that,' he teased, laughter tingeing his voice. She smiled despite herself and he looked around the room, thinking, trying to buy some time. She was right of course; she had to know. If not everything, at least something. He took a deep breath; her scent no longer seemed to affect him.

'What do you have to know?'

'Well for starters, why are we here? The truth.' She sat on the edge of the huge bed, looking up at him expectantly.

'To meet the Elders,' he replied quickly, 'That was an easy one.'

'Why Nicholas? What are you hiding?'

He sat next to her and looked at the floor. He was a fool if he thought he could fob her off so easily. He should know that by now. 'Okay the whole truth. We are here because we aren't sure what to do about you.'

'About me?!'

'I told you, you were special,' he smiled wryly, 'I just didn't realise how special.'

She looked confused. That still didn't answer the question and he knew it. She decided to change tack.

'Why did Eleanor call that white-haired woman sister?'

He smiled in relief. 'Because Sylph is Eleanor's sister, as is Arri.'

'Oh.' Eva's confusion increased as she digested this information. 'Then why did I feel they didn't like each other?'

'You caught that huh?' He frowned, just another thing to get used to. There was no harm in telling her about that. 'When Seton first came here all three sisters looked after him. They all taught him our ways. As the years passed, Arri and Eleanor fell in love with him, but he chose Eleanor. Ever since then there has been discord between the two sisters.'

Eva looked shocked. 'So that's the reason why?'

'Yes, but it didn't help that Arri opposed Eleanor's abdication from the Elders council to be with Seton.' He smiled. 'Love causes a lot of problems even for angels.'

Eva shook her head slowly. 'I guess. Does she ever regret it?'

'You've seen them together, do you think she does?' he asked, his eyes holding hers steadily, all the amusement gone now.

'No,' she replied slowly, 'but that was a big sacrifice.'

He shrugged. 'She thought the rewards were worth it.'

'Abdication, like what royalty do?'

'Kind of, the Elders are our version of the royal family. Eleanor's still part of the family but without the rights the others have.'

That explained her regal bearing and to some extent why Eva was in awe of her. 'Why couldn't they just accept Seton?'

He looked closely at her. 'We all live by the rules Eva. In vampire terms he wasn't good enough, having been a mortal and not an original Angel.' He looked away. 'We live and die by the Code.'

'Die? I thought you were immortal.'

'Everything can come to an end,' he answered softly and then he smiled. 'Is there anything else you are desperate to know?'

Yes, she thought. 'Why is this freckle on my wrist a problem?'

He had known she would ask him that. So why was he surprised? He knew she was overly curious, so how could he have dared to hope that she would forget?

'That freckle is special, but I'm not quite sure why. That's one of the reasons we are here. We have to talk to Sylph,' he said, trying to be as honest as possible.

'Sylph? Eleanor's sister?' Eva asked slowly.

'She is the Historian, the Keeper of the Past. She is the one who teaches us about the legends.'

Eva nodded, for some reason she liked the silver-haired lady she had seen. Of all the Elders, she had seen so far, she appeared the least frightening. She fidgeted slightly and he raised an eyebrow, his lips twitching.

'More questions?'

'Just one more, I promise. Who was the man who spoke to us?'

'Terence? He is the Regent, the head of the Elders.' He watched her face, noting the uneasiness. 'He may appear stern but he is fair and just. He has to be.'

'He has to be?'

'It's his gift, he was the Angel of Justice before the Fall.'

'But he seemed to control...' Eva broke off as Nicholas looked up at the door. Eleanor stood there silently watching them.

'We will talk later. Get some rest, you've had a long trip.'

She nodded, although she wanted him to stay, she didn't have the courage to say so, especially since Eleanor was looking increasingly stern. She watched as they left, closing the door quietly behind them. Eleanor still scared her and she wasn't sure why she didn't seem to like her. After hearing about her and Seton, Eva had felt sorry for her but seeing her just now had brought back the original awe. She thought back to when they were leaving Erie. She had been talking to her mother, trying to make her understand why she had to go to Italy.

'I don't want you to go,' Fey had said with finality.

'But mum, I have to. The Raynes have their reasons for taking me.'

'It's not safe Eva. What if those horrible people get to you again?' Fey had argued.

'Nicholas will protect me. I'm more worried about you,' Eva said, hoping to shift the conversation away from her.

'Me?' Fey shook her head sadly. 'I'll be fine.' And then she had gripped Eva's hand tightly. 'Promise me you will call me and escape if things get out of hand!'

'Mum!' Eva gasped at the pain in her hand and flexed her fingers gingerly when Fey finally let go reluctantly. 'It won't get out of hand, don't worry.'

Fey had shaken her head again and had been about to say something else when there was a knock at the door and Eleanor walked in without waiting for an answer.

'Are you okay?' she asked looking at Eva strangely.

She had nodded and looked up to see Eleanor's eyes now trained steadily on Fey who was staring at the carpet, refusing to meet Eleanor's gaze.

'Eva, could you excuse us?' Eleanor asked.

It was more of an order than a request and Eva had left the room hurriedly. She had hung around in the hallway, wondering what they were talking about when Eleanor had left a few minutes later, barely acknowledging her presence. She went back to her mother to find her sitting quietly by the window.

'Mum?' Eva was puzzled by Fey's ashen face. What had Eleanor said to make her look that way?

'Hi,' she had replied with a smile and then stood up to hug Eva tightly. 'Be careful in Italy my darling.'

After that she had spoken about Eva's departure and hadn't shown any further signs of being worried. Eva frowned, that had been very odd. Fey would never have agreed to let her go so easily, considering how anxious she had been before she spoke to Eleanor. A cold shiver slid down Eva's spine. Had Eleanor threatened Fey, to stop her daughter from changing her mind? She wouldn't put it past the ex-Elder, she thought with certainty.

Chapter 55

'Who are you and what were you doing at the house?'

Anna glared at her captors defiantly. She was cowering with fear on the inside but they were never going to know that. As a neonate she had heard the rumours. The Elites were murderers, eager to kill vampires like her rather than feed off humans. She clenched her jaw tightly to stop her teeth from chattering. She had also heard of their special powers and now had seen them with her own eyes.

First that tall one changing into a bat after defeating Luke who had seemed to be more than capable of defeating a man half his size, and then the one that had brought her here so fast. She hugged the wall protectively, keeping her eyes locked on the three vampires facing her now. She recognised the two boys from the house, but she had never set eyes on the tall tawny-haired female. She had fought against the boys when they had put her in the dark cellar, but when the female had smiled at her, a confusion had spread in her mind, and she had forgotten why she was fighting. She had remained that way until they had returned a few minutes ago, when again the female had smiled and her memory had been restored along with her urge to fight. Ashe moved forward and she hissed in warning.

'Why did you attack the girl?' he asked soothingly again.

She shook her head, her eyes darting around the cellar walls, trying desperately to find a way to escape.

'We won't hurt you,' Leonara added gently, catching the girl's frantic look. 'We just want some answers.'

'Are you with Darius' coven?' Eden asked curtly. He didn't quite understand why they were being so nice to her; she was the enemy after all, part of the Darkness.

After staring at them for a few more minutes she finally relented. They didn't look like they would harm her. If they wanted to they could have done that whilst she was confused earlier on. Maybe if she told them what they wanted to know they would let her go.

'My name is Anna, I belong to Darius' coven.' She narrowed her eyes suspiciously, watching them, trying to gauge their reaction to her words.

'I figured as much,' Ashe said looking at the others. They nodded. 'Why did you attack the girl? That house is within our territory,' he continued looking at her again.

She growled. 'I was thirsty!'

They all looked at her thin body and the increased paleness of her face and couldn't dispute that fact.

'Were you sent to kill her?' Ashe wondered.

She shook her head and her eyes filled with tears abruptly. 'I ran away,' she whispered, 'He would have killed me.'

'Who?' Leonara asked slowly.

'Darius,' she hiccupped.

'Why would he want to kill you?' Eden asked suspiciously. Killing off one's own coven didn't sound like a good idea and Darius was not a fool.

'Because I let the Elite go!' she almost wailed, 'It was my job to keep him occupied and I didn't...couldn't!'

'Elite?' Eden looked at the others.

They were all thinking the same thing; it had to be Nicholas she was talking about. She must have been one of the vampires that had tried to keep him away from Eva while the others tried to abduct her outside her apartment building a few months ago. They suddenly agreed with the girl, Darius wouldn't have thought twice about destroying her for her failure, they all knew he had a violent temper. No wonder she had run away, and where better to hide from the coven than in Elite territory?

'Do you have somewhere to go?' Leonara asked sympathetically.

Anna shook her head sadly. 'No.'

With no coven to rely upon and being in Darius' bad books at the same time was a dangerous situation to be in. The three Raynes exchanged looks, they couldn't let her leave and fall into Darius' hands. Besides she was the only evidence they had linking Darius to the attack on Nicholas. She had to stay with them until they figured out what to do.

+++

'You want me to believe that Nicholas Rayne; our most celebrated assistant district attorney; is involved with the massacre at that nightclub?' the chief of police looked across his desk at Chris in disbelief.

'In effect,' Chris agreed knowing how absurd it all sounded. It scarcely sounded plausible even to him. He hadn't even told his team about his suspicions and had asked the crime lab assistant who had run the number plate from the crime scene not to say anything either.

From the forensic evidence they had gathered it appeared that the car in question had been severely damaged. They still hadn't found it and he had no hopes of finding it in the near future. They had scoured every garage in Erie and beyond but no one had seen the black Mercedes SLK. With no further evidence against Rayne he couldn't expect his chief to support him, but he had to try.

The chief was shaking his head. 'Do you have any other evidence linking him to the case?'

'Other than talking to me on that night in person…no,' Chris admitted reluctantly.

'And you checked out the guy he was supposedly meeting that night?'

'Yeah, he checked out alright,' Chris replied wearily. Although when he had questioned the man he had seemed a bit vague but he had backed up Nicholas' story. The chief sat back in his chair.

'And you haven't found the car in question yet?' It was more of a statement than a question.

'Not yet.'

He sighed. 'Has it been reported as being stolen?'

Chris shook his head, he knew what his superior was getting at. They had nothing with which to charge Nicholas.

'Have you spoken to Mr. Rayne since the incident?'

'No, he isn't in the country. He is currently in Europe.'

'I see, well until he returns I'm afraid there's not much we can do.'

Chris agreed but he still had an uneasy feeling about the case. Something didn't add up. He would just have to keep looking.

Chapter 56

Terence looked around at the worried faces of the Council. The Raynes' arrival at the Reliquary, the Elders' headquarters under Vatican City, had caused enough of a disturbance for him to call a meeting. They all sat around a large central table intricately carved with religious symbols. Most of the Elders wore royal regalia but some were dressed less formally in fashions more suited to this decade. If he looked closely almost every century was represented around that table. He cleared his throat softly and the whispers ceased.

'As you are all aware, the Raynes' coven has found the One.'

The whispers started again in earnest and he frowned. That was enough to silence them again. As Regent he had complete power over them, but even he could not sway their decisions. He just hoped they would make the right decision this time. But what was the right decision? His eyes met Sylph's and she smiled.

'How do we know she's the One?' Arri asked the one question they all wanted answered. 'After all we have waited centuries for the legend to come true.'

Terence looked again at Sylph. 'The Keeper of the Past can answer that for you.'

Sylph looked around the room, her almost white-blonde hair shone like polished silver in the light. 'Eons ago when we fell from Grace and let our desires rule us, our kind procreated with mortals,' she took in the grim faces surrounding her.

An angry buzz met her words and she paused, waiting for silence. It had been the same years ago when the subject had last been broached. The Elders didn't like to be reminded of their past, of their mistakes, but that was her duty, to remember and avert a repeat of the past.

'Most of the progeny from those unions are known of; very few still live and are *Electismus*. (Vampire elites) Some of course chose to be Dark Ones,' she paused again as a collective growl emanated from the Elders. 'However some of the progeny were never turned.'

'Why was that allowed?'

'That is against the Law!' Eunomia interjected heatedly.

Terence turned to look at the Elder. Her face was indignant. Being the Angel of Lawful conduct he had expected her displeasure.

'It was justified at the time,' Terence's deep voice cut through their protests. 'The Elder in question was dealt with accordingly.'

There were furtive looks around the table, each one wondering if their neighbour was to blame.

'We are straying from the point. If you'll let Sylph continue.' He nodded at her and she looked around at the others before closing her eyes. Her face glowed more brightly than it had before, her hair became almost translucent as it flew around her, and her voice echoed around the room.

'Heed my words carefully banished Children of Heaven,' she said, her voice stern, unlike her usual gentle tones. 'The Progeny of Angels will decide your fate. But one will be more powerful than the rest. In that one your Salvation lies, for he can choose between the Light and the Dark and has the power to destroy either. The Mark on his hand will guide you to him.' Her voice faded and her face resumed its peaceful expression.

The silence that greeted her words was oppressive. Some of the Elders knew of the legend but had never heard the exact words. *What did it mean that a mortal would decide their fate?* Arri shook her head, *that couldn't be! A mere mortal dictating an Angel's fate? This was a cruel joke!* She glanced at Terence, hoping he would say as much, but he looked deadly serious. Her sister looked scarcely less.

'This cannot be! The Keeper is wrong!' Arri managed to gasp.

Terence sent her a withering look but Sylph was shaking her head. 'The past does not lie sister, what I said is the absolute truth as uttered by the Oracle.'

Arri was silenced, no one questioned the Keeper, and no one dared question the Oracle. She had already gone too far.

'And you think this girl the Raynes found is the One?' Eris; the Angel of Discord, asked sceptically.

'She bears the Mark. Our own kind have seen it,' Terence replied.

'An Elder must see it,' Arri intervened, 'to make sure.'

'Eleanor has verified it,' Terence replied tersely. He looked directly at her. 'She is your sister and was an Elder. Don't forget!'

'I haven't forgotten Regent,' she replied almost sweetly, 'but she lost that right when she chose beneath her and abdicated.'

He shook his head sadly; Arri would never forgive her sister for what she considered the ultimate betrayal. He could sense her feelings and they troubled him. She still felt strongly about Seton, but her love for him and her hatred for her sister created a volatile mix.

'Very well,' he conceded, 'Who better to validate the Mark than the Keeper herself?' He smiled at Sylph who bowed in acquiesance, before flying out of the room.

+++

Nicholas followed Eleanor towards a small door half concealed behind a tapestry depicting Zeus throwing lightning bolts from the heavens. Opening it they entered a small room, sparsely furnished. It was one of the smaller antechambers dotted within the Reliquary, leading to several other chambers of more importance. Eleanor motioned him to a seat and he sat down reluctantly. He would much rather have stood but her expression kept him silent. She hadn't spoken since leaving Eva and neither had he, although he desperately wanted to ask her what was happening with the Council and what the Elders had said.

As though her mind was running in accord with his she said abruptly, 'They have had a meeting. Sylph has been elected to verify Eva's identity.'

He looked steadily at her set face, not quite sure what to say. 'What does she have to do to verify it?' he finally asked in a hollow voice.

'Eva will have to show Sylph the Mark. If it is what we think it is, there will be another meeting.' She paused and moved uncomfortably. 'If not...' her voice trailed away.

'NO!' Nicholas jumped to his feet, 'I won't let them!'

She looked steadily at him. 'There is more...'

He kept silent waiting warily as she looked away from him. 'Being of the Hunted Bloodline, they won't let her fall into the wrong hands.'

'So...' he prompted her, fear squeezing his heart steadily.

She sighed. 'We have never had this dilemma before. Any of the Bloodline that have been in danger, have either had *Electismus* protection or have been dealt with by the *Phonoi*.'

He paled considerably. The *Phonoi* were the lesser spirits that had fallen with the Angels. They were used to destroy anyone the Elders sentenced. He had seen some floating above them when they had entered the Vatican, constantly at hand should the Elders need them. His eyes pleaded silently with Eleanor's.

'You were an Elder once, you must have some idea as to what they will decide.'

'I am not a Foreseer,' she replied softly, her eyes holding his, 'The vote can go either way.' She paused thinking. 'And there are some that may use Eva for revenge.' She bowed her head apologetically. 'I am sorry I cannot help you further. I may be able to intervene with the Regent, for Terence is an old friend, but if the Elders cast a vote, he too will have no choice but to abide by it.'

He clenched his jaw. He had never seen her so humbled and he knew she would blame herself for arousing the Elders' wrath against Eva. Arri would do anything to hurt her sister. *Spilling innocent blood is a crime*, he thought desperately. But would the Elders consider Eva's blood to be innocent enough to protect? He had to know the whole truth, which he was now certain was being kept from him and he knew of only one person who would be able to tell him.

Chapter 57

Eva had tried to relax, but she just couldn't. She kept remembering Eleanor's face when she had looked at Nicholas as they had left. Eleanor was frightening when she was pleasant, but in that moment she had looked positively lethal. It didn't help that she still had so many questions left, and worse, couldn't expect them to be answered. On top of everything her mother's sudden acceptance still puzzled her. She felt like she could no longer be sure of anything in her life.

She sighed and looked around the bedroom, there was nothing she could do except wait in this beautiful prison. After what seemed an eternity of waiting there was a soft knock at the door, making her jump. She called out in answer, standing up quickly, fully expecting Nicholas to enter. She was surprised to find Seton standing calmly outside.

He smiled and took her hand carefully saying as he did so, 'It is time for you to meet someone.'

An awful fear gripped her and she just managed to gasp, 'Who?'

'Sylph,' he replied and squeezed her small hand reassuringly.

The fear melted away from her features and she relaxed slightly. The gentle-looking silver-haired Elder hadn't made her want to run away. She was glad it wasn't one of the others; they all seemed to personify the cinematic portrayal of vampires and in her mind at least they didn't look like benevolent angels. She let Seton guide her along several passages before they entered a large room.

It was furnished like a typical living room, which surprised her. She had expected the same splendour she had seen in the other rooms, but this room was almost homely. Her eyes widened with relief when she saw Nicholas seated on a leather couch nearby talking to a silver-haired woman, whom she recognised as Sylph, in a low voice. He stood up as soon as he sensed her and turned round with a smile, which lit his face, making her gasp. She would never get used to how handsome he was, but that was just one facet, his kindness superseded everything. Seton led her forward and handed her to Nicholas, nodded at Sylph in greeting and then flashed out of the room, closing the door firmly behind him.

'Eva, this is Sylph,' Nicholas introduced them and then settled her on the couch before sitting down next to her. He kept a hold of her hand, which she found she liked, but it also crossed her mind that he might have done it to keep her from running away. His eyes shone with amusement, as though he had heard what she was thinking.

Sylph's pale silver eyes assessed the petite girl in front of her for a minute and then they lightened with humour.

'Don't be afraid child.' Her voice was soft, almost childlike and Eva instantly felt more at ease. She motioned towards a plate laden with sweetmeats. 'Help yourself,' she invited as she picked one up and bit into it.

Eva's eyes widened with surprise, she had never seen the Raynes eat human food before except for steaks, and Alena had told her it didn't give them energy. Here was an Elder who seemed to be enjoying the food just like a normal human. Sylph caught her surprised look and smiled in answer.

'Not many of us enjoy human food, but I confess I love it!' she admitted almost guiltily, making Eva laugh.

'I do too, especially the indulgent desserts!'

'Those are my favourite too,' Sylph agreed heartily, 'over indulgence may be a sin of sorts, but a beautiful one nonetheless!'

Nicholas rolled his eyes expressively as the two women smiled at each other as though sharing a secret. He had always liked Sylph and now he liked her even more for putting Eva at ease. But he knew they were here for a serious cause and he exchanged a look with the Elder as Eva leant forward to pick up a sweetmeat, unable to resist. They waited until she had eaten most of it before Nicholas cleared his throat.

'Eva, Sylph has been chosen by the Council to look at your hand.'

She looked up to meet his eyes. He couldn't see any fear in them now.

'Okay,' she agreed and looked at Sylph. 'Will it hurt?'

She shook her head. 'I'm not sure but I will do my best not to hurt you.'

Eva nodded, trusting her. She didn't notice Nicholas' obvious discomfort or the worried frown on his face as Sylph moved closer and put out her hand. Eva placed her right hand on hers and gasped in surprise as she felt an electric spark.

Sylph smiled reassuringly and turned her wrist slightly as she bent close to peer at the blue mark. Eva looked down too and the breath caught in her throat; the freckle had grown since she had last looked at it and now small blue veins stood out around it. She gulped, *so it wasn't just a harmless spot then?* She held her breath, waiting for Sylph to say or do something.

They remained motionless for a few minutes before Sylph touched the mark gently with a manicured forefinger, closed her eyes and murmured under her breath. Her finger glowed with a blue-white light where it touched Eva's skin, causing her to squint. Warmth seemed to spread from the finger as Sylph continued to utter words in an alien language. As she watched mesmerised, the spot grew larger until she could make out an intricate pattern.

She frowned; she had seen that pattern before recently. Suddenly it hit her; it was the same pattern that was engraved on the golden door leading into the vast Elders' Hall. She looked up to see Nicholas' drawn face. He looked partly uncertain now and partly relieved. So he had known what the spot was. She sighed inwardly in resignation; she had to accept that she might never be in the loop when it came to this sort of stuff, maybe because she wasn't one of them. She glanced at Sylph's intense face expectantly; but surely they would tell her everything now.

The Elder opened her eyes, assessed the pattern and lifted her finger away. The pattern immediately faded and shrank, but Eva could still see it. It looked more like an old tattoo, pale blue and faded deep into her skin, but still visible. She pulled her hand back and touched the area cautiously; it still felt warm from Sylph's touch. She looked up into the Elder's pale silver eyes questioningly. Her stare was returned steadily until she started to feel uncomfortable. Sylph didn't look pleased nor upset. Her face remained passive as she finally exchanged a knowing look with Nicholas.

'The legend has come true at last.' She turned back to Eva with a half-smile lighting her features. 'I believe I can now tell you what I dared not before.'

Eva looked quizzically at Nicholas, not daring to hope. 'You mean, you'll tell me everything I want to know?'

He nodded. 'We can't escape it now. We'll have to let you into our little secret.'

Sylph nodded, 'You are a very important part of our history, Eva.'

'I am part of your history? How can that be?'

'Nicholas has told you about some of it, but there is more…lots more,' she touched her temple, 'And it's all in here. Some of it even the other Elders don't know.' She sighed and sat back. 'Do you know why we fell from Heaven?'

Eva nodded she remembered what Nicholas had told her. 'The Angels wanted power.'

'Yes, eventually they did, but the original sin was love.'

'How is that possible?' *How could love be a sin?* she thought.

'Several Angels fell in love with their mortal charges. Some of the Greek myths about the gods are true. To be seen by their lovers the Angels had to become visible. Those that saw them, believed them to be gods,' Sylph explained slowly. 'We were never meant to be seen by mortals. We were the invisible guardians.' She shook her head. 'Those that were responsible were punished severely, many turned to the Darkness, but many more remained with the Light.

'The children from the mortal unions were sought out. These children did not possess the original powers of their Angel parent, only a product, a shadow, and therefore were weaker, their mortal and immortal bloods unable to co-exist in one body. They suffered terribly and were eventually destroyed for their own good. But legend tells of one child that we never found, one that lived on in the mortal world, none the wiser of its dual inheritance.

'This child had two special parents. One was an Angel Elder and the other, part of the Hunted Bloodline. Because of this, we believe the two bloods were able to support each other and not destroy the child. Over the years, the Elders forgot all about the child they hadn't found. Eventually this child grew up and had a family of his own, and generations were born, each with the same traits only diluted with more mortal blood.

'Generations later two mortals with the same traits met and had a child. This child had both bloods but they were stronger than in any of the others before it. Again they co-existed side by side, but as the child grew so did the power of the *Sanguis angelis* – Angel blood. The legend tells us that the children of Angels will decide our fate, but one will be able to choose between the Light and the Dark.' She looked keenly at Eva, 'The Mark on your hand is the Mark of the Elders, *Vestigium de Olympus* – the Mark of Heaven.'

She lifted her sleeve as she spoke, exposing her right arm. On the forearm Eva could make out a copy of the blue pattern she had on her own wrist. It was bolder and more intricate with silver star-like spots all over it, which glistened in the light, but it was essentially the same. She looked up into Sylph's face, her large violet eyes silently asking the question she already knew the answer to.

Sylph nodded, 'You are that child, Eva Tanner.'

+++

Anna had been moved to one of the guest bedrooms as soon as it was decided that she wasn't a threat. Leonara had spoken to Seton and he had agreed with them. She was to stay at the Mansion until they could deal with Darius. Once she was sure she wouldn't die at their hands, Anna relaxed considerably and even started to smile at her new found friends. She still wasn't quite sure what to make of them, but any enemy of Darius, she figured, could be counted as her friend. She was still wary of their powers, especially Leonara's. She hadn't felt that horrible confusion again but that didn't mean she never would. She didn't trust them that much.

She looked around the bedroom with wide eyes. This was a far cry from the dilapidated buildings she was used to. She hadn't had a shower in God only knew how long and when Alena saw her, she was practically ordered to throw away her filthy rags, as Alena put it, and get into something decent. She had meekly obeyed the female who was just as petite as herself. Who knew what powers she had?

Now dressed in clothes that had Alena's stamp of approval, she felt a lot better. But she was still weak. She ate the rare steak Alena brought for her with relish, devouring it with an urgency Alena had never seen before, which urged her to bring some more, and watched in amazement as they disappeared just as fast as the first one. She mentioned it to Kane and he shrugged.

'She was half starved when we found her.'

'Yes but at this rate she'll eat us out of house and home!'

'I think we'll manage,' he replied with a laugh.

She shook her head, she wasn't so sure. Later that night she checked on their guest. She liked the small vampire, and was hoping they could put her at her ease. She had looked terrified when Alena had seen her in the cellar. Her knock went unanswered. Puzzled she knocked again. Not hearing anything she opened the door cautiously and froze in horror.

Chapter 58

'Terence? I need to speak to you.'

Terence looked up from the scroll he was reading in surprise. He hadn't expected her of all people to seek him out. He put down the scroll and nodded a welcome. Arri moved closer.

'About what?'

'You said an Elder was responsible for Eva's birth. I want to know who.'

He looked at the red-haired Elder warily. He knew the Council had its own factions and ever since the breach between the sisters, he had been aware of a hostile undercurrent towards him. He didn't mind and wasn't particularly worried, but now that the most important decision loomed ahead of them he wanted some unity in the ranks.

'I cannot divulge that Arri, you know the rules.'

She grimaced. 'The rules? It appears you break them and uphold them when it suits your purpose!'

His usually calm pale eyes flashed with anger. 'You overstep your limits Arri!' he warned in a dangerous tone of voice.

Arri held his gaze for a second before dropping her own. 'I didn't come here to fight, merely for an explanation. The others want to know why we didn't search for the missing child all those years ago.'

'We had more important concerns, or have you forgotten the battles we fought?' he asked, his voice bitter.

'How can I forget?' she asked just as bitterly.

She thought of them often enough; the fear, the betrayal, the confrontation and finally the fighting. Even now she could hear the cries of war as each side faced each other on the high plateaus above the Holy City, all those centuries ago. Each one armed with their weapon of choice, each one hoping for a different outcome. The air had crackled with electricity as they used their powers against each other. Even now she could see her other half's face as he stood in front of her.

'Come with me,' he had said, putting out his hand.

'No, what you ask is a sin!' she had cried out desperately. 'We will lose our right to Heaven forever!'

'And be gods!' he countered triumphantly, 'Of our own free will.'

'It was never meant to be used in that way!' she had tried to plead.

'What use is free will if it doesn't free us!' he had asked, as he moved closer to her and took her in his arms.

She looked up into his beloved face; the face that had glowed with such fervour that he had truly resembled the god the mortals had thought him to be. The Angel of Healing, so handsome and fearful in all his glory. She loved him desperately, had loved him ever since Creation when they had been paired for eternity, until now. He hadn't been lured away by another's love but by his lust for power.

'Come with me, be my queen and we will rule forever, free,' he whispered, his eyes holding hers, his embrace brooking no resistance.

Her heart had melted and she had been on the point of capitulation, but something stopped her. As she stared at him something must have changed in her face, because his eyes shone with intense sorrow. She had seen his love, but now his eyes held a bleak look as though he had lost everything dear to him, mirroring her own feelings. They had always been like that, able to feel and hear each other's thoughts without uttering a word aloud.

I love you he sent with a deep yearning.

I am yours for eternity Zerachiel she promised in return and sealed it with a deep kiss.

They had stayed like that for some time, showing each other their love with a violent abandon, not certain if they could ever be together again. Then the trumpets of war had sounded and he had flown away from her, leaving her to join the Dark forces. She had called out in vain, and watched his golden light disappear into the grey clouds that were rolling forward, heralding death and to her a deep sense of loss and betrayal. She had lost her mate, the other half of her soul for what she believed was right. She stood up facing the rolling thunderclouds, a challenge in her eyes; she wouldn't let that sacrifice be in vain, she would fight. She had flown to the high plateau to join the army, standing ready for battle.

Looking around her at their faces, she had felt Zerachiel's loss even more keenly. With the fervour of battle they were terrible and beautiful to behold. Their golden faces were turned towards the rising sun, the rays reflecting off their perfect skin, their eyes blazing with a myriad of emotions. She had taken her place next to her sisters, holding her bow at the ready, one of her golden arrows already knocked into place. Together they had charged forward when the trumpets had sounded again, flying at their enemies with a single-minded wrath. They had destroyed several of their brethren who had chosen the Darkness, and watched with horror as their weapons reduced the Angels to dust.

Her arrows pierced the toughest armour, flying strong and true. She watched with a sense of powerless anticipation as the golden arrow arced in the air and then dropped towards its mark. Her heart ached as the arrow point rammed through the breastplate, causing another Angel to stop in mid charge, and fall to the ground, dead; turning away as he dissolved into a glittering dust cloud. She caught a glimpse of Zarachiel, or so she thought as she knocked another arrow in place. He was locked in combat with another. As she watched, the pair disappeared in the throng. She tried to fight her way through, to find him; to help him, but attacked from all sides she gave up and turned to fight for her own life.

She didn't know how long they fought, the horrors kept coming; the next one more terrible than the last as more of her arrows destroyed the Angels she had known for so long. When the dust settled and the survivors returned she had looked desperately for the one she hoped was still alive. As she searched the battlefield, she stumbled over the discarded weapons, and walked past the piles of golden dust that had once held such power, and she wept. Her tears falling down her cheeks unheeded, to mingle with the dust she hadn't bothered to wipe away, leaving behind dirty streaks on the pale skin.

Where is he? Don't be dead, don't be dead! she kept saying to herself, over and over again, as though it would come true if she said it enough times. *Be safe my love!* He would be safe, he had to be!

She flew aimlessly over the plateau, landing if she thought she had seen him, but every time it turned out to be nothing. Hours passed and the sun's last rays tinged the western sky with bloody streaks, which made her heart turn cold with dread. To her even the Heavens were mourning their loss. They had been fighting for days without succour, and day and night had rolled into one. She turned her head sharply, *was that a voice? In this place?* She flew forward, listening intently.

It's the wind, her brain said, but her heart refused to listen and urged her forward, desperately hoping. And then she saw him. A keening cry erupted from her, torn out of her by a force she couldn't control and she fell to the earth, stumbling next to him. He was lying next to his shield, gazing up at the sky, his beautiful face lined with pain. She lifted his golden head into her lap and bent over him, her long red hair creating a curtain around them.

'My love!' she whispered in a broken voice, her tears falling soft and swift on his upturned face.

He blinked and tried to smile, despite the searing pain spreading through his body. 'I am glad the Almighty gave me my last wish,' he whispered with difficulty.

Arri gulped, she could feel her heart rending into pieces. Shaking her head vigorously she said, 'It is not your last wish, I won't let it be!'

'It is, my heart, I feel the strength leaving me, the world grows cold and dark...'

'It cannot be!' she almost wailed. 'You and I...we are meant to live forever, together!'

He smiled and lifted a hand to touch her face gently. 'I will be with you forever, here.' He let his hand touch the spot just above her heart and she grasped it tightly, kissing it fervently.

'Heal yourself!' she suddenly commanded. 'Heal yourself like you healed all those mortals. Heal and stay with me. Please!' she begged, weeping desperately.

He tried to shake his head and failed. 'It's too late for that, I cannot...' his voice trailed away, but his eyes held hers, telling her silently how much he loved her.

'Repent!' she ordered, knowing she was grasping at straws, a terrible fear gripping her. 'Repent and you'll enter the Kingdom.'

He stared at her, sending his thoughts to her; he was beyond speaking now. *I have made my peace with Him and have asked for forgiveness. If we do not meet on Earth we will meet in Heaven* he promised and watched as her face glowed with relief.

She knew Raguel, the Angel of Fairness who dealt with Angels who had transgressed against Heaven and God, would be more lenient if Zerachiel had repented. He would then be allowed to enter Heaven and not be doomed to roam the mortal world as a common soul with no power, where she would not be able to find him. She leant closer and kissed him on the mouth with all the love she felt.

Suddenly she cried out in agony. She felt a sharp rending pain deep inside her and instinctively knew what it was. Their souls were separating. The bond created from the beginning of time was being broken and she was powerless to stop it.

She held onto him tightly, willing him to live but she could feel him leaving her, and as she watched his beloved face through her tears, it faded away. His eyes closed and he dissolved into golden dust. The pain she felt was unbearable and she crumpled to the ground, unable to lift herself, unable to walk. She didn't know how long she lay there as the thunderclouds finally let loose their torrent of water. The wind had already carried the golden piles of dust heavenward by the time the raindrops fell on her.

She closed her eyes, wishing to be dead too, asking the Creator with her entire being to take her too. But there was no reply. Later, much later, her eyes fell on her discarded bow and arrows. She lifted one of them and turned it so that it glinted in the dim light. Taking her own life was a cardinal sin but she would gladly face Raguel's wrath to be with her love. She lifted the arrow high, murmured the most powerful incantation she knew to make certain it struck true, and used all her strength to plunge it downward through her heart. Just as it was about to touch her skin it stopped and she looked up to see Eleanor and Sylph holding the arrow away from her.

She cried out in defiance and tried to wrench the weapon free, but they pulled it away from her and threw it out of her reach. She had begged them to end her suffering, but neither would listen. Instead they carried her back to the others, still crying and pleading.

Now her eyes, which had clouded over with the memory, cleared and she looked at the Regent. He was watching her sorrowfully.

'I am sorry; I should not have said that. Your loss was one of the greatest as was your sacrifice.'

She nodded, unable to speak. He would never know the pain she had felt - still felt or the betrayal when she saw Seton and Eleanor together. He still had Sylph, their souls were still entwined. She pushed away the twinge of envy. Zerachiel had chosen his fate, just as she had chosen hers. *Being in the mortal world changed you*, she thought. She had never known envy in Heaven, but then she had never felt such pain either.

Chapter 59

'What's happening to her?'

'I'm not sure.'

'Well we have to do something!'

'What do you suggest?'

Anna tried to open her eyes and failed. She didn't feel like she was in her body. She felt strangely at peace, but kept hearing voices, which continued to disturb her. She recognised them but couldn't quite place them. After a while they ceased and she breathed in relief; finally some peace. All of a sudden someone was lifting her head and then she felt an intense craving as she was made to drink a thickened fluid. Her eyes finally flickered open and she could make out hazy faces around her. She kept drinking until her focus returned and the faces she had seen took on the features of the Raynes.

Alena was sitting next to her on the bed, holding the cup to her mouth. Anna sniffed in appreciation; the blood smelt so good, not fresh, but still good. She gulped at it thirstily and before long the cup was empty.

'What happened?' she managed to ask, licking the blood from her lips. She felt rejuvenated.

Alena stared at her before saying, 'Don't you remember?'

Anna shook her head, her eyes looking around the room, searching for more blood. Not seeing any human around, she leant back, the craving still intense.

'You went into a coma after the fits.'

'Fits? I don't get fits,' she croaked painfully.

'Not normally, but you were very low on blood,' Alena explained.

Her eyes widened in surprise and then looked at the cup still held in Alena's hand. 'Whose blood is that?'

Alena smiled with a shrug, 'No idea, we got it from the blood bank.'

'The hospital?' Anna swallowed, feeling slightly nauseous; suddenly she didn't feel so good.

'Yes,' Alena nodded, 'no harm no foul.'

'I think we'll have to keep you on human blood for a while,' Leonara mused. 'You seem to have taken a reaction to pure animal blood.'

'Probably because you're not used to it,' Kane interjected from the doorway.

'We can't keep going to the blood bank!' Eden interrupted and Anna could see he was not pleased. She could sense his distrust as his eyes settled on her and then moved on. 'They will get suspicious!'

'We have no other choice!' Leonara replied with a frown in his direction.

'What about vassals?' Anna asked helpfully and immediately wished she hadn't. All the Raynes looked horrified. Alena shook her head in a firm negative.

'We don't keep vassals, it is against the Code.' She looked meaningfully at the others. 'We will have to take our chances with the humans. It's either the blood bank or nothing.'

The others shifted uneasily; they all knew what the alternative was. Alena was right, they couldn't get the blood from anywhere else, and if they didn't get it they would lose Anna.

+++

Chris stared at the witness testimonies for the hundredth time that day. There had to be something, something he had missed. He picked up Sarah's account and frowned. She claimed she had seen black-cloaked figures. If she was right, more than one person was responsible for the massacre. His mind flicked to the Rayne family again. But why be so careless as to leave a crumpled number plate at the crime scene and then flaunt their presence in the area? He rubbed his temples; it just didn't make sense. There hadn't been any fingerprints at the crime scene and forensics had drawn a blank. He stood up suddenly his mind made up; he had to go back to the alley, there had to be something else he hadn't seen.

When he got to the nightclub it was already dusk and the streets were coming alive with partying teenagers. He walked quickly to the alley. The stench of blood had gone but he could still see the stains on the concrete walls and the dirty ground. He switched on a flashlight and played it over the heaps of rubbish that had been thrown haphazardly. What was evidence and what was truly trash? It was hard to tell.

He walked further into the alley slowly. Reaching the end, he turned around. There was nothing here; it was all rubbish. He was about to move away when his eye caught sight of something half buried in the dirt. He bent down to pick up the circular object half-heartedly. It was a gold button and from the look of it quite a new one. He turned it over looking closely at it by the light of the flashlight. He could see something engraved on its smooth, shiny surface, but he couldn't make it out. Dropping it into a plastic evidence bag he pocketed it. It may be nothing, but it was worth a shot. He looked closely at the ground again as he walked back the way he had come. Not seeing anything he switched off the flashlight and started walking towards the nightclub. Now that he was off duty a drink would be welcome.

+++

ICE was packed with people dancing and drinking as he made his way through the queue waiting to enter the club. As he entered the building he could barely walk through the crowd towards the bar on the other side of the room. The bartenders were busily pouring drinks for the patrons when he finally reached the long bar which ran the entire length of the wall. He could just make out his fellow patrons' faces in the dim bluish half-light. The bartenders were illuminated by the bright neon lights suspended over the bar, making them appear like beacons from across the dance floor. *A clear invitation*, he thought as he signalled to one of the men.

'Scotch on the rocks,' he said before turning to survey the dancers.

His drink arrived and he sipped it, letting his eyes wander past the dance floor to the seating areas. The place was crowded tonight. He sipped his drink again, turning his head to take in the rest of the dance club. As his eyes wandered towards the stairs he suddenly caught sight of a girl walking towards them. She looked uncannily familiar, like he had seen her before but he was certain he never had. He kept his eyes trained on her as she walked up the stairs swiftly. Then it hit him and without a thought he walked forward, leaving his half – finished drink behind.

When he reached the landing, she had vanished. He searched the young faces around him but couldn't detect her in the crowd. As he turned to look again at the teenagers, he caught sight of her dark hair at the far end of the corridor. He moved forward, following cautiously as she walked up another flight of stairs to the second floor. When she reached the almost empty landing she looked around quickly before making her way along the darkened corridor to an office door marked private.

She slipped in and shut it firmly, oblivious of Chris as he peered cautiously after her from the stairwell. When he was certain the corridor was empty he stepped forward softly. He could have sworn it was her, everything about the girl reminded him of her, and yet there was something different and he couldn't quite put his finger on it. He had never seen her dressed so provocatively before. She was wearing a black miniskirt, leaving her long legs bare, and a black and red low cut top. But her hair had been a different shade of brown and it was cut much shorter. He frowned, something wasn't right.

Chapter 60

'We should tell her!'

'No, we are bound by our promise. Besides Arri would have a field day!'

'We can't hide it forever!' Eleanor argued.

'We can and we will,' Zophiel replied, his eyes steady on her worried face.

Eleanor tried to match his confidence and failed. He always had an answer for everything and he always seemed to have a plan. Even all those years ago when she hadn't been sure what she was doing was right, he had been adamant and bound her in the unbreakable oath. Being the Guardian of Oaths meant she couldn't go back on any promises and looking at him now she could tell he knew that better than anyone.

'She will find out sooner or later you know. She is the One and from what Nick says and from what I've seen she's very curious.'

'We were made to keep secrets,' came the steadfast reply, 'you should know that better than anyone.'

She looked at him suspiciously, why did she feel like he knew a lot more than he was letting on? He returned her look with a neutral expression, but she wasn't fooled. 'Don't worry Helios,' he soothed, using her Greek name, 'she is after all half mortal.'

'True she is *Dimidius Sanguis* (half-blood), but you forget the other half is *Cruor de Angelus*,' she replied smoothly.

'The blood of Angels,' he nodded, 'but how will knowing the past help her?'

'The past has always dictated the future, you know that.'

'And if it dictates her future we may all be destroyed.'

Eleanor eyed him warily, 'And yet there is always the chance that it will lead to our salvation.'

'You think she will help those who took her away? Who gave her to a stranger? Who altered her life so fully?' Zophiel looked at her sceptically as she tried to appear unaffected by this attack.

'If we explain…'

'She will never understand our reasons, never understand our fears.' He paused and looked into the distance thinking. 'But her love for Nick may still save us.'

Eleanor suddenly felt very cold, as though a cloud had gone across the sun and stolen all the warmth, how did he know about that? 'If the Council finds out…'

He looked at her, assessing her thoughts carefully as they flitted across her face. All the things she couldn't say aloud but was afraid of were right there. Finally after what seemed an age he said, 'They cannot object as they did in the beginning, she is as you said *Dimidius Sanguis*.'

Eleanor bowed her head in defeat. She knew he was right, Eva and Nicholas were bound to each other by love even if neither of them knew it fully yet. Eva would do anything to help Nicholas, but it wasn't Eva she was worried about now. She knew Nicholas would never let any harm come to her, as he had made clear before they had come to the Reliquary, and she feared for him. He may be foolish enough to…she couldn't finish the thought.

Chapter 61

'What news?'

The girl smiled and sat down on one of the leather chairs opposite the oak desk. She looked at the tall man on the other side, letting her gaze travel over his jet-black hair, piercing silver eyes and hawk-like nose. He had a lean face, his high cheekbones clearly visible, giving him a stern, aristocratic face that one could not easily forget. She had always been in awe of him and had been thrilled when he had selected her to be his assistant. She had learnt much in the past ten years. Her powers had progressed in leaps and bounds until she could challenge even him, but he kept pushing her to her limits. Even now as he sat looking relatively relaxed, she could almost see him thinking about her next task. Her muscles tensed deliciously, waiting, expecting an order.

'The police have found the number plate we left in the alley,' she said as she stretched her legs, answering his question. 'And the Raynes are still none the wiser. Some of the coven are in Italy and the Council is still debating about the human girl.' She smiled as he nodded his satisfaction.

'We may have to go to Italy to make sure it all works out as planned. But tell me my dear, how goes your task?'

She sighed, it was one of the most difficult things he had asked her to do so far. She closed her eyes and concentrated on relaxing her body. She could feel every inch of it and as she concentrated harder she felt light and airy as though she was floating. She could only do so much, and within a few seconds she knew she couldn't continue.

Vassagio watched as she disappeared into a mist, that hung over where she had been a moment ago and then she reappeared, her eyes still firmly shut, her disappointment plain to see on her expressive face. There was no doubt about it; she was very talented. He had known that as soon as he had seen her. He smiled to himself; his secret weapon was almost ready to be unveiled. She opened her eyes to see him still staring at her with an odd smile twisting his lips.

He nodded. 'Well done, but you must hold that form for longer and be able to travel.'

Chris had moved silently towards the office and now had his ear pressed against the door, keeping his eyes on the stairwell so that he could move away quickly if anyone approached and found him eavesdropping. He frowned, he could hear the girl and a man talking, and he was just able to make out the words.

Inside the room the girl sighed again, she felt so tired after her efforts. Vassagio changed the subject abruptly. 'Is Darius still in the area?'

She smiled, 'Yes, in fact I believe he is downstairs in the club.'

Vassagio nodded. 'He is hunting tonight, I may have a word with him.'

'I saw him take a girl earlier. He may have already left.'

The man laughed throatily, it was full of enjoyment. 'If I know him he will still be around. One girl will not satisfy him.'

'As we saw when he attacked the police,' she agreed. She had been horrified at Darius' appetite. He had killed more than his share and drained his victims to death, unlike the others who left some blood in their veins. She shuddered; she had never been tempted to drink from a human. Vassagio said it was a sign of how sophisticated she was; one of the reasons he had chosen her.

Chris frowned, *attacked the police? Were they talking about the massacre? Were these people involved? And who was Darius?* He could feel his anger rising. If these people were responsible he would make sure they paid dearly. He strained to hear more of the conversation.

Suddenly there was movement on the other side of the door. He stepped back and bolted as silently as he could down the stairs to the first landing. Grabbing a discarded wine glass, he pretended to stare down at the dance floor idly, keeping his attention inconspicuously on the couple walking down the stairs from the upper floor. The girl came down first, graceful as a model. Behind her was a tall man he had never seen before, tall and distinguished yet quite young, wearing a black suit, the only accessory being the gold watch on his wrist and the gold buttons on the jacket. His stern features however leant him the appearance of someone much older. As he watched they walked past him to get to the nearby stairs that would take them to the floor below. As they passed him, Chris turned back to the balcony, surreptitiously watching their progress. He hoped they were going to meet Darius whoever he was. He clenched his jaw; he would dearly love to know his identity.

+++

Alena looked around her again as she picked up yet another bag of blood. No sign of anyone yet. She left the room and walked down the corridor, moving so fast it looked as though her feet barely touched the white floor. She had volunteered to get the blood for Anna from the Erie blood bank situated within the local hospital. Getting in had been easy; the locks were easily picked and no guards came to this isolated part of the building at this time of the night. She walked swiftly towards the fourth storey window she had leapt through earlier and glanced down into the hospital car park.

Kane stood in the shadows, waiting for her. In the dark all she could see were his glittering eyes as he looked up at her. She whispered his name and he stepped forward, swiftly. She dropped silently from the window and he caught her, cushioning the blood bags from the impact of her fall.

'Good catch!' she complimented him as he let her feet touch the ground.

'Thanks. Did you get enough?' he asked with a raised eyebrow at the bags of blood in her arms. There must have been at least forty.

'I think so,' she shrugged, 'Let's hope she gets used to animal blood soon.'

He nodded in agreement. He wasn't comfortable with stealing the blood bank stocks but it was a hell of a lot better than getting it fresh. They left the hospital compound, flashing past the security cameras so fast they wouldn't appear on the film. They were so busy keeping the blood bags safe that neither of them noticed the man watching them from the shadows.

Chapter 62

Eva still couldn't believe what she had been told. True to their word Nicholas and Sylph had told her everything about the legend and her part in it. The information was staggering. According to Sylph she was a powerful hybrid; a combination of Hunted Bloodline and Angel blood, who had the best of both species. Apparently she also had powers she hadn't known about before. Nicholas mentioned her exceptional hearing, how she had managed to understand their high-speed conversation in the car on their way to the Vatican and even her courage when fighting off her attackers that night outside the lab so very long ago which seemed to reinforce everything she had discovered. She wasn't just a normal human; she was different and she wasn't sure if she was pleased or not.

All her life she had wanted to fit in, be normal; be like the other people she met, and she never had. Now that she knew why, she wasn't sure she wanted to know; *too late now* she thought. She could almost deal with the fact that she was different but to then be told that she would be able to decide the future was appalling. She had noticed Sylph's and Nicholas' manner changing around her. They seemed to treat her with more deference almost as though she was their equal and she wanted to shout out in denial.

She could never be like them; so beautiful or so powerful. Maybe they had got that part wrong. One part of her hoped that they had and yet there was a small part that wanted it all to be true. She glanced at her wrist, at the faint blue pattern still visible and sighed. According to the evidence, everything Sylph had said made sense.

She barely noticed when the Elder flew silently out of the room leaving her and Nicholas alone. She could feel his eyes on her, but she wasn't quite ready to meet his gaze. She felt him move slightly as he relaxed against the couch, still watching her closely.

'A lot to take in, in one day huh?'

She nodded, wondering what to say to him without sounding ungrateful or upset about what she had learnt. She could almost feel him smiling as he said, 'You know, it took me months to get used to the idea.'

'Really?' She looked up into his warm eyes more green than silver today and her breath caught in her throat. He looked so handsome and debonair sitting next to her against the brown leather upholstery, his skin almost glowing against the dark background. He nodded seriously.

'What did you do…when you found out I mean?'

'I went into denial,' he shrugged, 'and when I did get used to it, I felt like I didn't deserve it or in truth want it. So I decided to make the most of it.' His eyes focussed on something in the distance as he remembered the past.

'How did you do that?'

He shifted his gaze swiftly to her face. 'By helping humans…I decided to protect the weak and defenceless, so I became a lawyer.'

She now understood his anger when Jack Sharpe had gone free, thanks to the justice system and why he had sounded so bitter about rich criminals buying their freedom. It went against everything he was fighting for. She sighed, how could she help anyone else when she was still trying to help herself?

'What are you thinking about?'

'I'm wondering how I can help anyone when I'm so helpless.'

'You? Helpless? You must be kidding!'

She glanced up, certain he was laughing at her. But he looked deadly serious and if anything slightly shocked at what she had said. 'What do you mean?'

'You're not helpless Eva, far from it. You are the One! Don't you get it? You are the most powerful of us all!'

She looked at him in shock for a few minutes before finally finding her voice to say with disbelief, 'How is that possible? I'm human, I can't change into animals like you or control minds like Leo.'

He was nodding long before she had finished speaking. 'All of those are just parlour tricks compared to what you can do! You just haven't tapped into your powers yet. They are all still locked up so to speak.'

She shivered involuntarily. 'So you're saying I have to learn how to unlock them?'

'Yes,' he nodded, 'Thats why the *neonates* - the new vampires, come here to learn from the Elders.'

'Oh.' She didn't feel too bad now, but the thought of being in control of supernatural powers still made her queasy.

'Don't worry, we'll help you.'

She looked up at him, wondering, not for the first time, how he always knew what she was thinking. Maybe that was part of his talent? She decided to ask him; after all she may have the same ability.

'How do you always know what I'm thinking? Is that part of your powers too?'

He shook his head with a slow smile that had the blood racing in her veins. 'No but you seem to be very easy to read.'

She blushed and looked away from his intense gaze. 'So when do I start learning?' she asked with difficulty, trying not to think about how gorgeous he looked.

He sat back slightly. 'I'm not sure, but once Sylph lets the Council know you are the One they will no doubt want you trained pretty soon.'

Chapter 63

They had finally found her! Sylph still couldn't quite believe it. She knew what the Oracle had predicted but after so many years even she had started to lose faith in the prophecy. She felt ashamed of it now. How could she have doubted Iasoel, the Angel of Visions?

At the time most of the Elders had doubted her and Iasoel had left, but her message had been recorded and preserved in Sylph's mind for centuries. Now as she faced the Council of Elders, she could see their faith wavering. Would they still believe? She let her eyes travel round the chamber; the Elders were in the long room lined with the throne-like chairs. Several of the chairs were empty and she quickly skimmed past them. Instead she let her gaze rest on each face for a second before moving on to the next. Details were important and she was adept at noting them and recording them for eternity, to be used at a later date. It was this ability that had helped her identify the Dark Ones when they had first fallen from Grace.

Her eyes rested on an almost forgotten face and she froze. What was he doing here? After so long? Her mind reeled back to the last time she had seen him in the Reliquary. He was still part of the Council but he hadn't made an appearance for over two centuries. He must have heard about Eva, she thought, but she still wasn't convinced. He had left suddenly and no one had tried to find him. Rumours had spread like wildfire but nothing was certain. He bowed his head with a smile and she responded automatically, he was too powerful to shun. Her eyes moved on, noticing the sombre expressions. In return they all looked at her expectantly; some hopefully and some with anxiety. Her next words could change their beliefs and their world forever, catapulting them into unknown territory, and no one knew this better than her.

She finally looked at Terence and instantly felt at ease. He believed in the prophecy and the Regent held a lot of sway with the Council. But even from this distance she could detect the hostility emanating from her sister. Arri was watching her like a hawk. Sylph knew she would attract the greatest opposition from her and she steeled herself to meet it.

'Have you come to a decision?' Terence asked softly, instantly silencing the whispers.

She nodded and looked straight at the Elders. 'Eva bears the Mark of Heaven, she's the one we have been waiting for.' Sylph could see that they were equally divided in their reactions. Half were glad and the other half out-raged, and both were eager to voice their opinions. The only one who stayed seated and silent was the Regent. He was frowning deep in thought. A few minutes later he stood up and glanced at the two factions who were still arguing with each other.

'Silence!' he said in almost a whisper but each and every Elder heard it as though he had shouted the words at a high frequency. Their sensitive ears rang with the word forcing them to return to their seats and look at him. When he had their full attention he glanced again at Sylph who was standing a few feet away.

'The Keeper has spoken and now we must decide what is to be done.' He paused and glared at them, his face stern. 'A vote will be called for in due course, I will not tolerate an argument again, but we will hear your views.'

'If she is the One, she has powers we cannot hope to control,' one of the Elders mused softly.

Sylph looked at the man without surprise. Karael was right, Eva's powers would be difficult to control, and it was understandable that his mind revolved around protecting their interests; after all he was one of Heaven's Protectors.

'She is unable to use them at the moment,' Sylph informed the Council, 'she doesn't know how.'

'We can teach her,' volunteered another.

Sylph smiled at Nuriel, as the Angel of Spellbinding powers he was the one who taught the Neonates and controlled them if they went too far.

'And help her to become uncontrollable?' Arri asked sceptically.

'If we don't she may discover them on her own and become dangerous,' Terence replied.

'If we leave her in the dark she won't be a threat.'

'She may be a greater threat if the Dark Ones find her and sway her to their side,' Amitiel, the Angel of Truth retorted heatedly.

'There is no guarantee that she will choose the Light once her powers mature,' Arri said, 'Sylph told us she has the ability to choose.'

'As do we all sister,' Sylph replied in a gentle but firm tone of voice. 'I have seen her heart and it is pure.'

'But for how long? Do not forget we were the Children of Heaven too, once,' Arri responded acidly.

Terence sighed, 'Both arguments hold sway.' He glanced around the room. 'The decision is the Council's.'

Sylph looked at the Elders, fearful of their decision. If they decided to let Eva discover the powers on her own she may be in danger from the Dark Ones, but if they helped her to unleash them she may still turn on them. It was a gamble and Sylph waited with bated breath for their decision.

Chapter 64

It was a cold rainy day and as Chris looked out of the window all he could see were banked grey clouds hanging low, with no hope of sunlight breaking through. He was sitting at his desk staring unseeing out of the window. His mind was still racing from what he had seen at ICE a few nights ago. He had watched the girl and the tall man talking to another man with pale skin and intense black eyes. His features were classical in appearance and on anyone else may have looked quite attractive but they appeared to have a menacing twist about them that made Chris shudder involuntarily. There was no doubt in his mind that the man was the one he had overheard about outside the office…Darius. He had tried to find out more about him using the police database and had gotten nowhere. He didn't seem to exist, at least not in this state or in any of the surrounding ones.

As he watched, a tall woman had appeared next to Darius and he had blinked several times, wondering if he was imagining it all. She looked stunning and he hadn't been able to top staring at her. She seemed very close to Darius but he couldn't seem to care less. Chris felt an irresistible pull towards her and when she suddenly turned and looked at him he felt like he was the only one in the room. He didn't see Darius glaring at him or the aristocratic man next to him watching him thoughtfully. All he could think about was the gorgeous creature smiling at him so seductively.

All at once the entire group disappeared, leaving him to look around the dance floor desperately. After spending another hour looking for them in every room in the club, he had finally given up and driven home. Now sitting at his desk he couldn't stop thinking about the girl in the club. There was no way she was truly as beautiful as he remembered, he must have been more drunk than he thought; the alcohol must have messed with his head. But despite all the arguments he still couldn't get her out of his mind. Much to his colleagues' surprise he knocked off early and headed downtown. He had to see her again.

+++

She's not going to be here, he thought for the millionth time. And yet here he was, sipping his drink and watching the dance floor and the front door avidly like a man possessed. It had been five hours since he first arrived and the bartender was no longer asking him what he wanted; his glass was filled automatically now. *A bad sign,* he thought absently as he downed his drink. He had had more than he could handle but he still felt coherent enough to continue his vigil.

As he turned to place the glass on the bar, a slim hand covered his. He looked up in surprise and nearly fell off his stool. There she was, the girl he was looking for, looking if possible even more beautiful than he remembered, and she was smiling at him in that seductive way he remembered.

'Hi,' she said in a soft voice that sent chills down his spine.

'Hi,' he managed to slur back as he fumbled to sit on the stool.

'Have you been waiting for me?'

He thought about lying but why bother? His befuddled brain wouldn't be able to lie convincingly enough anyway, so he nodded instead.

She smiled and leant forward to whisper into his ear. 'Me too.'

He closed his eyes and inhaled deeply. She smelt of lilies of the valley underlined with an earthy scent he couldn't place. Whatever it was it was driving him crazy.

'Come with me,' she invited in that soft voice, and he leapt off the stool to follow her blindly as she walked towards the stairs.

He didn't know how he managed to climb them but before he knew it they were seated on a bed in one of the rooms on the upper floor, kissing. He could barely breathe as he felt her hands in his hair, holding him close. She let her mouth travel slowly down his neck and he sighed. This was heaven. Suddenly he felt a pin prick at his throat. His hands tightened on her face, forcing her back up to meet his lips.

'What was that?' he asked between kisses.

'Don't worry you'll like it,' she promised in a throaty whisper.

Before he knew it she had dipped her head again to his neck and he couldn't think straight as he felt her tongue lick at his skin. He closed his eyes and decided to let her do whatever she wanted. He felt a sharp sting and moved restlessly but her hands were ready and they moved slowly up and down his back soothing him and lulling his brain into oblivion.

+++

'Good job,' Vassagio congratulated her as he walked into the room a few minutes later, looking impeccable as ever in his customary dark suit. His eyes wandered over the detective's still form and then focussed on Marina sitting on a nearby chair.

'It wasn't easy,' she replied in a tortured whisper, keeping her eyes away from Chris.

'I know that's why I chose you to do it.' He smiled and walked towards the bed. Placing his hand on Chris's forehead he closed his eyes and concentrated. Images flashed before his eyes like a trailer of a movie showing Chris at the police station, Chris at a bar, Chris with Eva, Chris in the alley with the bodies and finally Chris with Marina. Vassagio smiled, she had certainly done a number on the detective. He had a strong mind but anything was possible. He pulled his hand away and turned to the silent female vampire.

'You must still be thirsty, satisfy it and then return. I have more work for you.'

Marina nodded and left the room hastily. The detective's blood had simply whetted her appetite; it had in no way satiated the thirst.

Chapter 65

Nicholas looked up as Sylph approached. 'What did they say?' he asked, his heart pounding; he didn't want to know, but he had no choice.

She sat down. 'They have decided to wait for a full Council meeting. Until then Eva will be taught by the Elders.' She smiled at him reassuringly but he didn't return it.

'So we are no closer to a resolution.' He looked towards Eva's sleeping form, 'We still have to wait for the final blow.'

'It's not certain how the vote will go. Terence has called for all the Elders to vote. We are waiting for the others Nicholas; this is good news. They may favour Eva. We still have time.' She touched his arm. 'She will learn about her powers, and once the Council knows her better they will vote differently.'

He sighed and looked at her, his eyes sad. 'When do the lessons start?'

'Tomorrow. She will be in good hands, but I would like you to be there too. She will feel safer.'

He nodded. 'I intended to even if you hadn't asked.'

'I thought as much.' She smiled meaningfully and stood up. 'I will let Eleanor know.'

She disappeared and Nicholas turned back to Eva. She looked so peaceful as she slept. He decided to let her sleep on the couch that night; he didn't have the heart to wake her. Let her have the luxury of good dreams, tomorrow may be very different he thought as he stretched his legs and leaned back to keep vigil over her.

+++

Sylph found Seton and Eleanor in their allocated room. As she entered she could see their agitated expressions, which resembled Nicholas'. She smiled to alleviate their immediate fears.

'What happened?' Eleanor asked quickly, gliding to her sister's side.

'Eva is to learn from us, Terence has called for a full Council meeting before a vote is taken.'

Eleanor sighed in relief and smiled at Seton. 'Nick will be pleased.'

'He understands the implications,' Sylph added slowly, 'The final vote is his worry.'

Seton sighed, 'It worries us all, what do you think Sylph? What way will it go?'

'I cannot answer that. For my part I am with Eva, but there are many who aren't.' She thought back to the meeting. 'Almost half of the Elders are against it.'

'No doubt Arri leads the dissent,' Eleanor said bitterly.

Sylph nodded. 'She is vocal with her refusal, but powerful Elders are on our side too.' She told them about the meeting mentioning Karael's and Amitiel's views. 'They are worried she will choose the Dark if we don't take her under our wing.'

Eleanor shook her head. 'I believe she will remain with the Light no matter what, her love for Nick will not let her hurt him.'

'Perhaps, but the Council are not aware of it as yet, and perhaps that's a good thing.'

'But it would put their fears to rest and help with the vote if they did.' Eleanor glanced at Seton.

He shrugged. 'You may be right, but if you're wrong you will put them both at risk, not just Eva.'

Eleanor looked away, he was right as usual, if the Elders got wind of the relationship there may be worse consequences. Her silence prompted Sylph to intervene.

'Some are already calling her a *Nephilim*.'

'No!' Eleanor turned to her sister, fire in her eyes, 'They were all destroyed in the Flood!'

'Perhaps, but we thought we had found all the *Dimidius Sanguis* but here she is,' Sylph argued.

'The *Nephilim*?' Seton frowned he had heard that word before.

'The cursed children of the Watchers,' Sylph explained, 'Abomination on Earth, half angel half human who tried to corrupt humanity and succeeded to some degree. To prevent them God sent the Flood which annihilated them.'

'I see,' he nodded, 'but where are the Watchers now?'

'They still hold their occupations as Shepherds of humanity, but their powers have been severely restricted, so they are not visible to humans anymore,' Eleanor replied absently.

'If the Elders believe Eva to be one of the Nephilim…' Sylph's voice trailed away.

'We cannot allow that to happen or else her fate is sealed,' Eleanor almost growled.

'I agree, there is strong distrust associated with that breed,' Sylph replied.

Seton looked at the two sisters, 'So we are agreed, no one will mention Nick and Eva's feelings for each other, and we will try to convince the other Elders.'

'Agreed,' both sisters chorused as one.

Chapter 66

She couldn't believe her eyes; there was so much space! Who would have known? The Vatican was immense, but the so-called catacombs or the Reliquary as the Elders called it, stretched for miles underground, covering an area the size of a small country. Some of the passages were dark and forbidding whilst others were light and airy. Several of the rooms resembled pictures she had seen of Venetian palaces in the guide books and others rivalled the splendour of the Romanov palaces in Russia and still more rooms reminded her of cells of torture. But everywhere a deep sense of peace permeated as though someone else was dealing with the cares of the world. She tried to worry about the Elders' decision but eventually gave up to the sense of utter contentment.

Suddenly she heard faint voices, almost like they were miles away but were still filtering through the walls. *Were those hymns?* She glanced at Nicholas who was walking next to her, with a puzzled look and he smiled.

'The Vatican choirs.'

'I thought we were several feet below them.'

He nodded. 'At times we are, but several of our passages run just below or parallel to their quarters.'

She shook her head; it was amazing what could be hidden practically under one's nose. They walked further and the gentle voices faded away. That morning Nicholas had greeted her with the news of the Council's decision. It had surprised her but she had been more surprised to find him sitting next to her on the couch when she woke. It never failed to amaze her to still find him next to her. Every minute she expected him to vanish into thin air. He seemed to sense her thoughts because he had leant forward and cupped her cheek ever so gently.

'Stop waiting for me to leave, I promise I never will.'

She had smiled, trying not to breathe or move. She wanted to stay like that forever with him touching her cheek, looking at her with those solemn silver-green eyes and leaning so close she could smell that amazing scent which delighted her senses. It seemed he felt the same way, because he had stared at her for what seemed an age and then he had moved away, almost reluctantly it seemed. She had had to shake her head to clear it, by which point he had already moved with lightning speed to the other end of the room, as far away as he could get and motioned to the plates of food already waiting for her.

'Eat,' he invited her, 'you will need your strength today.' Before leaving her to get ready.

+++

Now her hunger satiated and dressed in slim fitting trousers and a T-shirt, she followed him to an unknown destination, through a myriad of corridors and rooms. They finally stopped at a large wooden door. She looked closely at the carvings on its surface. They were intricately carved and didn't seem to have a beginning or an end, and closely resembled the mark on her wrist.

'It's the training hall,' he explained softly, 'they are waiting for us.'

Almost instinctively their hands moved to clasp the other's tightly. Without looking at her he uttered a few strange words.

'*Coelum obsequiem, patefacio!*'

The door creaked open slowly, the carvings glowing with threads of silver. Eva held her breath, not sure what she would find on the other side. When they walked through it wasn't anything like what she had expected. The room was a massive hall divided into smaller areas. Desks were grouped around certain areas while others held suits of armour and weapons. The décor was very basic, the stone floors and walls were bare, the only ornament a huge Cross hung on the far wall, sturdy iron nails visible at the ends of the shorter arms. She instinctively knew it was the original cross from the Bible. Her eyes wandered over the sparse furniture to rest on the group standing several feet away. Amongst them she recognised Sylph and Eleanor. Two men she had never seen before stood with them, wearing the traditional white robes of the Elders.

'Eva,' Sylph greeted her warmly as they moved closer.

She smiled at the silver-haired Elder; she felt so comfortable with her now. Sylph nodded to Nicholas by way of greeting and then turned back to Eva.

'You must meet your mentors,' she said and pulled her effortlessly forward to meet the two men standing silently.

'This is Karael, he is a Protector; he will teach you defence and attack.'

The tall dark haired man bowed low. As he lifted his head, his hair seemed to glow with red streaks like little flames. His eyes, though pale like the others', were steady and intense.

'Eva,' he smiled, 'A pleasure.' He spoke in a low firm voice; the voice of someone accustomed to giving orders and having them obeyed she thought.

She gulped and tried to smile; he looked dangerous. Sylph moved her on to the next Elder. 'Nuriel is the Angel of Spellbinding powers. He will help you with the spells.'

'Charmed,' the man responded almost tongue in cheek. Eva had a curious feeling that he was laughing at Sylph's pompous introduction of himself, rather than at her. She smiled back more easily for he had twinkling eyes, and a cheeky grin. His boyish looks put her at ease and as she turned to Sylph again, she thought she saw him wink at Nicholas.

'You will start your lessons today with me,' Sylph explained. 'You need to know the basics about us before you attempt any tasks.'

Eva nodded, still not sure if she really wanted to be here, but it seemed she no longer had a choice. The two men bade her farewell and vanished; Karael seemed to transform into a ball of flame, while Nuriel simply faded away, grinning cheekily at her all the while.

She found Eleanor watching her closely when she turned round. She looked curiously at the other woman, wondering what she was thinking. She thought the vampire looked uneasy. But then she smiled at her, and Eva blinked, she must have been mistaken.

'They like to show off for the neonates,' Eleanor said.

'Yes,' Sylph sighed, 'their vanity is beyond bounds.' But she was laughing as she took Eva by the hand and led her to a small cubicle. 'We will study history first, from the beginning.' The lessons had truly begun.

Chapter 67

She didn't know how long she stayed in the massive hall, but it seemed like forever. Sylph taught her about the Creation of Angels; how they were divided into nine choirs, the first choirs all protecting Heaven and God, while the last choir, which had the greatest number of angels, were created to protect and guide humans. It had been these angels that had faced temptation and succumbed to it. She learnt about the Watchers of Grigori; four immense angels sent to guide the first humans, who were also the first to fall in love with mortal women. Their unions created Nephilim, half human half-angel beings that tried to corrupt mankind.

She felt distinctly uneasy when she learnt about them and when Sylph asked her why she looked worried she asked, 'Am I one of these creatures?'

Sylph shook her head slowly with a gentle smile curving her lips. 'No Eva, you are nothing like them. They were abomination, almost like giants and they were evil. Your heart is pure, and you don't have Watcher blood. It is purer than that.' She looked away thoughtfully before continuing, 'It is true you are a half-blood, what we call *Dimidius Sanguis.*'

Eva nodded slowly, trying desperately to understand. 'So there are different types of half-bloods?'

'Yes, when our kind fell in love, their children had different qualities. Most did not survive because as you know their bloods could not co-exist. Yours is very different because each blood type fortifies the other.'

By the end of the day Eva had learnt everything she needed to know about the Fall and the Repentance and the War between the Light and Dark ones. Before she left, she turned back to Sylph with one last question.

'Nicholas told me the Angels that were destroyed in the War freed their powers and they found other hosts.'

Sylph nodded, 'Yes.'

'So vampires like Nicholas and Seton…they have these lost powers?'

'Yes.'

'How do you know which humans should be turned into vampires?' she wondered.

Sylph smiled and touched her head. 'We sense when the powers are ready to show themselves. The humans are born with them, and like yours are dormant for a while. But eventually Fate plays a hand and we come into contact with the chosen ones.'

She watched Eva's reaction. She had been surprised at how easily she had listened to and retained the information Sylph had taught her. She had also been pleasantly surprised at how astute her mind was when she asked questions and tried to understand the answers. Even now Sylph could almost see the questions developing in her mind and prepared to answer them.

'Are they all good?' Eva asked, thinking about Darius.

'No,' Sylph shook her head, 'you have already met Nick's brother. He was turned by one of the Dark when we found him, but he also chose the Dark.' She sighed. 'We don't always succeed, but there is always hope.'

+++

Sylph's words rang in her mind as she walked towards Nicholas, who had retired to a different cubicle to read.

'Hi,' he said, standing up and looking closely at her face, she looked tired.

'Hi,' she replied absently, falling into step next to him as they left the hall.

He sensed her pre-occupation and decided not to interrupt her thoughts. They walked silently towards their quarters. As they turned a corner in the passage, Nicholas stiffened and stepped quickly in front of her and halted, causing her to walk straight into him with a thud.

'Hey, wha…?!'

But he was too busy staring ahead. She peered round his shoulder to see a group of people standing a few feet away. They didn't look like the Elders, in fact they were dressed in very modern clothes and they appeared to range from mere teenagers to the mid-twenties. One was so young Eva thought she must be barely twelve years old. They were all staring back at Nicholas. Most looked surprised but a few were looking aggressive. They were all sniffing the air, questing, until suddenly a savage snarl broke loose from the youngest girl.

Eva gasped; the girl had looked so pretty and innocent a second ago, but now she resembled a ferocious creature. Her eyes were blazing a dull red; her mouth was gaping open to show sharp fangs dripping uncontrollably with saliva, which slid down her chin. She was crouching now and the rest were mimicking her. She felt Nicholas move, could feel his body tensing in readiness. A warning snarl ripped through his throat, causing some of the teenagers to cower in fear.

Eva shuddered in response, he looked terrifying and she didn't blame the youngsters for rethinking their actions. But several still stood their ground. Nicholas started pushing her backwards, away from him, making her stand close to the stone wall so that he could protect her better.

'Who are they?' she whispered from behind him.

'Neonates,' he growled in response not looking away from the crouching group. 'Stay behind me.'

Before he had finished speaking, a blur detached from the group and flew straight at him. Eva cried out in horror, but Nicholas was too fast. He caught the girl by the throat, shook her viciously and threw her back. Before Eva could shout a warning, two others flew forward and Nicholas turned with lightning speed to fight them off. The snarls and growls resembled a huge dog fight and Eva cowered close to the wall, watching with wide, fearful eyes as more of the Neonates plunged into the frenzy. Nicholas was busy fighting off at least five of them, and didn't notice the small girl duck under his defence and head straight for Eva.

She stopped a few inches away, sniffing appreciatively. Eva shuddered and moved closer to the wall, trying to shout to Nicholas for help, but no sound came out of her dry throat. The girl leaned forward slightly and Eva looked into her blue tinged dull red eyes, and knew the moment she decided to plunge forward. She lifted her hands protectively in front of her against the attack, closing her eyes tightly in fear.

Just as she braced herself for the impact she felt a curious tingling in her hands and then an astounded yelp. Opening her eyes slightly, she fully expected the girl to be on top of her, her teeth in her hands, but to her surprise the girl was nowhere to be seen. She looked at Nicholas who was still fighting. He turned to glance at her quickly with a smile and then resumed his fighting with greater intensity. Soon Neonates were flying left, right and centre, slamming off the passage walls and bouncing off the stone floor. Just as he was dealing with the last of them, Eva heard someone speak in a controlled voice.

'*Imperium animus*!'

The Neonates stilled and looked at the pale figure standing in the passage behind Nicholas. Eva followed their gaze and saw a tall man move forward slowly. As he did so, the Neonates shuffled back, regrouping. None of them uttered a sound as he approached. He flicked his wrist and they all turned and walked away, none of them looking back.

'I had it under control, Zophiel,' Nicholas almost growled, as he straightened to his full height. 'I didn't need your help!'

The man bowed slightly, 'Yes, but it was getting tiresome.' He smiled disarmingly. 'Will you not introduce me?'

Nicholas reigned in his frustration and looked at Eva. 'This is Zophiel, one of the Elders.'

'A pleasure to meet the One,' Zophiel said, smiling at her.

She felt he wanted to say much more, but for some reason unknown to her, he couldn't. He was just as handsome as the others she had seen, and he had the same pale, flawless skin, but his hair was a light brown, turning slightly grey at the temples, and his eyes were so pale, that they were almost transparent and only the edge of the irises glowed silver. She got the feeling that he was keeping a myriad of secrets that he would never divulge.

'She is strong isn't she?' he asked Nicholas, whilst still looking curiously at her.

Eva frowned, *what did he mean?*

'Yes, I didn't expect that to happen,' Nicholas agreed almost proudly.

Eva looked at him still frowning in confusion. 'Didn't expect what?'

'Didn't you see it?' He was looking at her now.

'I don't know what you are talking about,' she replied in a confused voice.

He shook his head. 'Eva you fought off that female Neonate.'

'What?!' She felt a bit faint all of a sudden. *He must be joking! There was no way I could have done that!*

'You flung her away with enough force to send her half-way down the passage,' he said, his voice tinged with awe.

'But I didn't do anything!' she insisted.

Zophiel stepped forward. 'Eva, when you lifted your hands did you feel anything?'

She nodded slowly, 'Just a tingling.'

'That was your power. When you are threatened your powers come into play to protect you. In your case a bolt of lightning hit the girl.'

'*Lightning came out of my hands?!*' She lifted her palms and stared at them in shock.

'Yes,' Zophiel smiled kindly, 'have you ever done that before?'

She looked up, her violet eyes wide as she remembered. 'When I was kidnapped by Darius, they tried to touch me and lightning shot out, but I thought that was from the charm Nicholas gave me.'

'That charm would have given them a shock, but it is not powerful enough to create lightning,' Nicholas replied.

Eva shook her head to clear it. 'But why were these people after me?'

'They are Neonates, new-born vampires,' Nicholas explained, 'they are still thirsty for human blood and will continue to be until they are taught otherwise.' He turned to Zophiel, 'This group is particularly blood thirsty!'

'Yes,' he nodded in agreement, 'They do appear to be more vicious, perhaps because they are so young.'

'Sophia and Nuriel will have their hands full,' Nicholas chuckled.

Zophiel nodded and looked at Eva. 'You are tired, get some rest.' And with that he flew down the passage, following the group of Neonates.

'Wow!' Eva breathed, 'That was crazy!'

'I agree, let's hope we don't bump into any more of them,' Nicholas replied as he steered her down the passage.

Chapter 68

He sat staring into space. He couldn't remember how he had got here, or where he had been or who with. But he suddenly had an overwhelming urge to find the Raynes. He looked again at the folder in front of him, searching for the address. It was just outside Erie. It wouldn't take him long to get there. He started to lift the phone receiver; he needed a warrant for their arrest.

'Hey Chris!'

The receiver fell back into the cradle. 'Hey.'

'What are you doing?' Joe was looking at him with the clear blue eyes that seemed to see everything.

'Nothing, working on the ICE case,' Chris replied absently.

'Did you get a new lead?'

'Kind of…yeah actually,' Chris shrugged, 'I think the Raynes are involved.'

'The Raynes? But you practically cleared Nicholas Rayne last week.'

'Yeah, but I was wrong. I think he is still a suspect.'

Joe looked thoughtful, 'So what made you change your mind?'

Chris frowned; he wasn't actually sure why he was suddenly suspecting the Raynes again. 'Uh, I'd rather not say just now.'

'Really?' Joe lifted his eyebrows. 'Surely you can tell me?'

'No,' he shook his head, not meeting his friend's eyes, 'Not just yet Joe.'

The other detective shrugged and smiled. 'Okay, guess I'll catch up with you later then.'

Chris nodded absently as the door closed behind his partner. He was trying desperately to remember, remember last night. He remembered the club and of course Marina…who could forget her? But afterwards it all became an indistinct blur. He vaguely recalled waking up in his bed, dressing and coming to work, but it felt like a dream. He sighed; he must have drunk more than he thought he had. His eyes automatically focussed on the folder again; time to get that warrant.

+++

Ashe looked across the room at Lainey, she was sitting at her usual desk in the corner, keeping herself to herself, the seat next to her empty. He could hear Taylor talking loudly to her group as they walked past him, headed for the centre of the room. *And the centre of attention* he thought. He ignored them as he walked past and could practically feel Taylor's annoyance. She had been trying to get his attention for the past two weeks and had failed miserably. Even now she was glaring at his back as he sauntered casually towards Lainey's corner.

What did he see in that nobody anyway? she thought, not for the first time.

Lainey almost jumped a mile when he dumped his books on the desk next to hers. *Who on earth…?* She froze as her eyes took in the lanky body and the totally out-of-this-world good looks. *Him again*, she almost groaned out loud. Ever since he had helped her at her home he had stayed close to her. She still didn't fully believe that she had fainted, and refused to believe that she had hallucinated about the girl in the bathroom.

Why was he still paying her so much attention? She let herself glance sideways at him, he was possibly the most gorgeous heartthrob in school and he could have hung out with anyone. So why her? She just couldn't understand it. She held her breath as he sat down and pretended to read the textbook in front of her, trying to ignore him. She knew he was watching her with a small smile.

'Hey Lainey,' he finally drawled, the smallest hint of laughter in his voice.

'Mmm,' she mumbled, flipping a page over without bothering to read it.

'That must be riveting stuff,' he observed in mock seriousness, and leaned closer to have a better look, far too close for her peace of mind.

She pulled away jerkily. 'Yeah.'

Mr. Thompson chose that moment to bring the class to order, preventing Ashe from making her feel more uncomfortable than she already was. She sighed with relief and turned her attention to the teacher thankfully.

At the end of the class, Ashe picked up his books and glanced at Lainey's profile. He didn't know why but he felt as though he needed to be near her, so he waited patiently until she had organised her books and stood up. He knew she was taking longer than usual in an attempt to avoid him, but he could wait. When she finally looked up at him, he flashed her a dazzling smile that made him blink.

'Mr. Thompson was on fire today! So what's your next class?'

'Uh, I'm not sure,' Lainey mumbled, trying to blink away the momentary blindness from his smile.

'Come on! You've had the same classes all semester!'

She sighed in resignation. 'Okay, it's history.'

'Hey mine too, walk together?'

She was hard pressed not to say no. He looked so happy. So she nodded instead and walked past him to the door. Taylor was standing in the corridor and as soon as she saw Lainey, she stepped forward, blocking her way.

'Look who it is, little Miss Nobody!' she purred in a sickeningly sweet voice as her group of girls snickered in response.

'What do you want Taylor?' Lainey asked tiredly, she didn't have time for this.

'Oh my! She speaks almost like an equal!' Taylor sneered and moved closer, making the other girl step back. 'But now that you ask I want you to stay in your place, away from Ashe Rayne...or else...'

'Why?' Lainey looked into Taylor's vicious eyes defiantly, even though fear was gripping her.

'Because he's mine!' Taylor hissed, leaning so close now that Lainey could feel her breath on her face.

'I doubt that,' came the smooth reply.

Taylor leapt back and looked up to see Ashe lounging against the doorway behind Lainey. He looked at Lainey covertly making sure she was okay. Other than looking slightly dishevelled she looked unharmed. He turned his silvery gaze on Taylor with a raised eyebrow.

'I believe you were saying something to Lainey, care to let me into the secret?'

Taylor flushed a bright scarlet. 'We were just talking, you know...girl talk.'

'I know girl talk,' he agreed, 'and that was no girl talk.'

He pushed himself away from the doorjamb and walked towards them. Lifting his arm he draped it deliberately over Lainey's shoulders, all the while maintaining eye contact with Taylor, whose face was turning an interesting shade of purple. He finally looked at Lainey's white face, leaned down and dropped a kiss on her cheek.

'You okay?' he murmured gently.

She nodded, too dazed from the kiss to object when he steered her away from Taylor and her now silent groupies, down the corridor, keeping his arm firmly in place. When they were out of earshot, Lainey looked up at him in bewilderment.

'What was all that about?'

'Just delivering a message,' he smiled back.

'Message?'

'Yeah, you know, we're friends and if they mess with you, they mess with me.'

'That sounds so corny! Plus why would you do that anyway?' she asked faintly, feeling oddly secure with his arm around her shoulders.

'Face it Lainey, we're going to be friends like it or not. Besides if it helps, our friendship will keep Taylor away from you,' he replied as they approached their next class.

She thought about what he had just said. It made sense, but she couldn't shake off the fact that Taylor had it in for her because of her new friend. Ashe took advantage of her preoccupied silence and escorted her to her usual seat before dropping into the one next to her with a suppressed yawn.

Chapter 69

Leonara drove through the wrought iron gates, turning the white Lamborghini Diablo just in time to prevent it from crashing into the metal frame. Having passed the gates she slammed her foot on the accelerator and sped down the drive-way at seventy miles an hour until she was inches from the central stone fountain, before turning the wheel sharply sending the car skidding sideways until it came to a screeching halt at the front door. Almost before the engine had died, she had leapt out of the driver's seat and flashed into the Mansion. She found the others in the living room already waiting for her.

'What news?' Alena asked, standing up quickly as she walked into the room.

Leonara shook her head. 'It's not good, we are now the suspects.'

'How is that possible?' Eden frowned.

'They have Nick's number plate and I detect foul play.'

'The detective?' Alena shook her head. 'That's not possible, he's a good guy.'

'Anything is possible if you add Darius to the mix!'

'But how...?' Alena's eyes widened as sudden understanding dawned. 'NO!'

'Yes! I saw his female leaving the detective's apartment last night. I couldn't be sure, but after this, I have no doubt!'

'We can't allow this,' Kane said grimly.

'What do you suggest? A fight?'

'We can't, it's against the Code,' Alena sighed, a worried frown on her elfin face. This was getting out of hand.

'We have to leave before they come looking for us,' Leonara's quiet voice broke the silence. It was exactly what the others were thinking.

'Leave our home?' Alena looked around the living room wistfully.

'We have done it before,' Kane replied gently, as he put his arm around her shoulders.

'But always of our own free will,' she argued, resting her head on his shoulder, 'this time it's a necessity!'

'Alena's right, how can we let humans run us out?' Eden's anger was etched on his face.

'We don't have a choice,' Kane said soothingly, 'If we don't we have to abide by their laws.'

Leonara nodded. 'Then it is settled, for our freedom we will leave. I'll arrange the flights.' She looked at the others with a mocking smile. 'Any requests?'

'Where to? Canada?'

'How about Rio? I hear it's teeming with lovelies!' Eden suggested, his anger diminishing rapidly, as the lure of an exotic country hit him.

'No, until we know what's happening with Eva we should go to Italy,' Alena said firmly, 'besides, we will have to get orders from the Elders.'

Leonara nodded in agreement. 'You're right, we still don't know what's been happening to the others.'

'It can't be anything bad and Rio is calling!' Eden pleaded with a winning smile thrown in Alena's direction. He didn't bother cajoling Leonara; she was immune to his boyish charms.

'You don't know the Elders well do you?' Alena asked, smiling back sweetly, but her eyes were deadly serious. She turned back to Leonara. 'We will go to the Reliquary Leo, as soon as possible.' She needn't have worried; Leonara was already on her way out of the room to make the arrangements.

'Where's Ashe?' Kane asked suddenly.

Eden rolled his eyes expressively. 'Bet he's with the human girl from school.'

'Are they working on a project?'

'Nope, he just likes her, I guess,' he muttered a tinge of bitterness in his voice. Ashe hadn't been around for a while and Eden was missing their usual forays on the racing circuit. None of the other competitors could match his prowess except his brother and it was getting boring when he won the races now. The challenge wasn't there anymore.

'Well, get hold of him, because we're leaving,' Alena told him as she and Kane flew out of the room to pack their belongings. The Mansion would be shut and their possessions put in storage until they returned. None of them had the slightest idea when that would be.

Chapter 70

Nicholas watched the suit of armour fly through the air and crash in a heap against the far wall. They had been practising for hours now and he could see she was tired but he dared not intervene. Every time he moved Karael shot a stern look his way that kept him silent. He dared not defy that look; he knew it far too well.

Instead he had to be content with standing on the sidelines. They had made it very clear; he was a spectator, nothing more. Sylph had sympathised with him initially but even she had agreed with the rule. It was the same for all the Neonates; they had to learn. In their world, although they were privileged, they had to be self-reliant against attack, and the way the Dark Ones were recruiting, they may have to fear that sooner rather than later. He had been proud of her during the Neonate attack in the corridor, but news travelled fast and before they knew it the Elders had thought it fit to catapult Eva into a more rigorous regime.

Neonates and Elites were constantly arriving at the Reliquary and would continue to pose a threat to the One unless she could fully defend herself without his help. He had insisted he wouldn't leave her side but it hadn't mattered, the decision had been made and for the past few days they had spent most of the daylight hours in the Training Hall with the mentors. They would have continued at night, but Eva needed to sleep.

He paced back and forth now like a caged lion, keeping an eye on her as she stood next to Karael, listening to his instructions carefully. He watched avidly as she tried to mimic his actions. He had lessons of his own to focus on as Sylph had reminded him the other day. Maybe he should concentrate on that instead. He looked at Eva again; she was in good hands, Karael was one of the best. He listened for the presence of other vampires in the immediate area. Not hearing anything he walked to the other side of the hall and pulled several screens into place to create a secluded area away from the others. Closing his eyes he concentrated, forcing Eva out of his mind and focussed on his task instead.

'Impressive!'

He looked up to see Nuriel leaning against one of the screens nonchalantly. He grimaced; he didn't want an audience.

'Easy now,' Nuriel cajoled, a wicked gleam in his eye, 'Tired of waiting for her already?' He motioned towards where Eva was still practising.

Nicholas shook his head and stepped forward, feeling the cold stone floor under his feet. He flexed his muscles experimentally and leapt forward, landing a metre away from the Elder. He didn't flinch.

'Excellent control,' Nuriel complimented the leopard pacing in front of him. He watched as it leapt onto a table and crouched low, its eyes gleaming in the dim light. Before his eyes, it transformed into a hissing spitting snake. He narrowed his eyes thoughtfully as the cobra swayed upright by several feet and showed its splendid hood. It hissed noisily before slithering to the ground and coiling on itself. In a second Nicholas was kneeling in its place, panting with the effort of the changes.

He looked up into Nuriel's sedate eyes and grimaced. 'I can't do it.'

'You can,' the Elder contradicted softly. He stepped forward and knelt next to him. 'It will come with practice, but you must let go. Ornias was the best shape-shifter and his power courses through you now.'

'Why can I only change into predators?' Nicholas wondered, almost whispering the words.

Nuriel kept silent watching him keenly. When Nicholas looked at him he sighed. 'Perhaps because you are using your powers in anger; use them with peace and you will change into more peaceful creatures.'

Nicholas shook his head, 'Peace?'

'Peace. You think too much. Remember your powers are connected to your emotions. You know that.'

Nicholas nodded slowly and closed his eyes. Nuriel stood up and moved away. As he watched Nicholas, he put out a hand and muttered a few words. Nicholas started to transform again and a second later a swan stood in his place, white and graceful. Nuriel smiled with pleasure but it didn't last long. Almost before he could nod his approval, the swan started spitting and its head and neck changed into the cobra's again. He shouted with laughter as the half snake half swan waddled towards him, still hissing and spitting. Several minutes later, amidst Nuriel's hysterical laughter, Nicholas transformed into himself and glared at the amused Elder.

'No more help, I beg of you!'

Nuriel guffawed and slapped his back. 'No more help old friend,' he promised with a chuckle.

Nicholas was about to reply when he heard a scream followed by a loud metallic crash. The two men looked at each other before flashing out of the cubicle.

Chapter 71

Eva watched as Karael destroyed the suit of armour with one flick of his wrist. She winced as the metal fell to the ground with a loud clanging noise that reverberated throughout the hall. He turned to look at her.

'Your turn.'

'But...' she tried to form the words, but couldn't. His eyes were hard as they watched her nervously lick her lips.

'Follow what I told you and you'll do it.'

She managed to nod and stepped forward a pace. He spoke aloud and the armour in front of them reassembled itself. Eva closed her eyes and concentrated like he had told her to earlier. She felt so tired. They had been at this for several hours and she had learnt several simple spells. Karael was a stern teacher but he knew how to tap into her abilities. Despite her initial reluctance she had to admit she was enjoying learning from him.

Karael had noticed her natural curiosity and to gain her interest had decided to show her some useful if slightly odd spells. He made her change water into wine and back again, saying it was a classic trick that had stood them in good stead. She had also managed to control a cat's behaviour and finally made a small chair move a few feet. She learnt that all the Angels, Elites and Elders, could do these parlour tricks but each excelled in one particular talent. He had looked thoughtfully at her as he said this, no doubt wondering what she would excel at.

Now as she looked at the menacing armour she shuddered, combat may not be her talent after all. She put her hands out and tried to concentrate. Nothing. She closed her eyes tight and tried to feel threatened. Nothing. Opening one eye cautiously she glanced at Karael who was watching her closely.

'Concentrate harder.'

She sighed, she was trying but it was so tiring. After a few more minutes she dropped her hands helplessly. It was no use; she couldn't do it. She felt rather than saw Karael move.

'Let's try defence, it is after all the best form of attack and less tiring.'

He sent the armour clanking back to its place against the far wall and summoned one of the huge battleaxes from the varied collection of weapons. For the next hour he demonstrated how he expected her to dodge it. She learnt fairly quickly, ducking and sidestepping with alacrity, surprising herself in the process. She waited as the axe came flying at her again. Standing on tiptoe she sidestepped it in one fluid movement, which sent the axe flying past her barely touching her.

That had been close, she thought.

Apparently Karael thought so too because he was frowning as the axe came back, faster than before. She was ready for it. She ducked and turned simultaneously, watching it move past her again. As she twisted round one of her feet snagged and she stumbled, losing her balance momentarily. She quickly corrected her stance and turned in time to see the axe a few inches away.

She screamed in panic and tried desperately to twist aside, hearing Karael's urgent chant as he tried to move the axe away from her. As she moved, she felt dizzy and felt herself losing her balance and falling to the ground. Just before she hit the floor and blacked out she felt an unbearably agonising pain and a heavy weight on her stomach and then...nothing.

When Nicholas and Nuriel reached the other side of the hall they found Karael on the ground, kneeling over Eva's still body.

'EVA!' Nicholas gasped and knelt next to the Elder. 'What happened?!' He stared at Eva's pale face, searching for any sign of life, fearing the worst. He felt sick as he tore his gaze away to look at Karael. An all consuming rage was building within him; how could he have let harm come to her.

Karael was busy checking Eva's hands and midriff and didn't reply immediately. When he did he said in a low voice that brooked no argument, 'Get Seton!'

Nicholas felt his gut wrench agonisingly as Karael moved his hands away to reveal a deep gash in Eva's midriff. Her clothes were soaked in blood that was now dripping onto the floor next to her. A medieval axe lay on the floor nearby where Karael had thrown it after pulling it out of her, its blade glistening with a dull red. Nicholas barely registered it as he stared numbly at the still figure.

Within seconds Seton had flashed to Eva's side with Nuriel in his wake. He glanced at Nicholas' angry, worried expression but didn't say anything. Instead he touched Eva, closed his eyes and murmured an incantation.

Oh God please help her, please don't let her die! Nicholas found himself praying fervently, something he had never done before as he watched Seton work. He knew his brother's powers were almost fully fledged but did he have enough control over them to save Eva? He cursed himself for leaving her for even a second, he should have been here; he should have saved her. It was entirely his fault; he had known she was frail, maybe too frail for what the Elders had in mind. He had seen how tired she was, why hadn't he risked Karael's displeasure and put a stop to the training? He tormented himself endlessly with the questions, sinking lower and lower into despair as the minutes ticked by.

Seton was still holding his hands over Eva, his eyes still shut, but the slight vibration in his hands intensified and they glowed white indicating how much effort he was exerting. The two Elders didn't move and when Nicholas glanced at them he could see how worried they were; she was after all the One, they couldn't let her die! He clenched his teeth, grinding them audibly as a few more minutes ticked by. He shut his eyes in despair.

Chapter 72

Surely it had been too long now, they had lost her; he had lost her, lost his soul mate. He crumpled to the floor, devastated, not caring what the others thought. Suddenly Seton sighed and Nicholas opened his eyes fully, expecting to see him defeated, but he was still kneeling next to her. His eyes were open and he was…smiling?! Nicholas craned his neck to see what was happening. And then he too sighed with relief.

The wound had almost closed, healing slowly. The blood flow had been staunched and as he watched, Eva's chest rose as she took a shallow breath. He straightened up and nearly whooped with joy. She was alive! He moved closer and lifted her head onto his knee, supporting it gently.

Karael and Nuriel exchanged a look but neither said anything; they were just glad she was still alive. Seton however looked worriedly at Nicholas, trying to get his attention, but he was too busy staring at Eva and silently vowing never to let her go and never to let any harm come to her.

As he watched, her eyelids flickered open. Once she realised who was next to her she managed a weak smile that tore at his heart. He bent his head low so that the others couldn't see how moved he was. Seton glanced at the two grim faced Elders and sighed, although the immediate danger was past, more may be lurking closer at hand. He stared at Nicholas but couldn't get his attention without drawing attention from the Elders. He had no choice but to hope Nicholas came to his senses soon, to show his true feelings would be disastrous. He stood up and moved towards the Elders, eager to steer them away from the couple before it was too late.

'What happened Karael?' he asked, turning so that the Elder had to follow his lead, until their backs were to Nicholas and Eva, who was still lying on the floor.

Karael shook his head, looking slightly shaken. 'I don't know. I was teaching her how to defend herself against a weapon and she was avoiding it superbly, but she seemed to tire and almost faint. It happened so fast, I couldn't stop the axe before it hit her.'

Seton nodded thoughtfully and walked slowly towards the other end of the hall, still talking about the accident, compelling the others to follow him. Nicholas barely registered their departure; he was still looking into Eva's eyes and stroking her hair away from her forehead. The colour was slowly returning to her cheeks. Almost without conscious thought he leant down towards her slowly. Not daring to think about what he was doing or the consequences.

Eva kept her gaze glued to his, her breathing increasing rapidly as she watched him come closer and closer. Just when she thought he would touch her he stopped and an uncertain light entered his eyes. She held her breath. There had been so many times recently when she had expected him to do something about the obvious attraction between them but he had always bailed out.

Not this time, she thought on a sudden impulse and lunged upward, catching him off guard. Her lips found his and clung desperately in a short kiss. She was still too weak to maintain her position and she would have fallen back if he hadn't supported her with a strong arm. She opened her eyes to see him staring at her in shock.

'Eva…,' he said hesitantly, shaking his head.

She stared at him, her violet eyes wide. He lifted his hand to her cheek and smoothed his thumb gently across her skin, still staring into those mesmeric eyes. He could see she was trying not to show how hurt she was and his gut twisted painfully. How could he make her understand he wasn't shunning her? That he was doing it for her safety? Suddenly a devil may care feeling hit him, he had denied himself for long enough, he deserved this. Pushing away all his natural cautiousness, and all the reasons as to why they shouldn't do this, he leant forward to cover her lips with his in a long devouring kiss that had them both gasping when he lifted his head again.

Eva nearly fainted again as he kissed her once more, letting his lips move over hers gently, teasing her. She couldn't believe how fantastic he tasted. She had thought his scent was amazing but what she was experiencing now was completely out of this world. She could feel a craving deep inside her, and for once she understood what an addict must feel like.

She moved forward trying to get as close as she could to him, deepening the kiss, not wanting to miss a single moment of it. Her entire being wanted to satisfy that craving, despite knowing she never could, and there was almost a sweet sadness in that knowledge. She could sense his restraint and yearned for him to be as out of control as she was. But he had the advantage; he didn't have to breathe. She broke away first with a gasp, sucking air desperately into her aching lungs and leant forward for more.

He didn't object when she kissed him again, holding her steady and kissing her back almost as fervently but carefully, terrified he would hurt her. He knew he had condemned them both to the Elders' wrath but with her in his arms he couldn't care less. He broke off the kiss and held her securely in his arms, preventing her from kissing him again. Sense was finally prevailing and he knew they needed to talk, but not here. He suddenly realised where they were and who was nearby.

Glancing over his shoulder he saw Seton and the Elders still walking towards the door. He sighed with relief; they hadn't seen them. He turned back to Eva who was still staring up at him with wide eyes, her lips still red and swollen from his kisses. He wanted to kiss that confused look off her face but he restrained himself. This was not the time or the place for it. So instead he hardened his heart to her pleading look and caught her face between his hands.

'We have to leave.'

'But...' she tried to struggle out of his hold.

'Eva,' he said softly and she looked at him, 'we can't do this.'

Her face fell visibly, pulling at his self-control dangerously.

He didn't want her, she thought miserably, *he never had. If she hadn't kissed him first he would never have thought about it.* She felt suddenly depressed and vulnerable. He looked so in control whilst she was still floundering from the aftermath. He cleared his throat and she winced, steeling herself for the final blow as he told her nothing could happen between them. She closed her eyes, waiting.

'We can't do this...not with the Elders here.'

She opened her eyes to see his earnest expression. He looked like he had been pushed to his limits, but before she could reply he swooped in to claim a quick kiss. As he pulled back the mischievous gleam in his eye belied his serious tone of voice. Her lips stretched of their own accord into a brilliant smile and she nodded slowly. He smiled back and lifted her bodily from the floor with ease, careful not to hurt her, although the wound had healed completely, leaving no scar. Only her clothes were stiff with dried blood and her T-shirt was torn. He watched as she walked a few steps, keeping an arm around her shoulders to steady her.

'How do you feel?' he asked in a low voice.

'Fantastic!' she replied with another smile. She glanced at the axe and shuddered. 'That was close. For a moment there I thought it was going to hit me.'

Nicholas stopped. 'Eva, it did hit you, right here.' He pointed towards her stomach indicating the blood. She looked down in surprise and gasped.

'Wha...?!'

'Karael pulled it out and Seton used his powers to heal you. I thought you weren't going to make it,' he rasped painfully, remembering how desolate and helpless he had felt watching her lifeless body as Seton worked on her.

She thought back. 'I know I fainted...I was so tired...I felt this crushing pain and then nothing.' She looked up at him searchingly. 'I thought I heard you calling me, but I was too far away...' her voice trailed away as his face became bleak.

Before she knew it he had pulled her into his arms, holding her securely against him as he buried his face in her hair, inhaling deeply, something he had wanted to do ever since he had first saved her. She closed her eyes and leaned against him, feeling his arms tighten around her as he kissed her hair. She had never seen him like this. He looked almost haggard with worry.

'Don't ever do that to me again,' he whispered into her hair. She moved her head slightly in agreement.

He glanced up and saw Seton looking at him sternly. The others had already left, and had missed his show of affection. He let Eva go and stood back as Seton came closer.

'How do you feel Eva?' he asked, his eyes taking in her dishevelled appearance. They travelled down to where the wound had been, making sure it had healed completely.

'Fine,' she managed to say in an even voice, although her heart was beating double time, eager to be held by Nicholas again, 'thank you for your help.'

'No problem, just be more careful,' he nodded and looked at his brother evenly, 'Maybe you should get some rest.'

Nicholas nodded and escorted her towards the door.

'Karael and Nuriel are letting Terence know what happened,' Seton said meaningfully as they passed him. Nicholas flashed him a grateful smile but Seton didn't return it; he looked very worried.

Chapter 73

'WHAT?!' Terence almost roared as Karael shuffled uneasily.

He had never seen the Regent so angry before except during the battles. Terence was standing up now, pacing back and forth on the dais. They were in the huge Elders' Hall and some of the others were shifting uneasily too. They all looked surprised at Terence's outburst but they understood why. The One could not be harmed, even if they didn't believe or understand the prophecy; she was still under their protection.

'How did this happen?' Terence asked, his eyes flashing with anger as he stared at Karael. He shrugged. 'She must have been more tired than I realised.'

'You were controlling the weapon. Then how did it manage to hit her?' one of the others asked.

Karael's eyes flashed dangerously at the Elder. 'What are you implying Rizoel?'

'Only trying to determine what happened,' the blonde-haired Elder smiled back but his eyes were deadly.

'If you think I intentionally tried to harm her...'

'You don't believe the prophecy...' Rizoel replied quietly.

Karael stepped forward menacingly his hand reaching under his cloak in a clear warning sign. 'If I wanted her dead she would've been.'

'Is that a fact?' Rizoel had stood up, his sword already unsheathed. 'If you weren't aiming for her how did she get hurt? Have you lost the ability of control?'

Karael snarled and pulled out his hand from under his cloak. With a sharp ringing sound his sword appeared, a bright red living blade as though flames were coursing up and down its length. 'Shall we test my abilities?'

Rizoel's smile was one of tightly controlled fury as he flashed down the steps of the dais his own sword a flaming streak of icy blue, as though it had been hewn from the centre of the coldest glacier. 'As you wish!'

'Stop!' Terence's voice halted them as they lifted their swords in readiness. He looked at the two Protectors, 'We cannot fight amongst ourselves. But Rizoel raises a good question; why could you not control the axe?'

Karael's eyes widened, 'You have to believe me! I tried!'

'And failed!' hissed Rizoel, refusing to back down from his fighting stance, his sword still glinting dangerously. 'She is under our protection!'

'I know and I would never harm her,' Karael retorted, still holding his sword in readiness. The two Elders glared at each other, neither willing to be the first to relent.

'Enough!' Terence commanded, 'Stand down.' He looked at Karael. 'I believe you, but the question still stands. If you weren't controlling the weapon, then who was?'

+++

Eva's eyes widened as she watched more and more people arrive and pay their respects to the Regent. She was sitting in the Elder's Hall with the Raynes. They had been asked to sit near the dais, surrounded by the Machai who, Nicholas had told her, were the spirit guards of the Elders. Spirits made up of light and shade, warriors able to become invisible at a moment's notice.

She glanced around her and caught Alena's eye. She had been surprised when the rest of the family had been present in the hall, as she had entered with Nicholas. There hadn't been time to say much but she was glad they were there. She felt safer with Kane's muscled body behind her next to Eden and Ashe's slimmer physiques. Alena and Leonara flanked her on each side, while Nicholas, Seton and Eleanor sat in front of her, almost shielding her from the crowds, and watching the new arrivals closely. Apparently all the Elders had been summoned to the Reliquary to decide her fate. She swallowed nervously as more and more Elders arrived with their entourages.

She gasped involuntarily as a huge group of slim, white clad women came forward. The woman in the centre wore a long flowing Grecian style white dress, with flowers twisting through her long pale hair, which almost touched the ground. She appeared to float forward, surrounded by the beautiful women who also had flowers in their hair. Eva's eyes widened as she caught sight of the sheathed swords slung round their waists.

It seemed the Elders represented every race and creed in the world. She looked around the hall letting her eyes move from the turbaned Indian warriors, to the black clad ninjas to the African tribesmen. Each Elder had a designated seat in the hall and once the Regent and the other Elders had greeted them, they made their way to their seat, their guards still surrounding them.

Eventually the last Elder walked forward, a petite Japanese woman dressed in a traditional kimono. Her face was peaceful but her quick eyes belied the complacence she portrayed. Her group of geishas personified that ancient custom with painted faces and fans, but after watching the other entourages, Eva was certain they too carried weapons hidden from view. She flashed past Eva, heading for her seat, but Eva caught her look of curiosity as she passed. They had all looked at the One curiously, some with trepidation and others with respect. She had noticed Eleanor nodding to each of them, keeping eye contact until they moved away. Nicholas and Seton had been tense throughout the process, watching the newcomers avidly. It was almost as though they were ready for any eventuality.

'Welcome.' Terence's voice boomed out, silencing the whispers and the rapid conversations in the myriad of different languages. He looked around at them and smiled. 'Thank you for coming at such short notice, as you know this meeting will affect us all in the future.' He glanced towards the Raynes. 'I would like to present to you the reason for your coming.'

As he spoke Alena and Leonara stood up each taking one of Eva's hands. They all moved forward, the Raynes keeping Eva in their midst, shielded from any potential attack. The hall was silent as every pair of eyes followed the group as they walked onto the dais to stand next to Terence. When he nodded they parted and Eva stood exposed for all the Elders to see. She was quivering with fear, not many of the faces looking at her appeared friendly. Leonara squeezed her hand gently and Eva lifted her head finding much needed strength from that assurance. One of the women stood up; it was the pale-haired lady she had seen with flowers in her flowing hair.

'Does she have the Mark?'

Terence nodded and Sylph walked forward to stand next to Eva at the edge of the dais. She took Eva's wrist and raised it high so that everyone could see it clearly. Eva felt the same warmth she had felt when Sylph had seen the Mark the first time. She could feel her skin pulsating, as the pattern grew bolder. Satisfied the pale-haired woman sat down and turned to whisper to her neighbour. The entire hall was buzzing with the soft conversations, reminding her of a hive full of bees. Terence nodded again and Sylph led her back to the Raynes.

'You may leave now.'

Before she knew it they were escorted out of the Elder's Hall through a side door nearby by two of the armed Machai. Once the door closed behind them she let out her breath. It had been a harrowing experience to have so many vampires staring at her with less than friendly intentions even though she had at least six of them to protect her.

Somehow Nicholas was now beside her, holding her hand as they followed the others down the corridor. He made her slow her pace and when she looked at him enquiringly he put a finger to his lips and glanced at the family. When they were several feet away, he pulled her through another door she hadn't noticed before and led her up a winding stone staircase. She followed him, trusting him to guide her through the darkness.

+++

They had spoken the night before about what had happened in the Training Hall. Nicholas had decided to keep the whole incident to themselves but she had questioned him as to his reasons, to which he had replied as clearly as possible.

'This isn't allowed.'

'Allowed? You mean…?'

'Yes,' he had sighed and held her face securely in his hands, staring deep into her eyes; silver clashing with violet, 'we cannot let anyone know about…us.'

'There's an "us"?' she had asked mischievously, trying to lighten the mood.

'Apparently there is,' he replied, a twinkle in his eye, but then he had reverted to being serious again, 'We can't risk the Elders finding out, not now that they are going to vote about you.'

She had nodded understanding. 'I get it, I'm a human and you're a vampire, an Elite.'

He had stared at her for several seconds, his eyes wide with surprise. 'Is that really what you think?'

She nodded slowly, uncertain now and worried by his intense stare. *Wasn't that the reason he had held back so far?* She knew the Elders frowned on unequal relationships such as Eleanor and Seton's. She would never have dared hope that Nicholas felt that way about her, but after what had happened in the Training Hall she had no doubts about his feelings, but maybe she was wrong. Her fears surfaced quickly. Maybe he hadn't felt like that at all. Maybe he had just been caught up in the moment and hadn't wanted to disappoint her after she had taken the initiative.

You are a fool, she thought despairingly, *he is gorgeous, practically an angel! How can he even like someone like me; a nobody?* She chewed her lower lip worriedly, waiting for him to confirm her worst fears. Something changed in his eyes and she stiffened, here it was, he was going to laugh at her and tell her she was indeed a fool for believing they could be together.

He smoothed away a tendril of hair from her cheek and shook his head, his lips twitching. 'Eva, you always doubt me.'

She could feel her stomach churning sickeningly, so he knew what she was feeling and thinking. That didn't make things any easier, she felt nauseous.

'I'm right.'

It was more a statement than a question and he stopped fiddling with her hair and looked into her eyes shaking his head again.

'No, you've got it backwards.' He sighed and leaned forward to kiss her cheek lingeringly. Her eyes closed involuntarily, feeling his firm lips moving against her skin.

'What do you mean?' she managed to gasp, fighting the urge to turn her head and kiss him properly. He moved back and she breathed a bit easier, trying to hide her disappointment.

'You are the One. The Elders will not tolerate us being together.'

'Because I'm half human?' she asked, knowing she was right, no matter how he tried to dress it up, she knew she wasn't worthy of an Angel's love.

'Because you're half Angel,' he replied with a wan smile.

'What do you mean?' she asked, the confusion plain on her face.

He sighed as though he was trying to make a very dense child understand a simple concept. 'You are by birth related to the Elders. You have Angel blood in your veins and an original power.' He watched as her eyes widened.

'But I'm half human!'

'So you keep saying, but you seem to be forgetting that that half is part of the Hunted Bloodline; another powerful element.'

'So you're saying—?

He smiled sadly. 'In effect you are a royal and I'm a commoner'

She gasped, she hadn't thought about it like that at all. 'But that's impossible! You are a vampire, have been for so long!'

'But blood is stronger than time,' he quipped.

She paled considerably, she supposed he was right, but all that had been generations ago! Surely that mattered? He seemed to understand what she was thinking and was already shaking his head.

'The Prophecy makes you more important than even the Regent. You hold their fate…my fate in your hands.' He caught her hands in his gently, reinforcing his words.

'But I want to be with you,' she said, blinking rapidly. She was getting too emotional, something she never did. She took a deep breath and steadied herself, she sounded like one of those soppy actresses she couldn't stand in those mushy love stories. His eyes were laughing at her as he watched her wrestling with herself.

Finally when she could trust herself to speak normally she asked, 'Do you want to be with me?'

He hadn't bothered to reply, preferring instead to kiss her so fervently she had been breathless for several minutes afterwards. 'Does that answer your ridiculous question?' he had asked, a piratical smile on his perfect lips.

'I guess.' She had looked at him, her eyes shining with happiness, still not completely confident. 'So we're keeping this under wraps?'

'For the foreseeable future.'

She nodded thoughtfully and then looked at him again, trying not to smile. 'I'm still not fully convinced. I think I need more assurance from you to fully believe you really like me.'

He had raised an eyebrow and then moved forward, so fast he appeared to be a blur, to silence her fears once and for all.

Chapter 74

Now he cautioned her with a finger to her lips and led her towards a narrow slit in the wall. They were standing on a small landing and when she looked through the slit she was shocked to see the Elder's Hall several feet below her. They were hidden just to the right of the dais, commanding a view of most of the Elders. They were still discussing Eva's Mark, when Terence held up his hand. Calling them to order, he waited until they were all seated before proceeding.

He spoke in Latin quoting verses from the Bible. Eva listened as Nicholas translated it for her. He then motioned Sylph forward. She repeated the Prophecy in a calm clear voice that didn't appear to be her own.

When Eva looked enquiringly at Nicholas, he smiled. 'She repeats what has happened in the past and uses that person's voice so there is no doubt as to who said the original words.'

She nodded understanding. 'Should we be here?'

He shrugged. 'The meeting is about you.'

She looked uncertain, it made sense, but there must have been a reason she hadn't been allowed to stay in the hall. Her thoughts were interrupted by what was happening below her. An Elder she didn't recognise was standing facing the dais. For some reason she felt a chill run down her spine and a feeling of foreboding clutched at her heart. Next to her, Nicholas had tensed too.

'Permission to speak Regent?'

Terence nodded and the Elder looked around the hall. 'My greetings to you all, it has been too long since we were together.'

There was a smattering of agreement as he turned back to the dais. 'We have seen the Mark and heard the Prophecy,' he smiled cordially at Sylph, who inclined her head, 'but how can we be sure she hasn't already chosen the Dark?' The hall echoed with his question.

Terence looked around at the others. 'She has been under *Electismus* protection long before either party knew of her true identity.'

'But what if the Elites were duped? What if she is really part of the Dark, and all this is just a way for her to gain our trust?' the man continued.

Nicholas stirred and when Eva looked up at him his face was a mask of anger. 'He's going too far!' he breathed.

Apparently some of the Elders thought so too because several stood up to counter this attack.

'Are you suspecting the One? After the Regent has proclaimed she is of the Light?' Amitiel asked in a low voice, dangerously close to a growl.

'How can you suspect the *Electismus* of being duped?' another asked angrily.

Arri stood up, her robe flowing around her like a dark cloud. 'We have seen it before, the Elites are not always to be trusted.'

'They have never let us down,' Terence interjected defensively.

'And what of Darius? He was an Elite but he has now turned to the Dark,' Arri asked him, her eyes flashing. Terence shook his head but before he could reply she continued. 'And is it not true that his brother is still an Elite? An Elite within the same coven that found the One?'

There was sudden silence in the hall after she had spoken, all eyes trained on Terence to see what he would say.

He was staring back at Arri calmly. 'Darius was never going to be an Elite; he didn't have any powers. You mentioned Nicholas. Yes, he is Darius' brother, we all know that, and we all know how different he is compared to his brother. His interpretation of the Code is stricter than ours in some cases. He would never betray us.'

'Do you protect him so strenuously because he holds Ornias' powers?' Arri asked slyly, her eyes narrowed with a small smile lifting one corner of her mouth.

Terence glared at her but when he spoke his voice was calm. 'Ornias was a good friend, but we all know that once we leave Earth, the host our power chooses has no relation to ourselves.' His gaze fell on Arri again with the directness of an arrow. 'You should know that better than anyone Ariel.'

Her eyes blazed with humiliation. He had used her original name, the one she never used now because it reminded her instantly of Zerachiel, he used to love that name. The Regent had riposted expertly, but she wouldn't turn tail and run. She wasn't made that way. Instead she decided to change tack and turned to look at the rest of the Council.

'Nicholas was human before. We all know they are emotional and remember their past life. Blood ties are strong for them, perhaps too strong in this case.'

'Do you have any evidence to support these accusations or is it all conjecture?' Amitiel asked her.

'I have some evidence.'

Everyone turned their attention towards the tall man who had stood up initially. He looked even more terrifying and Eva shuddered as she watched him turn to look at the Regent.

'As you know I haven't been at the Reliquary for some time. I have in fact been travelling and I happened to be in the same area as the Raynes' coven when they found the One.' He paused to let his words sink in before continuing. 'Whilst in Erie I witnessed the Raynes stealing human blood from the local blood bank.'

There was a collective gasp before the room exploded with the sound of angry exclamations and Elders rising to their feet.

'Silence!' Terence roared.

All the Elders sat back down shocked into silence and looked at the Regent. He turned to the tall man, 'If that is true then we would have detected it. The protection spells around the Reliquary won't allow any Dark One to pass.' He looked at the rest of the Council. 'Do you truly believe we wouldn't sense their betrayal, Children of Heaven?'

There were a few sighs and some of the Elders shifted uneasily as his earnest gaze passed over them.

He turned to look at Sylph. 'The Keeper was the first to notice the Dark Ones when we fell from Grace. I trust she has not noticed anything unusual about the Raynes?'

She stood up slowly and walked forward. Looking down at the Council, she shook her head, 'All present in the Reliquary are of the Light, none has partaken of human blood.' She turned her luminous gaze on the Elder in front of her, 'You are mistaken my lord, I have spent a lot of time with the Raynes and have yet to see any evidence of Darkness in any of them. As for Eva,' she lifted her head, 'she is of the Light, her heart and soul are pure.'

As she spoke, her eyes rested on the vertical slit in the stone wall above her and a shadow of a smile flitted across her face. Eva held her breath, Sylph knew they were there listening, she was sure of it. Almost immediately, Sylph turned to walk back to her seat. But the man was still standing unmoved by her words, looking at Terence evenly.

'If the Keeper believes their innocence then so do I. But why then steal human blood?'

Silence followed his words, broken only by Arri as she said softly, 'Maybe it wasn't for them.'

Over a hundred pairs of eyes focussed on her. She was looking at the dais contemplatively. 'The Keeper would sense if an Elder or an Elite had drunk human blood, but what of a *Dimidius Sanguis*? She is different from us in every way. Perhaps betrayal is not so easy to detect in her.'

Sylph opened her mouth to say something but then thought better of it and kept silent. A distinctly uneasy feeling assailed Eva as she watched the meeting unfold. *They thought she was a vampire like Darius?* She would have laughed if the situation hadn't been so serious. She could feel Nicholas' anger emanating from him in waves as he stood next to her, and she didn't blame him. After all his family's integrity had been called into question, and he was powerless to defend it.

Terence was now looking thoughtfully at Arri as she stood defiantly facing him. He could hear the whispers around him, several now questioned his judgement and yet a few still remained loyal. He glanced to his right where Sylph sat staring straight ahead, a stony expression on her beautiful face.

He knew she was controlling her temper; it wouldn't do anyone any good if they lashed out. He sighed inwardly, he had expected to be challenged, but he hadn't expected this argument. His eyes settled on the tall man. Vassagio had always been different from the rest of the flock. He had left them and struck out on his own. None of the Elders knew where he had gone. And now he was back amidst one of the greatest decisions in their history. He shifted uneasily, something didn't add up.

'What would put your suspicions to rest?' he asked cautiously, instinctively knowing the answer, knowing too that he would have to agree to it if he wanted his authority maintained.

Arri looked slightly taken aback, she hadn't expected it to be this easy. The smallest flicker of triumph flared within her as she drew out the moment.

'A trial by the Holy Flame,' she finally whispered.

Absolute silence met her words.

Chapter 75

Chris stared at the figures in front of him in disbelief. The numbers didn't make sense! Were they right? He didn't have to look at Joe to know he had double-checked the information already. He was meticulous with details. But the only other explanation that came to mind was too horrifying to consider.

'What do you think?'

He shook his head slowly; he didn't know what to think.

'Serial killer?' Joe prompted.

'This can't be the work of just one person,' Chris replied slowly.

'A gang?'

He frowned. 'Maybe.' He sat back tapping his fingers on the table unconsciously. 'What has the lab found?'

Joe flipped open another file studying it for a moment before sighing. 'Multiple wounds, some appear quite similar but they are still cataloguing them.' He looked up. 'Not your usual serial killer MO.'

Chris nodded. 'So which gun?'

'Gun?' his partner looked back at the file frowning, 'no bullets were found in the bodies.'

Chris' eyebrow lifted a fraction, 'Knife wounds?'

Joe shrugged. 'Forensics can't figure out what weapon was used, they're still working on it.'

'Any ideas so far?'

'Some of the guys think the wounds were from teeth and nails,' Joe replied sceptically. Personally he felt the techs were on some kind of drug if that was the best they could come up with. 'Like I said they're still working on it.'

'Hmm,' Chris looked back at the figures, 'Tell them to get a move on, we need to know what we're up against.'

'Right.' Joe stood up and headed for the door.

'Hey Joe?'

'Yeah?' He turned his head to look at his friend. Chris looked tired, his body seemed to sag and his skin looked unnaturally pale under his deep tan.

'Get them to check out this will you?' He tossed an evidence bag across the room. Joe caught it deftly and peered at the contents.

'Where did this come from?'

'Found it lying around. Get them to find out all they can about it.'

'Sure,' Joe shrugged and walked out of the office.

Chris sighed and swivelled to look out of the window. The sun was low in the sky and sent out a dull glow over the city. It was early summer and although the sun had finally made an appearance, it was by no means warm enough to walk outside without a jacket. He felt a chill and shivered. He must be coming down with something. For the past few weeks he had felt quite ill and tired to the point where it was now an effort to get out of bed in the mornings. He groaned, if it didn't resolve itself soon he would be forced to see the doctor, and how he hated being poked and prodded!

+++

Lainey ran down the steps and headed for her car. She had slept in and was now running half an hour late. *Great!* she thought, *just what I need!* It was the end of term and the last classes were wrapping up, ready for the exams scheduled to begin in a week's time. The first class today was one she really wanted to attend and now would probably miss or have to walk past the rest of the students and endure their rude remarks. She hit the accelerator and sped down the street narrowly missing a hapless dog as it crossed in front of her. She cursed the creature and kept going, swerving through the early morning traffic. Finding the only parking space in the school car park, miles away from the entrance, she jumped out and raced to the large square building just as the bell rang announcing the start of the day.

Phew! Just made it, she thought as she walked quickly into the classroom and headed for her usual seat, pointedly ignoring the rest of her classmates. Ever since Ashe had disappeared these past few days, her non-existent popularity had plummeted to the point where Taylor had stopped bullying her in the halls.

By the end of the day she had managed to get to all her classes, asked the teachers everything she needed to, before finally heading for the library. Grabbing a seat by the window she dumped her pile of books on the desk and selected one.

She usually studied at home, but lately her mother had taken to coming home early and badgering her daughter about how messy her room was whilst trying to mimic a nineteen fifties housewife. Lainey had had enough of trying to explain that she needed to study and didn't have the time to clean up or wear makeup. So to prevent any more arguments she had decided to be absent whenever her mother turned up and had taken to studying in the cluttered library at school instead. She flipped open her book and settled down for a long night.

Chapter 76

'Aw, you're not giving up already are you?' Eden shouted as he roared past his brother on a bright red Suzuki Hyabusa.

They were racing around Vatican City, heading into Rome. It had been Ashe's idea; to clear their heads he said. The Reliquary was too stuffy for his taste and being surrounded by so many Elders, stifling. He had bought the Hyabusa and the Kawasaki ZX Ninja and together they had left the Reliquary early that morning, intent on enjoying everything Italy had to offer. They had taken a few turns around the Vatican City walls, but the thunderous noise of their high performance bikes had prompted the Swiss guards to warn them off. They didn't need to be told twice and had sped into Rome.

Eden swung his bike round expertly and sped back to where Ashe had come to a stop at the side of the road and was staring into space, an odd look on his face.

'What's up?' Eden asked as he came to a stop and pulled off his helmet. His eyes raked his brother's form looking for a reason for his sudden refusal to move.

Ashe blinked and looked at him, his eyes focussing slowly. 'I'm not sure, but...' he paused thoughtfully, 'I have to go back.'

'But we just left,' Eden replied, his shoulders slumping.

'Not to the Reliquary,' he explained slowly, 'Back to Erie.'

'What?!' Eden's eyes narrowed suspiciously, 'Why?'

'I'm not sure. I just have this feeling that I have to be there now. That's where I'm needed.' He looked at his brother's sceptical expression and sighed. 'Okay, I know it sounds crazy but I had the same weird feeling when Anna attacked Lainey.'

Eden shook his head. 'You're right...you are crazy.' His eyes took in Ashe's worried face for a minute and then sighed. 'You know bro, if you're not careful you'll fall for this human and then all hell will break loose.'

Ashe sighed. 'It's not like that! I think...I think I'm supposed to be her guardian.'

'Guardian huh?' Eden laughed. 'Whatever you say bro. Let's get back so Leo can book you some tickets.' He started to put his helmet back on but Ashe stopped him.

'No, I have to go now and the others can't know where I've gone, otherwise they'll try to stop me.'

'Now? And how do you think you'll manage that?'

'Well...' he looked expectantly at Eden and he sighed in resignation.

'Okay, I guess.'

+++

Marina walked into the old building and headed for the rickety staircase. Within seconds she had flashed up the three floors and was walking into the shabby room. All eyes were on her as she swept past and came to a standstill behind the tall figure.

Darius turned round to smile at her, kissing her soundly before saying, 'Have you found them?'

She smiled. 'I think you'll like these.'

He nodded. He and the others had grown tired of going to ICE every night, besides the police were getting suspicious. He glanced at the rest of the coven who were lounging around the room. They looked well fed but even now the eternal hunger was apparent in their empty eyes as they watched him.

He turned back to Marina. 'Is it safe?'

She almost laughed out loud at the question. Ever since the Elites had left Erie, every place was safe for them. The police didn't matter, they were too slow and most importantly…they were human. Instead she smiled and nodded, her dark eyes shining with excitement.

'It's safe alright.'

He nodded and turned to face the rest of them. 'Tonight we feast!'

Loud cheering met his words.

+++

Lainey flipped another page and re-crossed her legs into a more comfortable position. It was dark outside now and the overhead library lights had been switched off leaving the study tables glowing in the pools of dim light thrown by the side-lamps attached to each desk. Several were occupied by students engrossed in their books, ensuring complete silence. That made the next few minutes even more poignant as several people entered the room.

Lainey barely raised her head as shadows flitted across the floor. *Just more desperate students*, she thought and continued reading. She heard a creak and looked up curiously. Most of the students were leaning over their books, but a few at the far end seemed to be slumped forward. She looked around to see a few people she had never seen before standing or kneeling next to other students nearby. As she watched another student seemed to fall face down onto the table.

She frowned, *what was going on? Who were those people?* She was about to rise when the girl sitting on the table in front of her, who had also apparently noticed the same odd behaviour made as if to stand up. In the blink of an eye one of the strangers was next to her; Lainey's eyes widened in shock as she caught a glimpse of strangely familiar dark flashing eyes and an abnormally red mouth. As she watched the stranger leant close to the girl, blocking Lainey's view so that all she could see of the other student was her arm. A second later the girl fell back in her chair with the stranger still leaning over her.

The man finally lifted his head and looked over his shoulder. As he turned, Lainey quickly looked down, pretending to study, her heart pounding. She didn't know who they were but they definitely weren't students of that she was now convinced. She waited, counting the seconds slowly before peeking through her lashes to make sure he wasn't still watching her. To her relief he was no longer there, and the rest of them seemed to be concentrating on the tables further away from her. She glanced round cautiously, should she just walk out and take her chances?

Her eyes fell on a small stain spreading around one of the students' collars nearby. It took her a second to realise it was blood. Before a scream erupted from her, she sucked in a deep breath. That image decided it for her, she didn't have a choice, it was either leave or…she swallowed, pushing the thought away quickly. She watched the strangers for a minute longer until she was sure they were busy and then slipped off her chair to the floor, taking her books and backpack with her.

She crawled under the table and stashed them in the shadows, waiting for a second to make sure no one had noticed her. No one appeared in her line of sight. Holding her breath, she moved gingerly backwards, heading towards the empty desk behind her shrouded in shadow. It was closer to the bookshelves and she hoped no one would come near it..

Crawling quickly across the short space, she almost dived under the other desk, half expecting someone to grab her jacket and drag her back out. But nothing happened. She peeked past the chair legs; the strangers were still moving along the far end of the room. She crawled to the other side of the table, which was in complete darkness and peeked out. The bookshelves stood only two metres away, towering above her, the narrow spaces between them dark and gloomy, leading away from the study area to the exit.

She could just make out the dull green glow of the exit sign above the door at the far end. This part of the library was deserted. She couldn't hear any sound, and the girl still seated two tables ahead was unnaturally still. Lainey tried not to think about why that was. She kept her mind focussed on getting out, because she knew if she didn't she would become hysterical with the horror of it all. Gathering herself for the rush across to the small space, that now appeared as wide as an ocean to her fear-filled eyes, she gave herself another second before sprinting across it doubled over, all the while praying that none of the strangers would spot her.

She disappeared into one of the narrow passages just as Darius turned round to search the room. The girl at the far end wasn't moving, but he expected that. He frowned, *why was the lamp switched on at the desk behind hers? There didn't appear to be anyone using it.* His eyes scanned the area around it again. *Wasn't there a girl there a few minutes ago?* He moved forward, still searching intently when one of the students behind him made as if to stand up. He turned in a flash and grabbed the young boy by the throat. The last thing he saw were Darius' razor sharp teeth coming closer.

Chapter 77

Lainey struggled to control her breathing as she crawled silently down the aisle between the tall bookshelves, her eyes darting back and forth, expecting one of the strangers to jump out at her. She was halfway down the aisle when she heard voices. Stilling instantly she glanced over her shoulder. The study area was still in shadow, the lamps glowing dully. Ahead the exit sign still beckoned.

The voices were coming from the next aisle and were moving toward her. From what she could make out they sounded like two students. She gulped, should she warn them? If she did she would be in danger too. She peered between the books to see who they were. Her eyes widened when she recognised two of Taylor's friends. What were they doing here at this time of night? Neither girl had ever set foot in this building, she was sure of it. She heard more footsteps and ducked instinctively, pressing herself against the bookshelf. Two boys she knew to be part of the soccer team turned the corner and walked towards the girls. It all made perfect sense now.

She watched as they moved further away from her hiding place, towards the study area, and closed her eyes. She had to get out of here! As she was gathering her courage for the final dash to the exit, she heard one of the girls scream.

She jumped to her feet and sprinted down the aisle, closing her ears to the increasing number of screams behind her. Reaching the end of the aisle, she barely checked the way was clear before speeding towards the exit. Once through it she ran down the three flights of stairs, two at a time, not caring when she stumbled in her haste. Reaching the bottom step she nearly flew into the solid wall unable to stop herself in time. Inches from it she was hauled backward, nearly falling onto the hard floor. Instinctively she started struggling, refusing to give up easily. If they were going to kill her anyway she was going down fighting.

'Hey, calm down!'

The voice that penetrated the panicked haze around her seemed familiar, but she couldn't seem to register it fully.

'Whoa there!'

Another set of arms wound around her, preventing her from flailing. Unable to fight she crumpled to the ground, exhausted and still panicked. She looked up, her eyes barely able to see past the tears that were filling up in their depths, expecting to see one of the strangers from the library ready to kill her. What she saw made her blink several times in astonishment. Ashe and Eden stood in front of her, looking as handsome as ever in their motorcycle leathers.

'You two?' she asked feebly.

Ashe knelt down next to her. 'Are you okay? What's going on?'

She swallowed painfully, her heart still beating rapidly from the panic and her mad dash to safety. 'They're...they're in the library,' she rasped, 'the others...they're...' she couldn't say the words. The tears she had been holding back overflowed and she sobbed, her head bowed.

Ashe looked up at Eden's stony face, before turning to her again. 'Lainey, who's in the library?' he asked, his voice firm giving her the strength she needed to stop crying and face him.

'I don't know, but they're...they're killing the students!'

'Are you sure?' Eden asked sceptically.

'I saw it,' she almost snapped at him.

'And that's why you were running?' Ashe asked slowly. She nodded in answer. He glanced at his brother. 'I think she's telling us the truth, I can sense them close by.'

A loud crash from three floors up drowned out his voice.

Eden's jaw clenched. 'We can't do anything to help them, we are outnumbered.'

Ashe nodded and turned to see Lainey staring at the stairs, panic in her eyes. 'Lainey, we have to leave, now!'

She didn't give any indication of having heard him, her body shaking uncontrollably with fear. So he bent down and lifted her easily into his arms. Looking at Eden he nodded. 'Ready.'

Eden caught hold of his hand and they instantly disappeared from the stairwell, just as a pale form flashed down the stairs, it's wild eyes staring, it's mouth an unnatural red, it's fangs glistening in the dull lighting and Lainey's scent still flowing in its nostrils.

+++

Before Eva knew what was happening Nicholas had caught hold of her and flashed down the narrow stairs. She blinked and found herself in their quarters. As she opened her mouth to ask him what he was doing, he set her down on a chair and then flew around the room in a blur. She had barely taken a breath before he was standing in front of her, his face unreadable, the packed bags at his feet.

'We're leaving,' he announced.

'Leaving?' she squeaked and then cleared her throat to say, 'Why?'

He looked at her askance. 'Didn't you hear Arri? They want you to go through the Holy Flame Trial!'

She looked confused. 'What does that mean exactly?'

He sighed and sat down next to her. 'The Holy Flame Trial is the most difficult test known to us. It hasn't been used for centuries because it's so painful. It differentiates between the ones of the Dark and the Light. The consequences are horrific.' His face was ashen as he said the words.

She paled slightly but fought to appear calm as she thought about what to say. Running away seemed like a good idea at this point. Before she could say anything however a pale blur entered the room. Nicholas was up and standing protectively in front of her so that she couldn't see who had come in until she spoke.

'Nicholas I…'

'Don't…we trusted them and now…' he shook his head.

'I know how you must be feeling but –'

'Save it, I've thought it through, we're leaving now!'

Eva peered around his legs to see Eleanor's pleading look. 'They will find you Nick. By running away you'll only confirm their suspicions.'

'You would rather she went through with the trial?' he asked grimly his eyes locked to hers.

She sighed and shook her head. 'Terence may still be able to get her out of this.'

Before she could finish Nicholas was already shaking his head. 'He agreed to the trial in front of the Council.'

'How do you know that?' she asked suspiciously.

'I was listening,' he replied, not a trace of apology in his voice, 'Arri and an Elder I've never seen before presented their case and won.'

'Describe the Elder,' she almost commanded. He did as she asked, her eyes narrowing when he finished. 'His name's Vassagio,' she said finally, 'I haven't seen him for years. Why is he back especially now?'

Nicholas shrugged. 'A coincidence?'

She pursed her lips. 'I don't believe in coincidences, especially not when it comes to him,' she looked thoughtful before saying, 'don't do anything rash Nick, I need to check something. Promise me you'll wait till I have more information.'

Nicholas hesitated; he knew what it meant to promise Eleanor anything. He wouldn't physically or mentally be able to do anything that violated it.

She saw his hesitation and smiled. 'Very well, don't promise, but please wait.'

He nodded and watched as she vanished through the door, leaving it to snap shut behind her from the breeze caused by her passage. Turning round he looked at Eva intensely. 'I wish we had got away before she turned up.'

'Why?'

He sighed. 'Because she has planted the seed of doubt in my mind; we should have stayed longer to hear more of the Council meeting.'

She nodded slowly. 'Where were we going to go?'

He smiled. 'Somewhere safe, where even the Elders would have difficulty finding us.'

'I see. But why was Eleanor so worried about that Elder…Vassagio?'

He lifted his shoulder slightly. 'I have no idea but…' his eyes glinted suddenly, 'I know where we can find out.'

Chapter 78

The Vatican covers an area of zero point four square kilometres, housing a population of eight hundred and twenty-nine people. As immense as it is above the ground, it is more so below it. Its catacombs stretch well beyond the city walls, as Eva found out a few hours later. They had initially gone to the Training Hall but within minutes of flashing around the room, examining the ancient tomes, Nicholas had shaken his head and led the way out.

Several minutes later he had released her from his hold, setting her down in front of a large iron door. Muttering an incantation she didn't understand he had opened it to reveal a massive room that seemed to rival some of the largest libraries in the world. From the stone floor to the arched ceiling bookshelves stretched the length and breadth of the room. She noticed some of the books were in English but most were in languages she had never heard of.

'What language is that?' she asked, pointing at a leather-bound volume, the writing practically obscured by age and dust.

'Sanskrit,' he replied absently scanning the shelves nearby. Not finding what he was looking for he moved back a few paces until he could see the books further up the wall.

Before Eva knew what he intended he had leapt forward and up, landing several feet above the ground. She expected him to climb a ladder, but she couldn't see one anywhere. Her mouth dropped open when she realised he was scaling the bookshelf using only his fingertips. He finally reached the exact area he wanted to and casually pulled out a few of the heavy volumes with one hand while using the other to anchor himself in place.

Once he had what he was looking for he cradled them carefully against his body. She drew in a sharp breath wondering how he would get down with his load. Hearing her, he glanced down with a wicked smile and winked before letting go of the shelf. He was still anchored, his feet planted firmly in the crevices before he flexed his legs and pushed out and away arcing his body before jack-knifing in midair to land on his feet next to her, the books still safely in his arms.

Eva had instinctively screamed in horror when he had leapt away from the shelf fully expecting him to plummet to the ground. She looked up at him in shock to see him laughing at her reaction.

'How did you—?

'Vampiiire!' he replied with a roll of his eyes. Seeing her still shocked expression he leant forward and kissed her gently. 'Silly child, stop worrying about me,' he chided, before moving towards a desk set in an alcove a few feet away, almost hidden from view.

She followed him, still not quite able to believe what she had just seen. She knew vampires could do some amazing feats, but knowing it was very different from seeing it with her own eyes. She shook her head; she had a lot to get used to. Nicholas had already flicked through two of the heavy books and was perusing the third one when she got to the desk.

'Here,' he said, indicating a passage on the yellowed page.

She leant forward to see it better and frowned. The symbols made no sense to her, but he seemed to be reading it easily.

'That's just Greek to me,' she finally confessed.

'You're right, it *is* Greek,' he replied with an amused laugh. 'It says here that Vassagio was the Angel of all things lost and hidden. It is in his power to find things.' He frowned as he read further down the page.

'What is it?'

'It goes on to mention that he was the one who found the Cup of Christ after the Crucification.' He didn't notice her mouth falling open in surprise.

'The Cup of…are you talking about the Holy Grail?'

'Yes,' he nodded, not bothering to still his hand as it flicked through the rest of the book.

'Wow!' she breathed, 'Do you know where it is?'

'No, but the Elders probably do,' he shrugged dismissively, completely missing her incredulous stare as he reached for another volume.

'Don't you care?'

'Why should I?' he looked up in surprise, 'It's a cup.'

'Not just any cup…it's the Holy Grail!' she breathed, 'The cup everyone's looking for!'

'Not everyone,' he corrected her with a knowing smile, 'Only mortals.'

She had to be satisfied with that as he searched through the rest of the books and finally shook his head.

'Nothing.' He frowned, 'Sylph would know but she won't tell me.' He looked at the book-lined walls, *where would he find the answers?*

+++

Vassagio walked down the passage, a satisfied smile on his lean face. His plan was working; he had effectively backed the Regent into a corner and forced his hand in the destruction of his most prized possession. It was a stroke of genius to join forces with Arri. Her brilliant mind made a mockery of most arguments and had decimated the Regent.

It had been pure bad luck for the girls to be born, one was enough but two? He sighed as he remembered what had passed. When he had learnt about them from Iasoel's prophecy he had been furious. Especially when he became certain someone was protecting them. It had taken him years to find their hiding place, his plan clear; kill them both. But then something had stopped him. He wasn't sure what, possibly a glimmer from his heavenly past.

Finding only one had angered him, until that odd glimmer had kicked in again and he saw the possibility. Killing them would be too easy and wouldn't accomplish anything, but if he used them for his own means then the odds were in his favour. And so he had spared the child, and continued to search desperately for the other. Sadly she had been too well hidden, but now, his smile widened, now it was time.

He grimaced as he thought of the past. He wouldn't have had to go to such lengths if he had realised Darius had had the girl in his possession. He cursed his luck again. She had evaded him then and again in the Training Hall a few days ago. He smiled grimly as he remembered the incident. It had been a nice surprise to find out that Karael had been given responsibility for Eva. He had always been suspicious of Vassagio, even on the Holy Mount, but he had thrown the Protector off the trail. So it had been a double victory when he had used his powers to control the battle-axe and attack the One, letting the blame fall squarely on Karael's shoulders.

He had waited just long enough to see her fall before flashing to a different part of the Reliquary. He knew Karael would have destroyed him if he had been found out. The Protectors were known for their notoriously short tempers. He had thought Eva had been dispensed with then, but news had quickly spread that she had merely been stunned. His smile was cruel now; she wouldn't…couldn't escape him this time, he would make sure of it.

Chapter 79

In a different section of the Reliquary Eleanor paced, thinking. Her perfect features creased with worry making her appear to have aged several years in the past few days; something that was virtually impossible for her to do. Since arriving at the Reliquary she had taken to dressing in the white robes worn by the Elders, despite Arri's obvious disapproval. Her sister was another problem she would have to deal with sooner or later, especially since she seemed to be getting closer to Vassagio. But at the moment her main concern was the reason for that Elder's involvement. Why was he against Eva? Arri's interest was understandable; it was a way to get back at her but she couldn't understand what was motivating Vassagio.

She turned and paced back the length of the room again, barely acknowledging Seton as he entered the chamber. He knew better than to disturb her train of thought and lowered himself into one of the chairs to watch her silently.

She thought back to when the Elders had lived on Olympus, the Holy Mount at the time. Vassagio had seemed more accessible then, finding the ancient relics, which were still stored deep in the Reliquary to keep them away from humans. He had been biddable then and she distinctly remembered that he had sided with the Elders rather than the Dark Angels, even though at the time Sylph had detected some reluctance in his decision.

It had been too chaotic at that time to pay much attention to that small detail, but now it surfaced and she frowned. Why had he been reluctant? The Light Ones had never craved power, especially not after what had happened on Olympus, when they had witnessed their fellow Angels playing with mankind like pawns on a giant chessboard for their own amusement. Was it this reluctance that had made him leave and pursue his own course? He had still retained his status as Elder and everyone had assumed he was searching for the ancient relics of power still lost to mankind. A sudden fear gripped her, but what if he hadn't? What if his time had been spent on a more sinister feat?

She glanced at Seton, should she tell him her deepest secret? But even as she thought about it, Zophiel's face swam into her mind's eye. Even if she wanted to she couldn't break her vow. Her gift was sometimes a double-edged sword. She sighed, there was only one Elder she could talk to about this.

+++

Seton had been watching her closely and could tell there was a battle raging within her but he couldn't understand what it was about. His guess was that it related to Eva and her relation to the Dark Ones. As he was thinking about it someone materialised out of thin air in front of him. He didn't have to look up to know who it was. Eden nodded curtly in greeting and waited for Eleanor to step forward, a puzzled frown on her face.

'Where have you been?' she asked him, taking in his dishevelled appearance.

He sighed. 'Erie.' When she turned a disapproving stare at him he continued defensively, 'Ashe and I were on our way to Rome, but he had this weird feeling something was happening in Erie.' He related how they had teleported to the city and found Lainey before escaping a confrontation with the coven.

'Who's coven?' Seton asked, instinctively knowing the answer.

Eden looked at him. 'Darius',' he replied flatly and turned to Eleanor, 'they are killing indiscriminately. They'll probably end up drawing too much attention, we have to do something.'

Eleanor's face was grim as she answered, 'We cannot make that decision; it has to come from the Elders.'

'Will you speak to them?' he asked slowly.

She nodded, they had enough to deal with but this new threat couldn't be ignored. 'Where is Ashe now?'

'In Erie with the girl, we didn't think it was a good idea to bring her here.'

She agreed with him and wondered vaguely about how Ashe had known something was wrong in Erie, but this wasn't the time for idle thought. The Elders had to be told about the problems Erie was facing.

+++

Lainey sat on her bed staring at Ashe's motionless figure by the window. He was as still as a statue, the only sign of life his quick eyes as they scanned the dark garden below. It was close to midnight when they had got to her house and found a note left on the hall table letting her know that her parents had left for a few days to visit a distant relation. That had been an hour ago and since then neither of them had spoken a word. She was still in shock from what she had seen and he appeared to be equally reluctant to talk about it.

But now that the shock was wearing off, her mind was busy and the silence was grating on her nerves. She opened her mouth to say something to the boy standing a few feet away and shut it again. What could she say? He looked so forbidding as he stood there, reminding her of a sentry on duty.

Dragging in a breath and as much courage as she could she finally said, 'What are you doing?'

'Watching,' he replied in that smooth voice that made her skin tingle.

'For?' she pressed hesitantly.

He turned his head a fraction so that she could see his eyes looking at her speculatively. 'Trouble.'

'You mean those people?' He nodded and was about to turn back to the window but she forestalled him with, 'Who are they?'

'You don't want to know,' he replied with certainty.

'I thought I recognised them, their eyes...' her voice trailed away as he raised an eyebrow. 'Their eyes were like that girl's, the one I told you was here,' she continued lamely.

He frowned, maybe he should tell her maybe then she would grasp the severity of the situation. A small inner voice reminded him that the Code forbade it. Code be damned, her life depended on him now.

'Lainey,' he moved closer, 'You did see that girl, and you're right, those people in the library tonight are just like her, but worse.' He paused. 'They are like animals and they are killing innocent people.'

'But why?' she asked, her eyes wide with confusion. So she wasn't going crazy and seeing people who weren't there. His confirmation gave her some relief. Of course there was still the matter of how they had managed to get here. All she had seen were flashes of light before she had found herself at the front door of her house. If that wasn't crazy she didn't know what was.

'Okay this may sound weird, and you probably won't believe me, but they are vampires,' he replied in one breath.

'Vampires? There's no such thing!' she scoffed incredulously, but seeing his serious expression, the smile on her face faded.

This probably wasn't the best time to tell her what he really was, he thought.

'You're serious?'

'Yup.' He turned back to the window to continue his vigil letting her come to terms with what he had said.

'Okay say I believe you,' she ventured finally after thinking through his reply, 'You are saying they are drinking human blood?'

He nodded not bothering to reply, not taking his eyes off the garden and the street beyond. He trusted his ability to detect the coven, but he wasn't taking any chances. He knew what excessive blood did to their minds. With nothing to stop them, fear was non-existent and they were likely to kill more and take crazy chances. He didn't relish the thought of fighting off an entire coven of vampires on a blood high. But without Eden he couldn't run either. A shadow moved further down the street and he turned slightly to follow the movement staring intently.

'But why come to the library?' she wondered aloud, oblivious of his sudden interest in the view.

'It's isolated and there are only helpless students there,' he replied absently, still staring at the same place he had last seen the movement. *It's nothing*, he thought, but something didn't feel right. 'Does this house have a basement?'

'Yes,' she nodded, wondering why he asked.

He stood still for a second longer, just enough time to see the shadow shift slightly and his senses to tingle in response before pulling her off the bed and into his arms. She barely had time to make a sound, let alone protest before they were flashing through the bedroom door, down the stairs and into the kitchen where he slid to a halt.

'Where's the basement?'

She pointed the way and he flew to the concealed entrance with her still in his arms.

'It's really heav...' she started to say as he bent to lift the door and then stopped as he opened it with the tip of his small finger. She didn't have time to react before they were flying down the steep stairs and into the empty darkness below.

Chapter 80

Nicholas had insisted that they behave as they normally would, so that the Elders wouldn't realise they knew about the Trial. It wouldn't take place straight away as several arrangements had to be made, so here she was. Back in the Training Hall with Karael, the Protector. She had progressed quickly once she had realised that she only had to get scared or panicked for lightning to fly out of her fingers.

So far she had annihilated several suits of armour and tried to attack Karael. Of course he had thwarted her attempt, but he hadn't been able to hide how impressed he was by how powerful she appeared to be. She wasn't physically strong but she didn't have to be; the lightning carried away any threat, she reasoned, but her tutor wasn't so sure.

'Your defence is strong,' he conceded reluctantly, 'but your attack is weak. You need to use your opponent's strength against them.'

So they had started using weapons, despite her initial protests. Now she lifted the sword he had given her. It was as light as a feather but deadly. The blade was so well honed that the edge was barely a third of a millimetre thick. She brandished it easily enough, hitting anything though, was another matter.

'Again!' Karael's voice rang out as she missed his sword for the third time.

She sighed, wishing Nicholas was there next to her, but he had decided to keep looking for information on Vassagio and had instead asked Alena to guard her. The petite vampire sat cross-legged on the stone floor, her bright eyes fixed on the duellists. Eva wondered vaguely why she was watching them so closely, but she had no idea that Nicholas had urged his sister to protect her at all costs if she wanted a certain favour from him. As Eva faltered again, Alena stood up and walked forward.

'Karael, perhaps she needs to rest.'

The Elder turned towards her, the red in his hair glinting brightly like small flames. 'She needs to train.'

'Yes, but she is after all only human,' she argued and turned away to wink at Eva so that Karael didn't notice.

'Fine,' he agreed reluctantly and lowered his sword.

'But I could use some practice,' she continued.

His pale eyes narrowed slightly and a smile touched his stern mouth as he inclined his head. Alena took the sword from Eva and smiled, before turning like a ballerina to take up her fighting stance in front of the much taller Elder.

Eva had barely reached the safety zone around the duelling circle when all hell seemed to break lose behind her. The clash of the swords was never-ending, the metallic ringing so loud she had to cover her ears. She turned to see two forms - one petite with red hair dressed in jeans and the other tall with flaming hair, dressed in white robes flying around each other, the swords moving so fast she couldn't see them.

She wanted to shout to Alena to be careful. The small vampire looked so delicate against Karael's larger, sterner form. But as she watched, she realised she needn't have worried for her friend, Alena seemed more than capable of holding her own. Eva sat down in a daze trying to make out the movements of the opponents and failed. Neither of them seemed to be losing. Finally after what seemed hours but was probably much less the duellists stopped and both vampires came to a standstill, neither out of breath. Eva uncovered her ears but they still seemed to be ringing from the duel, despite the deathly silence now present in the hall.

'Good,' Karael complimented Alena. 'Are your powers as good as your fighting?'

She smiled, 'I am always learning.'

He nodded. 'Show me.'

She dropped the sword, closed her eyes, muttering an incantation. Eva looked puzzled, *what was she doing?*

Suddenly Alena's eyes flew open and she flung out her hands and a dark cloud materialised above Karael, lightning streaking down onto the Elder. He sidestepped it neatly, ignoring Eva's cry of horror, only to have a torrent of water fall over him. Alena smiled and the water on the floor swirled around his body, enveloping him completely so that he was held several feet above the ground, threatening to drown him as it started to cover his head.

Just when Eva was about to scream at Alena to let him go, Karael vanished in front of their eyes and reappeared behind Alena in a hissing blue flame.

'Impressive,' he said.

Alena whirled around to face him, breaking her concentration and causing the cloud to disappear leaving the swirling ball of water to come splashing down onto the stone floor with a dull roar.

'I didn't realise you had that power indoors.'

'It's easier outside,' she confessed, breathing deeply, and Eva noticed her hands shaking slightly. She could feel her own accelerated breathing returning to normal when Karael nodded at Alena and looked over at where she was still sitting.

'Break's over.'

Chapter 81

Nicholas tossed aside the scroll and stretched his arms above his head tiredly. He had been searching through the ancient parchments for several hours and still hadn't found anything to incriminate Vassagio. Perhaps he was mistaken, he thought, after all Vassagio was an Elder, if his loyalties were compromised, surely the Council or the spells surrounding the Reliquary would have noticed. Was he still entertaining the suspicions purely because the Elder had spoken out against Eva? He shook his head, something wasn't right and perhaps he was giving it more importance than it deserved, but he couldn't start doubting himself now.

He lifted his head, letting his steady gaze travel slowly around the dusty room. It was rarely used and was filled with scrolls the world had long forgotten about. He picked up the ones he had discarded and placed them back on the shelves carefully before leaving the room, flashing down the corridors till he reached one of the doors leading out of the Reliquary. He needed time to think and he couldn't do that here. He quickly walked out of the hidden door, finding himself at the North side of St Peter's square. The place was filled with tourists and devoted Catholics, all intent on making the most of their visit.

He disappeared within the crowds, mingling easily so that no one gave him a second look. He strolled through the square, enjoying the feeling of freedom after being underground for so long. He didn't know how the Elders managed to stay in the Reliquary for long periods. The spells used to protect it seemed to suffocate him. Reaching one of the cafes he walked inside and ordered a strong cup of coffee. Lowering himself into one of the empty chairs he closed his eyes trying to put together everything he knew so far about Vassagio. He didn't know how long he sat there but when he opened his eyes his coffee was ice cold. On the verge of standing up his eyes fell on a girl sitting a few tables away, partially hidden from view.

What was she doing here? She shifted slightly in her chair and his eyes widened in surprise and then narrowed. The girl was dressed in a tight black skirt, a fitted white shirt and knee-high boots and her hair was short and looked wavier than he remembered. *How had she got out of the Reliquary,* he wondered *and why had she?*

As these thoughts flooded his mind, a tall man entered the small café and headed for her table. Nicholas had been about to move towards her when the man turned to look around the café, his face causing Nicholas to freeze in shock. This was getting more bizarre by the minute. He glanced again at the girl, *it couldn't be her,* he thought, he was almost certain of it. *Then who was she?* A small inner voice argued. He had to find out, but in the noisy café he couldn't quite lock onto their voices.

A passing waitress blinked in confusion, wasn't there a tall handsome man at that table a second ago? She looked down to see the large tip and shrugged pocketing it deftly, not giving Nicholas a second thought. He smiled to himself as he watched her walk away; humans were so predictable. He turned towards the couple and spread his wings. He preferred transforming into a bigger creature that was less likely to be affected by the small air currents, but to avoid detection this form would have to do. No one noticed as a black wasp flew unerringly across the room and settled on one of the picture frames on the wall.

'You shouldn't be here!' Vassagio ground out as he glanced again around the café.

'I had to talk to you about Darius,' the girl replied.

He shook his head quickly. 'You know not to mention that name here!'

She inclined her head and apologised, continuing with, 'They are taking over the city.'

He glared at her angrily. 'They are *what?!*'

'They are out of control,' she clarified, 'and the bodies are piling up.'

'That damned fool!' he grated. 'He'll spoil everything!' His eyes flashed accusingly at her. 'I left you there to make sure he didn't do anything like this.'

She sighed 'I couldn't stop him, that's why I had to let you know.'

He nodded knowing he had expected too much from her, but the fact remained that her presence in Vatican City could cause a lot of problems. He just had to make sure no one from the Reliquary saw her here, otherwise his plan would fall apart. He silently cursed Darius' wilful stupidity, *didn't he realise what was at stake? The fool!* For a few measly crumbs he was willing to forego the larger prize. They had to sort it out and he leant forward to talk to her, a plan already formulating in his mind. A few feet away on the nearby wall Nicholas folded his wings and listened intently.

Chapter 82

She could hear her breathing in the impenetrable darkness and tried vainly to control the gasping sound. She felt terribly self-conscious with Ashe so close to her, especially since she couldn't hear him breathing at all. She tried to see through the darkness but ever since Ashe had let the basement door fall back into place the deep gloom had surrounded them, leaving her practically blind. He hadn't said a word since letting her feet touch the floor, except to whisper in her ear to be quiet.

They had spent the time listening intently. She wasn't quite sure what she was listening for but Ashe's stillness kept her silent. Now was not the time for questions. She didn't really believe what he had told her about vampires, but she had no doubt about what she had seen; vampires or not those people were dangerous.

Suddenly he moved next to her slightly and she tensed, what had he heard? And then she heard it too. It was a deliberate knocking from…the front door? She made as if to move but his hand clamped down on hers in warning and she subsided. The insistent knocking continued for a while before ceasing abruptly; she let out her breath, they had gone.

Before she could finish the thought a loud crash made her jump, sending her heart racing and her breathing sped up again. She couldn't hear anything else but Ashe was tensing by the minute.

'They're searching the house,' he whispered close to her ear, 'whatever happens stay still.' She nodded quickly in response.

In the darkness the passage of time seemed interminable and she could feel her legs becoming tired, but she stayed upright, concentrating on her breathing. She was about to take another deep breath when she heard a distinct creak just above her head. The intruders, whoever they were, were now walking in the kitchen, directly above them. Ashe looked around him, clearly seeing his surroundings through the darkness. Vampires weren't affected by the dark, they could see just as well at midnight as they could at midday, so he could tell the basement was full of useless junk. He led her quickly towards a pile of boxes at the back and settled her behind them.

'Stay here no matter what happens next.' He waited for her to nod before turning to face the basement door, crouching low to the ground waiting. He could feel his senses going crazy with the smell of the others and his skin was tingling. It had never felt like this before, but then again he had never been in a situation like this before either.

The door opened sending a shaft of light into the darkness below and his eyes narrowed. He could make out at least three vampires standing in the opening. One of them, a heavyset male, started descending the steps slowly, ready to fight off any opposition. The others seemed content to wait upstairs.

'Here my beauty, I know you're down here!' he growled coming down the last few steps. 'Come out, we won't hurt you!'

Ashe tensed, the vampire would see him any second now. But he seemed oblivious to Ashe's presence as he continued to talk to the girl he believed was hiding from him.

'Come on girlie….we just want to talk…'

As he moved further into the basement, Ashe flashed forward aiming for the thickly muscled neck, expecting the man to retaliate, but it was as though he was invisible to his target.

He flew silently round the man looking for an opportunity before leaping onto his back and sinking his teeth into the thick neck. The massive man howled in panic and rage and tried to claw away whatever was attacking him. He swung round desperately, trying to see what was holding onto him but he couldn't see or smell anything unusual. He growled and twisted around again, trying to throw off whatever it was that was biting into the nape of his neck. He could hear the others shouting down to him but he was too panicked to answer back, instead he looked around for a weapon. Not seeing anything he headed for the far wall, intent on crushing his invisible tormentor.

Realising what was about to happen Ashe flattened his body against the man's back and forced his teeth further into the solid flesh, before clamping them shut like a vice. Ignoring the roar of pain he began pulling away with all his strength, using the vampire's body as a support. Abruptly the growls and screams were cut off as a screeching sound filled the darkness.

Ashe leapt off just as the vampire fell to the ground and dissolved into dust at his feet. He didn't have to look up to know his companions were racing down the stairs. He quickly flashed into the gloom, standing in front of Lainey who was cowering in horror. She couldn't see anything, but the noise was harrowing enough. Both of them waited for the vampires to come down the stairs and attack them as they listened to their frantic footsteps. Neither had any hope of surviving the ordeal.

Chapter 83

Eva sighed tiredly as she walked past the towering bookshelves. Training was over for the day but Alena had asked Karael for help with one of the spells, leaving Eva free to wander into the smaller rooms leading off the Hall. As though in a trance she moved through one room and then another, and before she realised it she couldn't hear Alena's sweet voice or Karael's strong gravely tones.

She looked around at the myriad of books; she had no idea where she was or how to get back. In the act of turning to retrace her steps she stopped abruptly, her attention on the hushed voices filtering towards her. She looked around one of the bookshelves to see two figures clad in the white Elders' robes standing at the other end of the room. From this distance she couldn't recognise their faces but she could hear their rapid speech easily enough. If she really concentrated she could understand the words, although for some reason they appeared muffled as though something was blocking the sound.

It seemed they were talking about someone they both knew, and she was about to leave when she heard Vassagio's name. *Why were they talking about him?* she wondered and leant against the bookshelf to listen more intently. She knew she shouldn't but Nicholas was worried about Vassagio and here was a chance to find out more about him. What she heard next made her eyes widen in shock.

'Vassagio is an Elder,' the man asserted firmly, his tone serious. 'Your fears are unfounded.'

'Are they Zophiel?' the feminine voice asked, 'Then why is he against my coven and Eva?'

There was a small pause before Eva heard the man say, 'It's impossible! We hid them both too well!'

Hid who? She wondered and why was Eleanor talking to the Elder she remembered from the confrontation with the Neonates earlier on?

She heard Eleanor sigh. 'Yes, but his gift is that of discovery. He has been away for so long, isn't there the slightest chance he may have turned?'

'That is a serious accusation.'

'No more so than the one made against Eva!' she retorted firmly, not giving an inch.

Zophiel stared at her for a full minute. 'You believe he has turned and has been looking for them all these years?'

'Yes.'

He shook his head, 'You have to admit it is going to be difficult, if not impossible, to prove.' She nodded and he continued. 'Eva is safe, thanks to Fey, but what of the other one?'

She shrugged. 'We lost contact with our allies a long time ago and have been searching for them since, but…'

'We have to find them. Even if Vassagio is innocent, the Dark Ones are rising and we'll need to bring her into the fold.'

'If only we had left them both with Fey,' she lamented softly so that Eva had to strain to hear her.

'And risk discovery? No, splitting them was the best option we had. I will send my Machai on the search, it is imperative we find her soon.'

Find who? Eva wondered, *and what did her mother have to do with all this?* Eleanor was speaking about her like an old friend. She leaned against the bookshelf a little more and didn't notice when one of the heaviest volumes toppled off the top shelf and slammed with resounding force onto the stone floor sending echoes ricocheting throughout the room.

Before she could blink Eleanor and Zophiel were standing in front of her, their stern looks turning to shock when they recognised her.

'Uh...' Eva gulped, her face turning a bright red with embarrassment.

'What are you doing here?' Zophiel asked her, his face an inscrutable mask.

She swallowed convulsively, neither of them looked pleased to see her, which didn't surprise her, after all she had been caught eavesdropping on what she knew was an important conversation.

'I was training with Karael,' she explained weakly, 'but Alena needed some help so I started walking and...' her voice trailed off uncertainly.

Zophiel looked unconvinced and exchanged a look with Eleanor. She smiled reassuringly at him and gestured to Eva. 'You are lost then, come I will take you back to Alena.'

Eva stepped forward eager to escape Zophiel's penetrating gaze; it felt as though he could see right through her soul and discover her deepest darkest secrets. As they left the room, Eleanor turned her head slightly and waved her hand. The door shut with a loud bang and disappeared into the stone wall, leaving no trace of its existence behind.

Eva blinked in surprise but didn't have time to ask her about it. The elegant blonde vampire had come to a standstill and was watching her closely, too closely. Eva's blood ran cold, would she use one of the spells against her? Even though she was the One, she knew she had committed a serious offence. She tensed wondering what she would do if Eleanor attacked.

But nothing happened for several minutes. She could feel the tension in the air and her heartbeat tripled, her rapid breathing sounding like thunder in the silent passage, and still Eleanor watched her contemplatively. Just as she was deciding on how to send out a bolt of lightning to defend herself Eleanor sighed.

'You still don't trust me.'

She turned and walked down the passage her feet scarcely making a sound, curiosity getting the better of her Eva followed a few feet behind.

'I...' she wondered how she was going to refute that statement when she knew Eleanor was right; she didn't trust her. She followed the stately figure down several more passageways, eventually finding herself in a small room. She looked questioningly at Eleanor who was now seated on one of the sofas nearby.

'I won't close the door if it makes you feel uncomfortable but I think you have questions that are best answered in private.'

Eva nodded and sat opposite her turning just in time to see the doors close on their own. Eleanor then lifted her hands and recited a short spell.

'What was that for?' she asked, forgetting her fear momentarily.

'To prevent anyone eavesdropping.' Eleanor looked at her strangely. 'Maybe it will work this time.'

'This time?'

'Apparently it didn't work when I was talking to Zophiel, or else you would never have heard us,' she shrugged, 'but it's too late to lament now, the damage is done.' Her bright eyes focussed on Eva's pale face. 'You have questions.' It was a statement of fact.

Eva swallowed, thinking back to what she had overheard. 'You were talking about my mother, Fey,' she said slowly. Eleanor nodded waiting. 'You spoke like she was a friend, like you had known her for years.'

'I do,' Eleanor whispered softly, causing Eva's heart to speed up.

'How?'

'It's a long story,' Eleanor replied dismissively, 'and most of it is not important.' Eva wasn't so sure.

'But how can you know her? I mean she's just a human and so much youn...' she faltered, not sure how to say what she was about to.

'So much younger than me?' Eleanor smiled thoughtfully, 'I suppose you could say that.' She sighed, 'Know this Eva, I will not be able to answer all your questions even if I wanted to.'

A puzzled frown creased Eva's brow. 'Why?'

'Do you remember my gift? Once an oath is made with me it is unbreakable.'

'So you have made an oath with someone about this?'

'Yes.' Eleanor smiled engagingly, 'But don't despair, I can tell you some of what has occurred.'

'Can you tell me why my mother stopped me from coming to the Vatican initially, but changed her mind after you spoke to her?'

'She just needed to see the advantages of the proposal, that was all,' Eleanor replied with an eloquent shrug.

'I see,' Eva breathed, knowing it had had to be more than that. Deciding to change tack she said almost casually, 'Why are you worried about Vassagio?'

If the other woman was surprised she didn't show it. 'We can't be too careful who we trust and Vassagio has been away from the Reliquary for so long…it is best to be a little cautious.'

'But isn't he an Elder?'

'Yes but we are not infallible. Do you remember the history of our past Sylph taught you?' Eva nodded. 'We fought other Elders who wanted power Eva, even Angels make mistakes.' Her eyes clouded over as she thought of that time. 'Terrible mistakes.'

'So you think he is with the Dark Ones?'

'Not precisely,' came the surprising answer. Eleanor watched the confusion reign on Eva's expressive face. She really was too curious for comfort. 'How do you think we haven't been detected by the good catholic priests living above us for so many centuries despite their digging and excavating?'

Eva shook her head, perplexed. 'I have no idea,' she confessed honestly.

'The Reliquary is protected by the spells of concealment. But it is also surrounded by spells that would detect the Dark Ones miles away. No vampire can exist near Vatican City without us being aware of them. If Vassagio was a Dark One we would have detected it as soon as he came near the Vatican. The Machai guard us too, and take on the shape of humans to dissuade anyone from finding us.' She watched as the information sank in.

'Then why are you still worried?' Eva asked, her wit coming into play; it just didn't make sense.

Eleanor sighed. 'Something doesn't feel right and Vassagio's talents are legendary. He hasn't been here for centuries but decides to turn up now and challenge not only us but also your right?' She glanced at Eva's solemn face and smiled reassuringly. 'But this doesn't need to worry you. Rest assured you will be protected at all cost.' She hesitated slightly before continuing, 'be assured too that you can trust me. I haven't been the most welcoming but my allegiance has never been in question and I pledge it to you now.' She bowed her head slightly, the dim light glinting off her sparkling blonde hair. When she lifted it, Eva stilled; she couldn't doubt the sincerity in that beautiful face.

Chapter 84

By the time Nicholas returned to the Reliquary, the Elders had decided to send Eden, Leonara and Seton to Erie. Their mission was to protect any innocents from Darius' onslaught and extricate themselves and Ashe from the city with the minimum of fuss. Eleanor's request for a full-fledged attack had been denied.

The Elders didn't want to create a war until they had gathered more information on the situation. A few innocents were dispensable if it meant their existence would still be a secret. Even the current killings would be difficult to explain away but a supernatural battle was a different story. Eleanor kissed Seton goodbye and watched as the three of them disappeared, Eden holding their hands securely. She understood the Elders' thinking, but the loss of even one innocent rankled at her conscience. She sighed, the greater good always came at a price, usually one a little too high to bear.

+++

Eden teleported them to Lainey's house and aimed for the backyard, sensing no danger in that area. As soon as their feet touched the grass all three were on high alert. Leonara searched for any active thoughts in the immediate vicinity that resembled a vampire's while the others spread out to check the rest of the yard.

'All clear,' Leonara pronounced, straightening up.

They all focussed on the dark house, the same thought running through all their minds; *where was Ashe?* They moved closer cautiously, still looking for any vampires lurking in the shadows. Not picking up anything unusual, Leonara glanced at the others in query. They had all expected to find at least some of Darius' horde. None of them believed for a second that they wouldn't eventually.

'Split up,' Seton ordered in a whisper.

They all headed in different directions Leonara scaled the back wall and disappeared into one of the open windows on the first floor. Seton flew to the front of the house to find the heavy oak door lying on the hall floor. It had been sheared cleanly from the metal hinges still clinging stubbornly to the doorframe. He could smell the rancid scent of vampires and stilled; *they had been here all right. The question was, were they still around? And if they were then where were they?*

Eden had opted against teleporting into the house, knowing he could end up in the middle of an entire crowd of vampires. Instead he opened one of the ground floor windows and swung through it, feet first, landing on the carpeted floor silently. Even before his feet touched the floor, his eyes were darting back and forth, taking in the room and its contents, his brilliant night vision making a mockery of the dense shadows. As soon as he realised he was alone, he flashed to the closed door and opened it slowly. The rancid smell hit him like a physical wall and he crouched expectantly, letting the door inch open slowly.

+++

Leonara had already scoured the master bedroom and the adjoining en suite before slipping into the long landing that ran around the first floor overlooking the hall below. Evidence of the others being in the house was everywhere. The master bedroom had been sacked thoroughly and the carpets were smudged with dirty footprints. But the most betraying evidence was the cloying smell of decay that tainted the air. She couldn't help inhaling it in an effort to find the source, but she felt sick. It was the smell that she had learnt to hate early on as a neonate; the smell of dried blood and disintegrating corpses, the scent of death. She moved stealthily forward, keeping her mind focussed on the task ahead and tried not to think about the stench around her.

She was about to enter another bedroom when she heard a gentle clink of glass against a hard surface. She stilled and listened carefully. Someone was definitely in the far bedroom and from the shuffling she could barely hear, they were moving around the room very fast.

Too fast for a human, she thought and instinctively crouched low before flashing to the closed door. She noticed it was slightly ajar and she pushed it a little more and almost gagged. If the landing had stunk this room practically reeked. She peeked through the small opening, her eyes narrowing when she saw movement.

The pale vampire was crouching over a pile of bed linen and clothes on the bed. The female was sniffing appreciatively at the bundle clearly addicted to the smell of her prey. Leonara scanned the rest of the room to see it had been completely wrecked. Clothes littered the floor, the few perfume bottles had been smashed and most of the furniture had either been turned over carelessly or been ripped apart. She looked again at the female who was still preoccupied with the clothes and frowned.

She was shivering? *No*, her eyes fell on the girl's hands; they were shaking uncontrollably. *Tremors* Leonara thought, the realisation hitting her forcibly. The vampire's entire body was trembling and when she lifted her head for a moment, Leonara could see she had dried blood on her face and her eyes were wide and staring the characteristic empty blackness ringed with bright red as her body tried to cope with the influx of too much fresh blood. In small doses human blood kept them healthy and fully functional but at some point it became as addictive and destructive as a drug. It intensified the vampire's abilities, enhancing speed and strength and brain functions.

Leonara could feel a tingle of fear, something she had never experienced as an Elite. This was no ordinary vampire; this one was high on blood, which made her fifty times more dangerous. Her strength would be tripled and until her body used up the excess blood its reactions would be lightning fast as would her thought processes. Even as she thought about it her senses picked up on the heightened activity in the girl's mind. Thoughts were flashing through it so fast she had to concentrate very hard to lock onto any of them; most were centred on finding more humans.

Leonara sifted through them as they flew past before picking up on a stray thought. This one was about Darius and the rest of the coven that were hunting elsewhere, apparently using Erie as their own personal playground. She froze; Ashe and Eden may have only seen a small part of what was really happening in the city. The girl stood up and glanced around the demolished room before walking towards the door and Leonara.

She had to act fast if she didn't want to face the lethal female. With every ounce of strength she directed a numbing effect at the girl's overactive mind. It made the vampire slow down slightly but she kept coming closer. Leonara focussed desperately on arresting the girl's thought processes. On any other vampire the intensity of her talents at that point would have floored them, but on the hyped up girl they merely caused her to stagger slightly as her hand came up to grab the door handle and pull it open.

Leonara didn't have a choice; she launched herself through the door, using the girl's initial confusion to tackle her to the ground, holding desperately onto her jean clad legs with all the strength she could summon. Before the vampire could recover, she manoeuvred herself so that she was sitting astride the girl, pinning her lower body to the floor. She was still exercising her mind control abilities when the girl threw up her hand and grasped Leonara's neck trying to crush it, her eyes glinting with malice.

Leonara grabbed at the hand, trying to wrench it away from her, but the girl's grip had the tensile strength of a hundred steel cables. Her fingers pushed together insistently so that

Leonara could feel her flesh, which was in itself as solid as concrete, buckling under the pressure. This had to stop and soon if she was going to survive, she thought.

She focussed on the dark eyes below her and aimed at the most basic brain functions. Throwing all her experience and strength on crippling them she sent the most powerful thought-altering effect she had ever attempted; this was now a matter of survival. The initial response was negligible, the claw-like hand still clamped to her throat getting tighter and tighter, depressing into Leonara's pale flesh forcibly. No matter how much Leonara clawed at it, it didn't seem to make any difference. The vampire was smiling now, her razor sharp teeth gleaming in the dim light as her other hand grasped Leonara's and pulled them away effortlessly.

Just as she felt one of the bones in her neck crack from the pressure, Leonara felt a slight give in the vampire's brain. The girl must have felt it too because her fingers slackened their hold slightly allowing Leonara to focus more of her attention on her thoughts. Suddenly the intensity she was employing seemed to increase and she felt the girl's brain give up its struggle just before it shattered inside the skull with such explosive force that the girl slumped backward, her fingers no longer holding Leonara's neck. She was still alive but Leonara knew she would never function again.

She slid off the broken body, her eyes haunted by what she had done. Just as she was contemplating what to do next, the girl's body started convulsing uncontrollably. Without a brain to control it, the body was left on its own to flounder in horrific throes. Not dead and not alive it was stuck between the two. Leonara closed her eyes, knowing what she had to do and before she could change her mind, she bent forward.

Grasping the girl's torso with one hand and her face with the other, she turned the head sideways to expose the neck and bit into the creamy expanse, crushing the pulsing carotid artery and ending the struggle. She turned away as the body dissolved into a pile of ash and walked out of the room, her tired mind refusing to think about what had just happened.

Chapter 85

Alena smiled in relief when she saw Eva walking towards her. She had been worried and had scoured half the Reliquary searching for her. She nearly danced forward, but seeing Eva's serious expression she stopped, the smile evaporating rapidly.

'Anything wrong?' she asked uncertainly, her eyes wandering over Eva looking for any injuries.

'No,' she replied looking distracted.

'Are you sure?' Alena persisted, noting the slight frown between her eyebrows.

'Yeah, I'm just tired.'

Alena nodded, 'No wonder, Karael is a harsh task master.' She took Eva's cold hand and led her gently along the passage. 'Thought I'd lost you for a bit,' she confided with a small laugh. 'Nick would've had my head, not to mention...' she stopped abruptly.

'Not to mention?' Eva prompted, intrigued by how quickly Alena's silver-blue eyes shifted away from hers.

'Nothing, it doesn't matter.' The petite vampire pulled her along the corridor quickly. 'Where did you go anyway?'

'I have no idea,' Eva confessed, not sure what part of the Reliquary she had been in. 'But I bumped into Eleanor and another Elder, Zoph...something...'

'Zophiel?' Alena nodded, 'Tall with really pale eyes?'

'Yup,' Eva agreed, remembering how those eyes had stared at her, their intensity frightening. 'Do you know him well?'

Alena shook her head without hesitation, her hair flying around her elfin face. 'No, he keeps himself to himself, just like all the Elders.' She smiled, 'Elites don't really measure up enough to talk with the Elders much you know.'

'Right...but Karael...?'

'He's different, as a mentor he has to deal with us, even as Neonates, all the mentors do,' she shrugged. 'Which is why he manages to control his temper so well.'

'What do you mean?'

'He's a Protector...his anger fuels his fighting skills. All the Protectors have very short tempers and none of the others are mentors. They'd destroy their students within minutes!' she laughed but Eva's throat had dried up.

'Has that ever happened?'

Seeing how pale Eva had become Alena smiled reassuringly, 'Don't worry, his neck would be on the line if anything happened to you.'

'Then why were you here today, looking after me?' she challenged, thinking back to how carefully Alena had been watching her. The reason for that amount of attention suddenly didn't bear thinking about!

Alena lifted a shoulder, 'Just extra safety and because Nick wanted me to. Plus I did manage to talk Karael into giving you a break. Don't tell me you're complaining!'

'Of course not!' Eva sighed, 'I really needed it, thank you.'

'I know,' Alena smiled and put a slim arm around her shoulders.

'I had no idea you could do all that stuff!' Eva continued, thinking back to what she had seen in the Training Hall earlier.

'That was nothing, you should see what I can do outside!' Alena shrugged dismissively, letting her arm fall away from Eva.

'And what's that?'

'Well, you know sometimes you get freaky weather conditions?'

'Yeah...'

'Well...' Alena looked at her, her eyes shining with a knowing gleam.

'No way!' Eva stopped in her tracks, 'That's because of you?'

'Not all of them,' she admitted, 'a few, and that was years ago.'

'So tornadoes and hurricanes?' Eva pressed, her heart sinking with a newfound fear of the petite girl standing next to her. Who would have thought she would be capable of such destruction?

'I haven't made one of those in years mainly because they weren't successful. But the ones I attempted weren't anywhere near populated areas. Besides, it's against the Code.'

'What is?'

'To cause damage or problems for humans; the Elders deal with that sort of thing very seriously.'

'Right.' Eva wasn't so sure and Alena caught her sceptical tone.

'I'm serious Eva, the Code is what we all live by. I have seen even Elders being severely punished if they go against it.'

'What is it?'

'A set of rules, I'm not sure Nick would approve but I might as well tell you. You'll find out sooner or later anyway.' She took a small breath. 'It all started with the Arc of the Covenant.'

Eva blinked, *would she ever stop being surprised?* 'No way! Are you talking about the one in the Bible?'

Alena nodded. 'Yes, it holds the Ten Commandments and the song of Moses.'

'I thought all that was mythology,' Eva breathed trying to concentrate on placing one foot in front of the other as they entered her room.

'I think most people do. Anyway like I was saying,' she plopped down on the large bed, 'the Angel Code or as the Elders call it *Codexia de Angelus*, was given to the Angels before the Fall and placed in the Arc. It is said that it is written in fire on a tablet of pure gold and blessed by God and the higher Angel Triads. It is one of the reasons the Arc is supposed to have so much power.' She glanced at Eva's shocked expression. 'Are you okay?'

'Of course, I have just been told the ancient secrets of what I thought was a mythical object...why wouldn't I be ok?' she gasped, her mind in turmoil. It was difficult to believe that everything she had thought was relegated to someone's overactive imagination might actually be true. She knew the location of the Arc was constantly debated amongst people she had previously thought of as cranks, but she had to ask. 'Do you know where it is?'

Alena shrugged. 'The Elders rarely give up their secrets, but I bet they know, and by association so does Eleanor.'

'Wow,' Eva breathed, 'have you never wanted to find out?'

'Not really, as long as it's safe and I'm sure it is, it's location doesn't affect me.'

'But how can you not be curious?' Eva asked, her eyes wide.

'Because not everyone is as curious as you,' came the drawling reply. Both girls turned to see Nicholas lounging against the doorjamb. He nodded to Alena. 'Protection detail over?'

'Just girl talk,' she replied slipping off the bed and walking past him. They exchanged a look, Eva couldn't place, before she left the room saying, 'I'll see you later Eva.'

She barely had time to reply before Nicholas had flashed to the bed and held her face in his hands. 'I missed you,' he framed in a husky voice as he lowered his head to kiss her soundly.

'I did too,' she replied when he finally released her, 'especially when I was with Karael.'

'Why? What happened?'

'Nothing, he's just a slave driver,' she sighed and watched as he settled next to her, his hand automatically reaching for hers. 'But enough about me, did you find out anything?'

He looked into her wide violet eyes thoughtfully. She didn't know their ways well enough yet to worry about Vassagio. Plus she had had a lot to deal with already. He shook his head. 'Not much, was Alena regaling you with fairy tales?'

'Might as well have been for all the credence I'd given to them before. I'm starting to think all the old myths and lost treasure stories are real!'

'You wouldn't be far off,' he told her seriously, hiding a smile with difficulty.

'Really?' she pursed her lips, her eyes glinting with a light he had come to expect. 'Going by what I know now, if vampires exist then werewolves do too?'

He burst out laughing; she looked so serious. When he managed to control his mirth he leaned forward and kissed her lingeringly on the mouth. 'Not quite.'

'Oh.' She had half expected him to tell her that not only did werewolves exist but also fairies and goblins; at this point she would have believed anything!

'Don't worry about all the things you don't know, you'll learn about them soon enough,' he consoled her, as his fingers smoothed away the slight frown forming between her eyes, now more certain than ever that not telling her about Vassagio and his suspicions about the Elder had been the right thing to do.

Chapter 86

On the ground floor Eden slipped through the living room door and found himself staring straight into the haunting emptiness of two dark, red-rimmed eyes. Before he could react the huge muscle-bound vampire flew at him, sending him flying backwards into the living room to slam against the far wall with enough force to cause a crack in the concrete. He barely had time to gain his feet before his body was hurled across the room to crash into the large mahogany bookshelves, sending the books crashing to the floor.

He opened his eyes in time to see the pale blur heading for him. He blinked and disappeared in front of the massive vampire causing him to halt in midstride and stare around in confusion. Eden reappeared behind him, still a little stunned from being treated like a rag doll. He couldn't believe how strong this creature was. His only defence was speed.

As he was thinking, the vampire seemed to sense his presence and swivelled around to see the empty room. Just as he was turning round again something jumped onto his back and he felt the stab of teeth at his neck. He roared and tried to grab at whatever was on him, his hands grasping vainly at empty space. He turned again and again something jumped onto him.

Enraged and a little scared he flew backwards, but by the time he had slammed his body against the wall his tormentor had disappeared. Eden watched as the wall shuddered from the impact without having any effect on the vampire who was still flashing around blindly. This time he had to aim for the most vulnerable part of the neck; this couldn't last for much longer. With that thought he teleported onto his opponent again and was about to sink his teeth into the thick neck when he felt a crushing hand grab his arm and haul him round to meet the fury of those black murderous eyes.

This isn't good, he thought just as another hand fastened around his throat and lifted him high. He grasped at the hand as it started to slowly crush his flesh. With his thoughts in disarray he couldn't concentrate enough to teleport. Vainly he tried to kick the man in the gut but it seemed to have no effect. As the pressure increased and Eden's vision became darker, so that all he could see were the vampire's obsidian eyes, the irises rimmed with fiery red, he pulled his thoughts together for one last desperate attempt. The vampire's fingers met with a sound like metal hitting metal, intent on crushing whatever was in their hold except…there was nothing. He was clutching at the empty air.

Before he could fully register what had happened he felt a searing pain. Just as he turned his head, Eden's sharp teeth met deep within his flesh, crushing half his neck so that most of it crumbled and fell to the ground, sounding like small bits of rock. The vampire tried to howl in agony, but before he could his face cracked like a shattered mirror before falling apart, followed by the rest of his body, leaving Eden to watch it turn into a large pile of dust. He didn't give himself time to think about what had happened. The noise would have been enough to draw the rest of the coven to the room. He had to find Ashe and the others before any more turned up.

Chapter 87

Seton had walked cautiously into the darkened hall and had been in the process of opening a door to his right when he heard a loud crash from the next room. He had abandoned his intentions and instead had headed for the other room. The noise was deafening as something was thrown against a bookcase or a shelf. He was starting to realise that it probably wasn't an inanimate object when he looked into the room to see Eden disappear just as a large vampire turned his back towards the door. Seton crouched ready to spring onto the man when he sensed something else.

Without a thought he reacted instantly, swinging away and barely escaping the pale shadow falling down onto him. If he hadn't moved when he did he had no doubt he would have been destroyed. The creature was now perched a few feet above the ground, it's nails digging into the paintwork on the wall to give it a handhold. The face was still indistinct but he could make out the curves of a female body. The thought gave him only momentary relief. He wasn't prepared for what happened next.

She slithered across the wall with an agility he had never seen. Before he knew it she had flung herself at him, catching him around the waist. Her weight caused him to over balance and fall to the ground with her. They rolled across the floor, her teeth snapping constantly at his face, her rancid breath surrounding him. Her eyes too were black with red rings and he glimpsed a sort of madness in their depths. There was no fear only a desire to kill. He clenched his teeth; he could expect no mercy from her. He rolled them across the floor until he was above her and then flipped his body into the air, kicking his legs high. The unexpected move tore her hands from their grip around his waist. Twisting in midair he landed on his feet turning quickly to face her…except she wasn't anywhere to be seen.

He glanced around and then froze as he heard a light scraping. Glancing up he was stunned to see her smiling down at him from the high ceiling. It sent chills through him for it was a demonic expression. He knew what was coming and tried to move out of the way but she was much quicker. She let go and fell through the air straight at him. He braced himself as her body plummeted down, nearly over-powering him.

He managed to stay upright as she snapped at his neck, her teeth just grazing his skin before he jerked his face away. Tensing his muscles he pushed her backward hoping to pin her against the far wall. Struggling against each other they moved inch by slow inch until her back was against the wall. But if Seton had thought it would weaken her and give him the advantage he had thought wrong. As soon as she felt the wall she tried to scale it and it took all his strength to hold her back. He lowered his head, his intentions clear his mouth open, but she twisted away with a savage snarl and pulled him closer.

Before he could move his face away she turned her head sharply. In trying to bite her he had left himself open and his neck was now unprotected. She automatically leant forward and he felt her teeth pierce his skin. He tried to pull back but her teeth were like barbs and she refused to let go. His eyes widened as the long fangs dug deeper. He lifted his hands and grasped her creamy neck, which shone like porcelain in the dim light, shaking with intensity as he whispered a spell. The girl was so intent on locking her mouth onto his flesh that at first she didn't notice that he was no longer holding her back. But then she felt it.

It was as though her body was boiling. The heat started at her neck and moved down, licking at her skin. She ignored it; she was about to kill and nothing else mattered. Her jaw started to close, sending her teeth deep into flesh and bone, inches away from meeting and ending another life. The mere thought sent a thrill through her. But they never did meet, her jaw fell open and a shrill scream erupted from her throat as her body convulsed agonisingly. The pain was unbearable and she felt as though she was in the middle of a raging fire. She slumped back still screaming as her body heated up and glowed a bright white, mimicking Seton's hands as they hovered a few inches above her throat.

Eden sped into the hall in time to see the white light reach the girl's face and light up her eyes. A second later her entire body dissolved as a bright blue-white flame engulfed it. Seton opened his eyes and stood back as the flame died down and with it the girl's scream, watching as the smouldering pile of ash fell to the ground in a heap.

'Wow!' Eden breathed. He looked at Seton noting the fang marks on his neck. 'You ok?'

'No harm done,' he replied and touched the wounds, which started healing instantly, leaving unblemished skin in their wake.

They tensed as someone flew down the staircase, relaxing only when Leonara came to a standstill next to them.

'Did I miss much?' she asked almost flippantly.

'You have no idea,' Eden informed her with a shake of his head.

'What about you?' Seton's eyes rested speculatively on her haunted features before she could mask them.

She shook her head quickly. 'Just one upstairs; I dealt with it.' She didn't want to talk about what had happened, and from what she could see neither did the others.

'We have to find Ashe,' Eden pointed out, 'and fast. If those guys are anything to go by, he's in a lot of trouble.'

The others agreed whole-heartedly, but try as she might Leonara couldn't lock onto her brother's thoughts. After another minute she gave up and turned worried eyes on Seton.

'I can't locate him, do you think…?' she didn't have to finish the sentence.

Seton shook his head. 'No, he's ok,' he frowned. 'Maybe he isn't here.'

Just then they heard a crash from the other side of the house and exchanged worried looks…Ashe.

Chapter 88

Ashe slammed the man against the basement wall again trying to pin him against it so that he could get to his throat. He was fighting a losing battle. The vampire thrashed violently, tearing at Ashe's hands. He couldn't see his attacker but he could feel the solid grip on his shoulders. The two struggled against each other just as the remaining vampire hurled himself at them, intent on killing whatever was on his companion. Ashe felt the rush of air and let go just in time, turning away as the second vampire flew forward, passing him with inches to spare. At full speed he crashed into his friend, causing him to roar angrily whilst he staggered backward in a daze.

Ashe was about to attack before catching sight of three more figures flying down the stairs. *Great*, he thought, *this is going to be one hell of a party*. With three more vampires to deal with he knew he wouldn't survive. His eyes picked out Lainey's scared face and he gritted his teeth; he wasn't going to give up just yet. Turning back, his eyes widened in surprise as they took in the scene unfolding in front of him. The newcomers appeared to be fighting his original opponents. He blinked to focus better and a smile crept across his handsome face, the strain of the past few hours disappearing as he realised what was happening.

Leonara had targeted the larger of the two, causing his attack to falter just as Eden teleported behind him to bite his neck. Within seconds another pile of ash was lying on the floor. He turned his head to see Seton fighting the remaining vampire. He wasn't large but he appeared to be in a killing frenzy as his eyes darted back and forth and he frothed at the mouth.

They were snarling and circling each other when suddenly the vampire flashed forward aiming for Seton's left arm. He pulled it away when it was just inches from the razor sharp teeth, feeling the splatter of saliva on it as he whirled with lightning fast speed, avoiding his opponent as he rushed past him in an indistinguishable blur. Ashe flew forward to help just as the vampire turned and headed back, still aiming for Seton who was now crouching low, his silver brown eyes fixed on the man. Leonara looked at the fighting duo intensely, concentrating on the vampire's thought processes, but from the speed at which he was moving it didn't seem to be having much of an impact.

Seton waited for him to come closer until he could have touched him and then he leapt high letting the man fly past below him. He twisted in midair and fell back to the ground, landing lightly on his feet. Turning he focussed again on his opponent watching him skid to a halt a few metres away and swivel around, an angry roar ripping through his throat. Just as he was about to move forward again he stopped and turned, a bewildered look on his face.

Seton couldn't understand what was happening as the man started twisting and turning desperately. He glanced at the others for a clue, but they looked as perplexed as he did. Leonara was still concentrating on him and Eden was trying to find a way to get to him without being hurt by the flailing arms. Seton saw his opportunity and ducked deftly under them, flashed behind the vampire and grabbed both his legs tightly, throwing him off balance so that both of them sprawled in a heap on the floor. With the man finally on the ground, Eden leapt forward, landing on his lower back, preventing the vampire from standing up. Just as he was about to reach for the muscled neck, a sharp screeching began, cutting through the furious snarls and growls. In a second Seton and Eden found themselves lying on a pile of ash.

'What the…?' Eden looked around in disbelief. He knew he hadn't destroyed the vampire and neither had Seton, then who had? He looked at his sister but she shook her head slowly.

A chuckle erupted a few inches away from him and he froze, *who was that?* He couldn't detect anything. Was this another enemy? Perhaps another vampire? The Raynes stood up looking around puzzled, ready to defend themselves if needed. From out of nowhere Ashe appeared looking dishevelled.

'Ashe!' He barely had time to move before Leonara had flung herself at him in a big bear hug. 'You're ok!'

'Yeah, thanks to you guys,' he replied, his voice muffled by her hair.

She stood back her eyes narrowed suspiciously. 'Where did you come from? I tried to read your mind and I got nothing!'

He shrugged. 'No idea, but these guys couldn't see me either, it was like I was invisible!'

Seton stood up, dusting off his clothes, his eyes roaming carefully over his brother. 'Your powers are growing, Ashe. Eden mentioned the feeling you had in Italy.' He glanced around the room with a frown. 'Where is she?'

Ashe nodded towards the boxes, he could see Lainey clearly but Seton was still frowning. 'Here.' He moved forward and took Lainey by the hand. He could feel his protective urges vanish as she stood up and walked forward, nearly stumbling.

'Ah yes,' Seton smiled warmly at the pale-faced girl; she looked scared. *No wonder*, he thought. He glanced again at Ashe and he nodded.

'She knows.'

Seton sighed; he couldn't blame his brother but damage control was needed. He nodded at Leonara and she moved forward and smiled gently at the girl. Almost immediately the fear melted away and her eyes became slightly glazed over.

'How long?' Seton asked her.

'A few hours,' she replied, 'she won't remember what has happened.'

'Good, we'll need that time.' He looked at Eden. 'Take her to a safe place, away from Erie and make sure there are no covens in the area.' He could see Ashe looking worried. 'She'll be safer away from here trust me. I need you here with the others, this isn't over yet.'

Ashe nodded and turned to Lainey one final time and touched her cheek. 'Be safe,' he murmured and stood back as Eden lifted her easily into his arms and disappeared. Ashe turned to Seton with a confused look. 'You said my powers were growing. I thought I already had all my powers!'

Seton shook his head with a dry smile twisting his lips, 'Clearly not. It seems to me that whilst you can detect others of our kind, you can also hide from them.'

'But you couldn't see Lainey even after I was visible,' he pointed out.

'I believe you are a Guardian, Ashe. Your protective instincts are the key. Which is also why you knew when she was in trouble, even though she was miles away.'

Ashe remained silent as he digested what Seton had said. 'It does make sense.'

'I for one am glad of what you can do now. We'll need all the help we can get to make it through this mess,' Seton replied, his expression grim.

+++

Marina's face contorted as a silent snarl whispered through her pale lips. Her red-rimmed eyes stared almost disbelievingly at the piles of ash littering the floor. It took all of her self-control not to burst into the room and attack the group of Elites. She was standing in the garden, peeking through a crack in the padlocked door that led into the basement. Darius had sent her to find out why some of the coven were taking so long to return. As far as she knew they were searching for one of the girls from the high school library that had escaped.

Darius hadn't been too worried, after all he said, who would believe her? And if anyone did investigate they would deal with them. Now looking at the Elites standing there so boldly, her rage boiled over. She couldn't smell humans in the immediate vicinity. The Elites must have set a trap and the others had fallen into it. Darius had to know about this. She made sure of their number before flashing down the dark street intent on alerting him before it was too late.

She found him crouched over yet another human. As she moved closer he lifted his head, a snarl ready on his bloody lips to warn off the intruder before he realised who it was. When he did he turned back to the corpse and finished draining it before standing up gracefully, a pale hand swiping across his mouth to remove some of the blood.

'What news of the others?' he asked huskily, the killing light in his eyes dimming slightly.

'They are gone,' she whispered, her eyes dropping to the ground warily.

'Gone?' he moved forward. 'Where?'

'I mean they're destroyed,' she clarified, her voice still low. She knew how furious he was going to be and she wasn't wrong.

His eyes glittered angrily and the paleness of his skin intensified as he bared his teeth. 'What?! How?!'

'The Elites...th...they're back,' she stammered, moving back a pace.

'WHAT?!' She winced as he roared the question at her.

'I found them at the girl's house. They must have set a trap' she continued hesitantly.

'A trap hmmm?' he asked thoughtfully, and then he started to smile, causing her to blink in surprise. She had been ready to fight him off. 'Well, we'll just have to turn the tables on them.'

'What...what do you mean?'

'They are in Erie now, our domain, we can't let them leave without a party can we?!'

'You want to attack them?!' she asked incredulously, her mouth drying up rapidly. 'But I counted at least three of them, there might be more!'

'Look around you,' he instructed and she glanced at the horde of vampires crowding around them, 'we clearly out-number them.'

'But the Code...' she insisted weakly, knowing it would enrage him, but also knowing that the repercussions would be severe if they went through with this crazy plan.

Darius smiled cruelly at her. 'I never thought you were a coward!'

'I'm not!' she defended herself, 'but what if we fail?'

'We cannot fail,' he replied and lifted his arms, 'We are now gods of all we survey! The Elites are nothing! We will teach them a lesson they will never forget!'

Chapter 89

Ashe stilled, his skin was vibrating again with an awareness he had come to dread. He and the others were sitting in Lainey's living room resting while they had a chance. Seton had outlined a plan of action for the next few hours, anticipating an attack before dawn. He now looked up at Ashe's rapt face and a cold determination filled him.

Ashe nodded slightly before saying, 'They're coming from the East.'

Seton turned to Leonara. 'Time to move.' His eyes settled on each of them in turn. 'Stay safe, we will get through this.' He had hoped Eden would have been back by now but he hadn't. They would have to manage without him for now.

They all flashed to various positions around the house. Seton took the front door, Leonara flew up the stairs; intent on influencing the enemy's thoughts from a vantage point. Ashe stayed in the living room trying to create the invisible force field around the others. All of them knew their defences were weak at best, but the thought of surrender never crossed their minds. As Ashe's awareness increased, he started to feel the protective urges again and his skin tingled. He hoped his newfound talent was working. Until he attacked or was attacked by the hordes sweeping towards them he wouldn't know for sure.

He whispered, 'They're here.'

It was loud enough for the others to hear and be prepared. Leonara concentrated on any thoughts in the vicinity besides her brothers' and put out a numbing effect, feeling it extending from her in pulsing waves. She glanced out of a window and frowned, several people were approaching the back yard. By the speed at which they were travelling, she knew they were part of Darius' coven.

The red eyes flared in the dark as they flew forward. She could feel their killing rage even from this distance. Focussing all her attention on them she managed to stop a few of the weaker ones that hadn't drunk too much blood. But the rest continued on their deadly quest. She sent a quick mental message to her brothers letting them know what was happening before she returned to her task.

Seton tensed, he could now see the crowd approaching and it stunned him. He hadn't expected such a large force. He crouched low hiding behind a large vase in the hall next to the damaged front door. *Let them come*, he thought.

+++

Eden paid at the reception desk and turned to see Lainey's still slightly dazed expression. He had transported them to a city well away from Erie and booked her into one of the five star hotels. He hadn't noticed any coven activities nearby as he had walked her into the opulent lobby. Now he escorted her to the seventh floor of the building to her room.

'Stay here,' he commanded in a low voice, 'You're safe and you're on holiday. Don't leave this room, I'll be back soon.'

She nodded, her mind programmed to heed his instructions. He left a wad of cash in hundred dollar bills on the table, and left her looking around the room. Having made sure the door was locked and chanting a few protective spells, he teleported back to Erie, intent on joining his siblings against Darius.

When he materialised outside Lainey's house his mouth fell open in shock. The house looked like it had been through a hurricane! Furniture was strewn across the lawn in pieces, all the windows were broken, the front door was non-existent and everywhere he looked dark shadows were crawling all over it with more arriving every second. The air was thick with the sound of snarls and feral growls and an occasional high pitched screeching. He desperately hoped that the others were all right.

He looked around him again; it appeared as though he was bringing up the rear of Darius' coven. Seeing a few stragglers he teleported swiftly behind them, crushing their necks before they could react. *Go to hell*, he thought as another one crumbled to dust. Just as he was about to teleport he sensed something behind him. As he turned he caught sight of a tall female, her light brown hair in disarray, her face which in another life would have been considered sweet, distorted by her ferocious snarl.

She was a couple of feet to his right, and heading straight for him. He twisted away, trying to throw her off her attack but she followed him round like a ballet dancer before launching herself onto him, her razor-sharp teeth snapping shut just inches from his startled face. Her long limbs twisted around him as she lowered her head again.

But he was now pushing her away with all the strength he could muster. Her red eyes told him all he needed to know. If he didn't get away he too would be a pile of ash on the muddy ground. He bit at her arms and she screeched in agony as he tore off chunks of her flesh, but still she held on, her grip crushing him. He managed to break off one of her arms, causing her to loosen her hold just enough for him to teleport out of her way and reappear behind her. She had fallen to the ground in astonishment and was trying to stand up when he leapt onto her back, sending her to her knees, and bit down savagely on her fragile-looking neck through her hair, a grim sense of achievement filling him as her body dissolved.

He stood up as he heard another fearsome screech. The weaker members of the coven were now nearing the house; he didn't have much time. Quickly teleporting from one to the other he disposed of them as fast as he could. Within minutes he had left over thirty piles of ash scattered across the muddy lawn behind him. But he knew he had barely made a dent in Darius' forces.

He teleported into the house, praying he wouldn't end up in the wrong place at the wrong time. He sighed a second later in relief; he had ended up on the first floor landing. Looking around he couldn't believe what he was seeing. Leonara was fighting off at least five vampires, stunning two just long enough to deal with the other three. When he glanced over the solid wood banister to the ground floor he could see Seton being attacked by another group. His hands were glowing a bright white, setting his attackers on fire if he touched them for too long. From the loud screeches and vicious bangs coming from the living room he assumed Ashe was hosting his own party.

He glanced behind him as another window shattered. In a blink of an eye he disappeared as the vampire flew in only to be disposed off before he saw Eden. For the next hour the Raynes fought off their assailants, slowly winning the battles whilst trying to survive. Half way through attacking another vampire, Eden glanced out of a window and gasped. Another larger horde was making its way down the street. Ashe would have detected them but was too busy using his new talent to pay them much attention. He crushed the girl's neck easily and disappeared before the ashes fell to the ground, teleporting next to Seton, careful to avoid his hands.

'There's another group coming to the house,' he yelled, ducking away from a charge as he felt the air movement behind him.

Seton's hands made contact, almost blowing up the vampire as she ran towards him, before turning to his brother. He could see the trepidation in Eden's eyes and felt his own unease. Dealing with normal vampires was bad enough, but these almost drugged up ones were lethal. It had taken a lot out of them to fight and there were still more on their way? He looked closely at Eden.

'You have to get help. We can't hold them all back alone! Go to the Reliquary and let the Elders know what's happening.'

Eden was about to refuse, but Seton's earnest expression stopped him. He didn't want to abandon the family, but even he had to acknowledge Seton's wisdom. He nodded and teleported back to Italy just as the first fresh vampires from the second group approached the house at a run, roaring with anger.

Chapter 90

'WHAT?!!' Eleanor's usual regal voice was transformed by the fury she felt. Before Eden could request any help she was out of the door and flying towards the Elders' Hall leaving him to follow as best he could. She barged through the massive double doors, ignoring the *Machai* guards on either side and flew to the dais. Terence looked up in surprise and was about to speak when he saw the fury etched on her face and sparking out of her eyes.

'We need to go to Erie,' she said with a finality he didn't know how to argue with and then related what Eden had told her. Terence's face paled as he listened, his flashing eyes the sign of how angry he was by what she had said.

'You have my support. Take what or who you need,' he told her and then added in a low voice, 'Teach Darius a lesson he won't forget!'

She nodded and flew out of the Hall to find Eden.

+++

Within minutes they were ready. Besides Eleanor and Eden who stood ready to transport them, Alena, Nicholas and Karael were also going. They clasped hands and Eden swiftly teleported them to Erie. Eva watched them leave, her eyes holding Nicholas' intently as he disappeared into thin air.

She could still hear his voice as he said, 'I have to go back to Erie to help Seton. You must stay here...safe.' He had kissed away the questions and worry plaguing her mind.

With the Raynes away and not even Alena for company, she felt completely alone. The Elders would still be here, and for all intents and purposes she would be safe, but something was niggling at the back of her mind. Despite the facts she could not stop worrying. Something didn't feel right, but she couldn't place her finger on it. Nicholas hadn't mentioned anything more about Vassagio and she hadn't asked. Being taught by Karael was exhausting at the best of times, but lately he had been pushing her constantly to learn more. By the time he let her leave the Training Hall she was usually too tired to worry about anything else.

For some reason no one had seen or heard from Vassagio for a while and no one seemed concerned. They had all accepted the fact that he had left the Reliquary and may or may not return. She hoped he wouldn't; there was something about him that scared her, possibly even more than Darius had. She turned and walked back to her quarters. With Karael gone she wouldn't be trained by any of the other Elders, although Nicholas had said that Nuriel, the boyish Elder she had met when she was first brought to the Training Hall, would train her in the art of spells. From what she had heard from Nicholas and Alena, Karael was good but Nuriel apparently was the master. As she walked down the old passageway, unknown to her, a pair of stony eyes followed her progress.

+++

The *Machai* moved around restlessly just as Terence stood up, a puzzled frown on his handsome face. He had felt it too.

Sylph, who had just entered the chamber, narrowed her eyes. 'What was that?'

'The spells...they've been disturbed,' he whispered.

Just as he spoke they heard the sound of several wings beating almost soundlessly in the still silence of the Reliquary as dozens of *Machai* guards rushed to the compromised boundary.

'A Dark one has dared to enter this place!' Terence prowled around the room restlessly, barely containing his anger.

'They will find him,' Sylph soothed, knowing that he already had enough on his plate with Erie in danger from Darius. Having their enemies attacking their most secure sanctuary was beyond bearing.

+++

'*Attero!*'

The command pierced the slightly shimmering almost invisible barrier cloaking the ancient stone walls of the Reliquary. They would be arriving soon; he had to work fast. He lifted his pale hands and started chanting.

'*Spiritus atrum unus.*'

A transparent form stood before him, only the eyes showing distinctly as empty black orbs. He smiled and flicked his wrist sending the apparition floating down the nearest passage. *That should keep them occupied*, he thought as he flew in the opposite direction. He had stayed away from the Reliquary for several days and only returned when he had heard about the Raynes leaving for Erie.

He had already sent the girl back to help Darius not to make a fool of himself. Now he had to deal with the other one. With the Raynes away and the rest of the Elders intent on helping Erie, preventing other uprisings and now dealing with his phantom vampire, this was the perfect chance he had been waiting for. He stilled suddenly murmuring an invisibility spell as a Protector approached, clearly angered by the supposed attack.

Rizoel had a hand on the hilt of his word as he paced forward, his bright eyes missing nothing. Vassagio strengthened his spell; he knew if he was found hiding, Rizoel wouldn't think twice about killing him. The Protectors' swords had been created in the same fire as the ones forged for the Archangels and just like them had the ability to kill angels easily. He stepped back just as Rizoel came closer.

What was that? He stopped and glared at the empty space on his right. Had something moved? His sharp eyes pierced the darkness easily searching for any inconsistency. But the emptiness appeared complete and the wall behind looked solid and unremarkable. His hand tightened on his sword, a dull hissing echoing down the passage as the weapon waited to be unsheathed. *Don't be ridiculous*, he chided himself after a minute longer. *If it was a Dark One you would have detected him by now. They don't have our powers*, he argued.

His hand relaxed and the sword became silent again as he continued on his way, still searching. Vassagio waited for several minutes before lifting the spell. That had been close; he had to be more vigilant. The *Machai* and the Protectors would be out in full force. He smiled, but they wouldn't be able to stop him, especially since they didn't know what he was up to. He turned and walked in the opposite direction to Rizoel, keeping a look out for any more Elders, heading for Eva's quarters.

Chapter 91

CALM DOWN! STOP! Leonara sent the commands desperately to the group surrounding her. From all the notice they took of them she might as well not have bothered. With the constant distractions she couldn't focus enough to make any one of them heed her thoughts. She whirled away, the sharp teeth aimed at her missing her shoulder by inches. *This can't go on much longer*, she thought, not sure if she was comforted or scared by the thought. She could hear the others thinking along similar lines.

My God, when will they stop?! Seton wondered from the ground floor.

Where the hell is Eden?! Ashe cursed silently.

Leonara was with Ashe on that one. She had seen him teleport downstairs and then away. She knew Seton had sent him for reinforcements but they needed them right now. Hopefully they would arrive before her strength ran out. Just as the thought entered her mind Eden appeared on the staircase below her. She barely had time to register the presence of the others with him before she felt the sharp sting of teeth entering her flesh.

She gritted her teeth, turning to see a particularly savage female next to her, her sharp almost serrated teeth deep in her forearm. *The price of deliverance*, she thought trying to ignore the burning sensation deep within her flesh as the venom spread out.

She knew she had only seconds before it poisoned her entire body, destroying her powers and thereby her status as an Elite. But worse than that it would take ages to recover; certain death in this scenario if she couldn't defend herself. She dragged her arm away viciously, eager to stop any more poison from entering her body, not caring that her forearm had cracked and disintegrated around the bite, her only concern was breaking the contact. As she pulled it out of the girl's reach, she screamed in agony before turning to face the girl again but she was too slow.

Alena had already flown to the rescue and secured the snarling girl from behind before biting down on her neck. The other vampires standing around Leonara fell back slightly, astonished by the sudden appearance of the Elites. But their blood lust was such that it swamped their instinctive fear and they rushed forward, snarling ferociously.

Karael, Nicholas and Eleanor had disappeared downstairs to help Seton and Ashe leaving Alena and Eden to deal with the vampires on the first floor. Eden was busy teleporting around the crowd as Leonara tried to stun the ones closest to her through the searing pain spreading along her arm.

'You need to get to Seton,' Alena said to her as she avoided another attack by pirouetting deftly, light as a professional ballerina.

Leonara only shook her head as she slammed another vampire through the wooden floor, sending splinters flying towards the high ceiling. Alena could see how much the venom was affecting her. Not wasting any more time she stepped between Leonara and the vampires advancing on her. They could tell she was weakening and she was fast becoming a very attractive target. Alena pushed her sister forcibly down the stairs as she backed away from the hungry horde.

'GO!' she shouted as she flung her hands out murmuring under her breath. All at once bolts of lightning cut through the air from above with deadly accuracy, hitting several vampires, setting them on fire. Within seconds half the crowd had disintegrated leaving the rest to falter in their attack.

+++

Leonara didn't see Alena's awesome display. She had stumbled down the stairs as fast as she could, looking for Seton. She finally saw him standing back to back with Eleanor. The sight of the ex-Elder fighting stopped her in her tracks. Eleanor was brandishing a sword that shone silver in the darkness, the intense brightness hurting her eyes if she looked at it directly for too long. Shielding her eyes she stumbled towards them.

Seton help! She sent weakly.

In the middle of blowing up a vampire he turned suddenly, leaving his victim to burn up in a slow blue flame, the snarls and moans still echoing hollowly.

'Leo!' he flew to her side, noting her rapidly weakening state.

She dropped to her knees as he reached her. Kneeling next to her, he closed his eyes calming himself before attempting to heal her. In the energized state he was in he could quite easily kill her. Eleanor flashed towards them, her sword held high. Leonara glanced up at her wearily, her foggy mind wondering why she would attack them. Just as she thought the gleaming sword would cut right through her it changed direction slightly and an astounded yelp from behind her made her turn her head in surprise.

The sword had cleanly pierced through the granite-like neck of the vampire intent on attacking her and Seton. As she watched the boy turned to dust leaving Eleanor free to deal with the others around them. A few metres away she could make out Karael in his white robes literally dancing around the room. His flaming sword never still as it plunged into the vampires' necks slaying them in great quantities so that one had barely hit the floor before another joined it. And yet it just didn't seem to make a difference to their numbers.

Just as she started feeling faint Seton placed his now cold hands against the wound, murmuring under his breath, his hands gradually becoming warmer. He chanted slowly his eyes still closed, his focus un-wavering. If he became distracted by what was happening around them his emotions would spiral out of control and he could destroy one of his own.

As the faintness started lifting Leonara opened her still cloudy silver eyes to see a large black creature flying from one vampire to the next. It took her a while to understand what it was she was seeing and then to believe it wasn't her imagination. As the creature flew around the room she blinked, a bat, it took her even longer to recognise it as being one of Nicholas' transformations. *What was faster than flying? Especially a flying creature that didn't attract a lot of attention?* She smiled as her mind locked onto his thoughts.

Take that, spawn of hell! Sleep in flames sucker!

You need to come up with better insults! She sent tiredly laughing at him silently.

Seton's hands were definitely improving her mental processes. She looked down to see the wound closing on itself. As she watched his hands she sensed something nearby and looked up to see a large vampire heading straight for them. She gasped; he had avoided the two Elders and was now intent on the crouched Elite. She shouted a warning and tried to stand up to defend Seton but his grip was too strong, his hands almost welded to her arm.

Look up! You're in danger! COME ON SETON!! She was screaming at him now with her thoughts, trying to get through to him but she kept coming up against a mental barrier. Still in a calming trance he just didn't seem to hear her or feel her struggles to be free. She glanced around for help. Karael and Eleanor were both occupied a few feet away. Trapped next to him, unable to help him and unable to break his focus she resorted to pleading aloud.

'Seton, please turn around!' But there was no response.

All she could do was watch as the vampire came closer and closer, knowing that within seconds he would attack and bury his venomous fangs into Seton's neck, ending his existence.

Chapter 92

She glanced back at the vampire and quailed; he was nearly on top of them. Summoning all her remaining energy she attacked his thoughts with all the desperation she felt.

STOP! She commanded.

He barely staggered and kept coming. She tried again and again but it just wasn't enough. She had never felt so helpless in all the years she had lived than she did at that moment. Here she was, an Elite with heavenly powers, powerless to help the one person she thought of as a mentor. The feeling crushed her like nothing else could.

He was now close enough to Seton for her to see the gleam in his eyes and she cringed, her eyes closing involuntarily as he leaned forward, expecting him to crush Seton's neck. When nothing happened to Seton's firm grip on her, she opened her eyes warily to see the vampire fending off a flitting shadow. She looked at Seton willing him to wake up, but he still had his eyes closed oblivious to the world and the immediate danger they were in.

She turned back to the fight now raging behind him, praying for Nicholas to come out of it unscathed. It seemed that the hatred the vampires harboured for the Elites was now transferred to this small animal. Nicholas felt the air moving near his left wing and he banked away steeply, narrowly avoiding the muscular arm swinging towards him, intent on crushing him.

He flew in a tight circle, astonished when the vampire followed him. He was much faster than Nicholas gave him credit for. He flew across the room, leading the vampire well away from Seton and Leonara, giving Seton time to finish healing her. But as he flew he knew he needed a plan. There was only so far he could fly in a straight line. He banked and flew to his right moving in a wide circle trying to outflank the immense man closing in on him. If only he could get behind him and to his neck.

He climbed steeply as another arm swiped at him, cutting him off from his intended route. He hovered several feet above the man, adjusting his wings with delicacy. As he watched for an opportunity the man seemed to lose interest and headed back towards Seton who was still crouching next to Leonara.

Come on, come on! Nicholas thought, urging Seton to come out of his trance, but he still seemed lost to the world. *Now or never*, he thought as he winged after the vampire, flying high and just behind him, looking for an opening. Seeing his opportunity he dropped lower, flying a few centimetres behind him now as he stalked towards his targets.

+++

Leonara screamed in horror. She had watched Nicholas lead the vampire away and fly high, the vampire losing interest and Nicholas flying behind him as he had come back towards her. Now her eyes widened in dread as she watched the vampire swing round suddenly, his outstretched arm slamming into Nicholas, sending him somersaulting out of control into the nearby wall.

She tried to struggle away from Seton but he was still holding onto her as the last bit of damage on her arm started to vanish. She looked up to see the bat flapping desperately, trying to get away from the huge vampire now standing over it, leaning forward to crush the small body. Miraculously it slipped between his fingers and flew up, its path unsteady as it got its bearings. She watched it fly further away with a sigh of relief, thinking it was going to escape, but it turned back at the last minute. She frowned, *what was he doing?* She turned to see the vampire heading again towards Seton. *That's one determined vamp*, she thought despairingly as he came closer.

Unfortunately Nicholas had seen him too and was heading back despite his injuries. The transformation was seeping his strength but he had to try, for Seton's sake. Leonara was sending out desperate pleas, trying to stop him, but he wouldn't listen and she was too weak to make him obey. All she could do was watch helplessly as he sailed through the air and landed on the vampire's neck. Just as he dropped his head to sink his fangs in, a large hand clamped down on his body, crushing his bones, which in his transformed state were a lot softer than in his usual form.

He heard Leonara scream and felt the air leaving his lungs, and then he heard his bones cracking before splintering apart deep within his body. His almost silent screech of agony, though inaudible to human ears, was like a banshee's wail. It penetrated the air, sending shock waves around the house.

Chapter 93

Most of the vampires came to a standstill in shock never having heard anything like it before. Feeling the small body go limp the vampire threw it against the wall with all the force he could muster, watching it to make sure it didn't rise again before turning with a cruel smile towards Seton and Leonara. She was now almost healed and trying to stand up. She couldn't believe what she had seen, but the killing light in his dark impenetrable eyes left no room for doubt and it fuelled her own desire to annihilate him.

Just as she was released from Seton's hold the vampire reached him. She leapt forward, flying through the air to tackle him. She braced herself for the impact just as her body crashed into his bulkier one. If she had thought it would knock him off balance she had been wrong. He stayed upright and she felt like she had hit a solid rock wall.

She almost bounced off, but the thick hand now circling her neck held her in place. She squirmed desperately, holding the hand, trying to pull it away to no avail. He was too strong. She gasped as his grip tightened willing him to let her go. Just when she thought he would finish her off he was distracted by a movement from his right. It wasn't much but it broke his concentration long enough for Leonara's thoughts to command his hand. It slackened and she fell back, staying out of his reach.

She caught sight of Seton moving in from the right to intercept the vampire before he could attack her again, but suddenly Eleanor flew between them, her silver eyes blazing with an all consuming anger. Leonara moved further back, she had never seen her so angry.

'Enough,' she said, her voice low, making it all the more authoritative. Her golden hair flowed around her face and down her back reminding Leonara of a statue of a pagan goddess. Eleanor lifted her hands her eyes shining like molten mercury and her hair flew back, as though caught in a gale.

Leonara frowned in confusion, *what was going on?* As she watched, Eleanor's body started to glow. Every part of her turned to a bright gold, and as she watched it grew brighter and brighter until it seemed to rival the sun. She had to turn away eventually as the brightness intensified, searing through the darkness, filling the entire house so that it shone out from all the windows as though the sun itself had been imprisoned within it. Leonara could hear screams and moans initially and then nothing.

When she turned back, the light had gone and Eleanor was kneeling next to Nicholas' still body, now transformed back into its human state. She glanced around her in amazement; *where were all the vampires?* The others seemed to be wondering the same thing because besides the Raynes and Karael no one else appeared to be in the house.

'What happened?' Ashe asked as he staggered out from the living room, his expression dazed and not a little confused.

Leonara shrugged before heading towards Nicholas. Ashe looked at Seton for answers but he too was flashing to Nicholas' side.

Karael passed Ashe, sheathing his sword. 'Impressive huh? She's still got it. Good old Helios!'

'Helios?' Ashe frowned.

'Yeah,' he jerked his head towards the group surrounding Nicholas, 'that's Eleanor's Greek name. Didn't you know?'

'She was the Sun god?' Ashe asked in disbelief his mouth dropping open when Karael nodded. The Dark Ones could not go out in sunlight. The intensity with which Eleanor had glowed would have easily destroyed them so that not even ash remained to signify their existence.

They moved towards the others. *What else don't I know about my family?* Ashe wondered as they drew closer. His breath caught as he saw his brother lying on the ground motionless. Although he had transformed back, Nicholas' body looked broken. His eyes were closed and he remained deathly still. Eleanor had lifted his head onto her lap and was now looking at Seton. They didn't utter a word; it wasn't difficult to understand that look. Seton lifted his hands and placed them on Nicholas' torso, concentrating as they warmed up again for the second time that night.

Chapter 94

Eva sat up suddenly, her breathing rapid, her skin clammy.

'It was a nightmare, just a dream,' she whispered to herself, her heart rate gradually dropping as her eyes focussed on her surroundings. She hadn't had a nightmare since arriving at the Vatican, which made this one particularly unusual and more frightening.

She had been walking with Nicholas hand in hand in a beautiful place she had never seen before. All she knew was that it was the most peaceful place she had ever been in with soft music playing in the background, and the sound of nature all around them. If she closed her eyes she could still hear the wind moving through the branches, the birdsong floating around them and the slight rustle of their footsteps on the lush green grass. Nicholas had been saying something and she had been laughing when suddenly he stopped and turned to look back. She followed his gaze to see a bright white light growing bigger from a pinpoint into a large circle.

'What is it?' she asked him.

It looked beautiful but a sudden dread seemed to descend on everything around them. The birds fell silent, the music stopped and all the world seemed to hold its breath.

'I have to go,' he replied and let go of her hand. That loss of contact threw her into a blind panic, such as she had never experienced before.

'No! You can't!' she cried out, trying to catch his hand again as he moved away. But he kept walking, smiling sadly at her, but still deliberately moving towards the light. How she hated that light. She ran towards him, but try as she might she just didn't seem to be getting any closer to him. His hand stayed just out of reach and she cried harder. She had this overwhelming sense that if she could only catch hold of his hand everything would be ok. But she just couldn't.

'You can't leave me!' she wailed despairingly, 'Please...don't go!'

Although the light still looked beautiful, she knew if he went to it, she would lose him forever. Despite its beauty it seemed to take on an ethereal menace she couldn't place. Thinking about it now she broke out into a cold sweat and started shivering; it still felt so real.

She switched on the bedside lamp, raking her shaking hand through her long dishevelled hair. She glanced at her watch; five o'clock in the afternoon. She must have dozed off and not realised it. No wonder her mind was so befuddled, she thought, trying to block out the image of Nicholas walking away.

'Please be alright,' she prayed fervently, as she stood up shakily and headed for the en-suite bathroom to splash water on her face.

+++

As she walked out of the bathroom a few minutes later she had a curious feeling. She couldn't quite place it but it was enough to stop her in her tracks. The room was lighted with several lamps but there were still patches of impenetrable darkness in the corners. *Was there someone there?*

She couldn't see anything, but the feeling persisted. *It can't be dangerous*, she reasoned but her mind refused to believe that. Shivers of cold fear slid down her spine and the now familiar tingling swept down her arms until it reached her fingertips. Her eyes probed the shadows vainly, while her body continued to tense. *You are safe here it's the Vatican for god's sake! Eleanor said no vampire could enter without the Elders knowing*, she reminded herself. *Calm down, there's nothing here!*

She willed herself forward, but as she passed an empty chair her entire body froze. No matter what she had told herself just moments ago her instincts knew different. She backed away rapidly, staring at the chair fearfully, ready to fight. *This is ridiculous*, her brain reasoned but her body refused to listen. Something was wrong, she just didn't know what. Automatically her hands lifted, small sparks of blue lightning already flickering at their tips, eager to rip into whatever she had sensed.

'Now now Eva, it's only…'

But whoever had spoken didn't get a chance to finish the sentence. A bolt of lightning flew out, streaking through the air and hitting the edge of the chair. Flames erupted instantly as Eva watched, her mouth dropping open in shock. But it wasn't the fire she was staring at aghast, it was the man who had leapt out of the chair, having materialised out of thin air and who was now trying to douse the flames.

Where had he come from? She wondered.

Having extinguished the fire with a spell, the white-robed man turned to look at her cautiously. She frowned, he looked apprehensive and then she realised why. Her hands were still held in front of her, the tingling still intense and the blue sparks still in evidence. She supposed she should lower them but something stopped her. *It might not be safe*, an inner voice whispered urgently.

She looked at him questioningly. 'What are you doing here?'

'I wanted to see you,' he replied in a smooth steady voice, but she didn't miss the cautious glance at her hands.

'Why? And why couldn't I see you before?'

'It's an invisibility spell,' he explained quickly.

She frowned. 'Why do you need a…?'

'To stop anyone seeing me here,' he cut in before she could finish.

'Why?'

He glanced again at her hands. 'Why don't we sit down and talk? You still seem on edge.'

I don't want to talk, she thought wildly. She didn't trust him, never had, and from what she had learnt from Nick and Eleanor and heard in the Elders' council, they didn't either. She thought about refusing his request and ordering him out of her room, but then thought better of it. After all, she thought, he was an Elder and much more powerful than her. He could overcome her quickly and who knew if her status as the One would be enough to protect her if the other Elders found out she had attacked him. She could sense time passing but her indecision held her rigid.

Chapter 95

He's an Elder, another voice argued. *How bad can he be? If he was that dangerous, surely someone would know by now. The other Elders wouldn't accept him. Even Nick and Eleanor, though not exactly fond of him couldn't find anything concrete against him.*

Her hands lowered and Vassagio's trepidation lessened. *She was tough*, he thought as he watched the conflict raging in her eyes. *I must be careful; one wrong move and I might not get another chance.* Besides he may end up being blown to bits, something he didn't want to dwell on. Although his powers were awesome, he knew that the powers she possessed could out-weigh his in the right circumstances. *I won't give her another chance*, he vowed as she lowered her hands further. The bolt of lightning had come dangerously close to him. He cursed himself for not seeing what might happen, but even he hadn't expected her to attack. *She's getting too powerful.*

'Okay why have you come here?' she asked, her voice a little unsteady.

He eyed a couch nearby. 'Don't you want to sit down?'

She shook her head vehemently. She still wasn't sure about letting her hands drop, but there was no way she was going to relax with this man. *Not man*, she corrected, *vampire*. He could move and react faster than she could ever imagine and she wasn't taking any chances. Maybe if she stayed standing she had a better chance of acting.

He shrugged and walked past her to the couch and sat down. She turned to face him but didn't go any closer. She was nearer to the door now. *Whatever good that will do*, her brain sneered, knowing he would probably be lounging against it in a flash if she attempted to leave. Suddenly the absence of her friends and Nicholas hit home with a tangible force. With miles of passageways who would hear her screams? Her body tensed further.

Vassagio seemed oblivious to her discomfort. He was looking around the room. 'This is a nice place.'

She didn't reply. He looked at her and smiled. 'To answer your question, I came to talk to you.'

'Why were you invisible?'

He sighed almost tiredly, 'To stop the others seeing me. I had to be sure no one knew we had talked.'

'What do you mean?' *Why would an Elder not want his peers to know he had spoken to her unless...* Her fingers tingled dangerously again.

He seemed to read her mind. 'I won't hurt you.' Her disbelieving stare spoke volumes. 'I came here to warn you.'

'Warn me? About what?'

He sighed shaking his head. 'Still so innocent,' he murmured under his breath, just loud enough for her to hear him.

What did he mean? She moved slightly closer, catching herself quickly before she moved too close. She had to keep her guard up; he wasn't to be trusted.

Looking up at her he could see the curiosity flare in her violet eyes. 'Eva you are the One! You have powers we have yet to see.' He paused. 'And that scares some of us.'

'Us?' *Who was he talking about?*

'The Elders. Your powers are legendary and still a mystery.'

She tried to laugh, but it came out as a strangled whisper. 'You're joking. The Elders can't be scared of me. They are the ones teaching me about my powers.'

'Precisely, they are the ones teaching you. They are in control...don't you see?'

She shook her head as she argued, 'But Karael has been pushing me to learn more and more. Why would he do that if they were scared?'

'To find out how far you can go, to see the extent of your powers in a place where they can control them.'

'This is what you're warning me about? That they are controlling my learning?'

'No, I have come to warn you of what will happen soon.'

Her confusion increased ten-fold. *What was he talking about?* 'What do you mean?'

'I don't expect you to understand at once. After all you are half human and it limits you. But the Elders, myself included, have always laid out our plans, our strategies if you will, years if not eons in advance. We consider all possibilities and eventualities, like chess players and wait patiently. You were always a possibility. There was always a chance you would somehow come to the Reliquary and now that you have, a strategy has been put into place.'

Eva's blood ran cold. It all sounded so clinical, so predetermined, as though she had had no hand in the events leading up to this moment.

He saw her look of confusion and smiled to himself. *Yes, come into my parlour, said the spider to the fly.* Outwardly his face was a mask of compassion. 'I can imagine what you are feeling. Fate played a hand, but it was helped immensely by what the Council wanted.'

'And what was that,' she asked, her voice barely audible as she grappled with what he had said.

'To have you here; to observe you; to see the full potential of the One.'

She took in a deep steadying breath; she had to know. 'And then?'

He shrugged. 'You must understand out existence depends on power. In our world we are the most powerful. But if something or someone more powerful came forward...' he sighed, 'let's just say not all of us would be thrilled.'

She stepped back a few paces, her eyes narrowed suspiciously, 'Like you?'

'I don't want to be the most powerful...I never have. That's one of the reasons I left Italy and ventured out alone. Ruling others no longer appealed.'

'Then why did you accuse me of being a Dark One in front of the Council? Why were you trying to turn them against me?'

'My dear, I was trying to save you,' he drawled, flicking dust off his shoulder, 'What better way for you to escape than for the Elders to banish you themselves?'

She frowned again. When he spoke like that it made her question what she knew. It had seemed so black and white at the time, but now she wasn't so sure. She didn't see him whisper a few words under his breath. She was too busy sifting through his arguments. Even as the thoughts were born to counter his explanations they seemed to disappear again. It was as if a dullness was permeating through her mind, making her stupid. She shook her head, trying to clear it. However one thought rose insistently above the rest, like a shining beacon of hope.

'Nicholas,' she gasped finally, 'Nick would never have brought me here if he thought it was unsafe.'

She wasn't prepared for Vassagio's reaction and visibly recoiled in shock as his incredulous laughter filled the room.

'You really are an innocent, aren't you?' he asked finally through his laughter. 'Nicholas is one of us. He's an Elite. He does what the Elders tell him to do.'

'He wouldn't hurt me,' she insisted desperately.

'Really?'

She looked at him warily. 'I trust him.'

He sighed. 'I suppose I'll have to spell it out. Where was he when that battle-axe nearly killed you in the Training Hall?'

'He was...' she paused trying to remember, 'He was training nearby.'

'Precisely. Why wasn't he watching over you?'

'He was…but then he moved away…'

'So that Karael could hurt you.'

'No! He couldn't have known what was going to happen!'

Vassagio snorted. 'He could have seen what was happening and stopped it but he left you alone with a Protector. He knows they have lethal tempers, but he still left you alone!'

'What does that have to do with…?'

'It has everything to do with what I'm trying to tell you. Karael is not a fan of the legends, especially the ones dealing with you. Everyone knows that and yet Nicholas left you in harm's way.'

She was starting to shake her head when he forestalled her with, 'Why didn't he confront Karael?'

'What?'

'Why didn't he confront Karael when you were hurt? Karael was in charge of that battle-axe. Why didn't he challenge him if he truly meant to protect you?'

The answer eluded her foggy brain. *I don't know! I don't know!*

'I'll tell you why…he was in on it and he couldn't question an Elder he was taking orders from.'

She tried to block out his words but he continued mercilessly.

'How do you think he found you? You think it was pure luck he stumbled on the One? No! He was ordered to hunt for you. To gain your trust and then to bring you here, to the Elders!'

'That's not true!' she almost screamed at him, willing him to stop. *Lies, all lies,* she thought angrily. *But what if some of it was true?* A traitorous voice asked. *It can't be,* she replied stoutly, *I know Nick. I love Nick.*

But suddenly she was questioning everything. Did he truly love her or was it all an elaborate strategy?

'And the icing on the cake,' Vassagio's voice pierced through her consciousness like a red-hot knife, 'He has left you here alone with the Elders. He has left you to your fate.'

'No, he had to leave to help Seton in Erie…' she defended him heatedly.

'Yes, to help Seton with an uprising caused by his own brother.' He stopped and looked at her pityingly. 'Did you truly not know? I confess I thought you may have pieced together some of the puzzle by now,' he sighed wearily, 'Guess I was wrong.'

Eva ignored his remark. Her mind was still grappling with what he had said. It suddenly made so much sense. Nicholas letting her watch the Council meeting so she would hear Vassagio and dislike him; his remarks about the Elder's presence being unusual. Not to mention Eleanor's apparent distrust for the Elder. It all seemed geared to make her fear and hate him, but what if he was the one who was trying to help her? What if what he said was true?

She shuddered; it didn't bear thinking about. She thought back further to the coincidental meetings she had had with Nicholas. He had just seemed to appear at the most convenient times. Had he been following her? Hunting her, as Vassagio put it? Her head was starting to hurt, and it still seemed oddly foggy.

She was still lost in thought when she felt someone nearby and looked up, startled to see Vassagio standing next to her. He didn't try to touch her but his eyes had a kind light she had never seen in them before.

'I know it's a shock for you,' he soothed, keeping his voice low, 'But we don't have much time.' He glanced around the room. 'You must leave.'

'Leave?' She suddenly heard Nicholas' voice in her mind clearly saying, 'You must stay here…safe.' She blinked. 'I can't leave.'

Chapter 96

She thought she saw a flicker of impatience in Vassagio's pale eyes but it was gone too fast for her to be sure. 'It's the only way to keep you safe. I can get you out and take you to a safe-house where they wouldn't find you.'

'Why should I go?' she questioned, her voice suddenly stronger, 'No one has tried to hurt me...'

'Yet,' he added with finality. 'Perhaps they were waiting for the right time. Remember, their strategies are well laid, like in a game of chess.'

As he said the words, the fog that had been lifting slowly settled back, dimming her ability to think clearly. For some reason her brain seemed to believe every word he had spoken so far. And yet...she shook her head, all this didn't feel right. *But it makes so much sense*, an inner voice whispered insidiously. *If I am as strong as Vassagio says I am, the Elders will no longer be the most powerful.* She could remember Nicholas telling her she was like royalty, almost on a par with the Elders, connected by blood.

But for some reason her heart refused to listen to reason. *I love Nick, he loves me*, it kept chanting insistently. *Nicholas told me to stay here...to stay safe.* She blinked in surprise; it was almost as though he was in the room with her, watching her. She blinked again she could almost see him standing directly in front of her shaking his head, his silver eyes sad.

Believe in me, he seemed to say in his deep voice, *don't go.*

'Eva...?' Vassagio's voice seemed further away now.

I love you, she thought desperately, preventing herself from reaching out and touching the apparition now materialising in front of her eyes.

Then stay, wait for me, came the soft answer.

But the fear Vassagio had ignited flared brighter. She shook her head slowly, *I don't know what to do! I'm hallucinating*, she thought, *but what a beautiful way to go insane.*

Vassagio was watching her closely. She was looking straight ahead, focussing on the empty air. It seemed as though she was communicating with an invisible person.

Impossible, he thought as a sliver of fear found its way into his thoughts. He knew it was possible, but it only happened between soul mates and only between Elders, connected by a bond forged in Heaven. If what he feared was happening, he had to act fast before it affected his plans. He murmured again, strengthening the spell affecting Eva's mind.

'Eva we have to go now!' he said, touching her shoulder.

It was like snapping out of a dream. One minute she was talking to Nicholas as though he was standing in front of her, and the next she was staring at the far wall of her room with Vassagio talking to her instead.

'We have to leave now, it's getting too late!' He gestured upwards.

She looked up to see shadows floating along the high ceiling. The windows high up in the walls seemed to flicker ominously.

'They are coming for you,' he whispered close to her, already guiding her towards the door.

'Who's coming?' she asked fearfully, following him instinctively.

'The *Machai* guards,' he replied, opening the door quickly before she changed her mind. 'They obey the Elders. We have to act fast.'

As he spoke she heard the fluttering of dozens of wing beats. He was right, something seemed to be coming closer and she didn't want to find out what it was. She remembered seeing the dark, almost transparent hooded shadows lurking in the Elders' Hall. They had looked menacing then, when they had been peaceful. She didn't want to know how terrifying they would be now.

'Where are we going?'

'A safe place,' he whispered before muttering a few words in a language she couldn't understand. 'We're invisible now.' He grasped her hand. 'Follow me.'

Before she knew it she was running full pelt down the numerous passageways, trying to keep up with Vassagio. As she ran the wing beats seemed to intensify and then die away. Her fear of the *Machai* lessened only to be replaced by a deeper more disturbing realisation; she was trusting Vassagio. It struck her that he had managed to convince her that everything she knew was a lie within minutes. Her mind reeled. How was that possible unless he had been telling the truth?

Whilst grappling with this she felt an intense sense of loss. *Nick!* her heart cried out. If Vassagio had been telling the truth it meant he was right about Nicholas too. *No*, she thought, *he must be mistaken. Nick isn't like that.* Suddenly the fog enveloping her mind lifted a little. *What am I doing? I can't leave! I have to talk to Nicholas; he'll know what to do!*

She stopped suddenly taking Vassagio by surprise. 'I can't leave, I have to tell Nick...' she made as if to pull away but he held fast.

'He doesn't care about you Eva!'

'You're wrong!' she insisted, 'He loves me!'

Vassagio nodded thoughtfully, realising she wouldn't move with that thought in her head. Despite his spell she kept thinking about Nicholas. Another sliver of fear swept down his spine.

'Maybe you're right.'

She looked up in surprise, *I am?*

'Perhaps he does care, perhaps I was mistaken,' he paused, 'but wouldn't he want you safe?' She nodded slowly, the fog settled back. 'He trusted the Elders. He doesn't know their plans yet, but I'll tell him, once I have taken you away from here. I will find him.'

Eva smiled and followed him again, her legs moving of their own volition, her mind numb. She seemed to forget why she had stopped, forgot the ache in her heart as she moved further away from her quarters. Nicholas' beloved face faded gradually as she ran further. Suddenly Vassagio stopped and opened a small door, she hadn't noticed, letting bright sunshine spill onto her face.

'Freedom,' he said as he led her out. The door closed behind them silently, sealing the Reliquary from prying eyes.

As Eva walked across St. Peter's Square she felt anything but free. An intense sense of loss hit her, but she couldn't decide what it was that she had lost. It was like her brain had shut off that part of her memories. But the feeling kept nagging at her consciousness insistently. She looked back once to see the stonewalls of the Vatican looming majestically in the distance and a tear rolled down her cheek as though her heart was mourning, even though her brain refused to acknowledge it.

Vassagio smiled to himself as he drew her further away, the plan was working perfectly.

Chapter 97

'Is he going to be ok?' Alena asked looking at Seton. He didn't answer; he was too engrossed in his task. She turned to Eleanor instead, who was still holding Nicholas' head securely on her lap, her head bowed. They had been like that for the past fifteen minutes.

She looked up to meet Alena's enquiring gaze and tried to smile, 'Seton will do his best.' But they all knew it didn't answer the question.

'Does this mean Darius' entire coven has been destroyed?' Ashe asked, trying to break the tension.

Karael nodded looking around at the mess surrounding them. 'Guess so, but just to make sure…' He flew into the various rooms and up the stairs, a mere white blur. Within seconds he was back shaking his head. 'Can't see any more vampires. Helios certainly did a good job!' Eleanor appeared not to hear the compliment.

'Well, as long as Darius is gone,' Leonara remarked.

'That would be the only good thing that's happened from this fiasco,' agreed Eden. He looked at Nicholas' still body sadly. And then he blinked and looked again. 'Uh…guys? Is he supposed to be doing that?'

The others followed his gaze, just as Nicholas' prone body became slightly translucent. It was almost as though he was fading away. Eleanor and Karael exchanged a surprised look. They both knew what was happening.

'How is that possible?' Karael asked under his breath.

Eleanor shook her head uncertainly, still watching as Nicholas solidified again, 'I've only seen it happen once but it was between Elders.'

Leonara frowned. 'What are you talking about? What's going on with Nick?'

Karael remained silent letting Eleanor field that one.

'It's complicated Leo. Let's just hope he comes out of this soon.' Just as she said the words, Seton opened his eyes and sighed. He looked exhausted.

'I've healed him as best as I can, but…' he shook his head, 'If he had stayed in his human form, it wouldn't have been so bad. We'll have to wait and see if he comes out of this.'

'But he's alive right?' Alena asked slowly, her eyes shining with unshed tears.

'Yes,' Seton nodded, 'Just barely. But only time will tell if I have managed to heal him properly.'

'How long?' Eleanor asked soothing back Nicholas' hair from his forehead gently, knowing he wouldn't be able to tell her, but she needed some hope.

He shrugged, 'As long as it takes.'

Suddenly Leonara thought of something. 'What do we tell Eva?'

The others stilled, no one had thought about that, and none of them wanted to be the bringer of bad news.

'The truth,' Eleanor finally said, firmly.

'But…she's just a hum…'

'She'll have to deal with it. God help her,' Eleanor responded curtly. She knew how upset Eva would be, but right now she had to think about Nicholas. If she thought about anything else she would lose control, and show how she was really feeling. That was not an option. 'We have to get him back to the Reliquary.'

Eden stepped forward instantly and lifted Nicholas effortlessly in his arms, ready to teleport to Italy.

Seton looked around the house. 'We'll have to clean this place up. The neighbourhood might notice, not to mention the family!'

The others nodded and flashed to different parts of the house, using spells and speed to restore it to its original state. Every single one of them glad to be of use, instead of standing around helplessly, willing Nicholas to wake up.

+++

A couple of miles away three figures came to a standstill on a deserted street.

'You tricked us!' Darius hissed, turning to the slight girl next to him. 'He's not here!'

'Would you have come otherwise?' she retorted, stepping away from him.

'Why have you brought us here?' snarled Marina from the shadows.

The girl turned. 'I have just saved your miserable lives! You may want to be a bit grateful!'

'*Saved us?* We were winning back there!'

'Fools!' she exclaimed, 'You were fighting Elites, not to mention two Elders! Did you really think you would win?' She laughed. 'Modesty was never your strong point!'

Darius was seething with barely suppressed anger. 'How dare you...?!' he moved forward in a flash, eager to grasp her neck.

But she wasn't standing there anymore. He whirled to see her sitting on one of the parked cars a few metres down the street, her head cocked to one side, a mischievous smile on her pretty face.

'Tut tut, Darius, you're growing slow!'

He flashed forward again, but just as he thought his fingers would clutch her flesh, she seemed to evaporate. All he could see was an area of mist hovering above the car, his fingers grasping at thin air. 'What the...?'

'You didn't really think Vassagio would have me around unless I had some talents, did you?' she laughed, her voice echoing eerily through the mist.

Before he could react, he felt himself being lifted high above the ground, the mist surrounding him. He rose several metres into the air, till he could see Marina as a small speck below him, looking up in horror.

'You have jeopardised the plan,' the sweet voice echoed around him, 'I should destroy you now!'

He gritted his teeth, waiting. He still hadn't got over how fast she was, and this latest trick was mind-boggling. *How was she able to do all this?* he wondered, especially since his senses had told him she wasn't a full vampire. More like a hybrid. A half-remembered memory surfaced. Someone else had smelt like that. Someone he had met recently...another girl. But before he could pinpoint who it was, he felt himself dropping like a stone, headed for the ground at a dizzying speed.

Just as he thought he was going to slam into it, he was lifted up again and a rueful sigh reverberated around him. 'But Vassagio is fond of you too and the plan is still incomplete. We could use you.'

He felt his body being lowered gently next to Marina who still looked aghast.

'Wh...who are you?' he gasped when his feet were firmly on the ground again.

The mist disappeared to reveal the girl again. She was smiling at the two fearful vampires. 'All you need to know is that vampire blood runs in my veins. And from now on you can call me Angelina.'

Darius froze. He suddenly knew who she reminded him of. *It can't be*, he thought, but the fear was already tightening its hold. *There can't be two of them.* Snippets of conversations he had heard as a neonate whilst at the Reliquary filtered through his mind; legends of the most powerful hybrid; Angel and human with powers rivalling those possessed by the Elders. He shuddered, now he knew why Vassagio favoured her so much. He looked at her and she smiled coldly, knowing he had realised who she was.

'See you later,' she whispered, blowing him a kiss, 'Stay out of trouble.' It wasn't a request. With those parting words she turned on her heel and walked down the abandoned street.

'What was that all about?' Marina asked, having finally found her voice.

'You don't want to know,' he replied in a dazed voice, hoping he would never see her again.

THE END

Blood Trials (Book 2)
Chapter 1

You know how some dreams are of valleys and flowers and happy moments? Where you have no worries or cares in the world? The sun is shining down from an azure blue sky, no clouds in sight and the temperature is just right? And everything seems so perfect in the world that you lose yourself in it and never want to wake up? This was nothing like that.

NICHOLAS!

He jerked instinctively against whatever was holding him, eager to be released so that he could answer that desperate call. But he was held back. Nothing he did seemed to make any difference. No matter how much he pulled and pushed or twisted, the bonds would not loosen. He tried again and again until exhaustion set in, and still....nothing. He had never experienced this level of helplessness before. What could be stronger than an immortal vampire? he wondered, as he tried again to become free.

He hadn't noticed it before but now that he thought about it...why was it so dark? Was he still in Erie? He couldn't hear anything. Maybe he was in the Reliquary. Even so why was it so dark? Vampires can see in the dark, this was different. This darkness was complete.

An intense fear gripped him. *What was happening to him? Was he even alive? Is this what happened to his kind when they died? Stuck in limbo with no powers, no basic functions, just a dull consciousness?* He couldn't hear the voice calling his name any more either. He was floating away...*he had to hold on! He had to hear that voice again! He had to try.* He focussed all his energy, trying desperately to listen, trying to make sense out of the cloying silence that surrounded him. He didn't know how long he waited, but all he could sense was...nothing.

+++

What was that smell? Her nose twitched as it tried to identify the scent wafting around her. It was vaguely familiar. It reminded her of a holiday she had taken in the mountains one year with a group of friends. The whole place smelt...well...different. There was no smoke or fuel fumes from traffic, nor any city smells, like food or garbage.

It had taken them a while to figure it out before it hit them...fresh clean air. Untainted, the way it was supposed to be. The rest of the group had inhaled it gratefully, but she had thought it smelt alien. Her views weren't any different this time.

The smell of pine, mulchy ground and mountain air was stifling. But it gave her a good idea of where she was - it definitely wasn't within a city. The haze surrounding her brain let up slightly so that she could think. The past few days had been a blur, not all of it pleasant. She had this constant ache in her chest she couldn't name and the insuppressible feeling that she had forgotten something, something important. She just couldn't figure it out and the more she tried the more it annoyed her. Just when she felt it was within her grasp it wriggled free and disappeared into that permanent haze she was getting used to!

But I don't want to get used to it! she thought angrily. Forcing her eyes open she looked around. She was in some sort of room; the walls were wooden and bare.

There was a small window on the far wall; the glass so dirty that she couldn't see out, but she knew what was outside - the smell said it all.

She closed her eyes again and relaxed against the bed. She had probably been here for a few hours, too exhausted to move. Happy not to think...not anymore. Her eyes may be closed but she was willing her brain into over-drive. It was sluggish, like an old car being driven for the first time after a long while. She thought back. The last clear memory she had was of a large golden Angel, staring at her, a spear in its hand. But it didn't scare her. It seemed to be looking at her almost sadly. It had seemed almost alive as she had walked past it. It reminded her of someone but she couldn't think who.

A few minutes later she had glimpsed an army of Angels assembled along a causeway. They had looked less alive, more like the statues they were. Castle de Angelus, she had read about it. The statues were placed on the causeway leading to the castle, created by Galileo and his students, they looked impressive. She forced her brain to continue along that path. Once they had passed the castle the speed had increased so that at one point she thought they were flying. They had rushed along the side streets, headed away from...?

She frowned, she knew they were running, but from whom? A distant memory of shadows on a wall flitted through her mind almost reluctantly. They were running from the shadows, she decided. But who was she running with? She frowned uncertainly. A beautiful hawk-like face morphed in her imagination and a name suddenly appeared...Vassagio.

She felt some sort of connection to it. It seemed her brain having recognised it wanted to believe he was a friend, an ally. Was he? Another part of her brain, the suspicious part, questioned that conclusion. After all, it said, she barely remembered anything at all. Perhaps he wasn't as friendly as she thought.

Suddenly images flashed into sharp focus; the Elders, the Council, the Trial by Holy Flame, her being abandoned in a huge room, Vassagio talking to her in a silken voice, telling her the truth about the Elders, then those shadows and finally their escape. It all seemed so logical, then why couldn't she shake that feeling of not being able to remember all the details? She lay back, snuggled into the pillows exhausted and let her mind return to its earlier numbed state. She would unravel her thoughts later...she had plenty of time.

Chapter 2

He smiled to himself, he could feel her fighting his spells. *Stop trying*, he thought, a cruel smile lifting his thin lips a fraction. *Stop trying to live, you're mine!* He glanced out of the window, by lifting his spells slightly he was able make her feel as though she was regaining her memories, whilst still being able to control exactly what she remembered. He had to convince her to trust him. He had never meant to bring her this far, but as luck would have it the Machai had been sent after them soon after they had left the Vatican.

Europe was no longer an option and Erie had attracted too much attention already. This had been the only safe haven he could think of...a solitary cabin deep in the wilds of Canada.

His luminous eyes picked out the slight movement of leaves as something walked past the cabin. He smiled, there was no fear. Even the animals sensed that he was a predator and stayed away. He felt a tug on his senses and reverted back to keeping the mental barriers he had constructed in Eva's mind in place.

She may have remembered too much already. He murmured under his breath, exhausting her mind and sending her into a deep sleep. *She was too persistent!* Since they had left the Reliquary she had been fighting the control he exerted over her. It seemed as though she instinctively knew she was being manipulated and resented it.

Never mind, he thought confidently, *you'll fold; they all fold eventually*. He had never been fond of poker but it seemed appropriate at the moment, as he watched her sleep.

+++

'It's a sign of her guilt!' Arri exclaimed angrily, her eyes blazing silver as she looked round at the other Elders. She could barely hide her pleasure at being proven right. Several nodded, but a few looked uncomfortable, among them Sylph and the Regent.

'We don't know what led her to leave,' Sylph interjected. She could read her sister's expression clearly. She was definitely not mourning Eva's departure. This Council meeting had been called once Eva's disappearance had been discovered.

'Ha!' snorted Arri, 'It's not hard to guess! She knew about the Trial and what it would reveal. She fled because she was afraid!'

'We don't know that!' Sylph argued, her temper rising.

'Actions speak louder than words,' Amitiel broke in.

'Why would she run then?' Rizoel asked. Sylph had no answer to that and remained silent.

Terence cleared his throat, calling everyone's attention. 'Until we find her these questions can have no answers.'

'We may never find her!' Arri exclaimed, 'I say we rule now!'

'What if her powers grow and she attacks before we can find her?' another Elder asked.

'We may not be able to defend ourselves,' Rizoel replied with certainty.

'It's worse than that,' Arri said, 'if she is indeed a Dark One and they drink from her —' her voice trailed away but none of the others could mistake the intended threat.

All at once voices were raised, suggestions were made and arguments erupted throughout the Hall. Terence watched as the white-robed Elders almost came to blows. It reminded him of a bygone age. An era which would never return. The white robes strongly reflected their Grecian past, except then they wore golden helmets to signal their powers. And yet even then they had argued over any decision that had to be made. He knew what had to be done, as much as he believed Eva was innocent he couldn't refute that fact that she had left the safe haven of the Reliquary.

He had no doubt she had been led astray, but until he found out why and by whom he couldn't prevent what was about to happen. *I hope you are safe Eva*, he thought as he stood up to face the Council. The Elders fell silent as he rose, his steely eyes demanding their respect.

'Arri is right, if the Dark Ones find her we won't be able to withstand them.' He ignored the triumphant light in Arri's eyes. 'As the One we were sworn to protect her. Now that she is outside our stronghold...willingly it would seem..we must act. I shall send the Machai guards to hunt her and bring her back.'

He looked at Arri's rebellious expression and said, 'We cannot harm the innocent and until we have proof of her alliance with the Dark Ones she will not be harmed, unless it is necessary to protect other innocents.'

His voice echoed around the Hall, ringing back from the stone walls with finality. None of the others challenged him. He nodded at Sylph who summoned the Machai who were floating outside the massive doors leading into the Hall, with a silent call. The doors opened and hundreds of Machai floated in. Most were still in their spirit form and looked suspiciously like black shadows surrounded by smoke. A few at the front of the group transformed themselves into human forms out of respect for the Regent.

'Seek out the One,' Terence intoned and they all bowed. 'But do not harm her unless she poses a threat.' They raised their heads when Terence flicked his wrist, and flew out of the Hall, their invisible wings beating against the air so silently that only vampires could possibly hear them, and only then if the Machai wanted them to. When he turned back to the Elders he found Arri looking less than pleased.

'The Machai?' she raised an eyebrow, 'they are good for protection...but hunting a fugitive?' she shook her head, 'we should send the Phonoi!'

Terence almost growled under his breath at her impertinence. 'We don't use them unless we are punishing one of our own or fighting an enemy. You know that as well as I do.'

'All the more reason to use them now...before it's too late!'

'The Phonoi only know how to hunt and kill. Their skills aren't suitable for this task,' he replied as patiently as he could, his anger sizzling under the control he applied.

She smiled sweetly back at him, 'She is a fugitive.'

'We have not decided what she is yet,' he said slowly, feeling his control slipping.

'Yet,' she agreed savouring the word on her tongue with anticipation, like a fine wine.

Chapter 3

'So what's wrong with me doc?' Chris asked as he buttoned his shirt.

Dr. Shepherd looked up from his notes with a slight frown between his bushy eyebrows. His face appeared older than his forty-two years, on account of the number of deep set wrinkles lining his otherwise youngish face. But at the moment he looked more puzzled than worried.

'According to the tests we've done, you're anaemic.' He shook his head. 'But you don't have any reason to be, other than that you are in good health.' He took off his rimless glasses as he spoke and set them carefully on the desk in front of him.

'And the memory loss?'

He shrugged. 'You're tired Chris, you said so yourself. You also mentioned all this started after the murder case.'

Chris nodded, 'Yes, when some of my colleagues were involved.'

'It must have been hard to deal with. Perhaps you are still feeling the effects of that,' Dr. Shepherd mused. 'In either case a blood transfusion will help with the weakness, your red blood cells are severely depleted, I'll give you some iron tablets as well.'

Chris nodded, but he wasn't convinced by the doctor's explanation. Yes, it had been a difficult case and he still felt anger when he thought about it but why would that affect his memory or make him feel listless and drowsy? Although recently he had felt a lot better. He couldn't quite put his finger on it, but ever since he had stopped dreaming about a certain beautiful dark-eyed woman, he had felt more like himself.

His memory was much better and he had felt his old determination returning. The police department had practically closed the ICE case but he had been adamant. It had to be solved. This was too close to home to be swept under the rug.

A few minutes later he had made an appointment for the transfusion and left the doctor's office feeling more rejuvenated and even more eager to solve the mystery that had haunted him for the past few months.

+++

The deep roar of the Honda engine drowned out the shouts of the panicked pedestrians as they scurried out of the way of the two speeding machines growling down the crowded street. To anyone else the riders looked like the typical spoilt rich boys that spent their free time in the Italian capital. It was only when they took a second to look at their solemn eyes that they had any doubts. The riders didn't seem to care who they offended. They flew through intersections as though they didn't exist, weaving effortlessly through the heavy traffic.

An hour later they were outside the city and heading East. Ashe let his bike have its head, reaching a speed well over two hundred miles an hour. The countryside rushed past him in a blur of colour but he didn't see it. His eyes seemed focussed on something else entirely.

Eden's eyes narrowed as he followed his brother's erratic flight down the dusty road. Ashe hadn't been the same since they had returned from Erie. But then none of them had. Nicholas' fall had weighed heavily on them, and the news of Eva's disappearance had completely thrown them. He sighed, he knew his brother was still thinking about Lainey. None of them had been allowed to leave Italy and Ashe had chomped at the bit more than the others. It seemed his new found guardian instincts wouldn't rest until he was near her again to make sure she was OK. He gritted his teeth and hit the throttle, roaring through the dust cloud now billowing behind Ashe's bike, intent on catching up to his brother.

A few hours later they roared past the Vatican City walls, ignoring the disapproving stares from the crowds and the grim looks from the Vatican guards. Entering the Reliquary through one of the secret passages they made their way to their allocated quarters, avoiding the Elders Hall. Neither had any wish to see any of the white-robed Elders; Angels who had fallen to Earth and were trying to repent and return to Heaven.

After days of chanting spells over Nicholas, none of them had improved his comatose state and the brothers had lost some of the confidence they had in the Elders' powers. Seton, their eldest brother, had rarely left Nicholas' bedside, trying desperately to bring him out of the deep sleep he had been in since the fight in Erie.

They found him now as they knew they would. He was staring at Nicholas' pale face, frowning as he tried to think about what to do to help him. Eleanor, his wife and an ex-Elder, sat opposite him on the other side of the bed, holding one of Nicholas' hands in her own graceful ones, her eyes closed as though she was praying.

'Any change?' Eden asked needlessly, trying to fill in the empty silence.

Seton shook his head not bothering to reply. Someone entered the room and Ashe turned to see Leonara, one of his sisters, standing just inside the door.

Seton looked up his frown deepening. 'Did you hear anything earlier?' he asked her.

She sighed tiredly. 'Just the same as before. His mind is still active but very disjointed. I've tried to rebuild its processes, but it is resisting.' She hesitated, wondering if she should continue.

'What is it Leo?' Eleanor asked, her bright silver eyes open now and staring at Leonara.

'The only thought that is constant is...Eva's voice,' Leonara admitted slowly.

'Perhaps that is what is keeping him here,' Seton said.

'And perhaps it is keeping him like this,' Leonara agreed, her voice tinged with anger. 'If she hadn't been found in the first place all this would not have happened!'

'Leo!' Eleanor admonished her, 'This is not the place!'

'It is the perfect place,' she contradicted Eleanor, 'We may never have been in this situation if Eva hadn't been found. Darius would never have attacked and Nick wouldn't have nearly been destroyed trying to save me and Seton!'

Seton stood up to his full six foot plus height, his eyes kind. 'You are not to blame for this, just as Eva is innocent. We don't know what would have happened instead. No one can predict the future except the Oracle.' He put a hand on Leonara's shoulder. 'Nick will come out of this; it's just a matter of time.'

She nodded but she couldn't stop herself doubting his words. She still blamed herself for Nick's state. If only she had been able to control that vampire's mind. Her weakness silenced her, especially when she saw what price Nicholas had to pay.

Although she had blamed Eva in the heat of the moment, she couldn't help but be worried for her too. She knew the Elders had sent their Machai after her. The only ray of light was that they hadn't sent the murdering Phonoi instead. She looked up at Seton. 'Have they found her yet?'

He instinctively knew who she was talking about and shook his head. 'Not yet.' He didn't seem upset about it nor pleased, for both emotions had penalties attached.

'We should look for her instead!' a voice said from behind them.

They turned to see Alena and Kane entering the room. Alena's short red hair shone in the candlelight as she walked forward, the usual spring in her step sadly absent.

'The Elders have forbidden it,' Seton replied as he turned back to Nicholas' prone body.

'There are ways...' Eden murmured under his breath.

'No!' Seton's eyes flashed in warning at his younger brother, 'You will not contradict that order.'

Eden bowed his head, but Alena didn't miss the telltale glint in his eye.

Chapter 4

Eva opened her eyes and shut them quickly as a shard of light pierced them painfully. She didn't know how long she had been sleeping. It could have been any time of the day for all she knew. She raised herself on her elbows and looked around. The room looked as spartan as before.

She was about to lie down again when she thought she saw a slight movement from a chair placed at the foot of the narrow bed. It seemed empty but...

'Who's there?' she asked, her voice breaking slightly on the dryness invading her throat. Her hands automatically lifted, even though she didn't know why they did. A gentle tingling started coursing down to her fingertips. *How odd*, she thought.

'It's only me Eva.' And before her eyes a tall man materialised out of thin air. She gasped and nearly fell back against the pillows. He seemed relaxed as he sat watching her, but for some reason she knew he wasn't. She also seemed to have this weird feeling of deja vu, as though all this had happened before. But before she could latch onto the thought it flickered away and she was left staring at the thin faced man with dull silver eyes, hawk-like nose and thin, cruel-looking lips. He appeared older but she couldn't see any wrinkles on his porcelain skin. He was smiling now, but it lacked the warmth it needed to appear genuine.

'How are you feeling, child?' he asked in a smooth deep voice. He was trying to appear calm but she had taken him by surprise once again by detecting his presence in the room. Luckily she hadn't attacked, and he had no intention of trying his luck a third time.

'Fine...I think,' she replied, slowly lowering her hands, although she didn't really want to. 'Do I know you?'

'Of course you do,' he replied, his smile widening to show sharp even white teeth, 'I am your friend. Don't you remember?'

Eva frowned trying to think back. An image floated through her mind and she grasped at it. 'Yes,' she said slowly, drawing out each syllable as a name popped into her mind. 'You are...Vassagio?'

'Yes,' he smiled back proudly, 'Do you remember anything else?'

'We were..running—'

'Yes, from the Machai.' He paused, 'they nearly got you, but—'

'But?' she prompted.

'I managed to save you. But it seems that the trauma has affected your memory.'

'The Machai?' she recognised that word vaguely, it still sent involuntary chills down her spine.

'The Elders' guards,' he clarified, seeing her frozen expression, 'they were ordered to...kill you.'

'But why?' she asked in a low voice, her head was starting to hurt again.

'Because they are afraid of you,' he answered, his steely eyes steady on her face. 'We were running away from them when they found us. Luckily I thwarted them and we escaped. But we will have to be careful. They are still out there.'

She nodded and winced as the pain at her temples intensified. She looked around the room again. 'Where are we?'

'In a cabin in the woods, in Canada.' He stood up and stared out of the grimy window. 'We are safe here for now, but I can sense the Machai getting closer.'

'What can we do?' A cold feeling of fear was already twining itself around her heart.

He turned then and she thought she detected a smile on his lips. But when she looked again he looked deadly serious. 'We will have to keep moving and if necessary fight. But you need to trust me if we're going to be successful.'

She nodded automatically. 'I do.' All the warning voices in her head suddenly silent now.

'Good, now get some rest, you will need it,' he said soothingly and watched as she lay back and closed her eyes. Soon, he thought, soon he would be able to put his plan in action.

+++

The lab technician rubbed his eyes tiredly. It was the end of the day and he had been staring down the microscope for the past two hours without a break. This was the last sample.

He placed the glass slide carefully under the lenses and yawned. All blood donations had to be checked thoroughly before being approved for use. He settled himself more comfortably on the chair.

Come on Pete, one more and you're done, he thought as he leant forward to look through the eyepieces. He adjusted the magnification gradually bringing the blood cells into sharp focus. The dented discs looked perfectly symmetrical as he scanned the sample. He didn't notice the slightly shiny appearance of the red blood cells.

Confident that everything was alright he lifted his eyes away from the scope just as thin silver threads started weaving around the blood cells, encasing them in silvery cages. He turned to the log book by his side and placed a tick next to the sample number he had just checked, barely glancing at the donor's name — Lainey Steel.

Chapter 5

She's in trouble, I have to help her! Nicholas moved restlessly. Time and space had no meaning for him anymore. It felt as though he was floating with no particular sense of direction. All he had were his thoughts and the undeniable feeling that something was terribly wrong. It had taken him a while to put a name to the voice he had heard.

Eva! He remembered her. Remembered too that he loved her. But she had been with the Elders and yet he couldn't sense her presence in this empty place. He knew there were others around him but he didn't know who they were. Occasionally he would feel something, almost like a touch, but it would disappear and he would be alone again.

I have to find her...somehow! He urged himself to move forward, through this interminable space. Open your eyes! Suddenly as though through second sight, he could see around him. He was...floating! Actually floating high above a bed on which a pale figure lay, surrounded by people he vaguely recognised. *What's happening?* he wondered, but before he could explore further, the old need to find Eva resurfaced even stronger than before.

He wanted to bid those people below him a farewell but there was no time. He could feel himself rising with incredible speed higher and higher, passing through the stone ceiling through the Sistine Chapel floor and then past the beautifully painted ceiling by Michelangelo. He barely had time to recognise the paintings before he was being propelled through the domed ceiling and out into the open air, high above Vatican City. He hovered, looking down at the crowds in St. Peter's Square and then beyond where the city walls divided the Vatican from the rest of Rome.

So he was in Italy, he thought. He turned to survey the area below him. Now that he was technically free, he had to discover how to use this new ability. As an animal he had been able to feel. But now feeling anything was a distant memory. It was thought that now dominated his actions. Everything was much brighter and clearer in this state, even more so than in his vampire life.

He let his mind wander. All of a sudden a strong image of trees flashed before him. *Trees in Rome?* He scanned far and wide, propelling himself around the city searching desperately, but all he found were ancient buildings. *No*, he thought, *that image is not in Rome. But how to get to it?*

He brought the image forward again. *Concentrate*, he thought. Using all the energy he could, he willed himself to scrutinise that image. The trees, they were...he frowned as a sweet, spicy smell wafted forth...pines! He had been to this area before. He thought harder, *it's a pine forest, but where?* There could be hundreds of forests around the world that resembled that image.

He let his senses guide him and then he heard it. A dull roar, barely audible in the background. Something leapt in his mind as he recognised the sound. *Of course!* he thought, it was so obvious! Summoning his strength he concentrated on that sound and willed himself to move. He couldn't believe how fast he sped through the air. All objects appeared like dim flashes in the background; night and day had no significance in the state he was in.

It seemed that even countries flashed by without check. He glimpsed the Eiffel Tower in Paris and Big Ben in London before he started flying over a large expanse of water. *The ocean*, he thought just as he glimpsed land in the distance. Before he knew it, he was hovering over a fragrant pine forest and the dull roar was much louder than before.

He turned slightly and focussed through the foliage until he could see the permanent white mist rising on the horizon — Niagara Falls. From the way the sky was lightening in the east he assumed that dawn was near. Turning again he focussed on the pine forest stretching far below him. Exhaustion was setting in and he could feel his thoughts becoming disjointed again.

What should I do? he wondered. If he became too tired would he return to the Vatican or fall into the immense green void below him? *I need a body.* The thought and the urge was so strong he reeled back in confusion. A body? From where? Was it even possible? His acute hearing picked up on a distant sound and he propelled himself towards it, ignoring how the earth flashed past in a haze below him.

Before he knew it he was descending faster and faster, diving down into the green forest that looked less inviting the closer he got. He kept dropping until he felt himself fall into something. Air rushed through him and with it a different consciousness; a mind completely different to his own. He opened his eyes, or rather someone else's eyes, and was startled to see colours as he had in his previous life as a human.

Am I in a human now? he wondered. He could feel the earth below him, the leaves brushing against him, and the slight chill of the coming dawn. *What am I?* he wondered, not for the last time, as he felt himself moving further into the pine forest surrounding him.

Chapter 6

'You have to fight!' Vassagio grated, making Eva wince. Ever since she had regained consciousness he had been teaching her to fight. He said she had abilities beyond the norm, but she had to find them. *How?* she wondered despairingly yet again as he moved forward threateningly.

She cowered before him and he stopped, mulling over this unexpected problem. He had seen her training with Karael, a Protector in the Reliquary, and she had managed to tap into her talents. Then why not now? Had his mental barriers affected her fighting too? He growled silently and flung away from her.

Risk her remembering everything in order to get her to fight and show him what she was capable of? It was a hard choice, one he had to make sooner or later. His frustration tripled until he wanted to scream with fury. He had to unlock her powers if his plan was to work. Very well, he thought and loosened the bonds he had entwined round her memories. He could feel the change in her almost instantaneously. She lifted her head and the old determined sparkle in her violet eyes returned.

He nodded with a smile. 'Again!'

Eva gasped inwardly as images flooded her mind. What was happening to her? She felt emotions she hadn't felt for a while. An old hunger filled her. What was she doing here? Why was she here? What were they doing? She tried to stop the questions but they kept on coming at her, demanding answers she didn't have.

Find out, a voice urged her. She looked at Vassagio's eager face. Yes, she would have to find out what was going on, but instinct told her he wouldn't help. *I'll bide my time.* she thought *and I'll get my answers*.

Suddenly something flashed in her peripheral vision and she reacted instinctively. Her hands lifted and almost before the familiar tingling reached her fingertips a white-hot bolt of lightning ripped apart the tree trunk heading her way.

Her eyes widened in shock and she sagged to the ground, suddenly tired. But oddly it wasn't her body that felt the fatigue, it was her mind. She heard applause and turned surprised eyes towards Vassagio who was clapping enthusiastically, his earlier ill humour gone.

'Well done, Eva. At this rate we will soon be ready to deal with those murdering Machai.'

Will we? she wondered, staring at the chips of wood smoking a few feet away, which was all that was left of the huge tree trunk. She had annihilated it without a thought. She glanced at her hands in abject horror. *What else am I capable of?*

+++

The nurse lifted the bag and hung it above Chris' head. The blood was warm now and she double checked the log book. The technician's ticks reassured her it was safe for the transfusion. Her finger flew along the row detailing the type of blood it was — O positive. She double checked Chris' blood type — O positive. Barely glancing at the donor's name she inserted the needle into Chris' arm, letting the blood drip slowly into his system.

'You'll feel better in no time,' she reassured him. He nodded his thanks as she left to deal with other patients. An hour later the bag was almost empty and the nurse had been right, he felt better. Much better, in fact he wanted to jump up and run out of the hospital. With difficulty he waited for the nurse to return. Ten minutes before she appeared he heard her footsteps on the floor and smelt her floral perfume.

Why is it taking so long for her to get here? he wondered, irritated by the delay. When she finally appeared with a friendly smile, he frowned.

'All set?' she asked jovially, checking the blood bag.

'Yeah, ages ago. Why didn't you come in sooner?'

'Sooner? I was dealing with patients in a different ward two floors above this one!' she replied with a confused smile. 'But I'm glad to see you're feeling better.' She eyed the redness in his cheeks knowingly. 'I've never seen a patient get on so well after a transfusion.'

Chris remained silent as he thought over what she had said. The second floor? Had he really heard her footsteps or was he dreaming? Maybe he was mistaken, after all, there were several nurses working in this ward. Half an hour later he walked into his office energised.

'Hey Chris!' Joe looked at his friend closely as he sat down behind his desk, 'You look a hell of a lot better!'

'Thanks.' Chris opened up a well-thumbed file. 'Anything new?'

'No.' Joe shook his head. He hesitated for a second, watching Chris stare at the open file. 'Maybe the chief's right. We haven't made any progress for a while. Don't you think we should close it now?'

'No,' Chris returned, not taking his eyes off the documents he had read hundreds of times before. 'We're missing something, Joe. We just need to find it...' He frowned. 'What happened to that button I gave you? The one I found in the alley near ICE?'

Joe shrugged. 'Nothing. It's a bit unusual but there's not much else we can find. Why?'

'It's just that I've seen that button before on someone.' Chris frowned as a vague memory of a tall man in a black coat came to him, but it faded away quickly. 'Keep looking, this isn't over yet.'

Chapter 7

Mmm! That was satisfying, Nicholas thought as he surfaced. When he started coming to full consciousness, if you could call it that, he began to realise what had happened. *Was I asleep? Where am I?*

The pine forest was flashing past him steadily and he could feel the loping gait of an animal around him. It wasn't as fast as a vampire but it had a fast-paced natural speed. *It's not a prey animal*, he thought, remembering the taste of blood a short while ago. It had to be a predator. A bear perhaps or a wolf? Either way it had seemed to have accepted the presence of Nicholas' conscious within it. He thought about what was happening, focussing on what he could.

He couldn't communicate with his host but he could feel and sense everything it did, like the feel of the earth, the smells around them as they travelled and the taste of a recent meal. *Perhaps I can steer it*, he thought suddenly and attempted to change the direction in which they were moving. The creature immediately stopped moving. He could feel its confusion. As he exerted his will the creature moved forward slightly and then veered to the left, following his commands. But as soon as he loosened the reins so to speak, the animal turned back to its original path, bounding up a cliff face with ease.

It's not even tired! Nicholas thought incredulously as he caught a glimpse of how high they had climbed. Whatever he was in it was clearly a very powerful animal and he was slowly learning how to control it. How had he managed to survive in it at all? The answer presented itself almost immediately as they climbed higher still. Having been able to transform into animals before as a vampire, his mind must be attuned to the instincts in animals, which would explain why this creature had accepted the intrusion so easily and why he was able to co-exist with it.

Although it felt alien and the creature knew of his presence both seemed to accept the other naturally. He decided to let the animal decide its path until he could understand more about how to control it, and more importantly until he had enough strength to implement it.

+++

Chris stared at the file and sighed. They were definitely missing something important, he could feel it. He was about to open the file again when he caught sight of a box placed against the wall. Lifting it onto the desk he emptied it. The evidence his department had collected a few months ago from a mass murder outside the hottest night club in Erie, ICE, was spread before him.

He shifted through it idly, thinking. After half an hour having examined each piece and re-read the reports from forensics, he started to lift everything back into the box. Maybe he was wrong. Perhaps the case should be closed. His eyes narrowed on a small evidence bag at the edge of the desk. A piece of metal was encased safely in the plastic.

He brought it closer; it was the button he had found a few nights later at the same crime scene; the same night he had seen the girl. He closed his eyes now and her face swam in front of him like a dream, half-realised. The only thing he could clearly remember was how beautiful she was, and with an involuntary shudder, her dead black eyes. He shivered again and the face faded away. Part of him yearned for her, but another part wished he would never see her again. He opened his eyes and frowned.

He was clutching the evidence bag with the button still within it, but there was something different about it. Something he hadn't noticed before. He brought it closer and his eyes widened. Within one of the holes a tiny speck of red glinted dully. Without a chemical kit he couldn't possibly identify the substance, but he was absolutely certain it was blood - human blood.

He turned the button slightly under the light, searching. It seemed he could see every grain on the surface of the button. He could almost make out the shape and size of the individual molecules making up the structure of the button. On the front of the button he detected another transparent substance he couldn't identify.

How is that possible? he wondered as he continued to stare at it. He glanced around the room and nearly gasped aloud. Everything was so clear, as though until then he had been looking through a fog and now it had finally lifted. A loud crashing startled him and he covered his ears automatically.

'Hey!' he yelled just as Joe walked in.

'What?' Joe looked as shocked as Chris.

'What the hell was that?!'

'What?' Joe asked again, clearly puzzled.

'That loud crash!'

'What crash? ' Joe frowned, 'I just knocked on the door.'

Chris stared at him long and hard. Was that what he had heard? It had sounded like a train crash!

'Are you okay?'

'Yeah, just a headache - I think,' Chris mumbled and looked at the button again. 'I want you to run this again.'

'But we already —'

'Do it again!' Chris snapped irritably, feeling immediately contrite when he saw Joe's hurt expression. He rarely lost his temper. 'I mean...I think we have missed something here, inside the button hole.'

'Where?' Joe squinted as he took the bag from him. After a minute he looked up. 'I don't see anything,' he confessed finally.

'Neither did I at first but I'm certain it's blood,' Chris replied and took the button back, staring at it avidly. 'I think there's some moisture on the other side as well. Get your best guys on this.'

'OK.' Joe still looked unconvinced. 'If you say so, but —'

'Joe, ' Chris looked at him earnestly, 'Trust me on this.'

Joe nodded and left with the evidence bag, wondering how he was going to get a serious response from the lab techs once he told them about what Chris thought he had seen.

Chris leant back in his chair. *What's happening to me?* Whatever it was, it might help to solve this case.

Chapter 8

'We need more!' Marina threw her victim against the far wall in fury. Turning she caught Darius' sceptical smile. 'The others are feeling the lack of blood.'

'They will do as I say,' his voice was low but still eerily cheerful.

Marina gulped and tried a different tack. 'I mean, perhaps we should move on.' She glanced at the crumpled body she had flung away. A homeless person no one would miss. 'They don't have enough blood to live, let alone enough to satisfy us.'

Darius' eyes flashed dangerously and he moved so fast he was in front of her in the blink of an eye, his nose almost touching hers so that she drew back in alarm. 'We stay until we are ordered otherwise.'

The memory of being defeated by the Elites was still strong in his mind. Most of his coven had been destroyed, the survivors flung far and wide. He had started recruiting again but there weren't many of their kind around and creating *neonates* would take time and patience. Plus there was the added worry of alerting the Elders. Ever since the uprising in Erie, their vigilance had increased and the Elites roamed far and wide eager to destroy any increasing covens.

He stared deep into Marina's hungry empty eyes, feeling her hunger as his own. They needed blood, but they couldn't afford to feed as freely as they needed to. He leant forward and kissed her still reddened mouth savouring the metallic taste of blood still apparent on them.

'We will get blood,' he husked, pulling away slightly. 'After all no one expects sick people to recover...do they?'

Marina looked confused for a second before understanding dawned. Her eyes glinted with satisfaction as she covered his mouth with hers again.

+++

'You must run!' the voice said close to her ear.

She flinched but didn't move away. It wasn't a harsh voice, more of a gentle soothing voice tinged with urgency. She had no idea to whom it belonged and yet it sounded familiar.

'Why?' she asked it, trying to see where it was coming from, but for some reason she couldn't.

'You are in danger!' it whispered urgently.

'From the *Machai*,' she nodded, 'I know.'

'You must run!' it repeated, the urgency increasing. 'Danger!'

'Vassagio will look after me,' she replied steadfastly,

'RUN!' the voice screamed at her and she jolted awake, breathing hard.

She looked around, looking for the origin of that voice, but the room was in darkness. She turned and gasped. Two luminous eyes stared back at her unblinking through the single window. She opened her mouth to scream for Vassagio just as those luminous orbs faded into the impenetrable darkness of the surrounding forest.

What was that? she wondered as a candle flickered to life and Vassagio stood by her bed. He looked scarily alert, as though he hadn't slept in days. *Do vampires sleep?* she wondered rubbing her own eyes tiredly.

'Are you ok?' he asked in that hard voice she had gotten used to.

She nodded and glanced at the window. 'I thought —' she stopped herself quickly. For some reason she didn't want to tell him what she had seen.

'What?'

'Nothing...it's nothing...just a bad dream.'

He stared at her for a long second and then nodded. 'Get some sleep, we have to work hard tomorrow.' *What was she hiding?* Try as he might he couldn't see what she had seen. Something was blocking him. *But she isn't strong enough to do that, is she?* He blew out the candle and watched as she settled down again. He had learnt not to underestimate her or Angelina. After all half-breeds could be extremely dangerous. He sat on the chair at the foot of the bed, his bright eyes open, watching her avidly, no sleep in sight.

+++

She woke up the next morning feeling tired. The whole night she had tossed and turned, the eyes at the window haunting her dreams. She hadn't heard the voice again, thank god, but the uneasiness remained. As she took up her stance in front of Vassagio she sifted through some of the memories she had salvaged the day before. They were still there. Not overly clear but there.

She analysed the feeling she had when she remembered each face from the past. With the Raynes she felt secure and safe, but the Elders were a different matter entirely. A myriad of hazy faces flashed past in succession; people she didn't know and yet each of them created feelings of fear and distrust. A pale figure with long dark red hair swam into focus, silver eyes flashing in challenge — Arri, beautiful and dangerous. In contrast a silver-haired siren smiled at her and instantly she felt comfortable.

She blinked and another pair of silver eyes danced into view. These were more serious but still kind with a latent fire slumbering in their depths — Terence, the just Regent of the Elders Council. Before she knew it a very different set of eyes were staring at her, silver but with flecks of green in their mesmerising depths. A bewitching smile flitting across rugged features set her heart rate spiralling, she knew him. Before she could explore any further, Vassagio's voice broke through her thoughts harshly.

'Concentrate!'

She focussed on the rock headed her way with difficulty. It sped towards her unerringly. She couldn't move out of its path fast enough. She tensed waiting for the inevitable. Her eyes closed automatically just before the rock hit her. But just as it touched her something pushed her forcibly, so that she fell sideways with a small cry as the rock crashed past, missing her by inches.

Ow! She sat up quickly wondering what had saved her. She couldn't see anyone nearby except Vassagio who looked more annoyed than relieved.

'You're supposed to attack it not dodge it!' he snapped, coming to a standstill next to her.

She thought he would have helped her up but he towered over her glaring down until she stood up, rubbing her hip unconsciously.

'That rock —'

'Would never have harmed you. I told you, you are too important,' he replied irritably.

She nodded slowly. Perhaps it was Vassagio that had helped her after all. Who else could it have been? She straightened as he vanished into the thicket next to her. Almost before she had regained her breath another rock whistled through the air. She destroyed it with a bolt of lightning and watched as the small chips fell harmlessly around her like snow.

Chapter 9

It was a few nights later; she could feel him near her. She frowned and turned away, but that inevitable feeling remained. Finally she opened her eyes to see — darkness, nothing else. It took her a while to adjust to the dim light coming through the dirty window It was still night time. Vassagio wouldn't have woken her up yet. She stood up, stretched and glanced around the room carefully again, hoping to see the reason she had awoken. She couldn't see anything unusual but she had learnt that that did not mean there wasn't someone there. She trusted her instincts more now, ever since she had seen Vassagio use his invisibility spell.

'Who's there?' she asked, proud when her voice didn't shake. She lifted her hands for good measure. 'Show yourself!'

'Eva?'

She stilled, her heartbeat increasing tenfold; that voice. No...it couldn't be. Had he found her after all this time? She narrowed her eyes, staring intently at the empty space from where the voice had come. Sucking in a much needed breath she stammered, 'V...Vassagio?'

'Eva, it's me.'

And then she saw it, a pale blur of a figure standing by the window. She recognised the voice, but the face was still indistinct. As she watched, the figure seemed to solidify sufficiently for her to make out flashing silver eyes in a lean face. She gasped as midnight black hair followed and the six foot plus man now standing before her smiled. All her old memories flooded back as though a barrier had been lifted.

'Nick?!' she gasped as she threw herself at him. He caught her effortlessly it seemed, folding his arms around her trembling body to hold her close.

'You came...' she mumbled, her voice muffled against his shoulder. He didn't reply, but his hand smoothed her hair reassuringly. After what seemed an age Eva lifted her face away to stare up at his beautiful yet stern features.

'Are you ok?' he asked, his voice husky. She nodded slowly, unable to speak. 'We have to leave.'

Her eyes widened in surprise. 'Why? Vassagio —'

'Is not to be trusted,' came the firm reply.

She glanced up to see his silver eyes flashing. For some reason she couldn't fathom he looked different; still Nicholas of course, but not the same as she remembered him. The feeling disappeared as he smiled again at her and gently cupped her chin, his eyes no longer flashing in the dark.

'Come with me Eva, for your own safety.'

She could feel herself melting as she stared into those intense eyes. She suddenly couldn't remember why she was resisting him...didn't want to remember if she was honest with herself. A silent nod was all he needed apparently, because as soon as she had agreed he barely glanced around the room before lifting her into his arms and leaping through the window which flew open as they approached. A spell she guessed as the cold night wind hit her face. It took her breath away so that she couldn't say anything as they flew into the darkness of the surrounding woods. Something howled but it didn't seem to bother Nicholas she noted. *After all*, she thought, *he is a vampire*.

They travelled through the night, not stopping for anything. She wished they would so that she could ask him what had happened in Erie, and perhaps he could tell her more about Vassagio. But he kept up the pace, moving so fluidly that he didn't seem to touch the ground or the surrounding bush. Despite the speed he kept her protected from any harm, brushing aside branches that would otherwise have scratched her, and cradling her against any jostles as he leapt from one side of a rushing stream to the other.

She must have slept after a while because when she woke up the sun was lighting the eastern sky and they had - stopped. She was lying on a moss covered bank, looking up at the dark green canopy of the woods surrounding them. If she listened she could hear the sound of water nearby. It took her a moment to realise what had happened. When she did she bolted upright and looked round for Nicholas, worried he had left her again.

But there he was sitting on a log, his back towards her. She frowned slightly, he looked so...still! Was he asleep?

'Good morning!' he said without turning towards her. 'Sleep well?'

'Yes, thanks,' she replied. Of course he wasn't sleeping. She wasn't too clued up on vampires' sleeping habits, but the tense way he was sitting spoke volumes about how stressed he was, or so she thought.

'There's food.' He motioned towards a flat slab of stone and her eyes widened.

Several fruits were laid there along with an incongruous plastic cup. She moved closer to examine the feast. Where had he got all this from? The woods looked barren of any fruit trees. He must have searched far and wide while she was asleep. She didn't hear him approach and visibly jumped when his voice sounded from just above her shoulder.

'Will these suffice?'

She looked up at him and smiled with a nod. He seemed friendly but she sensed a certain reserve in him. 'This is amazing! How did you manage...?'

He quirked an eyebrow at her, his eyes laughing openly at her. 'Never you mind. What do you want to drink?'

'I have a choice?'

'Of course!' He looked hurt at her lack of confidence.

'Coffee would be nice,' she said doubtfully, wondering how that was going to be possible while they were stuck in the middle of nowhere.

He smiled cryptically and handed her the empty cup. 'Get some water.'

She did as she was told and returned with the cup full of water from the stream nearby. 'I still don't understand how...?' she blurted out unable to resist.

'How is not important,' he replied without looking at her. He was staring into the woods, his eyes snapping back and forth not missing anything. 'Enjoy your meal.'

She opened her mouth to tell him sarcastically that she was still waiting on her coffee when the cup in her hand started becoming warmer. She looked down to see not the clear spring water she had collected, but a steaming brew of coffee. She sniffed it suspiciously still not convinced, but it smelt like any other coffee she had drunk hundreds of times before. Unable to resist she sipped it, and her eyes closed with satisfaction as the creamy liquid slipped down her dry throat.

It was the best coffee she had ever tasted...ever! She opened her eyes in time to see Nicholas turning away with a knowing smile. 'Is it OK?'

'Better than OK, its fantastic!' she breathed.

She couldn't see his face but she thought he was still smiling by the tone of his voice as he said, 'Glad you like it. Now eat. We have a long way to travel.'

She didn't argue, preferring to grab an apple from the slab of stone instead.

Chapter 10

Joe rushed breathless into the office taking Chris by surprise. 'How did you know?'

Chris stared at him for a second before understanding dawned. 'You found something?'

Joe nodded and handed him the paper he had been holding, 'Blood.'

Chris took the paper with a grim smile, he had known that. 'What about the other —?'

'Saliva,' Joe confirmed just as Chris' eyes flicked to the forensic report.

'The techs were stunned that you had seen that, even after they had given it a thorough work out.' Chris didn't miss Joe's confused look but he didn't venture an explanation. 'Want to tell me about it?'

Chris ignored the question and Joe sighed, 'Fine, whatever man. So what do we do now?'

'It's a man's saliva,' Chris murmured to himself, 'Have you run it through the database?'

Joe nodded. 'No hits yet.'

Not likely to get any either, Chris thought to himself. He frowned at the paper. 'Go back to ICE and get DNA samples from all the employees.'

'But —' Joe stared at him, 'We already cleared everyone who was there that night.'

'Do it again, I have a...feeling.' Chris' brown eyes met Joe's widening blue ones. 'Don't ask, I can't explain it.'

Joe shrugged. 'I guess I should give you the benefit of the doubt. After the button and all...' His voice trailed off suggestively but Chris kept staring at him blandly until he sighed in resignation and walked out of the office.

+++

Eva had never been so exhausted in her life. After eating, Nicholas had lifted her bodily into his muscular arms.

'Comfy?'

She nodded and wound her arms securely around his neck. 'I could keep up with you...if you walked,' she suggested shyly as her violet eyes met his piercing silver ones.

His pupils dilated slowly and he smiled. 'It would take too long, plus,' he shifted her weight slightly, 'we have too far to go to waste time!'

She nodded in understanding. 'The *Machai*.'

He gave her a blank look but remained silent as they took off. Trees and shrubs sped by. At one point Eva could have sworn she saw a huge grizzly lumbering along, at another a cougar's call faded almost as quickly as she heard it. It was cold and she shivered slightly. She felt rather than saw Nicholas glance down at her before a delicious warmth spread through her body. *Could he really change body temperature too?* she wondered idly. What else could he do that she didn't know of?

She didn't ask, besides she doubted he would be able to hear her over the sound of the rushing wind. At least she thought he wouldn't. For the moment she was just happy to be close to him after so long. To feel his arms wrapped protectively round her; to hear his strong voice and to look into those mesmerising eyes. She snuggled closer and took a deep breath eagerly and...frowned in confusion. She had been expecting the scent that usually made her knees weak as though she was addicted, but try as she might she couldn't detect it now.

How odd, she thought in confusion. Just as she opened her mouth to ask him about it the wind died down and they came to a full stop. She looked around dazed. Nicholas had chosen an open green area with a waterfall only a few feet away, falling from a rock face several metres high. She took a deep breath as her feet touched the soft green mossy bank

'Rest for a while,' he said softly, looking around.

She had the strangest feeling that he was currently in bodyguard mode. She cleared her throat as he completed his surveillance, and his eyes rested on her again.

'You said we had a long way to go,' she began, almost nervously as he stared at her. 'Where are we going?'

His eyes skittered away from hers for a moment as he replied, 'A safe place.'

His tone was so final she didn't have the courage to ask him anything else. He seemed to notice her hesitation and he smiled disarmingly, 'Don't worry, you are safe with me.'

As she stared at his charming smile and his glittering eyes she suddenly felt less than safe. The feeling quickly disappeared as his gaze warmed slightly. 'What would you like to eat?'

'What is there?' she asked in a strange hoarse voice, like it didn't want to come out of her suddenly dry throat.

One of those perfect dark eyebrows lifted. 'Anything you want.'

'Anything...?' She glanced around them with mock confusion. 'There's nothing here.'

'You don't need to worry about that Eva,' he returned and she found out she really didn't because within minutes there was a feast fit for a king in front of her. 'Take your pick,' he invited lazily as she stared at the food. It didn't seem real. What was more amazing was that she had just been thinking about the food that was now lying there.

She gulped as he said, 'You'd better —'

'Eat, yeah I know,' she murmured, picking up a bag of chips she had been craving since Italy. 'Should I bother asking?'

He quirked an eyebrow and walked to the edge of the clearing, leaving her to finish her meal alone.

Chapter 11

I wish I had brought more clothes, she thought idly as she washed her hands in the cold water of the pool. Every woman's wish, but in this case it was completely justified. She was still wearing the same pair of jeans and T-shirt she had left with when she had escaped from the Vatican. After several days, they seemed to have their own unique odour, and she could no longer tell the original colour of the T-shirt.

She had finished eating just in time to see Nicholas' figure disappearing into the woods at the far end of the clearing. Now she looked into the pale blue of the water, letting her eyes wander to the centre of the pool which was almost black and definitely a lot deeper. The water was so clear she could see the sandy bottom where coloured stones glittered like gems. She suddenly felt very tired and dirty and the water looked so inviting!!

On an impulse she stripped and walked into the cold pool, shivering as the freezing water splashed onto her relatively warm skin. She sank to her knees after a few more steps and yelped as the ice-cold water reached her neck. Taking a deep breath she dipped her head in and came up gasping. Despite the temperature, the water felt good and she rubbed at her skin vigorously, eager to escape the dull stickiness she was sadly getting used to. She washed her hair as best she could, engrossed in enjoying the feeling of being clean again.

After a while she looked at the clearing which still seemed empty. She moved towards the bank, glancing furtively around for a pale form. Not seeing anyone she reached for her clothes and her hand touched an unfamiliar piece of cloth. She looked down to see her hand clutching a soft white towel. *What the —?!* She glanced around again but the clearing still looked empty. Grabbing the towel with a shrug she hastily towelled herself dry and then looked around for her jeans. It was almost a relief to see them intact, exactly where she had left them. As she put them on she stilled; they were different too! They were clean! She put on the T-shirt which appeared to have finally regained its original colour.

'Better?' a disturbingly familiar voice drawled from behind her.

She whirled to see Nicholas lounging against a tree trunk watching her avidly. His gaze was so intense, she felt herself blushing involuntarily and wondering how long he had been standing there.

'Not long,' came the quiet reply and she looked up to see him standing much closer now. 'Don't worry,' he continued in that lazy voice that sent shivers down her spine, 'I didn't see anything.'

She nodded because her mouth seemed sealed shut with shock. She knew he was a complete gentleman, but his glittering eyes made her trust in him waver slightly. Having managed to unlock her lips she said, 'The clothes?'

'Needed a wash,' replied walking past her to survey the leftover food before she could retort. *Was that a veiled reference to how badly she too had needed a bath?* She was about to voice her opinion of him when he forestalled her with, 'Finished?'

She barely had time to understand the question let alone nod in answer before he clicked his fingers and the food disappeared. She blinked, *was that possible?* He turned slightly and caught her surprised look.

'Don't ask,' he advised, his voice tinged with laughter.

'I know,' she managed to say, just as a myriad of questions flooded her brain. *Close the flood gates!* the sensible side of her yelled desperately. But the wicked side; she didn't even know she had a wicked side; smiled and willed her to open her mouth and let them flow.

She swallowed and then surprising herself said, 'You seem...different somehow.' *Had she really said that out loud? Oh no!*

Nicholas stilled at her words, his silver eyes flashing dangerously at her. She suddenly wished she hadn't said anything, that look was enough to make her back paddle furiously. *But she had to know right?*

'Different?'

She nodded slowly, trying to ignore those platinum flashes. 'I don't know why, but...it's just...a feeling.'

To her immense relief and surprise he burst out laughing. 'You really are unique,' he managed to say between laughs. She waited for him to continue. *What was he talking about?* Finally he smiled at her. 'No matter how stern I appear to be, you don't seem afraid at all!'

'Should I be?' Eva asked, suddenly feeling scarily uncertain.

'No,' he shook his head, 'but it helps!' Her frown forced him to continue. 'You're right; I am different. Definitely different from Nicholas.'

She turned that round in her head slowly, trying to make sense of what he had said. Living for several months with the Raynes had taught her that not everything had the same meaning for vampires as it did for humans. But after a minute she was no closer to a resolution. She shook her head, 'I don't understand.'

'I didn't think you would,' he admitted wryly and glanced at some rocks nearby, 'Maybe we should sit. The chances of you falling over are pretty high after I explain.'

She didn't bother questioning his logic, her knees were already shaking. She sat down heavily on one of the rocks and watched as he mimicked her, his movements far more graceful than she could ever hope to be. She expected him to launch into the explanation but he sat very still and stared unnervingly at her with those pale silver eyes that reminded her of moonlight. She stared back staunchly, hoping he couldn't see her hands shaking slightly on her lap from sheer nervous energy.

After what seemed an age he sighed, 'Very well, I will tell you. After all we are far enough away and it might make it easier.'

'E...easier?'

He smiled conspirationally in reply. 'You weren't wrong. I am not who you think I am.' He winked slyly. 'I tried but I guess Nick is just too well mannered!'

Eva frowned, *why was he talking about himself in the third person? Was he on something?* 'You look like—' she desperately wanted to say "you" but instead finished with, 'Nicholas.'

'You are gracious, but no, I know my limitations and this,' he gestured at his body derisively, 'is merely a poor replica.'

Eva wanted to contradict his evaluation. She thought he looked great, just like Nic...she caught herself in time. What was she thinking? *He is Nicholas! Who else could he be?* She took a deep breath. 'If you're not Nick...and that's a big if...then who—?!'

'I thought you'd never ask!'

Nicholas or at least who she thought was Nicholas disappeared in front of her astonished eyes in an amorphous pale cloud that hovered in his place. She paled as the cloud slowly dispersed to reveal a tall youth in his twenties. He had electric blue eyes, startlingly bright in his lean face, longish tousled red hair and a bewitching smile. She gasped, he looked completely different and surprisingly...human. A small part of her sighed longingly; any way she looked at it she couldn't deny he was cute, and not just regular cute...hottie cute! The gleam in his eye hinted at a wicked side and she wouldn't have been female if she didn't respond to it with a delicious shudder.

'So...what do you think?' His voice wasn't quite as deep as Nicholas' she noted as he twirled in front of her.

He wore a black leather biker's jacket, white T-shirt over faded blue jeans, and Nike sneakers. It was a comfortable yet stylish outfit with enough of an edge to keep it from looking too young on him. She glanced at his laughing face, wondering if she was dreaming. Although his features were angular, his face seemed youthful almost jovial in nature. A slight stubble covered his cheeks and chin and to complete the look, a small diamond stud glinted in his left ear lobe.

'You look...' she started to say once she realised he was still waiting for her opinion, 'Different...nice.'

He sketched an elaborate bow and sat down opposite her his brilliant blue eyes searching hers. 'Thank you I do try.' He shrugged.

'So...' *Where did you go from here,* she wondered. 'You're a vampire?'

He shook his head, his eyes laughing at her openly now. 'Not a chance! I'm...something else.'

Eva frowned again at his teasing tone of voice. 'Will you tell me?'

'Not yet child,' he responded as though speaking to a very small child which was completely incongruous with his youthful looks, 'My orders forbid it. Besides,' he gestured to himself, 'Isn't this enough?'

No, she thought but nodded dutifully at him. 'OK.' She thought for a second. 'Where are we going? And don't say somewhere safe,' she pleaded as he opened his mouth.

He smiled at her, 'Good question. You'll know soon enough. Be assured however that it's safer than the Reliquary, child of Fire.'

Download/buy the whole book from Amazon by clicking on this link:
https://www.amazon.co.uk/Blood-Trials-Book-2-ebook/dp/B00DUHJDHG

Made in United States
North Haven, CT
03 December 2024